MW01154235

Placed Out

Children of the Train

Placed Out

Children of the Train

A NOVEL

JANET R. ELDER

Copyright © 2018
Janet R. Elder
janet.elder.fiction@gmail.com

All rights reserved. No part of this book,
other than a brief quotation, may be
reproduced in any form without written
permission from the author.

ISBN: 978-1975749514

Published by Janet R. Elder
Santa Fe, New Mexico

For Jim

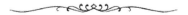

Wanted
HOMES for CHILDREN

∾∾∾∾∾∾∾∾∾∾∾∾∾∾∾∾∾∾∾

A company of
HOMELESS CHILDREN
from the East
will arrive on
THURSDAY, JULY 22, 1886

These children are of various ages and of both sexes. Having been thrown friendless upon the world, they come under the auspices of the Aid Society Home of New York. They are well disciplined, having come from an orphanage. The citizens of this community are asked to assist the agents in finding good homes for them. Persons taking these children must be recommended by a local committee. They must treat the children in every way as a member of the family, send them to school, church, Sabbath school, and properly clothe them until they are 17 years old. The following well-known citizens have agreed to act as the local committee to aid the agents in securing homes:

H.B. Cunningham   G.W. Weatherford   T.R. O'Rourke
J.N. Klemper   A.R. Billings

Applications must be made to, and endorsed by, the local committee.

∾∾∾∾∾∾∾∾∾∾∾∾∾∾∾∾∾∾

An address will be made by an agent. Come and see the children and hear the address. Distribution will take place at the

Depot, Thursday, July 22, at 11:30 a.m.

∾∾∾∾∾∾∾∾∾∾∾∾∾∾∾∾∾∾

Mr. L. Rice and Miss E. Darden, Agents
Homeless Children's Aid Society of New York, New York City

ONE

1

Ten-year-old Danny O'Brien wiped the sweat from his forehead with a tattered sleeve and vowed to himself that once he learned to pick pockets, he'd never fleece people again: it was too much trouble for too little gain. He glanced down at his half-empty rag collecting sack. No, it had to be done; he and his parents needed money, no matter how small the amount, no matter what he had to do to get it.

Standing in Madison Square at the juncture of Fifth Avenue and Broadway, he stared across the street at the Fifth Avenue Hotel, watching the well-heeled clientele who flowed in and out of the six-story, white marble building. He had heard that it had an elevator and that its dining room, an enormous one decorated with columns and chandeliers, was open from 6:00 a.m. to 3:00 a.m. His friend Patrick told him that all of New York's finest hotels had billiards rooms, telegraph and ticket offices, cigar and newspaper stands, even hair salons and floral shops.

Danny studied the hotel patrons, searching for signs of one who might be a likely victim. Silk-clad women wearing hats adorned with feathers, ribbons, flowers, and even an occasional stuffed bird, emerged onto the crowded sidewalk. Opening parasols and black umbrellas to shade themselves from the glare of the early evening sun, many strolled down Broadway towards "Ladies' Mile," a nine-block stretch between Madison Square and Union Square flanked with fashionable shops. Men in wing-collar shirts and smart suits strode down the street carrying walking canes or newspapers. Their bowler hats and stiff, straw boaters bobbed among the women's flora- and fauna-laden millinery.

Danny glanced at the clock that stood like a giant cast-iron lollipop on the sidewalk in front of the hotel: nearly seven o'clock. A single thought went through his mind: *I have seven cents to show for my day's work.*

In hopes of finding a dupe, he walked towards the street. Once there, he dodged trolleys, carts, cabs, and pedestrians, and made it safely to the small island in the middle of the intersection. A stately candelabrum-like gaslight stood in the middle of it, looking incongruous in the midst of the hubbub around it. He started to step off of the island but jumped back when a delivery wagon stacked with copper-girded beer barrels lurched towards him. When he saw an opening, he darted the rest of the way across the broad cobblestone street. A few feet from the hotel's entrance, he squatted by the curb, opened his ragbag, and pretended to busy himself with something inside.

After only a few minutes, the hotel's etched glass doors swung open and an older gentleman and his wife walked out. When Danny saw the man's gold pocket watch, chain, and fob he regretted even more that Patrick had not yet taught him the art of picking pockets.

The man smoothed the right side of his gray mustache as he looked down the street to his right. Then he unconsciously stroked the other side and looked to his left. A doorman in a maroon uniform with brass buttons stepped forward to offer assistance.

Danny was instantly alert. During the ten months since he and his parents had arrived from Ireland, he had learned how to spot an easy mark. Patrick explained that he should look for well-dressed passengers arriving at Grand Central Depot or for guests staying at hotels—expensive ones—because the easiest victim was someone who wasn't familiar with the city.

As Danny edged closer he heard the doorman call out over the noise of the street, "Yes, sir, Delmonico's is only one block, just a short promenade up Fifth Avenue to Twenty-Sixth, on this same side of the street." He pointed north of the hotel. "See that three-story building, the one with the striped awnings and the Pompeian columns at the entrance? That's Delmonico's."

The older man shielded his eyes from the glare of the still bright sun and peered down the avenue. "The darker building on the left?"

"Yes, sir, that's the one, and I think you'll find that Delmonico's has the finest food in the city." The doorman quickly added, "Second only to the dining room of the Fifth Avenue Hotel, that is!" He touched the gold braid of his cap in a two-fingered salute.

The man nodded, squared his derby on his bald head, and then offered his wife his arm. Like most of the women, she wore a long-sleeved dress in spite the heat. Only its pale green color made it look cooler. Tucked inside the brim of her hat above the mass of silver curls on her forehead was a spray of apricot-colored silk roses.

Danny stole an oblique peek at her and smiled. *Her bustle makes her look like a hen, and her hat looks like an upside-down flowerpot that's still got flowers in it,* he thought.

The woman took her husband's arm with one hand and with the other raised her parasol, and they began to saunter towards Delmonico's.

Danny fell in behind them, listening to her talk.

"—and I understand that twenty-five years ago, Morton, when the Prince of Wales visited New York, *he* stayed at the Fifth Avenue Hotel, and that Delmonico's prepared the food for a ball held in his honor. Of course, it was *the* social event of the season. They held it at the Academy of Music, and everyone wanted to attend." She leaned closer to him and lowered her voice so much that Danny had to strain to hear her. "And—can you imagine this—before they had danced a single quadrille, the floor collapsed from the weight of the people. Just simply collapsed." She paused as if to let the horror of the event sink in. "There was pandemonium, but young Albert Edward remained perfectly calm." She shook her head. "What do you suppose Queen Victoria would have done if anything had happened to her 'Dear Bertie'?"

Danny could tell she was going to continue the story, so he reached forward and tugged the man's sleeve. "Good day, sar!" Even in this short greeting, his rich Irish brogue bubbled through.

The startled couple turned to see who the voice belonged to.

In a gesture worthy of an opera tenor wooing the soprano, Danny swept his shabby cap from his head and clutched it to his chest with both hands. He started talking immediately, not allowing the man the chance to dismiss him. "The instant I seen you, I says to myself, that gent looks like a wagerin' man, he does. And I bet you a quarter, sir, I can tell you *where* and *when* you got your shoes!" Danny pointed to the man's two-toned, leather ankle-boots with contrasting toecaps.

The couple's gaze followed Danny's extended arm. They stared dumbly at the man's shoes as if they expected to see some obvious clue to their origin.

It was at that moment that Danny spotted Johanna Buehler among the pedestrians on the crowded sidewalk. She was walking towards him, coming up behind the couple.

Damn! he thought. *She could blunder in and ruin everything!*

She noticed him and raised her hand to wave, but he opened his eyes wide and then cut them to the side, a signal to stay quiet and to step into a nearby doorway.

She shrugged but did as he indicated.

Danny was pleased. He knew that from where she stood, she would be able to see and hear everything.

The man looked at Danny and frowned.

Danny knew that the man sensed it was a trick, but that he couldn't discern the nature of it. Danny set down his sack of rags. "Yessir," he reiterated, "I can tell you *where* and *when* you got your shoes." He watched the man's annoyed expression give way to curiosity.

Finally, the man gave a nod.

"A quarter?" When Patrick taught him how to pull this scam, he told Danny to be sure to get the man to agree on the amount first and to make the initial request a high one. He could always lower it if he had to.

The man exhaled a faintly exasperated sigh. "All right. A quarter."

"A quarter it is." With his brogue, Danny pronounced "quarter" as if it rhymed with "barter." He cleared his throat and drew in a breath. In a patient voice, he explained, "You got your shoes—on your feet—on Fifth Avenue—in New York City—on the first of June—in eighteen and eighty-five." He shot the man a smile that was dazzling in spite of a missing front tooth. After a low, sweeping bow he held out his hand. "My quarter."

"Why, you patronizing little beggar!" The man swatted at Danny with his derby. He took his wife by the arm and whirled her around. "Let's go, Bess."

Danny scrambled in front of them and blocked their path. "A bet's a bet!" he wailed. "You *cheated* me! You looked like a man of means and an honorable gent, but you don't pay your debts." He glanced over his shoulder to be sure that Johanna was still watching him.

The man jammed his bowler on his head. As if his hat contained raspberry sauce, a crimson flush started at the top of his head and cascaded down his face and neck. "Get out of here, you hooligan!" He shook his fist at Danny.

Danny leaped sideways. He saw Johanna gasp and cover her mouth with her hands.

Most pedestrians looked away or veered closer to the curb, but a few curious ones stopped to watch. A handful of vagrant children gathered, laughing and jeering at the red-faced man.

"He *looked* like an honorable gent, but he don't pay his debts!" Danny's tone was that of a howling animal, an animal that had been wounded.

Johanna slipped out of the shadow of the doorway and sidled towards the group of children. She stood on her toes to see over the girl in front of her.

"Imagine cheating a poor child! Have you ever *seen* such a shameful thing?" a grimy boy shouted for all to hear. Indeed, his words attracted a few more bystanders.

"For heaven's sake, Morton," the man's wife pleaded, "just give him the money! We're making an awful spectacle!" She dipped her parasol to hide her face from the street.

The man stuffed his hand into his pocket and hurled a few pennies onto the sidewalk.

Danny scampered to snatch them up, at the same time keeping an eye on the man and casting glances for a policeman. He grabbed his ragbag and slung it over his shoulder.

"Bloody little bastard!" The man's words brought hoots from the children. He wheeled and turned on them. "They warned me about you guttersnipes, you street trash..."

The woman rested one hand limply against her bosom. She shifted her parasol in front of her like a shield and peered into it as if to shut out what was happening around her. "Morton, *please!*" She was nearly in tears. She was humiliated, but there was more: Despite her disgust, the children's gaunt, dirty faces, their bruises and sores, and their shabby clothes pained her. Danny had seen it happen before. Sometimes it meant extra coins, but he sensed that would not be the case today.

"Morton, please!" echoed the children.

"Thunder and tarnation!" the man boomed. "I'll show you, you—" He sputtered and flailed his arms in front of his face as if trying to shoo away mosquitoes. Then he noticed a prosperous-looking couple was watching. He seized his wife by the arm and steered her down the sidewalk.

Danny strutted after them at a safe distance, aping the man's gait and hoping Johanna was impressed. "Hey, Mister! I'll give you some advice, and it won't cost you nothing," he shouted. The man ignored him, but Danny called out, "Never try to beat a man at his own game."

The man wheeled around so fiercely that Danny thought he was going to come at him. "Why, you little... I ought to—"

The woman tugged on his arm and held him back. "Morton, *please!*"

The children hooted, and began chanting "Mor-ton, Mor-ton." It continued like a drumbeat until the couple was out of earshot. A barefoot girl hobbled forward on a crutch improvised from a rag-padded board and touched Danny's shoulder. A sharp-featured boy who was missing several clumps of hair clapped him on the back. Then, as quickly as they had appeared, all of the children except Johanna disappeared.

2

"Danny!" Johanna sounded as exasperated as the wife of the man Danny had just fleeced.

He was still grinning as he strolled over to her and held out a meager handful of coins.

She glanced at the pennies. "Better put avay. Somebody take." She shook her head. "Vhat if he chase you? Catch you?" She pushed her stringy brown braids behind her ears. She wagged her finger in his face, but Danny could detect a trace of a smile on her face. "Someday, somevhon get you, Danny O'Brien!" Her German accent was as thick as his Irish brogue, and it gave her speech a musical quality that he liked.

"Nah, he was an old gent. And even if he chased me, he couldn't catch me. Besides, he don't know his way around New York." Danny said "York" in a way that rhymed with "park."

Johanna tilted her head towards Five Points, a crime-ridden slum on the Lower East Side, in the old Sixth Ward. Tenements had sprung up on the drained swampland decades ago, and ever since, the area had been home to the most impoverished immigrant families, including hers and Danny's. "You go home now, *ja*? Ve valk togezzer?"

Danny shoved the coins in his pocket and nodded; he knew the danger of being on the street alone, especially after the sun had set. He fell in beside Johanna, telling himself it was to help her, but secretly glad for her company. He felt better when she was around. They lived next door to each other on the fifth floor of the same tenement. Their families had moved in on the same day, only hours after the previous occupants had been put out on the street.

He left a large space between them as they walked. *If anyone sees me walking with a girl, I can always act as if I don't know her.* His common sense took hold, and his next thought was, *The sidewalks are so crowded that nobody's going to know we're together anyway.* A small sigh of relief escaped his lips.

They reached the intersection of Broadway and Twenty-Third. Danny moved his eyes from one storefront to another and wished he could read. One sign proclaimed, "Dr. Hall, Dentist (Painless)." Beneath the writing was an image of a large tooth. Danny wondered what kind of store it was. What did they sell there? At the store just beyond it, a painter was lettering something in gold on the door. Danny stopped to watch. "What does it say?" he asked.

"Steamship Office," the painter replied without looking up. He squinted and leaned closer to the door as he touched up the curves of the "O" in the word "Office."

Danny grimaced when the painter said "Steamship." All he could think was, *May I never again for the rest of my life ever have to set foot on any ship of any sort.*

As they walked along, he peeked sideways at Johanna. She was a year older and just as thin as he was, but it bothered him that she was taller. He had never seen her when she wasn't wearing the same threadbare black jacket, a man's coat, much too large, that draped about her like a scarecrow's costume. Its one remaining button drooped uselessly from a clump of frayed, twisted threads.

He stopped in front of a store window, cupped his hands around his eyes and pressed his face against the glass. He let out a whistle. "Will you look at this!"

Johanna pressed her face to the glass and gave a low murmur. The window was filled with a mechanical elephant whose trunk moved, a red wooden wagon, and a handsomely carved rocking horse with fringe for its mane. At the back was a shiny blue velocipede with a glossy leather seat. She tapped on the glass near a pair of dolls that were dressed in satin and lace and had velvet bows in their hair. "I vish I could give dose to Inga and Helga."

Danny nodded. "I know."

They walked in silence down Broadway towards Fourteenth. Although Danny couldn't read the street names, he could remember certain landmarks. Patrick had taught him the names of the major avenues and the numbers of the wider streets: Fourteenth, Twenty-Third, Thirty-Fourth. He knew Forty-Second Street because Patrick had taken him to Grand Central Depot. He knew that the next wide street was Fifty-Seventh, but he hadn't yet ventured that far north.

As they walked towards Five Points, he remembered what Johanna had said after they had lived in the tenement only a few weeks: "You should be on Vest Side. Most of Irish is in Irishtown. Paddy's Quarter is on other side of city." He now realized that she was still as ignorant of the insult as he had been at the time she said it.

There were, in fact, very few Irish families in their tenement. The ethnic majority in Five Points changed from time to time, but there was one constant: The newest arrivals in the country, the poorest of the poor, were the ones who ended up there, and even they stayed there for as brief a time as possible.

The sight of a wooden Indian in front of a cigar store caught Danny's attention, and he scrambled down the street towards it. "Watch this!" he called out to Johanna. He ran ahead, leaped up, and nearly touched the carved feathers of the headdress. He looked back and grinned at her.

She smiled in return.

Encouraged, he thumped the Indian on the chest as he waited for her to catch up. A scowling proprietor appeared at the door. "Get out of here," he bellowed at Danny and shooed him away with a broom.

Danny looked around him as he walked. He wondered if the West Side was any better. Each block they passed through was more rundown than the last. No longer did splendid buildings line the streets; instead, decaying ones and tenements blighted them. The sprawling shantytown clung to the edge of Manhattan, a ring of soured milk sullying the rim of a sparkling glass.

He coughed and rubbed his eyes. Particles of dried horse manure, coal dust, and cinder permeated the air and made them sting. Nearby mills, refineries, and tanneries belched sulfur, ammonia gases, and other fumes that irritated his nose and throat. Kitchen slops and human waste overflowed the gutters and created a stench that drew swarms of flying and crawling insects. The livery stables that dotted the blocks reeked of urine-soaked hay. Broken cobblestones, heaps of garbage, cast-off items, and an occasional animal carcass littered the sidewalks.

Danny scanned the street. Tenants sat on stoops. They smoked, drank, laughed. They loitered around doors. They jabbered and argued in languages neither he nor Johanna understood. He glanced at the tenement windows. Tenants fortunate enough to have windows sat beside them, looking out and fanning themselves in a futile effort to combat the heat that lingered even at dusk.

A warren of dark, narrow alleyways and side streets provided havens where down-and-out men gathered to drink and gamble, and Danny hurried past them. In one alleyway, he could see men crowded around an open crate, yelling and elbowing for a view. He knew what they were watching: vicious fights between waterfront rats that had been starved so they would attack each other.

He and Johanna heard an argument erupt, then saw knives flash.

She cringed as she flattened her hands over her ears and ran past the alley. She turned back to Danny. "I hate—vhat is called?"

"Baiting. Animal baiting." Patrick had taught him the word.

"Ja, der baiting. And I hate when men fights. Is always fight when gamble, drink." An inebriated ragpicker leered and reached out unsteadily for her. She wrapped her coat tighter around her and scrambled on down the sidewalk. "Hurry, Danny!" She was still trembling when he caught up with her.

3

Danny saw Johanna shove her hand into her pocket and feel for something. When he raised his eyebrows in an unspoken question, she pulled out her hand and opened her fist. On her palm rested two black buttons. They matched the solitary one that dangled from the front of her coat. She slipped her hand back in her pocket and continued to hold them.

Danny kicked a rusted coffee pot out of his way. Hands outstretched for balance, he tightrope-walked his way over the remains of a soiled, mildewed mattress. Then in a subdued voice he asked, "Is your mother still sick?"

Without looking at him, she shook her head yes. "And your *Mutter*—mother—she is better, *ja*?"

He twisted the frayed top of his sack and held the bag out in front, watching it slowly unwind. "No." He thought about the dream he had had again last night: His mother, so small and ill, grew fainter and fainter until she finally disappeared. To reassure himself that she was still there, he had crawled over to her pallet.

"Hey! Danny!" The voice floated out of the deepening twilight.

Danny squinted. He could barely make out the speaker, one of the scrawny boys milling around the steps of a shabby building across the street. His clothes were nondescript, and his toes protruded from yawning holes between the soles of his shoes and the tops.

Danny gave a smile of recognition and shouted back, "Hey, Alphonso!" His eyes traveled past Alphonso to thirteen-year-old Marco, but he lowered them before Marco caught him looking at him. Marco leaned against the wall, smoking a cigarette. His pockmarked face and the milky cast of his right eye heightened his air of toughness. Through gray teeth, he exhaled lazy smoke rings and watched them expand into nothingness.

Most of Marco's loose-knit gang, a tiny handful of the city's hundred thousand homeless children, survived by hawking newspapers. Marco scoffed at peddling the *Herald,* the *Sun,* or the *World* himself: he preferred to rob people. It was riskier and more profitable, and for that, he was acknowledged as their leader.

Danny considered saying hello to Marco but checked the impulse. He'd feel foolish if Marco ignored him or insulted him. Instead he called out to Alphonso, "Sell many papers today?"

Alphonso shrugged. "Enough."

"Have you seen Patrick?" He was eager to tell his friend about the man he had fleeced.

But this time it was Marco who answered. "Patrick's gone and he's never coming back."

Danny felt as if someone had thumped him hard on his chest. "Gone?"

"Got picked up and taken to the Home." Marco flipped his cigarette down and ground it under his heel to show the ease and speed with which Patrick had disappeared.

"The Home?" Danny repeated blankly.

Marco sneered. "Stupid Paddy. You don't know nothin'. The Aid Society Home. Any kid that goes to the Home…"

Danny found himself leaning forward, holding his breath.

"Well, let's just put it this way: Any poor bastard that goes to the Home ain't coming back." Marco circled his hand above his head and his entourage fell in behind him. "Stupid Paddy," he called out again over his shoulder.

Johanna turned to Danny. "What is 'Home'?"

He shook his head. "I don't know." He walked on, staring at the sidewalk and lost in thought. *How can Patrick be gone? What happens to boys who go to the Home?*

4

Danny and Johanna threaded their way down the street in silence. Over and over again she clutched and released the two buttons in her pocket. After a while, she made an effort to start up a conversation. "Today you get lots of rags?"

He shook his head no, but he was still thinking about Patrick. It was Patrick who told him about collecting rags, who explained that he could make more money that way than selling matches or begging. During the winter, his first in America, it was Patrick who showed him how to scour the docks and rail yard for pieces of coal to sell. Once, when a larger boy had knocked him down and wrestled his bag away from him, Patrick had hit and kicked the boy until he threw Danny's bag down and fled. Patrick had been his friend, and now he was gone.

Johanna volunteered, "I sold dozen apple today." When Danny did not reply, she filled in the silence. "I ask Frau Liebes—old woman live with us—I can sell paper flowers? Make more money? She say no, those girls are bad. Sell flowers is how they tell men they are bad. She say stay away when they tell you is easy way to make money."

Danny looked up when she suddenly went silent. She had stopped to comb through a pile of garbage near their building. She held up an apple core and smiled. *"Der Apfel."* Her stomach ached with hunger. The apples she sold were not hers to eat. She took a small bite and then offered Danny some. When he shook his head, she put the brown fruit in her pocket. "For Helga and Inga."

They entered the dark building and groped their way up the rickety stairs. Johanna kicked at a rat that scurried by. She took Danny's hand to steady herself as she stepped over an open-mouthed man who lay in a stupor.

In an attempt to shield herself from a stench that made her gag, she raised her arm and pressed her nose into the bend of her elbow. The smell of sweat, urine, filth, stale smoke, and beer mingled with pungent and sour cooking odors: garlic, cabbage, greasy sausage, sizzling oil, horseradish. More often than not, she and her mother and sisters made do with bread and weak tea.

When they reached the fifth floor, Danny and Johanna headed for adjacent doors that were indistinguishable from the other rotting, peeling ones that lined the narrow hall.

5

Helga and Inga, seven-year-old mirror images of each other, ran to meet Johanna at the door. She gave them the apple core. To their delight, she produced something else from her pocket: a crude doll with wilted green hair. She had fashioned it by tying a strip of cloth around a broken carrot and adding small sticks for arms. As she handed it to them, she looked past them at her mother and asked in a low voice, "Is she any better?"

Helga looked at the floor. It was Inga who spoke. "She just sits there."

Johanna walked over to the table where her mother sat. "Mama?"

Her mother did not lift her gaze from the cup of tea she was stirring. In endless circles she pushed a bent spoon, staring into the cup as if the pale liquid might reveal some fantastic secret.

Helga and Inga looked at their mother, then back at Johanna.

"Ist in Ordnung. Is all right," Johanna reassured them, but even she wondered.

Sidonie Buehler, a small woman with black hair and hollow eyes, continued to stare into the cup and draw circles with the spoon. Immediately after their arrival in New York, she had found work in a garment factory. The thirteen-hour-a-day job left her looking like a ghost. It paid three dollars a week, not enough to sustain them.

Johanna bit her lip and fingered the buttons in her pockets. *She changed when Papa died,* she thought. A shiver of fear ran through her. Her mother was thinner and paler than ever: even when there was a little food, she was often too exhausted to eat. She rarely spoke. She no longer sang, not even the lullaby she had sung to them every night of their lives in Germany. *"Das Schlaflied,"* the twins would beg, but there was only silence. Now it was Johanna who sang the lullaby to them.

For a split second, Johanna felt a rush of anger towards her father for making them leave Germany, and then for leaving them alone. She immediately felt ashamed and mentally corrected herself: *It wasn't his fault.*

She stood looking at her mother, but she was thinking about her father and the explosion aboard ship that had blinded him and destroyed his hands. Added to his physical pain was his anguish that he would not be able to support his family in America, and worse, that he would be a terrible burden to them. Johanna absent-mindedly fingered the shabby, black jacket she was wearing. Johann Buehler had taken it off, handed it to his oldest daughter, and said, "You must carry on for both of us, Johanna." A short while later, her father, for whom she was named, had made his way topside. Before anyone could stop him, he had climbed over the ship's rail and plunged into the icy Atlantic. She had worn his jacket ever since.

She became aware again of the sound of her mother's spoon clinking against the cup. As withdrawn as her mother was, Johanna still could not bring herself to think about a life without at least one of her parents.

She turned to her sisters. "*Wo ist*—" She switched to English, knowing their mother was depending on her daughters to learn the language of their new country. "Where is Frau Liebes?"

"There." Helga pointed to the hall, where a solitary window offered tenants the hope of a breeze.

Her mother had been grateful to find Frau Liebes to share the rent on their tiny room, grateful to find someone who sat day after day silently doing delicate handwork on garments destined for the wealthy women of the city. Given her family's increasingly desperate plight, Johanna wondered if there might soon be others moving in with them as well.

6

As Danny turned the wobbly doorknob to his flat, he heard his father's and uncles' tenor voices. Sometimes it was a bawdy song; tonight, it was a muted Irish ballad.

His uncles, Aodhan and Séamus, had come to America two years earlier than he and his parents. They had sent word to his father, "Bring your family to America, Ruadhrí. Life will be better here." When his brothers found work in the new country, the man who recorded their names had written them the way they were pronounced in English: Aidan and Shamus. In the same manner, Rory had acquired a new spelling of his first name.

The struggle against starvation in Ireland and the money sent by his brothers for the family's passage were inducement enough for Danny's father. Now the five O'Briens— Danny, his parents, and his uncles—shared a small room with a Polish family of five. Tattered blankets suspended from the ceiling and languages incomprehensible to each other afforded the families their only privacy. Danny was grateful whenever the Polish family went to visit the other Polish family on the next floor.

The singing stopped when Danny came in. His father waved him over to the table with the glass of rum he held. "Come in, laddie!" Danny glanced at the suspended blankets, pleased that no sound came from the other side.

The brothers sat in a haze of smoke around a small wooden table on top of which rested a half-empty bottle and a package of cheap cigarettes. Danny's mother rested on a pallet, hidden by a faded brown blanket that was tacked to the low ceiling.

His father wrapped his arm around Danny's shoulder and gave him a squeeze.

Danny didn't respond, but instead asked, "Is she awake?" Thoughts of her and Patrick seemed to swirl together.

"She's very tired, lad. It's almost time, you know."

He knew only too well. While they were in Ireland, she had lost four babies, and he had been terrified each time that she would die too. Even the voyage over was almost more than his mother could endure. In his mind's eye, he could see her lying ashen-faced and weak in steerage, or above deck clinging to the rail, empty-stomached but retching. For the first time he wondered if there had also been babies she had lost before he was born.

"…luck today?"

He heard only the end of his father's question, but he set down his ragbag, scrounged in his pockets, and pulled out the pennies and a few other coins. He placed them on the table and walked over to look in on his mother. She lay still, with her eyes closed. He decided not to disturb her. In the background, he could hear his father saying, "…know it should be the other way around, laddie. I should be earnin' the money."

With his index finger, his father arranged the coins in a row. "A man's son shouldn't be bringin' home more money than he does. But my back…" His voice trailed off, and he emptied his glass.

Danny nodded, unable to think of anything to say, and returned to the table.

His father had injured his back working as a carter and had been unable to work for the last two months. The slightest wrong move still caused a searing pain in his hip and leg. Rory poured more rum in his glass and rambled on, "I'm nearly well, you know." He turned to his brothers. "Ceara and I can both work after the baby is born."

There was silence for a minute, and then Aidan thumped his glass on the battered table. "I have good news. Shamus and I heard the railroad is paying a dollar a day, and what's more, the railroad has shanties it rents to workers. We're thinking it's a better opportunity, better than digging sewers and paving streets with cobblestones."

The color drained from Danny's face. "You're not going away are you, Uncle Aidan?" His voice broke. "You and Shamus?"

His uncle replied in a quieter tone. "Workers have to go to where the track is being laid. And it would only be for a short while, laddie."

Fragments of thoughts swirled in Danny's head. *Patrick. Mother. Aidan and Shamus. It's too much!* Danny swallowed hard; he dropped his chin to his chest.

His father downed the rest of the rum in a gulp and wiped his hand across his mouth.

Aidan pulled Danny to him and ruffled his hair. "It'll be all right. You'll see."

Shamus patted the seat of the empty chair between them, but Danny shook his head. He felt sad, hungry, tired. Knowing sleep would offer relief, he walked over to his mother and lay down near her feet.

7

Although there was no window to let the sunlight into their small room, Johanna sensed the day was dawning. She poured a trickle of hot water over used tea leaves and set the cup on the table. "Mama," she said softly, "it's time to get up."

But Sidonie Buehler did not get up. She lay on her thin mattress, glassy-eyed and immobile, oblivious to Johanna.

"Mama? Mama, are you all right?"

Inga picked up the alarm in her sister's voice. "Mama is *krank*—sick?"

Now it was Helga: "Mama is all right?"

Johanna knelt beside her mother and then cried out in rapid German, "Frau Liebes! Come quick! Something's wrong with Mama."

The old woman shuffled across the room and bent low. She passed her hand in front of Sidonie's face.

No response.

She looked at Johanna. "Once before in Germany I saw something like this. A woman in my village. This is bad."

"Mama! Mama!" Johanna shook her mother's shoulders, but Sidonie continued to stare with unseeing eyes.

Helga and Inga squatted on either side of their sister. They looked at their mother's face, then at hers, then back at their mother's, trying to understand what was happening.

When they saw their sister's tears, they burst into tears too.

In between sobs, Johanna took in gulps of air. "I have to go to the factory. They might let me take Mama's job until she gets better. I have to leave right now. If I'm late—"

Frau Liebes placed her bony, veined hand on Johanna's arm. "Child, wait. You don't know how to run the machine. Even if you got a job in the factory, what would you do with your sisters? You'd work from seven-thirty in the morning until nine at night, and you probably wouldn't earn the three dollars a week they pay your mother." The old woman looked at Sidonie again. In a softer voice, she said to Johanna, "Child, your mother may not get better."

Johanna clamped her hands over her ears. "No. She'll get better. She'll be fine." She crouched closer to her mother. "Won't you, Mama?"

Helga's chin quivered. She stood with tears rolling down her face, twisting a clump of her hair. Inga watched with large, watery eyes and wedged three fingers in her mouth to comfort herself.

"Johanna, you don't want to end up selling paper flowers on the street. If you and your sisters want to stay together and be safe, all of you must go to the Aid Society Home."

Johanna's head jerked up as if someone had snapped a puppet's string. "No! Children who go to the Home never come back. I heard this."

"Johanna, there's no other choice. The Home is for children who don't have parents, but it also takes in children whose parents"—she looked down at Sidonie— "whose parents can't care for them anymore. If your mother gets better, I'll tell her where you are, and she'll come for you."

"What if she doesn't? Doesn't get better, I mean?"

"Then I promise I will come and tell you."

8

Frau Liebes gestured for Johanna and her sisters to open the Aid Society Home door and go in. The building's drab stone exterior was a prelude to its equally drab interior. The wood floor of the foyer, painted black, added to the oppressiveness.

Johanna and her sisters huddled near the door as they watched Frau Liebes disappear down the street.

"Girls!" The Aid Society matron's voice startled them. Once she had recorded their names and other information Johanna provided, she motioned for them to follow her to an adjoining room. She studied each of them to estimate their sizes and then selected folded garments from a shelf. From another shelf, she pulled three thin sheets.

She handed Johanna the sheets. "You and your sisters take off your clothes and leave them here. Cover yourselves with these. You'll be given baths, and then you're to wear these garments." Into Johanna's hands she thrust three uniforms, long-sleeved black dresses with gray smocks to be worn over them.

Johanna's heart was pounding. Although her voice wasn't much above a whisper, her fear caused her to speak up. "Our clothes—my coat—we get them back? When our mother comes?"

"Those filthy rags? Certainly not! They'll be burned."

The shock registered on Johanna's face. "No! You can't! Is *my* coat! Was my father's coat!" She wrapped it more tightly around her.

The matron ignored Johanna and looked past her into another room. "Miss Dillingham, Miss Bartwick, come here, please. I need your help."

The two women appeared, and she signaled them towards Johanna.

"No," Johanna screamed as she flung the uniforms to the floor and put her arm up to shield herself. "You get away from me!"

Inga burst into tears. "Leave my sister alone!" she sobbed.

Helga hid her face in her hands and wailed.

"Stop it!" snapped the matron.

Their protests dwindled to whimpers.

Johanna's shoulders sagged when she looked at her sisters. They were terrified. It took only a second for her to make her decision. She pulled the one remaining button off her coat and felt for the other two buttons in her pocket. She let her arms go limp.

She kept her eyes on her sisters. "It's all right," she told them. *"Weint nicht.* Don't cry."

She offered no resistance as the women yanked the jacket down her arms and off of her.

But clenched in her fist were three smooth, black buttons.

9

"This is the girls' floor," the matron told Johanna and her sisters. "You'll use this bathroom to wash your hands and faces before meals."

Johanna looked at the long, water-filled trough and the row of thin, limp towels. She touched her still wet hair and fingered the spots where her braids had been.

Before scrubbing their heads with strong soap, the matron had cropped their hair. She had not bothered to unfasten their braids before scissoring them off.

As if to convince herself her braids were gone, Johanna ran her hand over her hair again. It barely reached behind her ears. She could still hear the sound of the blades as the scissors bit through the plaited strands. She looked down at her sisters and fought back tears. They looked like rats caught in a downspout. Then it occurred to her, *I must look the same.* She felt naked and ashamed. She glared at the matron, but the woman had already turned and was walking away.

"Follow me, girls. Hurry up," she barked over her shoulder.

Johanna shoved Inga and Helga along faster as they followed the woman down the long, dim corridor that bisected the second floor of the Aid Society Home. The matron stopped at a doorway and stood to the side so that the girls could see in. "This is where you'll sleep." Johanna and her sisters leaned into the immense, austere dormitory. Narrow, white-sheeted beds projected from the walls like the keys on a piano.

The matron pointed to her right. "Older girls sleep at that end." She pointed to the other end of the dormitory. "And younger girls sleep there." She bent down to Inga and Helga, putting her face close to theirs. "A monitor, one of the older girls, will check each morning to see if you have made your beds properly. If you haven't, she will have you make them again. Then you will be punished." She leaned even closer. "So you'd best do it right the first time." Although the twins didn't understand what she had said, they understood her harsh tone.

She continued down the hall. The sisters trailed behind her. "You younger girls will have different activities than your sister. Of course, you'll still get to see her at certain times of the day."

A tiny gasp escaped Inga's lips. She understood enough to be scared. Helga instinctively reached for Johanna's hand.

"But we must stay *zusammen.*" Johanna struggled to think of the word in English. "Togezzer."

"Toge*th*er." The matron corrected her but ignored her plea.

Johanna felt her chest tighten in frustration and anger.

"Johanna?" It was Helga's small voice. Johanna glanced down. She could hear the fear in her sister's voice.

The matron wheeled and again put her face close to Helga's. "You mustn't be such a baby!" She turned on her heels again.

Helga recoiled. Her bottom lip quivered. Her eyes filled with tears.

Johanna glowered at the woman. *"Witch!"* she silently screamed. She put her hand on her sister's shoulder and spoke in German, "It's all right, Helga. You and Inga will be together."

"Speak English! Don't make me have to tell you again." The matron snapped her fingers. "Let's go, girls! Don't dawdle." She moved on, pointing to this room and that as she recited the rules. "There are also monitors for the playroom and the playground, at the dining tables, in the chapel, and in each school room."

On the way to the dining hall, the matron gestured towards a large, empty room. "The girls' playroom. In bad weather, you sit on the floor and listen to Bible verses and recite them back. You can learn whole chapters that way."

She showed them a cemented area outside, adjacent to the playroom. Treeless and grassless, it was surrounded by a high brick wall that partitioned it from an identical boys' playground on the other side. "This is the girls' playground. Girls and boys have different playgrounds."

"What about *Brüder und Schwestern*—brothers and sisters?" Johanna interrupted her. "When *they* see each other? Be toge*th*er?" She made a point of pronouncing the last word correctly.

The woman pursed her lips and clasped her hands in front of her bosom. "Nothing good comes of mixing boys and girls." Her frown deepened. "Especially boys and girls who lack a moral upbringing."

Johanna did not comprehend anything except the woman's disdain, and she felt vaguely insulted. It was clear from the matron's tone that she considered the matter closed.

"The chapel is there." She pointed to a set of heavy wooden doors but didn't open them. "Boys and girls attend chapel together, but they sit on different sides."

She consulted the round gold watch that hung from a black cord and rested on the pleats of her starched blouse. She frowned and snapped it closed. "The midday meal has begun." Seeing they did not know these words in English, she pantomimed putting food into her mouth.

Johanna's hunger momentarily overrode everything else. Her eyebrows went up in expectation.

Helga hoped she had understood the matron's gestures and her sister's expression. *"Ich bin hungrig,"* she whispered, rubbing her stomach.

Johanna put a finger to her lips to silence her but nodded.

They entered an enormous, high-ceilinged dining hall in which a sea of 600 children sat in silence. The center of the room was empty. Narrow wooden tables were placed end to end in long rows on either side of the room. To discourage conversation, the children sat on stools along the backsides of the tables so that everyone faced the middle of the room.

"Girls sit on the girls' side," the matron instructed them. "And talking is not allowed anywhere except the playrooms and the playground."

"But—" Johanna began.

"Talking is *not* allowed!"

10

It took only a few days for Johanna and her sisters to discover that meals were dreary, perfunctory events. They offered sustenance, but they were little more than the tea and bread they were used to. Three times a day they were given a cup of milk and two slices of bread. Sunday, however, provided a small but welcome change: soup and a molasses cookie. And Sunday held the promise of another bright spot: It was the one day of the week visitors were permitted.

The hope of having a visitor filled Johanna's mind as she sat on the playground, oblivious to the chatter of the other girls. *It's been almost two weeks. Mama must be better by now.* The one o'clock bell sounded. *There's still time for her to come.*

"Johanna! You have a visitor."

She jumped at the sound of the matron's voice, as if the woman had read her thoughts. She rose unsteadily, feeling the same dizziness as when Frau Liebes had left them at the Home. She was afraid to get her hopes up. Clutching the three black buttons in the pocket of her uniform, she held the rail and slowly descended the stairs.

Please let it be Mama. Please let it be Mama.

When Johanna saw the Frau and not her mother, Johanna's wail reverberated to the top of the stairwell.

Frau Liebes came over and put her frail arm around the girl.

"Mama? Where's Mama? What happened?" Johanna demanded.

"She just lay there, getting weaker and weaker. She wouldn't eat or speak. The landlord wanted to put her out on the street the very day that you left."

"But she's sick. She needs help! And they put her out? In the heat?"

The old woman hesitated. "Johanna... Johanna, they took her to Bloomingdale Hospital." She turned her palms up in a gesture of helplessness. "There was nothing else to do, nowhere else for her to go."

Johanna pulled away from the old woman and sank onto a bench. "Oh, Mama," she sobbed. She wiped her cheek with the back of her hand. "Frau Liebes, please, we have to get her out! Once I heard women in our building talking. They said Bloomingdale Asylum is for crazy people, that they take people there because they're possessed. They said—" She pressed her fingertips over her mouth to muffle her own sobs. "They said they lock them in cages and throw buckets of cold water on them. They said they beat them and leave them naked and starving. They said there's always shrieking and screaming...." She took the old woman's hands in her own. "Frau Liebes, Mama's not evil or crazy. She's sad. She's exhausted and sick, but she's not crazy. And if she stays there, she'll—"

The old woman sat down on the bench beside her and looked down at the floor. "Johanna, your mother died three days after they took her there. I found out yesterday."

The frau continued to talk, but Johanna could no longer hear. For several minutes, it seemed to require effort just to breathe. Finally, she raised her eyes to meet the old woman's rheumy ones. "What did they do with her? With her body?"

The frau shook her head sadly.

Johanna clutched her arms across her chest, rocking and softly moaning.

The frau put her hand on Johanna's and squeezed it. "I'm too old and too poor to take on any children. I barely survive on what I make from doing piece work." She squeezed Johanna's hand again. "You still have your sisters. You still have each other." She stood up and stroked the top of Johanna's head. With slow steps she made her way out the door and down the granite steps.

11

For the next several nights, Johanna pressed her pillow over her mouth so that no one would hear her crying. *Helga and Inga must be as frightened as I am,* she reminded herself. Even though she explained that they would not see their mother again, her sisters continued to say, "When Mama comes..." and "After we go home with Mama...."

With the hope of being reunited with her mother gone, Johanna found time passed even more slowly. Along with scores of other girls, she marched silently in single-file lines through daily activities regulated by a clanging bell.

In the classroom, she sat in her assigned row and spoke only when called upon. She stared at the words in the dilapidated reader and speller. She copied arithmetic problems on a worn-out slate and struggled to focus on the numbers. Like all of the older girls, she also went to sewing and cooking classes.

During the rest of the time, she worked in the airless sewing room in which the uniforms were made or in the stifling bakery. She sat making buttonholes, sewing buttons on uniforms, and hemming towels, and wondered whether the boys' work of caning chairs or mending shoes was any more pleasant. *At least I'm not in the laundry room,* she told herself. But her next thought was, *Might as well be.* The harsh, antiseptic smell of the laundry pervaded everything: the clothing, the bedding, even the floors.

She looked forward each day to the few minutes when she was with Inga and Helga. "When is Mama coming? When are we going home, Johanna?" Inga asked again that afternoon.

Johanna did not mention their mother, but reminded her sister again, "This is our home now." To herself, she bristled, *Home! "Home" is not a word they should use for this place!*

Yet within a few weeks after she and her sisters arrived at the Home, someone else she knew arrived, and it began to feel a little more like home after all.

12

Danny bounded up the tenement stairs two at a time. He was hot and sweaty, but exhilarated from the Fourth of July parade, from the flags, and from the rousing music that reverberated in his ears. He patted his pocket to be sure the small paper flag was still there. He smiled. *Mother will like it,* he thought.

He flattened himself against the narrow stairwell to allow a large man who was descending the stairs to squeeze past him. In his arms, he bore something wrapped in a threadbare, mud-colored blanket.

Danny frowned. *Someone dies in this awful place almost every day.*

When he reached the fifth floor he stopped in his tracks. The Polish family stood in the hall, the three children pressed around their mother, clinging to her skirt. Danny's scalp prickled, and his breathing became shallow. Other tenants stood around his open door and talked in low voices.

The realization hit him. *The blanket.* His knees went weak. For a moment, he felt strangely detached, as if he were floating. *It was our blanket.* "No!" he shouted as he ran towards the door.

His father stumbled into the hall. His eyes were red, and he smelled of rum. Tears spilled down his face. "She's gone, boy. Your mother's gone."

"But she was asleep when I left this morning. How could…" He wiped across his eyes with his sleeve. The next realization hit him even harder. *I didn't even get to say good-bye.*

"The baby's alive. A girl." His father's words were barely audible.

Danny charged at him and pounded on his chest with his fists. "It's *your* fault she died! You brought us here! We never should have left Ireland."

Rory did not try to fend off his son's blows or refute his angry accusation.

Danny abruptly stopped hitting his father but clung to the front of his shirt. "The man on the stairs. With the blanket. Where is he taking her?"

"She has to be buried."

"It's not right! There should be two days of waking." Danny's mind reeled. *No wake. No keening to mourn her. It isn't right.*

He pushed his father away and dashed down the stairs and into the street. The man had loaded his bundle into the wagon and climbed onto the seat, but when he saw Danny, he paused.

Danny rushed over to his mother's body and stroked the blanket. *There must be something,* he thought. *The flag!* He tucked the small red, white, and blue rectangle inside a fold of the blanket.

The man turned back around and flicked the reins. The wagon rumbled forward.

Danny watched the wagon until it disappeared from sight. *America was supposed to be better.* He bit his lip and wiped his eyes.

Several children had gathered to watch.

"Get out of here!" he yelled and shoved his way past them. He grabbed the rim of a nearby ash barrel and flung it sideways, sending up a cloud of acrid, black dust. As he barged down the street, he stomped a broken chair in his path, splintering it. Then he kicked the fragments. When he came to an alley, he turned in. He slumped against the wall and slid to the ground. He rested his elbows on his knees and covered his face with his hands.

His mind ricocheted from one thought to the next. *Johanna. I can talk to Johanna. She'll understand.* Then he remembered. *She's gone.* That she had been gone for weeks. *I didn't get to say good-bye to her either.* He found himself wondering who else was going to disappear from his life. He sat in the alley, twisting and untwisting a piece of wire he found on the ground beside him. Lost in his own thoughts, he did not hear the factory whistles, the clopping of horse hooves on the cobblestones, or even people's voices.

Then he heard a baby wail.

He struggled to his feet. Danny tried to recall his father's words. *The baby lived? A girl? Is that what he said?* Danny retraced his steps to the flat.

His father sat slumped over the table, his head cradled in his forearms.

"Where is she?" Danny demanded.

Rory raised his head and gave Danny an unfocused stare.

Danny came over and stood in front of him and repeated his question. "The *baby*. Where is she?"

"The old German lady, next door." His father waved his hand in that direction. "She has her." Then he added, "I named her Mary Ceara. For the Blessed Virgin who spared her life and her mother."

Danny reached the door, but hesitated with his hand on the doorknob. He turned to face his father. "The Blessed Virgin didn't spare *mother's* life. She didn't help mother before, with the other babies." He slammed the door behind him.

Frau Liebes showed Danny the pasty, red-haired baby who lay sleeping in a box. On her left shoulder was a small, irregularly-shaped brown mark. Danny touched it gently. It reminded him faintly of a shamrock.

Frau Liebes pointed to the baby. By piecing together words in broken English and gesturing, she made Danny understand that Bridget O'Toole would nurse the baby tonight, but only tonight. Bridget had two babies of her own. The frau struggled to convey the rest of her message: His father had said he didn't know what to do. She had told him that the baby must go to a foundling home, that she would die unless she did.

But Danny was no longer listening. He ran his finger beneath Mary Ceara's shriveled ones. *Sister. My sister. I have a sister,* he thought. He stroked the baby's pinched face, searching it for traces of his mother. Silently he repeated "Ceara," the name that now linked his mother and his new sister.

Mary Ceara gave a reflexive jerk and opened her eyes.

He was startled. Unlike his parents' brown eyes, and even his own, her eyes were pale blue.

"…to der Foundling Home," the frau repeated.

At the second mention of the word "Home," Danny looked up. "Home? What kind of home?"

"Foundling. Place for babies vhat don't got mutters. Iss like *wo*—like vhere— Johanna, Inga, Helga vent, but for babies. I told your *Vater*, take her dere… if baby live tru *der nacht*."

Danny walked back to his flat and sat down across the table from his father. He noticed that he held his mother's rosary in his hand. For the first time, it occurred to Danny that his father must be in pain, too.

Rory rubbed his reddened eyes and scratched his stubbly jaw. "Danny," he began, "you know I can't take care of Mary Ceara. She'll die without…" He pulled the bottle towards him and drank out of it. "I'm taking her to the Foundling Home. In the morning. It's a place where—"

"Frau Liebes told me," Danny cut him short.

"Danny…" his father began again, but the way he said it, the slight hesitation, caused Danny's scalp to prickle again. He held his breath, but in a flat tone, all his father said was, "They'll take her and tend to her."

Danny felt a wave of relief and exhaled. "Then we'll be getting her back when she's bigger? When she's stronger?"

"Danny…"

The same ripple of fear. The peculiar angle of his father's head. The odd cast of his eyes. Danny's breathing quickened, and he braced for whatever was coming.

His father spoke slowly, as if producing the words was painful. "*We* won't be going to get her. I can't feed *you* either, Danny. And I see what happens to laddies who live on the street."

A cold feeling started in Danny's feet and crawled up his legs like vines. He felt incapable of moving, as if he were bound to the chair and rooted to the floor.

With his finger, his father traced and retraced a scratch on the scarred tabletop. Without looking up, he said, "You'll be better off at the Aid Society Home. Frau Liebes said that's where she took the three lasses when their mother got sick."

Danny noticed he didn't say, "and died." He sat clenching and unclenching his jaw.

"It's not as bad as it sounds. Shamus and Aidan and I have a plan. We talked about it a few days ago. We were afraid your mother… might not make it."

Danny folded his arms defiantly across his chest but did not speak. *There's nothing more you can do to me,* he thought. *There's nothing left you can take from me.*

Rory held out Ceara's rosary to Danny. "Take this. It's not much, but it's something of your mother's."

Danny shook his head no. "The Virgin Mary failed her. You failed her, too. You keep it." His chair made a nerve-fraying scrape as he shoved it away from the table. He went over to the empty pallet where he had left his mother sleeping that morning. He dropped to his knees and ran his hand over it. Then he lay down on it and curled up into a ball.

13

Things will be better when Aidan and Shamus get here, Danny told himself. He had been anxious for them to arrive because his father refused to say anything about their plan until then. He and his father had said almost nothing to each other since Rory returned from the Foundling Home that morning. When Danny heard their voices, he jumped to his feet and ran to the door.

"The baby's gone," he blurted.

Aidan put a hand on Danny's shoulder as they walked over to the table. "I know," he said gently. "I know." He adjusted the wick of the smoky lamp, struck a match, and held it to the wick.

Danny watched, and waited for him to begin talking. He had noticed that even though Aidan wasn't the oldest, he usually took the lead.

He lit a cigarette with the same match and exhaled a stream of smoke. "Danny, Shamus and I won't be working for the railroad after all. Laying track pays a dollar a day, a good wage to be sure, but there's no real future here." He drew on his cigarette and exhaled another column of smoke. "We've decided to try our luck out West."

Shamus interrupted and took over his brother's explanation. "We didn't come here to America to spend our lives breaking our backs and being spit on. Aidan and I have a chance to sail to Galveston."

Before Danny could ask any questions, his father joined in. "I'm the one who's going to work on a railroad crew, Danny, but only for a year, mind you. I can live cheap in a shanty near where the track's being laid."

Questions swirled in Danny's head, but he started with, "Where's Galston?" *Is it anything like County Galway?* he wondered.

"Galveston," Aidan corrected him. "And it's in another state, called Texas. It's far away, but there are opportunities there."

Danny didn't know any more than he did before Aidan answered.

He wanted to ask another question, but his father went on. "Danny, if I take the railroad job, I can stay in New York—meaning the state—and I'll be nearer to you and Mary Ceara."

Danny's expression did not change, so Rory pressed on.

"You'll eventually go West on a placing out train. Charlotte Sullivan runs the laundry at the Home. She's heard them talk of sending trains to Texas. She says that she might be able find out from someone which train they put you on." Rory glanced up at Danny and then averted his eyes just as quickly.

Danny clutched the sides of the chair seat to steady himself. "I'm going on a train? Where? What are they going to do with me?" His mind raced ahead. *Was there some place they took children? Children who had no mothers? Bad children?*

"They call it 'placing out.' Children go West on the train. The train stops in different towns and…" The pause that followed was too long.

"It stops in different towns, and *what?*" Danny shouted.

He could barely hear his father's answer. "And people take children from the train to live with them."

Danny leaped to his feet, knocking his chair over backwards. "I don't want to live with someone else in some other town!" He began to cry. He didn't care if his father and uncles saw his tears or if the Polish family heard him. "How are you going to find me?" He sought his father's eyes with his own. "I'll never see you again." He turned first to one uncle and then to the other. "Uncle Aidan?" he implored. "Uncle Shamus?"

Aidan stubbed out his cigarette. "We'll try to find out what train you're on. But you'll have a job to do, too, Danny. We want you to try to avoid being placed out until the last stop. That way we'll have a better chance of finding you."

Danny swallowed hard. He righted the chair and sat down again. He tried to console himself. *They have thought about me. They're going to try to find me.* He looked at his uncles. In a softer voice, he asked, "How do I keep from being placed out until the last stop?"

Aidan gave him a broad smile and winked. "Just act the way you usually do."

His father resumed speaking. "Frau Liebes told me the Foundling Home don't put babies on placing out trains until they're at least a year old. I may have to give Mary Ceara up to them, but I'm hoping to earn enough money to take her back before she's a year. After I get her back, we'll come find you, Danny. We'll be a family again. I promised your mother—" He couldn't finish the sentence.

"We'll *all* be together again," Shamus proclaimed as he encircled an arm full of air. He leaned over and tapped Danny on the chest. "If you're put on the train to Texas, why, you'll be headed for the very place where your old uncles are!" He made it sound as if he and Aidan would meet him at the depot.

"But Uncle Shamus, you and Aidan swore you'd never go on a ship again. Not after crossing the Atlantic." He shuddered at the memory of sleeping four to a bunk, of waiting for hours—and sometimes even fighting—to use the cooking fire or have a sip of foul water. "*I'll* never go on a ship again!"

"This is a different kind of ship, a merchant ship," Aidan explained. Then he turned to his brother. "Rory, we'll try to get in touch with you by Christmas to tell you where we are. Until we're together again we'll try to get in touch every year around Christmas time."

Rory nodded. "I hope to God in heaven it works. At least Danny and the baby will have food and shelter, even if…" Once again, his voice trailed off.

"Father, when do I go to the Home?" Danny's voice already sounded far away.

Rory stood up to get another bottle of rum off a shelf, but also to keep Danny from seeing his eyes. "Tomorrow," he said over his shoulder. His voice was husky with emotion. He uncorked the bottle and poured some amber liquid into the three dirty glasses. He slid one towards each of his brothers and raised his glass. "For once, maybe luck will smile upon the O'Brien clan and we'll all be reunited in Texas."

14

Danny lay on the floor in the dark, listening to his father and uncles snore. He moved closer to his father. *Soon it'll be morning,* he thought. *Today's the day.* He took a deep breath, exhaled slowly, and waited for the sun to rise.

That morning he held his father's hand as they climbed the long, broad steps of the Aid Society Home. He had to fight the impulse to break loose and run.

The admission process took only a matter of minutes. A tall woman in a dark blue dress opened a large book and dipped her pen in the ink. "The child's name? Your name?" Then she recorded Danny's age and his parents' names, including his mother's age—twenty-six—at the time of her death. She wrote "Irish" in the last column, and then gave Rory a paper to sign.

He made a mark.

When he handed it back to her, she stood up. "We find it best not to draw this out." Danny and his father rose numbly to their feet. The woman motioned for Danny to go with her.

Danny ignored her and wrapped his arms around his father's waist. He buried his face against his shirt and clung to him.

Rory ran his hand over Danny's hair, then leaned down and took his face in his hands. "We'll be together again, in Texas. You'll see."

Danny nodded, wanting to believe it as much as his father.

Rory wiped his nose and eyes on his sleeve.

Then the matron took Danny by the shoulder and disappeared with him through a doorway. Danny did not look back. He knew if he did, he would cry.

15

He had been looking for her. He thought he saw her that night in the dining hall, but she was far away and all the girls were dressed alike. On Sunday the 600 children lined up for chapel. It was as the girls began filing into their side of the chapel and silently filling up the pews that Danny saw her.

"*Achoo! Achoo!*"

When the violent sneezing continued, children began to turn and look. The matron was instantly on her way over to Danny. She had already whipped him once that morning for talking.

"*A-a-a-achoo!*"

A few of the boys and girls started to giggle, then dozens of them. Some moved out of line to see who was causing the welcome commotion.

"Children! Children! This is a place of worship!" The matron's tone was menacing. "Johanna! You're a chapel monitor. Do your job!" She pointed to the disarray at the end of the girls' line.

Johanna walked back to the younger girls, including Inga and Helga, who were struggling to suppress outright laughter. She had just herded them back into a straight line when she jerked her head up at the sound of another startlingly loud and comical *achoo*.

That's when she saw him.

The matron grabbed Danny by the ear, but he gave Johanna a wink and a huge grin before he was led away.

For the first time since she arrived at the Home, Johanna smiled.

16

After nearly a year at the Home, Johanna had no reason to expect any day to be different from previous ones. But after breakfast one summer morning, the matron told her, "You won't be going to school today. Go directly to the playroom. Now."

Johanna was frightened, but she felt better when she saw her sisters and two dozen other girls shuffling into the large, empty room.

The matron motioned for them to sit down on the floor in rows. She moved along the rows, looking at each child and making marks in the ledger she was holding. Finally, she closed it and cleared her throat. "You're going to spend this week learning manners, girls, because next week you will be leaving on a train to meet your new parents and your new families."

Johanna understood only the last part. Her thoughts spun. *She didn't say "placing out," but that's what she means!* Johanna had been at the Home long enough to learn the term "placing out" and to know what lay ahead. *What if bad people take my sisters and me? What if I never see my sisters again?* Another thought struck her like a knife. *Danny. I'll never see Danny again.*

The matron clapped her hands. The girls stood up for their first lesson: how to say please and thank you.

The week passed quickly, a week filled with lessons on how to be polite and smile when they were introduced to someone, how not to fidget or scratch, and how to eat in a quiet and mannerly way. On June 6, the girls were awakened earlier than usual. They were given baths and their hair washed. Each received a new pair of shoes and a new dress. Johanna helped her sisters put theirs on.

"*Schön!* Pretty!" marveled Inga, forgetting that there was ever a rule about talking. She ran her hands down the front of her skirt and tapped the toes of her shoes together.

A matron circulated among them. From her left forearm dangled a set of cards with strings looped through one end. Around each girl's neck she put a tag that bore her name and a number. With the seriousness of a scientist labeling specimens, she announced, "You're to wear these until you're placed out."

17

As they left for the train station, Johanna stared back at the Home. Although there was almost never a chance to speak to Danny, she had found it comforting to know he was there. Now she felt sorrow at the prospect of once again being separated from him. *You were my only friend, and I didn't even get to tell you I was leaving.* She had not even seen him during the past week. In fact, every part of their normal routine had changed once their time for placing out had come. *Good-bye, Danny.* She silently mouthed the rest of her thoughts: *Good-bye, New York. Good-bye, Mama.* She dabbed away a tear before her sisters could notice.

Grand Central Depot was noisy and dirty. The twins hung close to Johanna: The enormous trains with their plumes of black smoke and their screeching, hissing sounds alarmed them.

"Fire?" Helga asked anxiously. Children who had lived in tenements knew that smoke meant fire, and that fire brought injury, death, and destruction.

"No. No fire. It's all right."

Inga stared open-mouthed at the sight of the engine. "So big!" she uttered in disbelief. Indeed, the wheels on the engine were almost as tall as she was. "How does the train know where to go? What if it takes us to the wrong place?"

Johanna frowned and was considering the matter when she saw a young woman approach the group. The matron said, "This is Miss Darden. She is an agent of the Home. She will be your chaperone on this trip." She saw their blank expressions and said, "Miss Darden will be traveling with you on the trip." Then she pointed towards the back of the train. "Mr. Rice has just arrived with the boys. He will be going on the trip as their chaperone." The matron wished the girls and the agent a good trip, and then turned and walked away.

Johanna leaned over and looked down the platform. She could see boys lining up. They, too, had on new clothes and wore tags around their necks.

Miss Darden turned to the group and spoke for the first time. "Girls, please line up in pairs and hold your partner's hand. Follow me. Let's get aboard."

The other girls moved towards the train. Johanna and her sisters continued to watch what was happening around them, unaware that the line ahead of them had moved away. They watched the luggage and trunks being carted to and from the trains. When the heavy door of a freight car slammed shut, Inga jumped and put her hands over her ears. "Do we have to get in one of those, Johanna? I'm *scared.*" She blinked back tears.

"It's all right," Johanna replied in a distracted voice. The truth was that she didn't know. The thought of traveling in a freight car frightened her, too.

Miss Darden came over to Johanna and her sisters and wagged her finger in their faces. "You weren't paying attention, were you?"

Johanna felt her face flush. Helga and Inga scrambled behind Johanna and peeked out.

"The other girls have already boarded. *That* car is the one for the girls." Johanna was relieved when Miss Darden did not point to the freight car. "Hurry up now."

Johanna grabbed her sisters by the hand and pulled them towards the train. She felt woozy as she climbed the metal steps. *This train is going to take us even farther away. Take us to…?* She stopped her thought and walked down the aisle, steadying herself by holding onto the back of each seat as she passed it. "There." She pointed to an empty row. "We'll sit there."

Inga called out, "I get to sit by the window!"

Johanna nodded to Inga and let her go in first.

Helga looked disappointed.

Johanna settled herself on the wooden bench and Helga plopped down beside her. The seat was hard and the passenger car was hot. "You'll have lots of time to sit by the window, Helga. It's going to be a long trip."

Even with the windows open, Johanna felt as if she were suffocating. A familiar thought rolled through her mind: *There's no one to take care of them but me. Papa and Mama are gone.* She strengthened her resolve.

Just then, the train made a grinding noise, emitted a deafening whistle blast, and lurched into motion. The twins squealed and pressed their hands over their ears. They ducked and hid their faces in Johanna's lap.

"That's just the sound the train makes." Johanna tried to sound knowledgeable and brave.

The twins giggled with relief and sat up again.

Once out of the station, Johanna still felt as if she had bees in her stomach. *Wir sind schon dran. It's begun. We can't go back.*

To distract herself, she leaned past Inga and held her cupped hand out the window. The air rushed against her fingers. It felt wonderful and free.

Miss Darden walked down the aisle, counting the children and mouthing an inaudible number as she pointed to each.

Johanna studied her. She was tall and stern looking. Faint rows of wrinkles across her brow made her appear older than her thirty years. *She might be pretty if she smiled,* Johanna thought. *Maybe she was just worried about getting all of us on the train. Maybe she'll be nice once the trip gets under way.*

A younger girl, scared by the motion and the clatter of the train, was crying. Miss Darden frowned, but then sat down beside her. When she put her arm around the girl, the girl began to cry even louder.

Johanna's head hurt. She tapped Inga on the arm. "Change places with me for a minute. I need some air."

Inga stood up and squirmed past her.

Johanna slid over and stuck her head out the window. She looked forward. Then she looked back. Her heart leaped. She saw a familiar face leaning out a window in the last car.

It was Danny, and he was grinning at her.

TWO

1

"I hear they're giving away orphans today, off the train."

Oleta Mutt acknowledged Zebbie Parker with a curt nod but did not look in her direction. It annoyed Oleta to be told something she already knew.

Zebbie continued, "We're in need of a boy to help us, don't you know. A good, strong one."

Oleta still did not respond. Instead, she lifted the faded, drooping brim of her sunbonnet and dabbed her damp forehead with her sleeve. She leaned forward to peer down the tracks. In the distance, a train was emerging from a haze of shimmering heat that was capped with a cloud of black smoke.

Moments later the train ground to a sparky, metallic stop. Like sparrows released from a cage, children poured out of the stuffy car onto the wooden platform of the depot. Traces of soot smudged their faces. Two weeks of travel from New York had left them looking exhausted and dirty. A trio of German girls straggled out last, Johanna flanked by the twins.

"Why, look at them two!" exclaimed a man's voice in the crowd. "They look like a matched set!"

The three sisters possessed the same delicate bone structure and their mother's dark eyes and dark hair. Their once pale skin was now red and peeling, no match against the Texas sun that daily bore through the open train windows.

Johanna squinted against the glare. *Where are we?* she wondered. The train had taken them through a landscape that was more brown than green. Only the rivers and streams that cut through the central Texas countryside were outlined with leafy trees and flanked with ribbons of patchy green vegetation. Crops of cotton and corn struggled in the heat, and everyone agreed that the summer of 1886 was hotter than usual.

"Do I *have* to go if someone picks me?" Helga whimpered to Johanna.

"Yes, you know you do. We *all* do," her sister responded in German. Then she softened her reply: "But maybe someone will take all three of us." She surveyed the meager crowd who had gathered and tightened her grip on Inga's and Helga's hands when a man pointed to them. Each stop represented a new threat. Twice she had pleaded with couples who wanted only her or the twins. She had persuaded them to take other children since they couldn't take the three of them. Now she felt frightened all over again. Her head ached.

Inga coughed and leaned against Johanna. "I'm hot," she complained hoarsely.

"I know." *It's as hot as it was in New York,* Johanna thought to herself. *But at least it doesn't stink here.* A warm breeze provided a momentary change, but not much relief.

Helga stared at the townspeople with unabashed curiosity. She suddenly became animated. "Look, Johanna!" she exclaimed. "It's Papa!"

2

At the sight of the man's head, Johanna, too, was startled, but when he turned towards them, she realized what a foolish thought it had been. "No, Helga. He *looks* like Papa, but that's not Papa." She reminded her younger sister, as she had so many times before, "We won't see Papa again. He died." Her mind drifted, as it so often did, to thoughts of their father and mother.

Johanna now understood the despondency her father must have felt when he realized he would not be able to take care of his family. *I miss you so much. I would have found a way to help you, Papa.* When he gave her his jacket, he told her, "You must carry on for both of us." Johanna silently berated herself. *If only I had understood.* When she learned of her father's death, she put the coat on. She had worn it almost daily until it was taken away from her at the Aid Society Home. All that remained were the three black buttons she had struggled to keep. *Mama drowned, too,* she thought. *She drowned in Papa's death, in fear, in hunger, in poverty. She drowned in sadness, a darkness she slipped into until she was unreachable.* Johanna recalled her mother staring with eyes that did not see, recalled her mother no longer speaking or responding to her or her sisters. *Bloomingdale Asylum.* Johanna felt her teeth clench when the hated name crossed her mind. *Mama, you loved us. It wasn't right what happened. You—*

"Children, line up!" The shrill sound of the chaperone's voice obliterated Johanna's thoughts and made her jump. Miss Darden was harried. A week earlier, Lloyd Rice, who had been in charge of the car with the boys, had slipped on the steps of the train and broken his ankle. Ever since, Miss Darden had been coping with the remaining children by herself. "Danny O'Brien, I'm talking to you, too, young man! Get over there where you belong. And take off your cap."

Danny ignored both instructions.

Like a hen fluttering to settle in a roost, Zebbie jostled to get a front-row view on the station platform. She elbowed her husband and pointed to some of the boys. Oleta was more interested in the girls. She was sizing up several of them, envisioning each in turn carrying out orders she gave them.

"Children, line up! Girls on this side; boys on the other," Miss Darden exhorted them.

In a futile attempt to arrange the children in a row, she signaled for some of them to move forward. "Line up," she snapped, "or you'll never be placed out! This is nearly the last stop. You *know* the last stops are in Texas."

I'm glad, thought Johanna. She was exhausted, and the heat made her feel limp. They had wound their way across the miles south and then west, disembarking at preselected towns for placing out. The unlikely group of young travelers had endured train changes whenever the gauge of the track changed, which was often. Soot and cinders floated through the windows like delicate black feathers. They left splotches on the children's clothes and sometimes burned them. The summer weather forced passengers to leave the windows open, even though the heat intensified the acrid odor of the train smoke. The clatter of the wheels ceased only when they pulled into a depot. Even so, the sound seemed to reverberate in their heads long after the train had stopped.

Nor did the feeling of motion cease when the train stopped. When Johanna dozed off, the rolling sensation caused her to dream that she was on the boat from Germany. She awoke with a start when the dream ended abruptly with the explosion that injured her father. At other times she would emerge from an uneasy sleep, shaken by the image of her mother standing on the deck of the ship, gazing at the black water.

Johanna scanned the sparse crowd but avoided looking directly at anyone. Instead, she pretended to study the depot, as if she were scanning the landscape to select a site for a picnic. The long wooden structure was muddy yellow trimmed in faded green. She studied a white sign that bore the words "SULPHUR CREEK" painted in black. Silently mouthing syllables, she was glad now for what little instruction had been given to them at the Aid Society Home. A rusted railroad logo dangled above a sign that announced hoped-for arrival and departure times. Scarred, tall-backed wooden benches, like worn bookends, bracketed the door to the waiting room. An idle freight wagon stood at the far end, awaiting the trunks, luggage, and cargo that did not often arrive.

Miss Darden struggled to maintain her composure. At the time of his accident, Mr. Rice had reassured her, "The only stops left are the ones in Texas, and you have experience as an agent." She responded to his kind words with a weak smile. To herself she thought, *Then you aren't aware of the incident in Nebraska, in Schuyler, two years ago… or worse, the one in Fredonia, Kansas, when a child in my care died. Wandered onto the tracks and was killed.* She closed her eyes and swallowed, sick at the memory. *"No more mistakes, Miss Darden." That's what they told me.* To herself, she repeated their warning under her breath, *No more mistakes, Evangeline.* She looked at the children around her. Although only a handful remained, she doubted her ability to place them all. She was plagued by the recurring thought, *What will happen if I fail? If I can't place them?* Inga coughed again, and Miss Darden cast a nervous glance in her direction. *The changes in temperature—hot and stuffy aboard the train during the day, but often drafty at night—could they be causing Inga's sickness?*

Miss Darden surveyed the ragged line of children and sighed. It was no straighter than a saw edge. "At least *try* to keep the line straight," she urged. "And the older girls and boys need to help the younger ones wipe the soot off their faces, please."

They look dreadful, she told herself, *like they just climbed out of a coal bin.* She wanted them to look appealing, but the weeks on the train were taking their toll. When the train was in motion, the noise was unrelenting. The train seats were inhospitable to small bodies. She had watched how some of the children learned to snatch bits of sleep at odd moments. Others stared out the window, glassy-eyed, until exhaustion overcame them. When she could arrange it, the brood slept in town meeting halls, churches, or schools. In one instance, the children who had not been placed were taken home for a night by members of the community. She knew from looking at the children's faces when they returned to the train the next morning how much they had enjoyed the luxury of washing up, eating a hot meal, and sleeping in a bed. But she also knew that these young travelers were always aware that mile-by-mile they were moving farther and farther from everything, and possibly everyone, they had ever known. She could see it happen as the days went by: that knowledge weighed them down like a sodden wool blanket.

3

On a discouraging day like this, she had to remind herself of the reason she undertook these difficult trips. It was the same desire that first led to her work at the Aid Society Home, the hope of a better life for wretched children. Grieving relatives handed them over, like wilted bouquets, to foundling hospitals, orphans' asylums, and homes for destitute children. Poverty-stricken parents, usually immigrants and unwed mothers, tearfully signed over legal guardianship of some or all of their offspring. *Yes, she promised them, your children will remain here until we can place them out with families in the West. They'll have an opportunity for a good life in the country, away from the hunger, disease, and poverty in New York. Their life in the country will be a healthy one, filled with fresh air and honest labor. They'll be with families who welcome them and can provide for them.* She knew that most of the parents who relinquished their sons and daughters clung to one hope, a better life for their children.

Sometimes babies and children were left on the institution's doorstep under the cloak of darkness. Evangeline's eyes rested on a thin boy. *Charley O'Donnell was one of those,* she thought. Like Indian war paint, dirt and soot smudges still streaked his cheeks, despite an attempt to remove them a moment earlier. *Charley doesn't look much cleaner now than he did the morning we found him.* She shook her head at the thought.

Another small sigh escaped her lips as she mentally retraced her three years with the Aid Society: When she could no longer endure the wrenching process of admitting orphaned and relinquished children to the Home, she had asked to become a placement agent on the trains. For the last two years she had escorted homeless children to destinations across the Midwest. She acknowledged to herself that in this capacity, she had made certain mistakes. The same familiar doubts began to resurface. *Did I utterly misjudge myself? From the beginning, was I too weak, too naïve, too idealistic? Did I then make a bigger mistake by becoming an agent?*

The children's restlessness brought her musing to an end, and she renewed her attempt to straighten their irregular line. "Beatrice, move forward. Thomas, move down a little. Don't crowd!" But the children seemed no more capable of maintaining a simple row than of marching in a military formation. Some of them stared at the ground. Others stared boldly at the small crowd, searching for a kind or sympathetic or interested face. A few children feigned indifference or boredom, but still stole glances at those who had come to look at them. Charley stepped forward and began loudly reciting the alphabet. "A, B, C, D, E…" He called each letter out clearly, hoping to attract favorable attention to himself.

"Charley, be still! You, too, Danny!"

Charley reluctantly moved back into line, disappointed not to have gotten past E, and scared that he would once again be overlooked. He protested, "But Cullan got picked just because he could sing and dance!"

It's true, she thought. The boy had delighted an older couple with an Irish song and a brief but spirited jig. Charley had been crestfallen when Cullan left the train. She was annoyed that the only other remaining Irish boy, eleven-year-old Danny, would have nothing to do with six-year-old Charley. Miss Darden, however, ignored Charley's protest.

Miss Darden glanced at her watch. It was 11:30, the time listed on the Aid Society Home's announcements of the train's arrival and its purpose. The townspeople had grown quiet and were waiting for her to begin. Although she had delivered the same remarks scores of times, she always felt shaky until she was under way. She cleared her throat and took a breath. "Notices were sent to towns along this railroad line informing you that you would have the opportunity to choose one or more homeless children to join your family."

She digressed just long enough to say, "Although the Homeless Children's Aid Society has placed thousands of children with families throughout the Midwest during the past three decades, this is the first time we have placed out children in Texas. I know this great state will prove to be the land of opportunity for these orphans." The crowd murmured its approval.

Danny snorted and scoffed at the last remark.

The agent shot him a peevish look. She continued to speak, to cover the awkwardness caused by his embarrassing response. "It is the belief of the Aid Society that it is easier for a child to start a new life if all existing family ties are cut. Although we make exceptions and will honor your requests, we prefer to place siblings out to different families."

"What's 'siblings'?" shouted a lanky, slow-talking farmer.

"Brothers and sisters—"

"Children who have the same parents and who should stay together." It was Danny again, his sarcastic, faceless voice emerging from beneath his cap. Johanna had to suppress the urge to lean forward and look in Danny's direction. She could feel her lips forming a small smile.

The agent whirled in Danny's direction. She fought to stifle her anger. In a contained voice she said, "That will be enough, Danny!" *I'll never place him!* she silently despaired. *Who's going to take an awful boy like that?*

She turned back to the crowd. Without hurrying, she reached up and tucked in an errant strand of auburn hair that had blown loose. She wanted to show that she was in control, even though Danny was doing his best to prove otherwise. Her light blue dress helped give the impression that she was calm in spite of Danny's outbursts and cool in spite of the heat. Then she answered the man's question. "We discourage you from taking siblings, children from the same family, sir. We think it's better if brothers and sisters go to different families when they're placed out. I'm sure you can appreciate the problems, sir, that might arise from placing siblings in the same home."

He nodded his understanding.

At the same moment, almost imperceptibly, Johanna shook her head "No."

4

Inga coughed and slumped against her older sister. *Hurry up, Miss Darden,* Johanna mentally urged her on. *Tell them that they have to feed us, have to take care of us when we're sick.* She pressed her hand against Inga's feverish cheek, then stroked it. *We're supposed to get a common school education. They're supposed to take us to Sunday school. They have to do this until we're seventeen...* Johanna knew the agent's recitation by heart and silently ticked off each item as Miss Darden said it.

Johanna's eyes wandered to two leaden-faced women who were nodding their approval of the Sunday school requirement. She overheard one of them remark, "Like as not, those orphans are heathens. Probably never heard of the Bible."

Johanna could feel the corners of her mouth curl in disgust. She had to choke back the impulse to shout, *I bet I know more Bible verses than you do!* How many long winter afternoons and rainy spring ones had she and her sisters spent sitting on the hard playroom floor in the Home, parroting back verse after verse after the matron droned them? It made Johanna's tailbone hurt just to think about it.

Now Miss Darden was saying, "You will be given a card that states your obligations. A representative from the Homeless Children's Aid Society will correspond with you or come through next year to see that the children are being cared for properly." She felt a flash of guilt saying that. The reality was that despite good intentions, the Aid Society was not always able to meet that goal. "I will keep a similar card with each child's placement information to take back to the Homeless Children's Aid Society."

"Just wait and see if anyone *ever* comes!" Danny taunted.

Miss Darden had endured enough. She walked over to him and grabbed his ear, pinching it until it was a brilliant red. Johanna winced and pressed her hand to her own ear in sympathy. Danny flinched but made no sound. Miss Darden turned her back to the townspeople as she excoriated him through clenched teeth.

When she was satisfied she had made her point, she turned to the crowd but left her hand on Danny's shoulder, just in case. She adjusted her stance so that the sun was not in her eyes and continued, "We want the placements to succeed. For this reason, we ask local committees of respected citizens—ministers, judges, bankers, newspaper editors—to review the names of those who might wish to become foster parents and to approve the applications of those deemed suitable."

The same man interrupted her again. "What about the other way 'round? What if the *child* don't work out?"

Miss Darden could hear Danny mutter under his breath, "You throw 'em back. Like a fish you don't want." She tightened her grip on his shoulder in case he was considering saying it again, louder.

"The child can be removed or placed with a different family if these conditions are not met or if the child proves unacceptable to you. You are not required to adopt the child, although you may do so if you wish. Parents who turned their children over to the Aid Society because they could not adequately provide for them have relinquished custody of their children to the Aid Society. Of course, all of our records are kept strictly confidential. At no time would any child, including babies and very young children, ever be given information as to their actual parents or the placement of any of their siblings." As an aside, she added, "And, of course, you may change the name of any child you take."

Helga sighed and shifted her weight from one foot to the other as if she were standing on a hot griddle. "Be still," Johanna whispered. "She's almost through." Johanna felt another surge of anger at the people who were unabashedly scrutinizing them. These strangers could determine their fate, and she and her sisters would have no say in the matter. *At least we've made it this far together,* Johanna comforted herself. Märta, a pleasant Swedish girl, had been placed out at the first stop. Her younger brother was still on the train. Separated by such great distance, how could they ever hope to find each other again? At that unhappy thought, Johanna unconsciously squeezed her sisters' hands.

People had begun fanning themselves with anything handy. The children had also begun to fidget in earnest. Miss Darden knew that whenever she reached this point in her presentation, the children's anxiety escalated.

She hurried to conclude her remarks. "These orphans are good children"—she felt foolish saying that with her hand still clamped on Danny's shoulder, so she let go of him—"who, through no fault of their own, are homeless." Still seeing a few puzzled expressions, she explained: "Let me remind you that we use the term 'orphan' for any child who is homeless or who has been relinquished to us, even if the child has one or both parents still living. Many of the parents are recent immigrants who were simply unable to provide for some or all of their offspring."

Johanna choked back more resentment. "Unable to provide…" Her mother had worked thirteen hours a day and was still "unable to provide." Her father's accidental blinding and maiming left him "unable to provide" for his family—and distraught enough to end his life. Johanna felt tears sting her eyes, so she looked down at the ground.

Miss Darden's voice again. "Several of the children speak with accents. Some still speak very limited English. Nevertheless, we hope that you will give them a chance for a new life, away from the poverty and harshness of their lives in New York. We believe that a loving Christian family, fresh air, and discipline will enable these children to become productive, responsible adults." She knew firsthand what it was like not to have a family of one's own. Her voice dwindled to half its volume. "Please look over the children now. Talk with them and make your decision."

The selection process made her uncomfortable. Invariably there were disappointments: a child hoping to be chosen, but who was not; a prospective foster family not obtaining the child of its choice.

A sprinkling of townspeople, along with several farmers and their wives, moved towards the children. Almost as a reflex, Johanna took a step back. Some couples were accompanied by their own children, whom the orphan train riders studied intently. One could almost read the thoughts of the children from the train: *Did the family's own children look happy? Well fed? What would it be like to have that boy as a brother? That girl as a sister?*

Other bystanders stayed at a distance, satisfied to watch and glad for any novelty that broke the monotony of a dull summer day. Danny peered at them. They reminded him of the parade-goers he had seen in New York: delighted to watch the confetti being scattered, and more delighted that someone else would have to clean it up.

An onlooker cupped his hands around his mouth. "Don't pick a pig in a poke," he joked in a loud voice.

"Be sure to check their teeth!" guffawed the blacksmith.

Miss Darden wrinkled her brow in disapproval. She resented those who viewed the children as chattel and who saw this merely as an opportunity to acquire unpaid labor and farmhands.

"F, G, H, I, J, K, L, M, N…" Charley resumed his loud recitation of the alphabet.

Johanna now clasped her sisters' small hands even more tightly. Her own hands had grown clammy, and her mouth felt dry. *Please let us be chosen by the same family,* she prayed. Miss Darden had warned her that while twins were usually adopted together, she would probably go to another family. Still, Johanna remained hopeful. *Wasn't it just yesterday that four brothers and sisters were taken by the same family? At the very least,* she told herself, *Inga and Helga will be placed out together.* She reminded herself that it had almost happened when they stopped near the Louisiana-Texas border town of Bois d'Arc. After a short discussion, however, the couple decided against Helga and Inga, and settled instead on a brother and sister. And hadn't the other set of twins, curly-headed four-year-old boys, been placed out almost immediately, both to the same family? Johanna exhaled and felt herself relax slightly.

Several children were already walking away from the line with couples who had selected them. One young husband and wife escorted a little girl towards Miss Darden. The child stopped licking the peppermint stick the woman had given her and held up her prize for the other children to see. Helga's mouth watered. Johanna watched the couple with keen interest, and then smiled. *They really want a little girl,* she thought. She noticed two couples vying for Nikolas, whose newly missing front teeth gave him the winsome grin of a jack-o'-lantern.

Johanna looked at the children on either side of her. Just as she and her sisters desperately wanted a chance with a decent family, so did each of them. An older boy was doing a handstand. Johanna could tell from his expression that even he recognized it was a demeaning attempt to gain someone's—anyone's—notice.

"Choose me! Choose me! I'm a hard worker!" cried Piroska, a gangly Hungarian girl of fourteen. Seeing the unusual level of activity and tension among the other children, Johanna thought, *Miss Darden's remarks about the final stops being in Texas frightened all of us.*

5

As Miss Darden watched, she recalled the scare she'd had two-and-a-half weeks earlier in a town just this size. She had alighted from the train. It was a bright day, but except for the stationmaster, the depot was deserted—something that had never happened before. Alarmed, she called to him, "Where is everyone?"

Danny leaned out a train window and lent an unwanted chorus. "What's wrong? Where are the *people*?" he demanded. "Doesn't anybody here *want* us?" He had a way of upsetting all the children. They crowded around the windows, chattering and speculating.

At that moment a band had begun to play in the distance, and the stationmaster shouted back, "Everyone is at the Fourth of July parade, lady."

"Yes, of course," she responded, feeling foolish but relieved. She had lost track of the date.

"Folks'll come around soon as it's finished." Miss Darden was weary, but she felt obligated to explain to the children about the holiday. *After all,* she had told herself, *most of them are immigrants.* They continued to peer out the windows on the platform side of the train. "The people are at a parade," she had explained. "Today is the Fourth of July, Independence Day. It's a special day that celebrates our nation's birthday. It celebrates freedom. Everyone in America is free—" She had been startled into silence when Danny abruptly slammed a window shut, crossed his arms over his chest, and closed his eyes.

Miss Darden was still reflecting on Danny's odd reaction when she was jolted back to the present, back to Sulphur Creek. Two brothers clung together, making a noisy disturbance and refusing to be separated. She hurried over and put a hand on each one's shoulder. "Boys, let go of each other."

The smaller boy shouted, "He's my brother! I'm not going without him!"

"Dillon, you *have* to." Her tone was soft, but resolute.

"No! I won't!" Now he was sobbing hysterically. "Kieran! Kieran!" He locked his arms tighter around his big brother.

Miss Darden dreaded scenes like this. She kept thinking she would become used to them, but she never had. The townspeople stopped talking and stared. The other children watched in silence, each imagining the moment when he or she might be taken away from a brother or sister and from the others on the train. Johanna felt sick every time it happened.

The agent looked at the couple who wanted Dillon. They stood by, awkward and helpless. "I'm afraid we'll have to separate them," Miss Darden said to the husband. Another man hesitated, then stepped forward to help.

The husband nodded slightly, and then forcibly unclasped Dillon's hands while the other man restrained his brother. "We want the younger one. Just the younger one," the husband explained in a remorseful voice. As they pulled the children apart, the small boy erupted into a kicking, flailing flurry of arms and legs.

"We can't take on two more," his wife apologized to Miss Darden. Then, to the struggling child, she soothed, "It'll be fine. You'll see."

The child collapsed into an exhausted heap. "Kieran," the boy sobbed to his brother, "don't let them take me." The other man kept his hands on Kieran's shoulders.

Kieran stood with tears rolling down his cheeks. He jerked one shoulder, then the other free of the man's grip. In words that he seemed to pry from his throat, he choked, "It'll be all right, Dillon." He glared at the couple. "You do right by him, or I'll—"

"Kieran, please get back on the train!" Kieran did not move. Miss Darden wished devoutly for Mr. Rice. Kieran watched the man pick up his crying brother and carry him to their wagon. Once aboard, his wife tried to put her arm around Dillon. He turned his back to her, his eyes fixed on his brother. Her husband walked over to Miss Darden and signed some papers. A minute later, Dillon drove away with his new parents.

"Kieran! Never forget me!" Dillon clutched the side of the wagon and continued to cry out, "Remember me, Kieran! I'll remember you!"

Kieran could hear his brother even after he disappeared from view. He shoved his way past the rest of the children and climbed back on the train. Crying, he curled himself into a ball on one of the seats so he couldn't be seen by those outside.

Miss Darden sighed but did not follow him. *It's for the best,* she told herself. *It's for the best.* A commotion near the train ended her silent mantra. It was Danny. Again.

6

Since Mr. Rice's departure, Danny had been a chronic source of irritation and anxiety. Despite Miss Darden's constant reprimands and threats, he refused to believe that any of the rules applied to him. Worse, he remained oblivious to the danger of his antics. Too many times she had watched him delight and excite the other children by leaning out one window far enough to tap on the glass or make a face in the window behind him.

Now Danny was walking up and down the line mimicking the townspeople who were inspecting the children as if they were livestock. At the sound of his brogue, Johanna jerked her head in his direction. He leaned towards a frail boy who was a little younger than he. "How much coal can you shovel in a day? If it's less than a ton, laddie, I can't use you!" He pretended to test the boy's muscle by pinching his scrawny arm, and the boy flexed his bicep to join in the game.

Although compact like his father and his uncles, Danny exuded energy. Moving on to a wisp of a girl, he again simulated an adult's booming voice. He paused before her and demanded to know, "You don't eat more than once a week, do you, lassie? I don't want to have to waste money feeding you." Flattered by the attention, the child giggled "No" and looked bashfully at her scuffed, high-buttoned shoes.

Miss Darden collared Danny. He made a face of mock terror as she marched him to the end of the line. "You stay right here, young man, and you don't move! This is the last warning, Danny!" Although her words were threatening, her tone was hollow. She shook her head and walked away.

Most of the townspeople, however, refused to venture near him: to discourage them, Danny called out, flailed his arms, spit, wore his cap low on his forehead. He made a grotesque face at a man who quickly abandoned his attempt to remove the cap.

Danny was content to be at the end of the line. *No one will bother me now,* he thought. *Uncle Aidan would be proud. I'm going to make it to the last stop.* He slumped in relief.

Charley, who had finished reciting the alphabet and started over again, was selected by a widow and her widowed mother-in-law during his second recitation. They led him towards Miss Darden, each holding one of his hands. The younger woman was already smoothing his hair, while her mother-in-law used her free hand to dab at his soot-smudged face with her handkerchief.

He was beaming. "My name is Charley," he announced. "I'm six years old, and I know the alphabet."

"You certainly do!" Still wiping his cheeks, the older woman said, "My boy was named Charles."

"I already had a bath in New York," Charley protested as she continued her efforts to tidy him up.

"It'll take us a month of Sundays to get you clean!" she laughed.

Charley was wondering who and where her "boy" was. But at that moment she tucked her embroidered handkerchief in her sleeve, bent over, and opened the silver filigreed locket suspended around her neck. Inside the oval were two sepia-toned pictures: an older man with a bushy mustache and mutton chop sideburns, and a younger man who looked much the same, but with only a mustache. The collars of their military uniforms were visible at the bottom of the pictures.

Pointing to the faded image of the young man, the woman said in an emotion-filled voice, "My son Charley was a fine, young lad like you. When he grew up, he became a soldier like his father." Her eyes shifted to the picture of her husband, and she touched her finger to his picture. "My husband, Francis, was killed in '74, fighting the Comanches and Kiowas at Palo Duro Canyon." A faraway look settled over her. "He was a tall, handsome Irishman. He liked to read, and he knew his Bible." She continued to drift, one thought flowing into the next. "He was a captain in Colonel Ranald Mackenzie's 4th Cavalry. I'm proud to say it was the finest, most respected Indian-fighting regiment of the Army."

When she looked up from the locket and into Charley's face, she realized he was staring at her as if mesmerized by her voice but baffled by her words. Aware that her disjointed reminiscing had only confused him, she closed the locket with a soft click. "Well, we'll sort it all out later, won't we?" she cooed, and stroked his face.

Her daughter-in-law picked up the thread of the conversation. "My husband Charles was a brave, honorable man. We always hoped for a fine, red-haired son like you." Although Charley was perplexed as to who was related to whom and in what fashion, he did understand her final words and the older woman's gentleness. He buried his face first against one woman's skirt and then the other's. Hugging and being hugged, he felt a warm flood of relief wash over him.

Evangeline Darden hesitated only momentarily to rationalize placing the boy with the women. *They're widows, but Charley would have a good home. And the younger one is sure to remarry. Besides… this is nearly the final stop.*

Danny watched Charley as he climbed into a simple carriage with the two women. He could see his red head bob as he chattered. He turned and gave Danny a jubilant wave. Danny watched them go. Once they drove off, Charley did not look back.

At Charley's departure, Danny felt a sense of loss even though he had considered himself too grown up to be friends with a "baby" like Charley. To his surprise, he also felt a genuine pang of jealousy. He had done as his father and uncles had asked—made himself so disagreeable that no one wanted him—but each time he saw a child leave with happy, smiling parents, he wondered if he was doing the right thing.

Danny was still considering the matter when he saw a weather-beaten farmer and his worn-looking wife moving along the line of children. They examined each child carefully, feeling this one's arms and legs and checking that one's eyes and mouth. After comparing several boys, they narrowed the selection to two. Eventually the farmer and his wife, satisfied with the soundness of a husky Polish boy, agreed: "This one." They walked over to a makeshift table Miss Darden had set up. Zebbie looked in Oleta's direction to make sure her neighbor knew they had found what they had come for.

"His name is Stanislav," Miss Darden informed them. She took their application and printed the boy's name and age on it. Turning the sheet towards the farmer and pointing to a blank line, she said, "You'll need to sign here."

He wrote "Herbert M. Parker" in large, loopy script.

Danny was watching the Parkers. He felt antipathy for them; he could see that Stanislav was scared. "Stan!" Danny called out. Stanislav turned to him, but Danny could think of nothing else to say. Instead, he gave a small, sad wave. His stomach ached. It hurt each time another friend disappeared. He, Stan, and Arthur had made up silly rhymes and songs on the train. In hushed voices and through muffled snickers, they chanted, *"Evangeline and Lloyd/ Where can they be?/K-I-S-S-I-N-G"* and *"Old Mr. Rice/fell off the train/broke his ankle/and now he's lame."* With Stan's departure, Danny was the only one of the three who was left. Skinny Arthur Boston had been picked a few days earlier by an old, stony-faced couple. Arthur was clever and full of tricks. He was the only person who could make Danny laugh. Now, there were no boys on the train Danny wanted to sing with. Instead, he told himself, he would just sing "Mary McCrae," the song he sang when he felt doleful. And he would listen to Johanna sing her lullaby to her sisters each night.

Miss Darden shook hands with Stanislav. She started to say, "Make Mr. and Mrs. Parker glad that they chose you," but changed her mind. "I wish you a good and happy life, Stanislav." She looked directly at the Parkers when she said the word *happy.* The couple, who had not yet spoken to him, walked away, the boy trailing behind them. He was chewing on a thumbnail and sneaking furtive glances back at Miss Darden. For a split second, their eyes met, and she could see his fear. She looked away. *It happens so fast,* she thought. *He doesn't know whether to feel happy or sad.* She shifted her eyes to the Parkers. *Neither do I.*

Zebbie smiled triumphantly as she passed Oleta. "Hope you find one," she said in a voice that oozed smugness.

Oleta pretended not to hear her. She and Angus continued to move slowly along the line, with Oleta taking the lead. Angus was tall, bleary-eyed, and like the rest of the farmers, sun-baked. The top half of his left ear was missing. The scalloped edge looked alarmingly like it had been made by a row of human teeth.

Oleta was humorless and heavyset, with short arms that made her look even stouter. The papery skin on her plump face was puckered like a dried apple. Her brow was overshadowed by a straw hat adorned with two tired-looking silk flowers, and it was soiled and frayed where she had repeatedly held it while securing it with her hat pin.

"This one might do," said Angus, referring to Sofia, a dusky Greek girl.

Oleta shook her head no. "Looks like she might eat too much." Oleta moved on down the line and paused in front of Johanna.

Johanna swallowed and interlaced her fingers with her sisters'. Their hands were soaked with perspiration.

Danny's face fell when he saw the couple linger in front of Johanna and her sisters. He tried to edge closer to hear what they were saying.

"This one is small. Don't look as if she'd eat much," Angus told Oleta in a commonsense tone of voice.

She talks about me as if I'm not here, Johanna silently bristled.

Oleta eyed Johanna. "You know how to sew?" Oleta stitched the air with an imaginary needle.

Johanna gave a curt nod, but it angered her further to be talked to as if she were retarded or ignorant. A few minutes earlier, the woman who called them heathens had moved past her quickly when Johanna announced in an ingenuous voice, "I know Satan."

"You cook?" Oleta stirred an imaginary pot with an imaginary spoon.

Johanna nodded again. "Bread." She was instantly angry at herself. Pride had caused her to try to make herself more appealing to these awful people.

"You speak English," Oleta said in surprise.

"Ja," Johanna replied, still upset. She felt her face flush with embarrassment at having answered in German, so she added, "We learn English at the Home."

Oleta seemed satisfied. A look passed between her and her husband. "She'll do."

"You, girl," said Angus to Johanna, motioning for her to follow.

Johanna took a deep breath. "Let's go," she whispered, taking her sisters with her. When Angus turned and saw the three of them following him, his face clouded.

He waved his hands as if swatting away horseflies. "Not them!" he bellowed. "Just you!"

"But they're my *sisters,*" blurted Johanna. She lifted their linked hands to show they were a unit.

"Don't want 'em," Oleta shot back, already turning and walking away.

When Danny heard this, he shouted, "You old biddy! Why do you want to take her away from her sisters?" Although Danny's cap shadowed his face, it was as red as Angus's, and he was quivering with rage. Johanna gave him a desperate, grateful look. Even though he had known Mary Ceara only a few hours, he understood something about having a younger sister.

Miss Darden's voice pierced the air. "Young man! You get back on the train NOW!" Only when she began moving towards him did he obey.

"Please!" Johanna begged, hoping either the man or his wife might yet relent.

The twins watched Johanna's face, trying to understand whether or not they were going with her. She was still holding on to them.

Angus narrowed his eyes. He glared at her and roared, "She said *No!*"

It was done.

Johanna sucked her lips in and bit down. This was the moment she had dreaded. Tears trickled down her dusty cheeks and streaked her sunburned skin. She turned loose of her sisters' hands and reached into her pockets. Extracting two black buttons, she bent down and closed one into their right hands. In German she said, "Keep these always! They're from Papa's jacket. I have one, too. Now, put them in your pocket." She kissed Inga and Helga, and joined their hands together. She clasped her hands over theirs and choked in a small, strained voice, "I love you! Stay together!" To impress upon them the importance of her words, she repeated, "*Zusammen! Together!* Together you will be all right."

Reluctantly, Johanna released their tiny hands and hugged her sisters one last time. She looked in despair at Miss Darden. "Please, Miss. I know you are not supposed to, but keep my sisters together. Please!"

Miss Darden swallowed and her jaw muscle tightened, but she did not reply.

Danny watched from the train. He hid his face behind the edge of the window so no one would see that he was crying. Up until this moment, he had convinced himself that he, Johanna, and her sisters might somehow end up in the same place in Texas. Now the absurdity of his hope was undeniable. He wiped his eyes and peeked out the window again.

Helga had burst into tears. Inga's sobs were interspersed with ragged coughs. Not wanting her sisters to see her distress, and unable to endure theirs, Johanna walked hurriedly in the direction of the Mutts. Angus was already at the table with Miss Darden. "Johanna Buehler, age twelve (12)," the agent wrote on the paper. Looking up at Angus, she asked, "Will you see that this child is fed and that she goes to school?" Then she added, "She's had some schooling at the Aid Society Home."

Angus nodded in assent.

Oleta stood off to the side. Johanna remained stiff and silent behind her. Sofia took the twins by the hand and held on to them as the girls sobbed. Hearing Inga's raspy cough, Johanna felt her heart constrict into a tight knot. The crying grew louder, and Miss Darden finally gestured to Sofia to take the girls back onto the train.

To Johanna, Miss Darden babbled, "It may not seem like it now, but someday you'll know that this is for the best." She felt the color rise in her cheeks, ashamed to be saying something that even she did not completely believe.

Johanna stared at her with contempt and then looked away. She felt numb, as if she were standing outside the situation, watching. She had explained to her sisters many times that she might have to go with a different family, and that no matter what, it would be better than the three of them staying in the overcrowded Aid Society Home. Now she wasn't sure. She reached inside her pocket and clutched the button from her father's coat.

Johanna clenched her eyes shut and swallowed hard. *Let this be over quickly,* she prayed. Then she peeked out, relieved that her sisters were no longer in sight. She had the urge to run back to the train, but the futility of it stopped her. *What good would it do? I couldn't hide under a seat. If I tried to hang on to something, they'd pull me away like they did Dillon.* She felt her eyes water. She wiped them and cupped her hand above them, pretending to shield them from the sun. She put her other hand in her pocket and stroked the button between her finger and her thumb.

Johanna glanced down at her dark blue dress. Her sisters were wearing brown and gray ones. Their dresses were now stained and dirty, and they smelled rank. Once again, she wished she and her sisters were back at the Home, dressed in identical drab but clean dresses and smocks. *No!* She pushed the thought from her mind for once and for all. *This has to be better than the Home.*

Johanna watched Angus Mutt pull a small piece of folded paper from the pocket of his soiled overalls. He glanced at it uneasily and then at Oleta. She gave a single, small nod of encouragement, but her sour expression remained unchanged. Miss Darden understood—this was not the first time she had seen this sort of thing—so she excused herself to go talk to another couple.

Danny looked closely at Angus and Oleta, determined to remember their faces because they were taking Johanna away. He wanted to be able to recognize them or describe them well enough to find her again one day. His eyes rested on Angus's notched ear.

He brightened when he saw that Johanna was looking at him. He had always been able to make her laugh, even when she had spoken almost no English. Johanna had been delighted over Mr. Rice's unanticipated departure because it forced Miss Darden to put all the remaining children in the same car. It had given Johanna and Danny time to talk about the deaths of their mothers, about life in Five Points, about their voyages across the Atlantic, about their lives before sailing to America, about the Home, about their hopes.

In spite of her feelings a minute earlier, Johanna gave Danny a small smirk. He was aping Angus Mutt's clumsy attempt to deal with the paper Miss Darden had placed in front of him. Even with traces of tears in her eyes, Johanna smiled at Danny and then rolled her eyes skyward.

She thought again about their conversations. Faced with an unknown destination and an equally unknown future, Danny always talked grandly about how he, his father, his two uncles and his new sister would someday be reunited in Texas. "We have a plan," he confided. Johanna liked to picture them meeting at a train station, shouting and hugging and crying tears of joy. "We'll all be together again," he proclaimed. "And we'll live in a house. And we'll have real beds."

Danny's earnestness and enthusiasm always drew Johanna in. "Yes," she declared, joining in his vision, "a bed for *each* of you! A soft one with lots of warm blankets in the winter." With her mind's eye, she could see the imaginary dwelling coming to life. "And a kitchen, of course. With a fine stove."

"And more food than we can eat, piled high on a big table."

When the word "table" ran through her mind, Johanna looked back at Angus, who was still standing in front of the table. After Miss Darden walked away, he had unfolded the scrap of paper he plucked from his overalls. Johanna stared, hoping to see what it was. Angus picked up the pen, inked it, and referring to the scrap of paper, copied his name letter by letter on the sheet Miss Darden had given him. He compared the paper scrap and the page one last time. Satisfied, he set the pen down. He carefully refolded the piece of paper along the creases and returned it to his pocket. In disconnected, uneven letters, he had scrawled "A. Mutt." He glanced at Oleta, who gave him another nod.

Returning to the table, Miss Darden blotted his signature even though the heat had already dried it. She picked up the form and inspected it. Danny strained to hear. "Thank you, Mister… Mutt," she said, making the inevitable comparison between his name and his face. To complete the information, she wrote "July 22, 1886" at the bottom. Then she handed him a card. "These are the Society's requirements of the families who take children." Although her words had an empty ring, she said, "I'm sure Johanna will be happy with you and your family." And then, "She's a good girl." There was a slight pause during which she struggled with herself. Suddenly she blurted, "And so are her sisters. Are you *sure* you won't consider taking the two of them as well?"

Johanna flashed her a look of gratitude, but Angus shook his head no, turned to Oleta to be sure, and then walked towards the wagon. Oleta and Johanna followed, Johanna looking back at the platform where she had seen her sisters for the last time. She raised a hand of farewell to Danny. She felt as forlorn as she had when Frau Liebes told her of her mother's death.

Miss Darden absent-mindedly fingered the page she held as she watched Johanna and the Mutts climb into their wagon. People such as the Parkers and the Mutts made the agent feel discouraged about the free home program. Even though a local committee was supposed to assess prospective foster parents in each of the towns, she knew that those who served on the committees were reluctant to declare any neighbor, friend, congregation member, client, subscriber, or voter unfit. It could damage friendships, not to mention businesses and careers, especially those of the committee members. Besides, most of the applicants already had children of their own. How could a committee declare them "unsuitable"? Rarely was any applicant disapproved. It distressed Miss Darden to admit that despite the goal of finding good homes for the children, some of the children ended up as maltreated, unpaid labor, toiling in strangers' fields, shops, or homes.

Miss Darden gathered up the papers for Johanna and the three other children placed out at Sulphur Creek, and put the sheets into a portfolio. The stop in Sulphur Creek had taken less than an hour. She shepherded her remaining brood back onto the train.

As soon as the agent boarded, Danny demanded to know, "Are the Muds going to treat Johanna good?" Danny stared hard at Miss Darden, who wondered if her expression betrayed her own doubts.

"Mutts," she said distractedly. "M-u-t-t. Their name is *Mutt*. I hope so." The way Angus yelled at Johanna had concerned her, too.

"What's the name of this place, anyway?" Danny pestered her.

"Sulphur Creek. Now no more questions, Danny!"

Mutt. Sulphur Creek. Mutt. Sulphur Creek. Danny repeated the words over and over to himself like a litany, determined to lock them in his memory.

"Only a few more stops," Miss Darden told the children wearily as she tried to resettle them on the train. "Let's hope we can place every one of you."

8

Miss Darden and Mr. Rice had begun the journey with fifty children. Now there were only a handful. Although all of the older children wondered, none of them had the nerve to ask: What happens to those who do not get chosen by the time the train reaches the end of the line?

Evangeline Darden found herself wondering the same thing. This trip was different from the hundreds that had snaked their way across the Midwest farmlands since the middle of the century. The orphan trains were known and welcomed there.

For the first time, she had the uneasy feeling that she might run out of towns before she ran out of children.

9

"Her name's Hannah," Angus drawled to Oleta as they climbed into the wagon. Johanna did not realize at first that he was referring to her. Instead of the softer sounding "Yo-HAH-nah" that she was accustomed to, he produced a two-syllable word that began with an unpleasantly flat, nasal sound. His strange pronunciation and the complete disappearance of its first syllable rendered her own name unrecognizable to her. Johanna continued to stand beside the wagon, confused as to where she was supposed to sit.

"There." Oleta pointed a sausage-like finger towards the back of the wagon.

Johanna climbed in unsteadily and sat down among rags and pieces of straw. She blinked back tears, fighting off nausea and dizziness. Afraid to ask, but more afraid not to ask, she ventured one last time, "What about my sisters?"

Without bothering to turn around, Oleta answered, "You have two *new* sisters and a brother. You don't need them two of yourn. Forget 'em."

Stung, Johanna understood the last two words, but struggled to assimilate the meaning of the rest of what Oleta had said. She slumped in exhaustion against the side of the wagon, rested her clasped hands on her knees, and pressed her forehead against her hands. Then came the terrible thought which up to now she had been able to hold at bay: *I may never see Inga and Helga again.*

After bumping along for a few miles, Angus turned the wagon down a narrow, rutted road that ended in front of a nondescript wood house. At that moment Johanna grasped what Oleta had said earlier: Two girls burst out the door, banging it shut behind them. Yelling and giggling, they pointed to Johanna and took turns climbing on and off the wagon wheel that was closest to her. She would come to learn that they were eight and nine years of age, although both were nearly as tall as she was. They were joined by a large, slow-moving boy who emerged from the barn.

"Girls!" Angus bellowed. They fell silent and stopped rocking on the side of the wagon for a minute, but then quickly started up again. "I told you to quit! Git over here!" he roared. Instead, they scampered to Oleta, who ran a hand over their heads and smoothed their brown braids.

"Now girls, you calm down, you hear?" Oleta said.

They ignored her, too.

Spotting the unrepaired fence, Angus walked over to his son and began yelling at him. "I told you to have that fixed by the time we got back." The boy raised his head, but not his eyes. His face reflected no surprise, and other than a slight flinch, he displayed no reaction whatsoever.

The sisters stared at Johanna. Their parents had told them they were going to get a girl to help in the house and on the farm. Johanna squirmed under their brazen scrutiny. "Is *she* what you got?" asked Ruby, incredulous. "She don't look very strong."

"Looks like a stick scarecrow," Opal contributed.

Angus turned to his daughters. "This here's Hannah," he said tilting his head in her direction but not looking at her. Johanna climbed out of the wagon and stood holding on to the side, as if it might somehow give her strength. Then to Johanna, he said, "This here's Ruby and Opal. Them's your new sisters."

As if to complete the necessary formalities, Oleta pointed to her son and added, "And this here's Cletis, their good-for-nothin' brother." She turned to Johanna. "You're to help me with these two young'ns, 'specially when I'm feeling poorly. I 'spect you to be hardworkin' and obedient." In a dry tone she sniffed, "Try to be deservin' of our kindness." To be sure Johanna understood, she added, "We didn't have to take you in."

Johanna did not understand what Oleta meant, but it didn't matter. She was no longer listening. Instead, she was thinking about her own mother and about what Frau Liebes had said the day she told Johanna her mother had died: that she was lucky, that at least she still had her sisters. Now she no longer had them.

Now she didn't feel very lucky. The loss of her sisters seemed unbearable. And despite the Aid Society's goal of a better life for the children, Johanna's last bit of hopefulness had evaporated. She had a terrible feeling that her life was going to get worse, not better. She could only guess about her sisters' fate.

THREE

1

It was nightfall when the train clattered into the tiny town of Salt Box and announced its arrival with a sibilant whistle blast.

"Children, arrangements have been made for us to stay overnight at a nearby church," Miss Darden told the few remaining children. A ripple of excitement went through them. They knew by now that this meant they might have a better meal.

The Aid Society agent walked the children to a whitewashed structure where the minister's wife fed them cold cornbread and buttermilk. Although they found almost anything a welcome change from the endless bread-and-mustard or bread-and-jelly meals on the train, some of the children grimaced at the first taste of buttermilk.

Later, as they stretched out on the hard benches that served as church pews, a disappointed child complained to anyone who was listening, "I thought we might have a hot supper."

"Just be glad these benches don't make noise and move all night long," another child replied.

Inga was too ill to eat and lay listless on a bench. Helga began to sing the lullaby that first their mother, and then Johanna, sang to them. Afterwards she cried as she listened to Inga's labored breathing and wished for her mother and her older sister. Waiting to fall sleep, she played in her mind the scene she had played so often during the past year. It was always the same: Their mother would suddenly appear. She had come for them, explaining that a terrible mistake had been made, that she wasn't dead at all, and that her daughters certainly did not belong among these orphans. The other children would watch them enviously as they swept out the door with their mother. Helga would cast a sympathetic glance in their direction, unable to hide her feelings of joy and superiority.

The following morning, Inga seemed better. Miss Darden gave her a plum that one of the churchwomen brought. The older children knew to help the younger ones wash their faces and tidy up. Miss Darden assembled her charges at the front of the church and scurried to greet the handful of citizens who had begun to trickle in the door at the back.

While the other children studied the townspeople entering the church, Danny slipped behind the pulpit. It was a hollow, three-sided podium with a cloth draped down the backside. Danny could see where the sides of the wooden lectern had been worn smooth by the grip of the preacher's hands. When he pulled the cloth up, he saw three dusty hymnals that lay inside on the floor. He shoved them against the sides of the podium's cavity to create more room. By crossing his arms over his chest, hunching his shoulders, and tucking his head, he was able to squeeze into the small space. He nudged the cloth until it dropped back into place. Suddenly, Danny felt a sneeze coming. *The dust.* He pinched his nostrils with his fingers in time to reduce the sneeze to a tiny, convulsive, but silent movement. Relieved, he wiped his nose and waited, hoping not to sneeze again.

He remained like a sentry frozen not at attention, but in a contortion. He strained to hear Miss Darden. Because there were so few townspeople there, she dispensed with her usual presentation. Instead, she spoke informally, and in a matter of minutes, the selection process was under way.

A couple and their five children had waited impatiently for Miss Darden to finish. Then they hovered around a one-year-old like iron filings around a magnet, delighting in her delicate fingers and toes and stroking the soft curl of blond hair at the nape of her neck.

"Is this our new sister?" one of the children asked.

Their mother nodded. "Yes. She's finally here. Our prayers have been answered." This placement had been prearranged with the Foundling Home, with the baby sent in Miss Darden's care to the waiting family.

"Many a family would have taken this precious baby," the agent told them. "More than once, I had to have an older girl take her back on the train."

The woman smiled at the agent. "We're so grateful to you. I've run out of babies of my own. My youngest is seven." She handed Miss Darden her letter from the Foundling Home. Unconsciously, the woman touched the small gold crucifix at her neck. "We're a devout Catholic family. It will be a great joy to have a baby in the house again."

Her husband smiled in agreement. "Besides, this will even up the number of boys and girls!" he laughed.

The paperwork completed, the family left in a tight knot with the baby at its center. The children in the church were heartened by the family's animated banter.

"Let's call her July!" exclaimed the one of the boys.

"No! Julie!" insisted an older girl.

"Or Jubilee!" suggested another boy.

Their mother settled the issue. "I think Mary Julia would be a fine name."

"I get to hold her first," the youngest boy implored his mother.

"No, I'm bigger. I get to," declared his sister.

Miss Darden stopped to watch the family depart. She allowed herself a moment to bask in their happiness and the baby's good fortune before returning to the task at hand. *It's imperative that I place all the remaining children at this stop*, she reminded herself, although she hardly needed reminding. Salt Box was the last town in which she was authorized to make placements. San Antonio, the final stop, was large enough to provide numerous foster families, but the Aid Society did not place children in cities. As the hour progressed, Evangeline Darden felt her spirits rise. One by one, children were taken. Only Danny—*where is that child?*—and the Buehler twins remained.

2

Quiet and fearful without Johanna, Helga and Inga stood near the front of the church, holding hands.

Of those who had turned out to select a child, all had left, except for one couple who had just walked in. The man looked at Miss Darden. "Is this where them train orphans are?"

Evangeline Darden felt her skin prickle as she gave a reluctant nod.

Stup Dill shuffled to the front of the church. His wife Althene trailed silently behind him. He stopped in front of the twins and studied them, looking slowly back and forth from one to the other. Other than the color of their dresses, they were as indistinguishable as matching salt and peppershakers.

Then he announced, "Them two'll do." Stup pointed to the twins with blunt fingers that were all of equal length. The first three fingers of his right hand had been chopped off flush with his little finger. A raw-boned man with coarse features and sparse, cropped hair, Stup said to no one in particular, "Two of 'em could probably do as much work as one scrawny boy. 'Sides, Mashburn don't want no brother."

"Thought you wanted a boy to help with the hogs," ventured Althene in a barely audible voice.

"Actually, we do have a boy here," Miss Darden volunteered as she scanned the church for Danny. Danny had dozed off, the sound of all conversations muffled by the wood and cloth walls of his hiding place.

Ignoring the agent, Stup turned and glowered at Althene. "Changed my mind. These two girlies appeal to me," he said, pointing his stubs at them again. "Besides, no boy brat off this train would ever be a real Dill. I already got a namesake in Mash."

The twins did not understand what he was saying, but they recoiled from him and held hands more tightly. He looked fearsome; his gruff voice, unwashed body, and truncated fingers made him repugnant.

Althene said nothing more but stood meekly behind her husband. Her pinched, squirrel-like face and thin wisps of hair peeked out from under a bedraggled, weathered sunbonnet. Her head was perched on a scrawny neck whose tendons stood out, as if locked in a chronic, unvoiced scream.

Stup clomped over to Miss Darden. She still felt uneasy and reluctant, yet she was desperate to place the last of the children. The agent wrote "Inga and Helga Buehler" on a paper. She turned the sheet towards Stup and pointed to a blank line. *At least they're going to the same family,* she told herself. She had concluded that although it was the Home's preference that siblings be separated, the girls would fare better if they stayed together, especially with the Dills. Stup held the pen awkwardly between two of his truncated fingers and his thumb, and pressed a heavy X onto the page.

She took the paper and pen back. "What is your name, sir?"

He shot her a suspicious look.

"I have to write it on the form," she explained.

"Stup Dill."

Miss Darden looked quizzical. "Mashburn Dill," he corrected himself with a grunt.

"But everyone calls me Stup."

Miss Darden wondered at the name Stup. It sounded like an unpleasant elision of "stump" and "stub," accurate descriptions of what remained of his fingers. Still wondering, she printed "Mashburn Dill" beneath the X.

"Inga is the one in the brown dress. Helga is the one in gray," she told Stup, although she looked at Althene when she said it. Stup did not appear interested. She continued, "They came from Germany about two years ago. Their older sister told us they're eight years old."

Stup signaled to Althene to take the two terrified youngsters to the wagon. She muttered at them under her breath so that Stup would not hear, "Bad blood is what you are. Got enough trouble without you." The twins did not understand her words, but they sensed her displeasure and clung tighter to each another.

Stup lifted Helga into the wagon as if he were launching the tiny, terrified child, but when he lifted Inga, her birdlike chest began heaving with wheezy, raspy coughs. He set her back down and pressed his hard, callused hand against her pale, feverish face.

"This one's sick!" he bellowed at Althene. "Can't you do nothin' right?"

3

Althene responded with a helpless, shamefaced look. She compressed her lips. They curled down at the corners so that her mouth looked like a ragged strip of apple peel.

Grasping Inga by the shoulder and half lifting, half steering her, Stup marched her back to the church as if he were an army officer leading a charge. Helga began to scream, "Inga! Inga! *Zusammen!* Johanna said *zusammen.*"

"Stop your gibberish!" Althene hissed. In a fierce, but controlled voice, she sputtered, "Don't make him mad." Then shaking her head and looking heavenward, she muttered, "Don't need this trouble."

Gulping air by the mouthfuls, and trying not to cry, Helga crouched in the back of the wagon as far as possible from the plank that served as the driver's seat and peeked over the side of the wagon. Althene sat at one end of the board, close to the edge of the wagon. Helga kept her eyes on Inga. After Stup yanked open the door of the church and disappeared inside with Inga, Helga began to whimper and moan. *Mama will come,* she repeatedly told herself. *Please, Mama, please.*

"This one's sick." Stup roared at Miss Darden, as if she had tried to palm off ailing livestock on him. "Don't want her." With that, he shoved the child towards her, spun, and strode off before the stunned woman could reply.

Inga dissolved into a sobbing, coughing heap on the floor. "Helga," she gasped over and over again. Miss Darden helped her to her feet and then sat down on a bench beside her. The agent felt frightened and ashamed—and guilty.

Helga stared in horror as Stup emerged from the church alone. She rose to her knees. "You git back down in that wagon!" he bellowed at her, swatting the air with his truncated hand.

"But Inga—" she said in a broken voice.

Stup approached the wagon. He glared at her but did not speak. Dwarfed by this angry giant who blocked her view of the church, she felt herself wither beneath his hateful eyes. She cowered and sank down.

The wagon creaked as Stup climbed on. He slapped the horses with the reins, and they jerked into motion.

"Stay here," Miss Darden instructed Inga. She gathered her resolve, telling herself, *I'm going to confront Mr. Dill and demand he return Helga.* But by the time she went outside, the Dills and Helga had vanished. She walked slowly back into the church, clutching a handful of wilted ruffles at the throat of her dress and looking somber.

Inga tried to rise to her feet but collapsed.

"Inga!" she gasped and ran to the child. *Danny! Where was that boy?* "Danny, I need you!" she screamed. For the first time, she found herself hoping that he had not run off. "Are you still here?" Then in a defeated voice, she wailed to the missing boy, "Why do you do these things?"

Danny lifted the cloth that covered the backside of the pulpit and peeked out. Everyone else other than Miss Darden and Inga had left. It wasn't a trick. The eleven-year-old emerged from his hiding place, painfully straightening his cramped limbs. His muscles seemed to have gone to sleep as well. He rubbed his arms and neck trying to ease the soreness and restore circulation and feeling.

The agent shot him a split-second look of exasperation, but then immediately held out her handkerchief and gestured to the basin of water used to tidy up the children earlier that morning. "Dampen this. Hurry!"

For once, Danny did as he was told. He handed her back a dripping cloth. "Will she be all right?" he asked in a subdued voice.

"Let's hope so. Bring me the basin." She cradled Inga in her arms and pressed the wet cloth to the child's fiery cheeks and forehead.

A sick feeling gripped Danny's stomach. "Where is Helga?"

The agent didn't look up at him when she answered. "Placed out." She spoke in such a low voice that Danny could barely hear her. Abruptly she changed the subject. Still without looking at him, she held out the cloth in his direction. "Dip this in the water and wring it out again, Danny."

When Miss Darden pressed the newly dampened cloth to Inga's face, she saw the child's eyes briefly flutter open. Danny was as relieved as the agent was. When he was satisfied Inga was alive, he told Miss Darden, "I want to go to San Antonio." It was the same thing he had told her so many times before.

"Why?" Her frown deepened at his silence. It frustrated her that he would never tell her the reason. *Now I'm stuck with him,* she brooded, but she was too drained from the scare with Inga to chastise the boy. *It's useless to reprimand him.* In a flat tone, she merely replied, "I don't know what I'm going to do with you, Danny. Now, San Antonio *is* all that's left, the end of the line, and I'm not authorized to place children in cities."

Danny had heard her explain on countless occasions the Aid Society's policy of placing children only in small towns and rural areas: their goal was to remove orphans permanently from the pernicious influence of cities.

Miss Darden sighed. She continued to sit on the floor, rocking Inga gently and making no attempt to preserve her dignity. She gave Danny a defeated look. "I may have to take you and Inga back to New York," she murmured.

Danny sensed she was scared. He made a sour face and turned away, but secretly he felt more frightened than ever. Little by little, his bravado had faded as he watched his companions disappear one-by-one with their new families. And now it looked as if he might end up where he had started. In New York. Alone.

4

Mama! Helga cried out again in her head, as she rumbled along in the back of the wagon. But at that moment, she realized once and for all that her mother was not coming—ever. She felt the same panic, the same desperation, as when she had gotten separated from her mother as they and hundreds of other immigrants flooded off the ship and stepped ashore at Castle Garden in New York.

The Dills rode back to their farm in silence that was interrupted only by Stup's cursing one of the horses when it stumbled. Helga tried to gather the courage to jump out of the wagon and run back to the church, but the leap looked too frightening and she was confused by the turns they had taken. So she crouched in the corner of the wagon, twisting a clump of her hair. She stared mutely behind, as if this would maintain some invisible link with Inga.

When they came to a sign whose lettering had faded away, Stup turned down a dusty road that led to a ramshackle house. Two mongrels, one of them limping, sidled up to the wagon. Stup grunted as he got down. With his boot, he knocked one of the cowering dogs out of the way. The dog yelped, startling and scaring Helga, and slunk off.

Stup gestured towards Helga. "What's her name?" he demanded of Althene.

"Hilda." Althene's voice was timorous.

Helga knew enough English to understand the question. *I'm glad they don't know my name,* she thought with a streak of defiance. *I don't want them to know it. It's mine, and I won't tell them! I won't speak to them.*

She jerked when she saw two pairs of frightened eyes peering out a dirty window of the house.

Stup saw them also. "You get out here!" he shouted. Instantly, two skinny girls with matted hair, freckles, and pale eyes appeared outside the door. They were barefoot and clad in frayed, skimpy dresses that exaggerated their gauntness.

"You finish your morning chores?" Stup roared.

They nodded in unison, keeping their eyes downcast.

"Where's Mash?"

The taller of the girls pointed past the house in the direction of the creek. "Fishing," she said in a small voice.

"Bring him and me something to eat," Stup ordered, and walked off towards the creek. "And be quick about it."

There was a flutter of activity from Althene, Lettie, and Nita. Althene was almost to the door when she remembered Helga. She turned and beckoned to her. "Get in here, Hilda. I don't want you, but I didn't have no say."

Helga made no reply, but cautiously climbed down from the wagon. Althene was so accustomed to her daughters' silence that it did not occur to her that Helga understood only part of what she was saying.

Althene put greasy salt pork, beans, and bread in a pail and handed it to Lettie. "Take a pail of fresh water with you, too. Now scat!"

Taking the pails without speaking, the child disappeared in the same direction as Stup. Helga stood in silence watching the girl's angular profile grow smaller in the distance as she lugged the pails towards the river.

Althene turned to Helga. "You won't be needing those traveling clothes no more." Helga understood only when Althene thrust a ragged garment at her and motioned for her to remove her dress and shoes and give them to her.

Helga crouched in the corner, her back turned to them, and changed clothes. She took the button from her pocket and put it in the pocket of the dress Althene had given her. She clutched it in her fist.

Althene thrust an empty flour sack at her daughter. "Nita, you gather corn husks, leaves, and twigs to stuff a pallet for Hilda to sleep on." She looked at Helga and frowned. "And take her with you."

The pair walked a short distance, Helga trailing along in silence behind Nita. Helga watched the strange girl, and then she too began collecting leaves and stuffing them into the sack. She shrieked when she saw a rabbit, frightened by the intruders, bolt from beneath a bush. *"Was ist das?"* Then, seeing that Nita did not understand, she pointed in the direction the rabbit had gone, and asked, *"Vhat?"* It was as if all the English she had ever learned had evaporated.

Helga thought that Nita could not talk. She was taken by surprise when she heard a small voice say, "Rabbit."

Helga watched the terrified animal dart in crazy zigzags. "Rabbit," Helga repeated the word. She stared at Nita who had not once stopped her anxious work or glanced up, and repeated the word, "Rabbit." For the rest of her life, Helga would think of the fearful, skittish Dill girls as "the rabbits."

5

The girls continued to toil in silence the rest of the afternoon, Helga mimicking Nita's and Lettie's actions. They gathered the stunted ears of corn that clung limply to the stalks. They worked in the scanty garden, chopping weeds. As they neared the back of the house, Helga's senses were assaulted by squealing and grunting sounds and a terrible odor that sent waves of nausea rolling through her stomach. She clasped her hands over her mouth. When she was able, she again choked out the question, *"Vhat?"*

"Pigs," replied Nita. She pointed to the source of the stench, several large pens filled with the animals. Nearby was a dilapidated barn. It was cobbled from the same grayed boards as the house. Cramped and dirty, it held a steep V-shaped corncrib, two horses, a mule, a cow, and a few chickens.

Off to one side, Helga noticed Althene. She had strung a rope between two trees. Over it she had hung a threadbare rug. Wielding an odd-looking implement, she was beating it mercilessly.

Helga met Mash at supper when he and his father returned, empty-handed, from fishing. Mash was stout like his father, and shorter than his older sisters. He wore a sullen expression on his porcine face.

"What do you call her?" Mash asked, pointing his thumb in Helga's direction. Without waiting for an answer, he gave his assessment, "She's even bonier than them two." He rolled his eyes disparagingly at his sisters. Talking through a mouth stuffed with bread, he asked about Helga as if she were not there. "Does she talk?"

Helga again felt fear flood through her. Her scalp tingled. Her heart hammered. Her stomach burned.

Despite revulsion at seeing the boy shove food into his mouth with filthy hands, Helga realized how ravenous she was. She had not eaten since morning. Althene motioned for her to sit at the end of the table with her and her daughters. Stup and Mash sat at the other end where the food was. As soon as the two of them had finished eating, Althene and her daughters picked among what was left. Then Helga was given what little remained. The bitter greens were seasoned with salt pork, but Helga ate the soggy leaves anyway. Her stomach still felt empty, but she left the chicken feet in her tin dish, unable even to touch them.

That evening, she lay on the rough pallet listening to Stup snore. Since morning, she had lost her other sister and her name. Tears slid down her grimy face leaving streaks in their wake. Holding her frail arms across her chest, she rocked herself back and forth. "Johanna… Inga… Johanna… Inga…," she repeated softly to herself. She no longer called her mother's name. Afraid to make a sound, she began to hum in her head the familiar, comforting lullaby until she fell into an exhausted, uneasy sleep.

During the night she was awakened by a small commotion and a muffled cry, but in the dark she could see nothing. She shivered despite the July heat. She wrapped her arms about herself more tightly, wanting to believe it was the bad dream she had been having about rabbits and pigs that was causing her to tremble.

FOUR

1

Evangeline Darden had a problem: She was headed for San Antonio, and she still had two unplaced children, Danny and Inga. Sitting on the train's hard bench, she mentally chided herself. *Every child should have been placed by now.* The weight of her failure rested heavily on her. *I can't make any more mistakes.*

Suddenly she felt sorry for herself. She stared out the train window at the Texas countryside, a landscape made blurry by her tears. *I wish Mr. Rice were still here. If I hadn't been left all by myself with all of the children, then...*

She looked down at Inga. The child was sleeping, her head resting in the agent's lap. She was troubled by the child's labored breathing. She looked across the aisle at Danny and studied the small, slumped figure. She wondered what he was thinking.

She inhaled sharply and sat up straight. *Be an adult, Evangeline,* she told herself. *You're just going to have to manage as best you can.*

2

Danny sat alone, his cap pulled low on his forehead. He was trying to stave off feelings of desperation and despair. All along, he'd insisted he wanted to go to San Antonio, and he'd done everything possible to make that happen. Now it was about to. Had he gone too far, behaved too badly? Had he cheated himself out of living with a kind family in the vain hope of finding his uncles halfway across the country? Additional anxious thoughts flooded in on him. Shamus and Aidan wouldn't be at the train station, of course. In fact, they might not even be in Texas. There were no couples there waiting to meet the train and adopt children. Would he simply be left at the San Antonio depot by himself? Or would he have to make the long, terrible trip back to New York? Suddenly his father's and uncles' plan for all of them to meet in Texas seemed absurd. Danny slumped lower, lost in his miserable thoughts.

The train whistle jolted him back to reality. *We're nearly there.* Again, he considered his situation: He had succeeded in making himself so habitually objectionable that, indeed, no one had wanted him. Now he had no idea how to make himself appealing. When the full realization that other than Inga and himself, the rest of the children had been placed out in the last small town, panic engulfed him. He fought the impulse to cry out, "Hey, what about me?" Now he was about to be stranded in San Antonio with Miss Darden.

When the train stopped, Miss Darden stood up. She turned to Danny and leaned close to his face. "Stay on the train with Inga. She's too ill to walk. I'll see if I can find the name of a minister or a priest who might help us."

3

Miss Darden climbed down from the train and looked around. After so many small towns, the number of people and the bustling activity at the station came as a shock. She spotted the stationmaster at the other end of the depot and made her way to him. She was within a few feet of him when she glanced back and saw Danny flitting about the platform. "*Danny!* Where's Inga? I told you to stay with her!" Her voice was frantic.

"A lady is watching her. She said she and her husband came to meet someone on the train, but they didn't show up." His lilt gave the words a matter-of-fact tone. Then, in a more anxious tone, he demanded of the beleaguered agent, "What's going to happen to me? What if no one here wants me?"

Miss Darden realized people were staring at them, but she didn't care. She motioned to a depot bench and shouted at Danny, "Sit down on that bench! And don't you *move* until I come back!" The vehemence in her voice surprised even her, and it startled the stationmaster. "Sir," she called out, "I'd be obliged if you would see that he stays on the bench. I have to tend to a sick child on the train." She made a palms-up gesture of helplessness and headed back through the crowd to the passenger car.

The ancient stationmaster peered at Danny and frowned. "I'm busy, lady, but if I have time…" When he realized that he was talking to the back of her head, he became silent and returned to his duties.

Dragging his feet, Danny shuffled over to the out-of-the-way, tall-backed bench and plopped down on it. The bench was hard and had been worn smooth at intervals where it had received the most use. Danny's feet did not reach the ground, but instead dangled over the edge. It made him feel very small. He swung his feet back and forth in restless arcs. He told himself it was ridiculous to think that he might see his uncles among the throng at the station. He knew that. Still, he found himself searching the faces around him.

The agent reboarded the train. Anna Jäeger, a plump, middle-aged woman with creamy, pink skin sat holding Inga's head in her lap and stroking her face. Inga was feverish and slipping in and out of consciousness. Anna held her more tightly whenever the child coughed. Albert, Anna's rotund husband, softly fanned the air above Inga with his hat.

Anna gently scolded the agent, "Your beautiful daughter, she is very ill. You should not leave her like this. Is not right." She was alarmed at how hot the child was and at the rusty traces of dried blood at the corners of her tiny mouth. Anna said something to Albert in German.

Before Miss Darden could respond, Inga's eyelids opened and her eyes rolled back. "Helga. *Zusammen. Zusammen.*" Anna put her ear closer to the child's mouth. She heard only Inga's last word before the child lapsed back into semiconsciousness.

Surprise registered on the couple's faces. "*Zusammen*," Anna repeated and looked up at her husband.

Albert turned to Miss Darden. His brows furrowed as he looked at her auburn hair. "You are *German*?"

"No—no, I'm not. But *she* is. And she's not my daughter." Then in a lower voice, "She's an orphan." The dam of her pent-up anxiety broke, and Evangeline Darden gushed out an explanation of the placing out program and her role as an agent. As if now talking to herself, she continued, "I'm not sure what to do with Inga—the child's name is Inga—but before I do anything, I must get her to a doctor." She turned to the man and raised her eyebrows to form a question. "I wonder, Mister—?"

"Jäeger. Albert Jäeger. And this is my wife, Anna." It came out as "YAY-ger" and "Dis iss my vife, Onna."

"Mr. Jäeger, I wonder if you could assist me. Perhaps you could direct me to a doctor? If your wife will stay with Inga for a few more minutes, I'll see if I can arrange a wagon. Then if you would be so kind as to carry the child to the wagon—"

Anna's eyes flew to the agent's face. "This beautiful child has *no* one? No parents? No home?"

The agent shook her head. "Do you know of a doctor who might—"

"What will happen to her?" Anna demanded, her troubled eyes already filling with tears. She smoothed Inga's hair away from her damp brow.

"Well, as soon as she's better, I suppose I'll try to place her out at one of the towns on the way back to New York." The agent exhaled a burdened, exhausted sigh. "To be honest, I've never had this happen before. We've always placed all the children. No one was willing to take Inga because she was ill." Again, the agent felt the sting of failure.

"Albert…" Lifting her eyes to meet her husband's, Anna announced her decision in a firm voice: "This child needs us."

"Anna, we're not young. Besides, she may not—," Albert, still speaking in German, struggled for the right words, "—may not get well."

"She *needs* us." Anna was adamant.

Albert looked tenderly at the frail child, at her delicate features, and at the long black lashes that fringed her closed eyes. "*Ja*," he acknowledged, "she needs us." He looked at his wife of many years and already knew in his heart he had capitulated. "If it is meant to be…" He did not finish his sentence. He turned back to Miss Darden and spoke in English. "This child—*we* could take her, *ja*?" To be our *daughter*?" At the sound of the word "daughter," he felt a wash of emotion run through him.

Anna clasped her hands over her heart, breathless and fearful that Miss Darden might say no. "The children we hoped for many years ago…" Anna's voice trailed off. "We were not blessed in that way." Then she poured out a poignant plea. "Please. We have big house—for children we once thought we would have. We are older than most parents of child this age, *ja*, but we would be good parents. Albert, he has good business—sausages and smoked meats. And Albert—," she looked up at her husband, "show what you keep in your pocket."

Albert reached into a baggy coat pocket and produced a tiny wooden pig and a duck. "Always I carry some animals I carve. In case I meet a child who needs a toy," he explained.

Anna gave the agent no chance to reply but hurried on to press their case. "To Germans, Miss, family is everything. With her,"—she touched Inga's cheek—"we would be a family. And *she is German.* God has meant this to be." Anna beseeched Miss Darden with her voice and her eyes.

Once again, Evangeline Darden fought with herself. *They're good people, people of means. They're German. But I'm not supposed to place children in cities. But what if I don't place Inga and she dies in my care? What if I lose my job?* She felt defeated. *What does it matter—I've already broken the rules.* Her head was swimming. She looked at the Jäegers' earnest, imploring faces. "Yes," she heard herself declare, "but there are conditions you must fulfill and a paper you must sign."

Albert nodded, his face aglow. He lifted the child in his arms. "Don't leave us, *mein Kleines,*" he whispered.

Anna wept joyful tears as she fussed over Inga. "Now everything is complete. Is the way it should be." In broken English, Anna sketched their life for Miss Darden while the agent prepared a paper for Albert to sign. The agent understood the rudiments of her story: Nearly three decades earlier, political oppression and a potato famine had driven the Jäegers from their home in the lower Rhine valley. Now in their late forties, they had spent most of their lives in Texas among the thousands of Germans who immigrated to San Antonio and re-created the culture of their homeland there.

Albert picked up the story. He explained that he had brought to this country the profession he could no longer use in Germany after his family's meat packing business failed. Now, fellow immigrants in San Antonio couldn't get enough of the spicy sausages and smoky hams produced by Jäeger Meats. At the beginning, Anna had also worked. She baked sugary, buttery pastries and created exquisite needlework to sell or give in trade. But as Albert's business prospered, she ceased baking and sewing other than for themselves or for pleasure. "But the children, they know when they stop by our house," he smiled in his wife's direction, "Anna will give them *springerle, pfeffernuesse,* or some other delicious cookies." Albert beamed and patted his ample belly. Then his expression faded as he concluded their history in a subdued tone. "Our only disappointment is that no children were ever born to us."

The agent nodded sympathetically and handed Albert the paper to sign. He signed it, smiled, and handed it back to her. She found it difficult to swallow, much less to speak, so she simply clasped Mr. Jäeger's hand in hers and nodded again.

She watched Albert Jäeger carry his new daughter to their carriage and gently hand her to Anna. Once in the buggy, Anna cradled Inga against her and stroked Inga's warm face. Anna felt vaguely troubled. "Albert, what did she mean, *zusammen?* Together with whom?"

"When she gets better, we will ask her. But first we must make her cheeks pink with health, not fever." At that moment, Albert felt his optimism start to grow, and he turned his thoughts to the future. "She will have a featherbed, Anna. And on the headboard I will carve *Deo Data.*"

"Yes," Anna murmured, never taking her eyes off the small, limp figure, "*Deo*

Data. Given by God." And she began to hum a song she had not hummed in decades, a German lullaby.

4

Danny glanced around the depot. Although San Antonio's was bigger and busier than most, it could have been the depot in any of the towns they had passed through. Sitting alone on the bench, he felt insignificant, but at the same time conspicuous. In each stop, he had hated the shame of arriving with a group of "orphans." He hated the curiosity and scrutiny of the prospective foster parents, the kaleidoscope of unfamiliar faces, the anxiety of seeing one child after another disappear, the fear of not knowing his fate. *Where is she?* he wondered. He nervously scanned the platform and the train door for the hundredth time.

After Evangeline Darden watched the Jäegers depart with Inga, she shifted her gaze out another train window. *Danny!* To her horror, she realized that she had forgotten about him. She climbed down the metal steps of the train and felt relieved as soon as she spotted him. He still sat scrunched in the corner of the bench, almost hidden from view. *Would those people have taken him?* She turned the question over in her mind but consoled herself with the thought that he probably would have acted up and they wouldn't have taken him. She was glad she had not asked. *They seemed touched by Inga's illness and by the fact that she was German. No, I'll just have to work out something else for Danny.*

She made her way over to Danny. Although he did not like her, he sighed with relief when she reappeared.

"I thought maybe you weren't coming back," he said in a small voice. He hoped that his fear wasn't obvious. He glanced up at her from beneath the brim of his cap. He suddenly narrowed his eyes in concern. "Where's Inga?"

The agent started to say "Inga has been placed," but changed her mind. *What good would come from his knowing I've violated another rule?* She chose her words carefully, telling him only part of the facts. "Danny, Inga is very ill. She may not live. A man agreed to take her to a doctor."

At the sound of her words, Danny teetered and reached for the edge of the bench to steady himself. In his mind's eye, he could see Johanna hearing the devastating news. It made his stomach hurt.

Now everyone is gone, he thought. *Even Inga.* In a weak voice, he asked, "What's going to happen to me?"

Miss Darden removed his cap. She could see he was trying not to cry. For the first time, she saw Danny for what he was: a very frightened boy. *Now it's just the two of us,* she thought. *I've made a muddle of things, and I'm frightened, too.* She had no answer. She did not look at him, but instead sat down beside him. Feelings of sadness and failure overwhelmed her. Without warning, she burst into tears.

She sat sobbing. Danny felt embarrassed and helpless. *Did I make her unhappy?* he wondered. He edged farther from her, wishing he could disappear.

5

A man's loud voice inquired, "Ma'am?"

The agent looked up, wiping her eyes with her twisted handkerchief and struggling to regain her composure.

It was the stationmaster, an old man dressed in a black uniform trimmed with polished gold buttons and frayed gold braid. As the stationmaster, he felt it was somehow his responsibility to come to her aid.

Miss Darden stood up unsteadily and steered the old gentleman a few feet away from the bench. She blotted the corners of her eyes as she talked to him in an emotional voice. Periodically, she gestured in Danny's direction. Danny couldn't hear what she was saying, but the old man spoke in such a loud voice that he could hear practically every word that he said.

The old man shook his head no several times and shrugged his shoulders. Danny heard him say, "No, I don't think so." Then, "Well, if it's only for the night," and "If it's all right with Mrs. Bromley." Finally, he scratched his head above one ear and sighed in resignation. "She never turned nobody away in her life. I don't reckon she'll start now." The man still shook his head, but it was clear that an agreement, however fragile, had been reached. Danny held his breath as Miss Darden walked back to him.

She dabbed her red nose with her handkerchief. "Mr. Artis Dunside, the stationmaster"—she gestured with the hand clutching the handkerchief towards the old man—"has agreed to let you stay the night with him, Danny. He'll bring you back to the station with him tomorrow morning. We'll decide what to do with you then."

Danny suddenly felt like a cracked pitcher: not really good for anything, but somehow wrong to cast off. He leaned around her to peer at the diminutive, mustachioed railroad agent. "Does he have a wife?"

"No. He boards in a house that's nearby. He says the owner, Mrs. Bromley, will put you up for the night. He says she's a good-hearted woman who's never turned away anyone in need." Miss Darden looked at the stationmaster and then back at Danny. In a quick, nervous voice, she warned, "You be a good boy. Don't make any trouble for him."

Danny did not reply.

She clasped him by his shoulder and prodded him to his feet. "I want you to come meet Mr. Dunside. *Be nice.*" She took his hand, but he pulled it free. They walked over to Mr. Dunside. Danny deliberately lagged behind Miss Darden and tried to appear as indifferent as if she were inquiring about the train schedule.

The stationmaster finished chalking a revised arrival time on a large board. Then he turned and awkwardly shook hands with Danny. "Don't know nothing about children," he shouted at Danny. The boy did not respond. After an uncomfortable silence, the old man blared, "The Southern Pacific—the last train—is due at 6:00 p.m." Waving towards the bench Danny had just abandoned, he yelled at a puzzled boy, "You can wait over there until I'm through."

To signal Mr. Dunside's hearing problem, Miss Darden looked at Danny, opened her eyes wide, and discreetly tapped her ear with a fingertip.

Scrutinizing Danny with a wary eye, Artis Dunside announced in a voice that could be heard over any incoming train, "I sure hope this ain't a mistake." He looked at his pocket watch and walked back towards the tracks to signal the conductor.

Danny glared at Miss Darden. He spit his rebuke at her: "What you do is *bad,* giving away children."

The agent turned her head aside, as if she had been slapped. She did not look at him, nor did she reply. Instead, she hurriedly gathered her valise and the folio of placement papers, and without so much as a backward glance, she fled the depot.

6

Evangeline Darden spent the night at the Gladstone Hotel. Despite the luxury of a real bed, she slept fitfully. Early the next morning, she took her belongings and left the hotel.

She moved numbly towards the depot. When a stray lock of hair drifted across her face, she made no attempt to tuck it back in place. Her eyes looked bleary, and her normally careful attire was mussed and rumpled. As she walked down the street, she passed a livery. The smell of coal, horse manure, and sweat emanated from the open doorway. A few yards later, she stopped. She turned around, walked back, and went in.

"Mornin'," the blacksmith called out. As soon as he finished pumping the bellows, he removed a red-hot horseshoe from the fire with his tongs. He clanked the horseshoe down on an anvil and wiped the sweat from his forehead and neck. The smithy hooked his thumbs under the straps of his heavy leather apron. "Something I can do for you, ma'am?"

Miss Darden did not acknowledge him or even seem to hear him. She walked over to the fire and shoved a portfolio of papers into it. She stood as if mesmerized. The flames leapt up, crackled, and consumed the pages. She watched them collapse into curls of black ash. *It's done,* she thought. A shiver ran through her.

"Something wrong, lady?"

The agent raised her eyes to meet his, but it seemed to be an effort. "I want to go west, but I don't want to go by train. Do you know a way I can get to the next town?" Her voice was devoid of energy or emotion. *I can catch a train west from there,* she thought to herself.

"I reckon I can help you work something out." The blacksmith gave her the name of a local person who was traveling that way. He walked her to the door but kept a watchful eye on her. "Ma'am, are you all right?"

When she didn't respond, he pointed up the street. "Stop in that office with the black and white sign. Ask for Mr. Overmeyer. He's leaving in his wagon this afternoon." She nodded and walked away in the direction he had pointed.

"Where you headed?" he called out.

Without looking back, she replied in the same flat voice, "California."

7

It would be the turn of the century before the Homeless Children's Aid Society sent another trainload of children to Texas. The Society was bewildered: No agent's records were ever received or found. It was as if the children on the train in the summer of 1886 never existed.

Indeed, other than the children themselves who were scattered in the train's wake, there was no proof that their journey had ever occurred.

8

"Best meal I ever ate," Danny blurted through a mouthful of fragrant, steaming dumplings. With his sleeve, he wiped the rich, buttery sheen from his lips.

Mrs. Bromley took pleasure in watching Danny eat. "Would you like another helping, dear?" she asked. He stuffed himself, washing down the hot dumplings with glasses of milk and licking the gravy off his fingers. "Use your napkin, dear," she said gently and pointed to the cloth that lay untouched beside his plate.

After supper, Danny slept like a post until Mr. Dunside roused him the next morning. Mrs. Bromley was amazed the boy could eat so large a breakfast after the supper he had consumed. He wolfed down a plate of biscuits with syrup, punctuating the bites with large gulps of sweet milk. She suspected that he stopped only because the plate was empty.

"Good luck, Danny." She waved as he and Mr. Dunside left for the depot. "Maybe we'll see you again." Then she called out, "Wait!" A moment later, she reappeared with some ginger cookies wrapped in paper and handed them to him.

The July heat began asserting itself early in the morning. Danny climbed back on the now familiar bench to wait for Miss Darden. He surveyed the platform. Artis Dunside consulted his watch. It was precisely 7:30. *Late.* He frowned and clicked his teeth in disapproval. He believed people, like trains, should be punctual.

Smoky locomotives chugged in, disgorged passengers, trunks, and goods. As soon as they were refilled and the passengers had boarded, the trains lumbered out again. Danny studied the passengers who got off and those who greeted them. More than once he found himself sizing someone up, instinctively assessing whether the person would be gullible enough to fleece. He wondered where the departing passengers were headed. The thought ran through his mind, *Surely none of them is fool enough to go to New York.*

Danny squirmed. He had learned how to tell time at the Aid Society Home. He looked up at the large black numbers on the Regulator clock: 8:30. *Where is she?* he fretted.

Out of nervousness, he began nibbling on the cookies. He broke each cookie into small pieces to make it go further, a habit left over from living at the Home, of trying to make the weekly Sunday cookie last as long as possible.

Danny saw the aging stationmaster look in his direction and shake his head. The disgruntled expression on his face made Danny feel like a piece of unclaimed baggage that no one knew exactly what to do with.

Midmorning, Mr. Dunside offered Danny a dipper of water. "Maybe she got detained," he mumbled, but it sounded half-hearted.

By noon, both Danny and Mr. Dunside knew that Miss Darden was not coming.

"I hate her." Danny choked out the bitter words. Then, in a broken voice, "She doesn't care about me. *Nobody* does." He fought back hot tears.

"Look here, there's no reason to carry on," the half-deaf stationmaster shouted to Danny. He could deal with grown men; it was crying women and children who made him feel helpless. "I think Mrs. Bromley took a shine to you. I reckon she'll let you stay with her until we figure out something to do with you."

FIVE

1

I didn't get foster parents, but living here ain't so bad after all, Danny admitted to himself after the first few weeks. He reflected on the odd composition of the household. Mrs. Bromley, a widow, was pleased to have the income from renting a small spare room to Artis Dunside. In turn, the old stationmaster was grateful to have a place to live that was only a mile from the depot. The other occupant of the house was Dilue, a mysterious woman whose appearance had shocked Danny. Because she rarely spoke, and little was said about her, Danny wondered if he would ever learn the circumstances of her life.

Crowned with a cloud of billowy white hair, Mrs. Bromley was a diminutive woman who smelled of soap. Her rich voice and energetic bustling belied her seventy-five years. Danny quickly learned that she was a sensible, cheerful woman who did not tolerate lazy or intemperate habits in anyone.

When Mr. Dunside returned home from the depot with Danny for the second time, Mrs. Bromley placed a cot in the attic for the boy. After she showed Danny where he was to sleep, she said, "I expect you may be with us for a while. While you're here, young man, you're to make yourself useful. I expect you to run errands, work in the garden, and do any other chores I need help with."

Danny frowned, looking around the attic and feigning indifference to her words. He was about to reply, "Can't make me" when she said, "Now, come with me to the kitchen for milk and cake." Danny held his tongue.

She was an excellent cook who liked to see others enjoy her cooking. "You need to put some meat on your bones," she announced to Danny, "and I intend to see that you do." Danny was only too glad to oblige. For the first time in his life, he discovered what it was like to have enough to eat, and it felt good.

2

Barely a week had passed when Mrs. Bromley informed Danny, "I've arranged for you to work at the Muehlenberg Mercantile. You start Monday. Mr. Muehlenberg bought Abner's store—my husband's store—after he died." Danny had seen a small, silver-framed photograph on the table in the parlor. The face in the sepia-toned photograph was that of a sober-looking man with hair parted down the middle. Danny had assumed, correctly, that it was the late Mr. Bromley. "Mr. Muehlenberg is a fine man, a hard-working German, who has been very kind to me over the years. The store is only a few blocks away. It's important that you learn a trade and earn your keep, dear."

Danny shrugged. "If that's what you and Mr. Dunside want me to do." To himself he thought, *What if I make mistakes? What if Mr. Whatever-his-name-is fires me?* Danny lay in bed that night, kept awake by those troubling thoughts.

Danny was nervous at first, but Mr. Muehlenberg took time to explain his duties and patiently answered Danny's questions. Danny learned quickly. Once school started, he worked at the store in the afternoons and all day on Saturdays until Mr. Dunside finished at the depot. Just when he felt he had begun to fit in, he did something that could have changed everything.

3

One September evening when Danny arrived home from Muehlenberg's and walked into the kitchen, his face went ashen. Neatly displayed on the table were a top, a small sack of hard candy, and a penknife. He stood in the doorway staring. His mind raced. *How did she find them? I hid them beneath my bed, rolled up tight in my jacket.*

"Danny."

He felt his scalp prickle at the sound of Mrs. Bromley's voice. He hadn't even noticed her. She sat in the corner, solemn and erect, in a straight-backed chair. He kept his eyes lowered, too ashamed to look at her. He swallowed but could not speak. He felt something that he had never felt—not even once—during the scores of times he had scammed and robbed people in New York: He felt shame over trying to take advantage of someone.

Mrs. Bromley stood up slowly. Her five-foot stature might as well have been a towering six feet. She walked over to the table and touched each of the objects on it. "These are from Muehlenberg's…" she began. She spoke slowly, distinctly. Danny wasn't sure whether it was a question or a statement.

Still too ashamed to raise his eyes, he nodded mutely.

The realization hit him like a bolt: *I don't want to have to leave here. Worse than that, I've disappointed her. She's given me a home, fed me… trusted me. Mr. Muehlenberg trusted me, and I cheated him.* He felt panicky.

Danny looked up at her. She seemed much older and frailer than she had that morning. He began to fidget.

Without looking at him and without hurrying, Mrs. Bromley walked over to a shelf and picked up a piece of paper and a pencil, and a covered milk-glass dish. She carried them to the table and sat down.

"How much does Mr. Muehlenberg charge for a penknife?"

Danny was puzzled. "Two bits."

She wrote it on the paper and looked up. "The whirligig?"

He answered, and she noted the amount.

"The candy?"

She totaled the figures, then removed the lid of the dish and emptied the money onto the table. Danny was aware that she was revealing to him where she kept the money in her house. As she went down the list, she pressed her index finger on one precious coin after another, sliding them into a separate pile. When she had totaled up an amount equal to the cost of the items, she pressed her hand flat over the pile, shoved it into the middle of the table towards Danny, and looked him directly in the eyes.

He shifted uncomfortably from one foot to the other. The silence became intolerable. *That's Mrs. Bromley's lace money,* he thought. He ached with guilt; he had watched her spend hours every evening making the smooth wooden bobbins dance to produce a tiny bit of spider web lace. To earn extra money, she sold it at Mr. Muehlenberg's store. Danny looked at the coins on the table and felt his face burn. *How many hours did she work to earn those?*

She continued to look Danny in the eye. He prepared himself for a lecture, for Bible verses—or worse, dismissal from her home. "Is Mr. Muehlenberg still at the store?" she asked.

Danny nodded. Even though it was late, the proprietor generally stayed to tally the day's receipts and post the accounts.

"Take this list and the money to Mr. Muehlenberg. Tell him thank you for sending my order home with you." She did not smile.

Her eyes met his just long enough to see the wonder in them. "And Danny—"

"Yes, ma'am…"

In a dignified voice, she instructed him, "Tell Mr. Muehlenberg *I'll* let him know whenever I need something else." She nailed him with her gaze until she was certain he understood her meaning.

Danny's relief was almost palpable. "Mrs. Bromley—" he began, but again fell silent. He felt sick at heart. She looked hurt, not angry. "Mrs. Bromley, look here, I can put these back," he blurted. "Mr. Muehlenberg probably ain't even missed—"

"*No.*" she cut him short. "I *want* you to keep them. Put them on the little table in the attic where you can see them, where you can enjoy them."

Danny swallowed. "Yes, ma'am. And I'll tell Mr. Muehlenberg you won't be needin' anything else." He spoke so quietly that she could barely hear him.

She nodded once. "Take these to the attic. Then run on down to the store. Supper will be ready in half an hour."

Danny picked up the top. Its smooth, solid wood no longer felt pleasing to his hand. He gathered up the other items, knowing that the horehound drops would have no flavor and that the penknife would bring him no secret joy. The coins seemed to burn his palm.

He walked out of the room, grateful not to have been thrown out of the house but burdened by shame. *Things will be different,* he said out loud to himself. *I'll be different.* And he meant it.

4

Before long, Danny knew the names of the mercantile's regular customers and most of the suppliers. He worked hard. Mr. Muehlenberg praised him, which caused him to work harder.

Danny would often play a game, trying to predict what certain customers would buy before they asked, or trying to guess where a stranger was from. Whenever an Irishman came through, Danny would ask if he had run across Aidan and Shamus O'Brien. The responses were always disappointing. Danny explained who Aidan and Shamus were and implored the men to be alert for any word of his uncles. "Remember their names," he would beg them. "Maybe you'll hear something by the next time you come through."

Albert Jäeger was a Muehlenberg customer whose visits Danny eagerly anticipated. The jovial German often delivered in person sausages and cured meats to the butcher shop down the street from Muehlenberg's. "Going in person is good for business," he would tell Anna, but both he and his wife knew that it was really because Albert liked to visit with his friends.

While he was in the neighborhood, Mr. Jäeger sometimes came into Muehlenberg's. He would puff on his pipe and chat for a few minutes with Mr. Muehlenberg while Danny filled his order: a kettle or crock, a length of chain, or perhaps a whetstone.

The aromatic smell of smoked meat and spicy sausage clung to Albert like perfume. It not only made Danny's mouth water—Mr. Jäeger always smiled and tossed him some jerky for helping him load up his purchases—but the fragrance sent Danny on a mental voyage to the place Mr. Jäeger called "the Rhine land."

Invariably, Mr. Jäeger's accent made Danny think of Johanna. When Danny was putting bags of salt into Mr. Jäeger's wagon one afternoon, he volunteered, "I know a girl from Germany."

Mr. Jäeger nodded approvingly, but gave the matter no further thought. Most families in that part of San Antonio were German. "*Ja?*" he laughed. "There *iss* lots of us!" He handed Danny a penny. "Now you put the rest of the things in the wagon—*ja?*"

Danny worked diligently. Talking with people energized him but stocking the shelves and sweeping the floors were drudgery. Of all his tasks, he most preferred unloading new merchandise. Each unopened box seemed laden with promise. Some goods were shipped through the port of Galveston and brought the rest of the way by train. Even though Danny was not sure which direction Galveston was, he knew that it had been Aidan and Shamus's destination, and handling the boxes made him feel he might actually find his uncles. He found it comforting to run his finger over the word "Galveston." Danny was beguiled and tantalized by the label on every carton that had been transported by ship or train. Each hinted at adventure and a life more exciting than working in a store.

5

Danny's day-to-day life settled into a routine. He had a good place to live, could eat his fill, and he was attending school—and Sunday school—regularly. But Danny had concluded that, as Mr. Dunside himself had acknowledged that first day at the station, the elderly bachelor didn't "know nothing about children."

After Danny's arrival, however, and to Artis Dunside's own surprise, faint stirrings of a paternal nature had surfaced in the old man. Artis told himself, *Yessir, I owe it to that boy to tell him what I've learned in this life. Give him guidance.*

The stationmaster, however, had no idea how to talk to the boy. Without exception, what came out of his mouth were proverbs, aphorisms, maxims, adages, or other snippets of accumulated wisdom. "Well begun is half done," he would shout at an appropriate moment. Or, "A man's word is his bond." "The good Lord gave us two ears and one mouth, so we should listen twice as much and talk half as much." At the dinner table Mr. Dunside counseled, "Waste not, want not." Regarding threats from a bully at school: "The soup is never eaten as hot as it's cooked." When Danny borrowed—without permission—Mrs. Bromley's magnifying glass from the parlor table, Mr. Dunside chided, "Neither a lender nor a borrower be." And when the boy complained about an afternoon spent in the menial task of cleaning Mr. Muehlenberg's storeroom, the old man clucked, "Digging a hole is the only job where a man gets to start at the top."

Before long, Danny could tell when an aphorism was coming. Mr. Dunside would stroke his chin with his thumb and then loudly intone one of his terse pronouncements. The old man also had the nervous habit of consulting his watch, even when not at the depot. A dozen times a day he extracted it from his pocket to polish the already gleaming crystal.

Within a few weeks of Danny's arrival, the old man had ceased mentioning a permanent placement for Danny with another family. And despite Mr. Dunside's eccentricities, Danny realized he liked the old gentleman.

6

Mrs. Bromley never mentioned the top, penknife, or candy to Danny again. She noticed that they remained untouched on the table in Danny's tiny room. Nor did she ever mention the episode to Mr. Dunside.

Week after week, Danny made a point of doing anything that Mrs. Bromley asked, promptly and without complaint. She was aware, too, that although Danny never said anything about it, he replaced the money in her glass bowl. *Might as well admit it,* she thought to herself one day as she watched Danny drying the dishes, *I'm plumb foolish about that boy.*

7

Danny's relationship with the stationmaster, although courteous, nevertheless remained stiff and awkward. That changed one night, however, when Danny asked Mr. Dunside, "Do you know where Galveston is?"

"Indeed!" roared the half-deaf stationmaster. "Galveston Island," Mr. Dunside mused. "Used by the pirate Jean Lafitte when he was raiding Spanish ships seventy years ago. Germans settled first in Galveston and the Rio Grande Valley. Searching for decent farm land was what drew them to this part of Texas: New Braunfels, Fredericksburg, Sisterdale, Boerne, Comfort—"

"But where is *Galveston*?" Danny interrupted.

"Wait here."

The old gentleman returned with a worn map. He unfolded it on the kitchen table and gently smoothed out the creases. He thumped a spot on the Texas coastline. "Galveston!" he thundered. "Shipped cotton, sugar, hides, farm goods. John Magruder and his Confederate boys recaptured the city from Union troops by hiding behind cotton bales on riverboats. Young Dick Dowling and his Irish lads in the Davis Guard, a crack artillery company, they helped retake the port."

Mr. Dunside absent-mindedly glanced at his pocket watch and began winding the stem. As if reciting from an unseen book, the stationmaster talked steadily about Galveston for fifteen minutes before he finally ended with, "Outbreak of malaria there pret' near every summer." Seeing Danny's astounded face, he chuckled, "Good thing you didn't ask about San Antonio, boy. You know, they say this town was laid out by a drunk Spaniard on a blind mule."

Danny grinned, but sat transfixed. "How is it you know so much about Galveston, Mr. Dunside?"

"I went to sea as a young man. In fact, I was a sailor for most of my life. I was a boatswain, or bo's'n, the warrant officer in charge of the deck crew," he thundered.

It had never occurred to Danny that Mr. Dunside had any life prior to working at the depot, or, for that matter, that he had ever been any age besides the age he was now.

Mr. Dunside ran his finger over part of the map again. "It was my health that forced me to seek a drier climate. That was the end of my life at sea." Danny could detect the regret in the old man's voice. "I rode the rails for years as a conductor, trying not to feel landlocked. I eventually got too old for that, but by that time, I couldn't give up the railroad. So I settled in San Antonio and started working at the depot."

Mr. Dunside told Danny that although he had worked on trains that traveled through several states, he chose Texas as his permanent home in 1881. "Yessir, that was the year the second railroad came to San Antonio. The International and Great Northern—but everyone called it the Insignificant and Good for Nothing," he chuckled. "I first came through San Antonio in 1877, the year the Southern Pacific inaugurated service to the city. San Antonio held a two-day celebration. By the way, Danny, there was lots of Irishmen that worked on the east-to-west section of that railroad."

Mr. Dunside fished out his pocket watch and dangled it by its chain. "Railroader's watch," he said with pride. "A person can set his watch by the movement of the trains." Danny looked quizzical. "Railroads *have* to know the right time. If they didn't, there'd be terrible wrecks. We couldn't make switches. Passengers wouldn't know when to show up at the depot."

"But how do the different depots all agree on the time?"

"That's a fine question, boy. The railroad already thought of that. In fact, you can thank them for the national time system. It gives us the official time. They created the system in 1883." With his fingernail, Artis attacked an imaginary spot on the crystal.

"Yessir, the system went worldwide the next year." He was beaming.

Danny studied Artis's watch with a new interest, awaiting the rest of the explanation. Artis handed him the watch so he could examine it more closely.

"Did you know the railroad tells us which types of watches we can use? Even have rule books on their care and maintenance. And they send men to inspect them regular, too. Everyone is required to have a regulation watch—conductors, yardmasters, engine foremen, brakemen, firemen, agents—"

"But how do *they* know what the *official* time is?" Danny interrupted again.

"The telegraph. The stationmaster receives the official time and sets his clock on that signal. The trains and crews check with the stationmaster and set their watches at every station." Artis looked at Danny's earnest face. He felt warmed by the boy's interest.

Danny held the watch carefully in both hands as he returned it to Mr. Dunside.

The old stationmaster found himself saying, "Perhaps *you'll* work for the railroad one day, boy." What he thought but didn't say out loud was *And perhaps this watch will be yours one day.*

8

For much the same reason that Danny liked unloading boxes from faraway places, Artis Dunside liked the anticipation he felt every time a train pulled into the station. Throughout the years, that had never changed.

Practically every evening after the "Galveston evening," Mr. Dunside, at Danny's instigation, regaled him with stories of early railroading in Texas, mostly how little of it there was: only 700 miles of track by 1870. "The first railroad company, the Buffalo Bayou, Brazos, and Colorado, bragged that their Engine No. 1, the General Sherman, was the first locomotive in the state. And they boasted mightily about their track, all twenty miles of it!" He shook his head and chuckled at the memory.

On another occasion, Mr. Dunside detailed the irony of the South's need for railroad track to be laid in Texas so that the Confederate troops could receive supplies. "The trackage was sharply curtailed because the Rebels needed metal even worse for guns."

Danny laughed when Mr. Dunside told him about the TM&C line, "so called because its equipment consisted of two mules and a car," and of the line called "the Great Sweetgum, Yubadam, and Hoo Hoo."

"Did I ever tell you about an engine dubbed 'the Bull of the Woods'?" the old man asked Danny one evening. "Got its name because of its inclination to jump the track," he explained, laughing at his own story.

Over time, he profiled other railroad lines that ran through Texas: the Fort Worth and Denver City; the Houston and Central Texas; the Gulf, Colorado and Santa Fe; and the Texas and Pacific. From listening to Mr. Dunside and scrutinizing the maps, Danny soon developed a railroader's knowledge of Texas, able to recite in order the major towns that dotted the bigger railroad lines. It had not escaped him that the information could be valuable if—when—he went searching for his uncles or if he tried to find Johanna.

Years of railroading were the cause of Mr. Dunside's partial deafness, and although he bellowed rather than spoke, Danny accepted it as the price of hearing his stories and learning about places he hoped he might someday see.

For their evening chats, Mr. Dunside began to invite Danny to his small room. The room was sparse and immaculate, and it contained fascinating evidence of Mr. Dunside's travels at sea and on land. The old man would turn through his atlas, point to a city, a state, or a country and tell Danny everything he knew about it. "You can't never know too much," he advised the boy. "Books and maps"—he patted his treasures—"why, there's a whole education in them." He thumped Danny gently on the chest. "You remember that."

The hard-of-hearing stationmaster was unaware that his tiny cubicle of a room amplified his voice no less than if he were shouting into a box canyon. Danny learned he could buffer this by propping his head in his hands and discreetly plugging his ears with his fingertips.

With callused fingers, Mr. Dunside also spent hours patiently teaching Danny to tie sailor's knots. He watched with satisfaction whenever Danny produced a complicated knot. "I couldn't tie that any better myself." He placed his hands on his knees and looked Danny square in the eye. "You recall what you said the first time you tried to learn a simple knot?"

Danny grinned. "Yessir. I said, 'I can't do this! It's too hard! And it ain't any fun!'" His grin broadened. "And then I flung that twisted hunk of rope on the floor."

"And you remember what I said?"

Danny stroked his chin the way he had seen Artis do a thousand times and cleared his throat as if he were making a great pronouncement. "You said, 'Danny, if something is difficult or boring after five minutes, then spend *ten* minutes on it. And if it's still hard or boring after ten minutes, then spend *twenty* minutes on it. And if it's *still* that way, spend half an hour on it… then an hour. Sooner or later, it will *become* interesting—and easier.'"

Mr. Dunside was gratified and not a little flattered that Danny had taken his words to heart. "That's a lesson that months at sea teaches you. If something is hard, spend more time on it. If something seems boring, you have to discover what's interesting about it. And look what you can do now," Mr. Dunside said, pointing to the intricate knot Danny held in his palm.

Sitting on his own bed at night, Danny had practiced and mastered the cat's-paw, lubber's knot, and hawser bend. He had learned the bowline bend and cuckold's neck. It had filled him with pride when he could finally manage the nail knot: it tightened when it was pulled, and it didn't slip. Soon he was even using some of the knots at Muehlenberg's. But each time he tied one, it reminded him there was a whole world out there, one that he had not yet seen.

9

Back in September, less than two months after Danny's arrival in San Antonio, the city had a visitor who had captured the boy's imagination. At first Mr. Dunside made Danny try to guess who had come through the depot. "Arrived today under army escort on a special train from Bowie, Arizona," he offered, knowing that the clue would be tantalizing, but of no help. Impatient to spill the news, Mr. Dunside finally announced in bursts, "Geronimo! The Apache chief! With two and a half dozen braves! They just surrendered to the U.S. Army, to the Tenth Cavalry, to the buffalo soldiers." Mr. Dunside quickly explained about the regiment of Negro soldiers and hurried on. "No, sir, I wouldn't want to tangle with any of them Indians, you can be sure! They've been taken to Fort Sam Houston and are being held in the Quadrangle," he said, referring to the fort's oldest building. Mr. Dunside pulled a map out of a drawer, unfolded it and pointed to the lower right corner. "I hear that in a few weeks they'll be transferred to Fort Pickens, Florida."

"Show me the route." Danny studied the map as the old man traced out the train route.

Danny loved hearing about Mr. Dunside's experiences, both past and recent. But part of the price of learning about Mr. Dunside's colorful life was that the old gentleman, at Mrs. Bromley's insistence, required from Danny a quarter of an hour of "Bible reading" each evening before he would discuss his travels. Sometimes Mr. Dunside read—shouted—and Danny listened. At other times, Danny read—shouted—and Mr. Dunside listened.

In addition, Danny was required to memorize scripture each week and recite it on Sunday. Danny suspected he had Mrs. Bromley to thank for that as well. Both Mr. Dunside's and his own regular church attendance were attributable to Mrs. Bromley; she would countenance nothing less. But occasionally, like little boys conspiring behind the barn, Danny and the time-conscious stationmaster "forgot" the precise time at which they began the quarter-hour of Bible reading and were able to complete it in less than ten minutes.

Danny's interest in learning was fueled by the informal education Mr. Dunside afforded him. Attending school, however, was less enjoyable. His arrival on the train and his brogue made him a target for ridicule. He'd been in periodic fights since the first day of school. A classmate, a husky German boy named Otto, regularly tried to provoke fights with him by muttering "Irish bastard!" and "Unclaimed freight!"

At first Danny tried to ignore him, but it only encouraged Otto to escalate the taunts.

"You belong in Irish Flats with the rest of the micks, O'Brien!" Otto sneered, referring to the heavily Irish section of the city near St. Mary's Church. The Flats were famous for rowdy all-night parties, protracted whiskey-soaked wakes, and uproarious brawls.

Danny's hot temper eventually took over. After-school fights with Otto became a regular occurrence. At the cost of countless bruises, scrapes, and bloody noses, Danny slowly gained some proficiency as a fighter, but he was still no match for a boy who stood a head taller and weighed twenty pounds more.

Mr. Dunside encouraged Danny to defend himself ("If you need a helping hand, look at the end of your sleeve"), but counseled him never to inflame a bully further ("Don't write a draft with your mouth that your fists can't cash"). Finally, though, the white-haired man was forced to concede, "What you're doin' now ain't working, Danny. You got to out-think that feller. You let him rile you and make you go to swinging blindly, he's going to win. Besides, most of the time, it ain't worth the time or the trouble to whip a jackass like him, even if you could."

Danny suspected that Mr. Dunside's diminutive stature had caused him to arrive at this viewpoint early in life. He told Danny, "Over the years, I've dealt with everything from drunken, hot-headed sailors to angry train passengers. I concluded that it's easier to plow around a stump than through it."

Danny had, in fact, watched the stationmaster calm the irate, placate the frustrated, and bluff the bullies. "Bullies are always cowards," Mr. Dunside explained. Danny was interested in the old man's advice, even though Danny knew from experience that a distraught woman or a sobbing child could reduce this same man to a puddle of helplessness.

"Now, the way I see it," the old man continued, "you could just try to steer clear of that Otto feller." Mr. Dunside stroked his chin, and Danny prepared himself for an aphorism. He was not disappointed. "If you can't hunt with the big dogs, you best stay on the porch."

Danny rubbed his sore arm and nodded.

Mr. Dunside cocked his head to the side, and after pausing to be sure that he had Danny's attention, added, "Of course, you got some other choices."

"I'm listening."

"You can turn that German boy around by making him beholden to you. Or you can out-bluff him." He sucked air between two of his teeth as if trying to remove a kernel of corn from them. "Yup. Either one of 'em will work."

Mr. Dunside never knew which Danny chose or how he did it, but one night Danny announced that there wouldn't be any more fights with Otto. All he said was, "Me and Otto come to an understanding."

The old man could tell from Danny's tone that the matter was settled and that Danny felt pleased with the way he had handled it.

The bantam-sized stationmaster beamed with pride. "I bet you did! Yessir. I jus' bet you did!"

10

It was Mr. Dunside who stoked Danny's curiosity, who revealed to him the wealth of knowledge that books and maps contained, and who first made Danny think of himself as smart. "You continue to read and learn, you might one day ma-tric-u-late"— Mr. Dunside said each syllable distinctly and looked pleased—"at Corn Hill College. It's near Austin." He handed the flattered boy a newspaper, tapping an article with a callused, double-jointed finger.

Danny smoothed the paper out on the table and moved the lamp closer. He immediately noticed that the article reported the college had "preaching twice a month, Sabbath school every Sunday, and prayer meeting every Sunday night." Danny wondered if Mrs. Bromley had brought the article to Mr. Dunside's attention. Danny finished reading the article aloud. Besides describing itself as "healthy, pleasant, and accessible," Corn Hill College proudly advertised that there was "no grog shop within 15 or 20 miles."

"Well, that's a might peculiar," the old sailor mused. "I heard once that wherever there's a good pub, a college eventually sprouts up nearby." Mr. Dunside grinned and winked.

Danny hooted, surprised and delighted by this unknown aspect of the man. He tingled with stealthy pleasure over a joke that he knew Mrs. Bromley would disapprove of. Enjoying a newfound sense of camaraderie with Mr. Dunside, he suddenly felt very grown up.

Mr. Dunside's sense of responsibility quickly reasserted itself, and in a more serious tone, the sailor-turned-railroader advised Danny, "There's something to learn from everyone, boy. Pay attention. Ask questions. Listen more than you talk. Then you'll know what you already know, as well as what the other feller knows."

11

In late January, Mr. Dunside came home and announced to the small household that another famous person would soon be coming through the Sunset Depot. And once again, he made Danny and Mrs. Bromley guess. When they gave up, he leaned back and folded his hands across his chest. "Sarah Bernhardt."

"Who's that?" Danny asked, frowning.

Mrs. Bromley's right eyebrow was arched in faint disapproval. "An actress. A *French* actress." Mrs. Bromley had an unfavorable opinion of the theater; she associated it with the unsavory vaudeville theaters sprinkled throughout the city. The plush Grand Opera House had opened on Alamo Plaza the year before, and Mrs. Bromley was still reserving judgment on it.

"A *famous* French actress," Mr. Dunside corrected her. "She's traveling from Mexico back to the East. She'll be coming through on February 2."

After arguing with herself for several days, Mrs. Bromley succumbed to curiosity. Under the guise of taking Mr. Dunside a forgotten handkerchief, she went to the depot that day. She took Danny with her, and they arrived—"as luck would have it," she would later explain—just moments before Sarah Bernhardt did.

Mrs. Bromley was captivated and pronounced the actress "a fine, cultured lady." When the actress declared San Antonio "the art center of Texas," she captivated Mrs. Bromley completely. For days afterwards, the talk in the Bromley home was only of Sarah Bernhardt.

To Danny, the world seemed now, more than ever, full of possibility. It was filled with intriguing people—from Indian chiefs to French actresses—and wonderful, faraway places. Seeds of curiosity and wanderlust had been planted in him by his family's move to America, his being taken to Texas, by his uncles' voyage, by the exotic visitors to San Antonio, and by tales of his elderly mentor's travels.

Although neither Mr. Dunside nor Danny knew it at the time, these seeds would flower in less than two years.

SIX

1

For several weeks after he arrived at Mrs. Bromley's, Danny had spied on Dilue, peeking around corners so she would not spot him. Because she always sensed his presence and spoke to him, it took him a while to realize she was blind. When he asked Mrs. Bromley about the mysterious Dilue—he never heard a last name—she replied only that "Dilue had an unhappy early life. She's lived here a long time now, and she's been happy."

Danny had gasped when he first beheld the woman. Most of her nose was missing; her nostrils were two open holes. Her ears were damaged, and she had scars on what little of her body was visible. Her light blue eyes were unnerving, and more so because they were unseeing. The only other eyes Danny had seen that were such a pale blue were those of his baby sister, Mary Ceara.

Dilue's posture was ramrod straight. She traveled silently and effortlessly through the house, never bumping into an object. Other than to go into the back garden, Dilue did not ever leave the house. During the summer, she would traverse the rows of the garden, fingering the vegetables deftly, then picking only the ripe tomatoes, beans, and squash. She would sit on the back porch shelling black-eyed peas into a large crockery bowl and never drop one. Sometimes she sat on the porch for hours in perfect stillness and solitude, gazing sightlessly into the distance.

2

It seemed to Danny that Mrs. Bromley, Dilue, and Mr. Dunside were a strange triumvirate. There were no two people more respectable than Mr. Dunside and Mrs. Bromley, yet Danny was aware that it was Dilue's presence that made it possible for Mr. Dunside to board in the widow's home without so much as a hint of impropriety.

While mulling about propriety, Danny was struck by the oddness of an adult female, Dilue, being addressed by her first name. Neither he nor the proper Mr. Dunside referred to her even as "Miss Dilue." In contrast, Danny realized that he had not ever heard Mrs. Bromley's first name.

Dilue contributed money to the household by weaving cane seats for new chairs and recaning ones that needed repair. People left chairs on the front porch. They disappeared inside the house and days later reappeared on the porch, refurbished.

Sometimes in the evening, Danny would sit and watch Dilue work. In her scarred but sure hands, the strips of cane seemed to glide into place. Mrs. Bromley had once said to Danny that Dilue had a kind of "knowing" in her hands.

It seemed to Danny that Dilue also had another kind of knowing. She knew when it was going to rain. She knew when it was nightfall. She knew when someone left a chair outside the front door for her to re-cane. She knew without tasting the milk when it was on the brink of souring and exactly when biscuits needed to be taken out of the oven. She knew when someone entered the room. She sensed when Danny was happy or upset or sad.

It would be two springs hence that Danny would leave San Antonio, and Dilue knew Danny was going to leave even before he did.

3

During the long, gloomy Sunday afternoons when the winter weather made it unpleasant to go outside, Danny would tell Dilue what he could remember of his mother, his father, his uncles, and the baby sister he barely knew. He would struggle to recall his early memories of Ireland. He would pour out his recollections of his days at the Aid Society Home, of Johanna and her sisters, and the train trip West.

Dilue listened and rarely spoke, but Danny felt she understood.

"They can never take your family away," she said.

It did not occur to Danny at the time to question who "they" were or whom it was that made up one's "family."

It would be many years later on a moonlit night, lying beside a campfire on the open range and thinking about Dilue's words, that these questions would surface in his mind.

4

Danny's restlessness manifested itself slowly but inexorably, like a leaf unfolding. His disquiet was most pronounced in spring. Two years had passed; Danny was nearly fifteen, and Artis Dunside recognized the signs. As a young man, hadn't he himself signed on as a ship's mate? He reluctantly acknowledged to himself that it was time.

After church one Sunday, he asked Danny to join him in the parlor, a room they rarely went into. He gestured to the two chairs, and they sat down. He wasted no words and no time. "Danny, you want to be going, don't you?"

Danny stared at the worn rug. With his heel planted, he moved the toe of his shoe back and forth in a small arc. "It ain't you, Mr. Dunside. Or Mrs. Bromley. You both been good to me. Better than you ever had to be."

Mr. Dunside replied, "It's all right, boy. You got to live your life." After a brief silence, the old man asked, "When?"

"In May." Danny stared at the lace antimacassar that covered the chair arm and traced the pattern in it with his finger. "That'll let me finish my schooling. It'll give Mr. Muehlenberg time to find a new boy for the store." It was plain that Danny had already given the matter thought.

"I see," said Mr. Dunside, with a slight dip of his head. "Well, that will be fine." And then, "Better let me tell Mrs. Bromley."

Danny nodded.

"Do you know yet where you'll go?"

"Galveston."

Again, Mr. Dunside nodded, pressing his lips together. He understood the boy's reason. After a moment, he rose unsteadily to his feet, and Danny jumped up to help him. Mr. Dunside grasped the boy by both shoulders and looked him in the eye. "I hope you find them, son." Then he dropped his hands, straightened himself, turned, and walked out of the room. Suddenly, Artis Dunside, ex-sailor and railroad man, seemed old and fragile.

Danny felt deflated and guilty. He heard Dilue in the kitchen and went in there. "Dilue—" he began.

But she silenced him with two words: "I know."

5

The day before he left San Antonio, Danny waited until Dilue went into the garden, and then he slipped into her closet of a room. The space was so small that he could encompass it in a glance: a bed, a dresser with a washbasin and a pitcher, a comb and brush, a chamber pot. Her two dresses hung on pegs attached to the far wall.

Silently opening each dresser drawer, Danny peered at the contents. From the bottom drawer he lifted out a packet tied with a cord. He loosened it and unrolled the papers. They were accounts from a newspaper dated 1843. He picked one and began to read. He blanched as his eyes drifted down the column.

> Dilue Dancy, age 12, was taken captive by the Comanches during a raid in September of 1840. The young girl watched in horror as her father had the soles of his feet cut away. The attackers then tied him behind one of the Indian's horses, and he was made to run for miles before they tired of this sport and killed him. The girl's mother was also forced to watch, after which she was defiled, mutilated, and scalped. Dilue's younger sister, Laurel, was taken hostage along with her. Later, when two Indian captives were killed by angry settlers, the Comanches retaliated by stripping

Laurel, staking her out, and skinning her
alive.

Danny sank to the bed. He sat for minute until he had regained his composure and the wave of nausea had passed. When he was able, he looked down again at the newspaper clipping.

> The child was finally freed after two and a half years of daily beatings and torture at the hands of her savage captors. The Comanche men regularly debased her, and she was routinely wakened by their pressing chunks of fire against her flesh, especially her nose. San Antonio merchant Abner Bromley and his wife, Eleanor, have taken the terrified girl in to live with them. Mrs. Bromley is tending her wounds and caring for her. The child has begged to be hidden from sight forever.

Numb and shaking, Danny slipped the yellowed pieces of newspaper back inside the covering, retied the cord with trembling hands, and replaced the packet in the drawer. Then he went to his room and did something he had not done since his mother's death: He buried his face in his pillow and cried until the burning in his eyes and aching in his throat forced him to stop.

At dinner that night, Danny could not eat. He could not look at Dilue, even though she could not see him.

As she left the room, she said in a voice loud enough for only him to hear, "Sometimes it's better not to know."

SEVEN

1

"Oleta, give yourself to the Lord!" the black-frocked man beseeched her. "Yes, Oleta, do it for the Lord!" he cried, his inflection rising. Reverend Elrod Jeeters sank to his knees at the thirteen-year-old's feet. He realized at that moment that he found her bare toes attractive, too. "Kneel down beside me here," he urged, patting the soft ground. He slipped off his shiny broadcloth coat and smoothed it out like a blanket. "Give me your hand," he said, pulling her down beside him.

"But—"

"Hush, now, honey. I got to listen to the Lord's instructions. Sometimes he sends me these poker-hot feelin's, and I got to obey."

With that, he covered Oleta's mouth with his. He kissed her repeatedly, stifling every protest before it could escape her lips. After a minute or two, she no longer bothered to protest. She liked him: Unlike her father and brothers, the reverend was clean-shaven, and although unschooled, his manner was as smooth as his face. His words were sweet and his tones mellifluous. "Just lay back here…" His hands moved over her, first touching her neck, and then fumbling with the buttons of her dress. "You want to be converted, don't you?" he coaxed.

"Oh, yes! Yes!" she cried, caught up in his fervor.

The reverend's cries of "Hallelujah!" and "Amen!" reverberated through the woods.

He rolled back beside her on the spongy ground, savoring the moment, the sunshine, the soft breeze, and the fragrance of the pine needles that cushioned them.

Oleta sat up and grinned at him.

He pulled his trousers up and buckled his belt. "Whoooey, honey! Say, you don't got any sisters, do you?"

"Nope." She tugged at her outgrown dress so that it came down closer to the tops of her knees. "Just brothers. A whole mess of 'em." Oleta fastened the buttons down her front. When she glanced up at the reverend, she was surprised that the color had drained from his face. He looked peculiar around the eyes and puckery around the mouth.

Elrod Jeeters rubbed his face with both hands as if he were washing it. "Younger or older?"

"Younger or older what?"

"Brothers. Are your brothers younger or older?"

"Older. Ever' last one of 'em!" She shook her head. "And they think jus' 'cuz they're older they kin—"

He cut her off. "Oleta, honey, you can't go tellin' ever'body about this afternoon."

"Why not?"

"On account of it's a sacred thing, givin' yourself to the Lord." He was speaking fast, and his voice was now half an octave higher.

Oleta stared in fascination as his Adam's apple danced up and down, and blood pulsed through the veins in his neck.

"Oleta, look at me! If you go tellin' your ma and pa and all them brothers about today, it'll take the holy plumb out of it."

"Ain't got a ma. Ma died three years back." Oleta looked at Reverend Jeeters again and grinned. A small trickle of sweat ran down her sunburned face. "I like you better than that old preacher that usually come through the hollers. He just jabbered, jabbered, jabbered. Like to have talked ever'body's ears off!" She reached for the reverend's bony hand.

"Well, I'm pleased you feel thata way 'bout me, honey, but I can't be stayin'."

Oleta's face fell.

He hurried on. "You know I got 'the call.' The Lord has told me to spend my life itineratin', travelin' around and spreadin' the Good News."

Oleta's lower lip protruded as if she had just sucked a lemon. A slow blink signaled that tears were imminent, and if the reverend was any judge, loud wails as well.

"Now, now, now. Don't you be sorrowin' over me." His voice was soothing again. He grabbed his Bible off the ground. "Here," he said, thrusting it in her direction, "you kin keep this f'rever if you swear on it not to cry and to keep what happened today 'tween you, me, and the Lord."

Oleta opened her eyes wide, the welling tears instantly vanishing. She bobbed her head up and down and reached for the Bible.

The reverend pulled the book towards his chest. "Promise, now?" he repeated, not turning loose of the book until she swore silence. The ersatz preacher mentally bargained for his future: *Lord, you get me outta these hollers without bein' shot by her pa or one of them brothers, and I swear I'll stop convertin' young girls.*

Elrod Jeeters wanted to be sure his departure from the holler would be uneventful. "Here, tell you what, honey. We'll choose you a Bible name for you to add to your own." He took the book back from her. "Let's just open the Good Book." He fanned the pages. "And pick out a holy word. All the words in the Bible's holy, of course." The reverend flipped the book in her direction. "Now you just point to a word."

Oleta closed her eyes and pointed to a word: "verily." The preacher's schooling was less than Oleta's three years' worth, and after studying the word for several moments, Reverend Jeeters solemnly announced the word from God: "Ver-ILL-ee."

He put on his coat and his broad-brimmed black hat, slung his grimy linen bag over his shoulder, and mounted his bedraggled horse. "Behold the Lamb of God that takes away the sins of the world."

Oleta wasn't sure if he meant himself, his horse, or Jesus, but she nodded and smiled at him, still clutching her Bible to her breast.

That night by the light of a lantern, Oleta was a study in concentration as she carefully inscribed "Oleta Verily Starns" inside the cover of her new Bible. She filled with pride as she gazed at the name she had written in large, labored letters. She vowed if she ever had daughters, they would have Bible names, too.

2

With no sisters and six older brothers, Oleta Starns had spent her life cooking, cleaning, sewing, and taking orders from men. By the time she was fifteen, she was more than willing to marry seventeen-year-old Angus Mutt. *Having one man tell you what to do,* she reasoned, *is better than seven of them.*

The newlyweds' struggle for subsistence in West Virginia and rumors of cheap land in Texas induced them to bundle up their few possessions and head west. Among the belongings the young bride brought with her were her two most cherished ones: a straw hat with flowers on it that had belonged to her mother and the Bible given to her by an itinerant preacher.

Angus and Oleta Mutt's farm sat east of San Antonio on hilly, densely timbered land that sometimes made Oleta and Angus forget that they had left the hollers. The rich soil sported buffalo grass, slender-stalked bluestem, and purpletop. Oak and pecan trees abounded. To Oleta's delight, peach trees and vegetables thrived in the sandy loam. Angus benefited from the long growing season and rainfall that spread throughout the year. What he hadn't anticipated was the backbreaking years of effort it would take to clear the land and pay off the debt.

A son, Cletis, was born to Oleta and Angus the year they arrived in Texas, but it was four more years until Oleta gave birth to the daughter she wanted. When Ruby was born, Oleta started at the beginning of the Bible and selected the word "Genesis." Painstakingly inscribing her Bible for the second time, she scrawled beneath her own name her daughter's birth date and "Ruby Genesis Mutt." After considerable puzzling, Oleta concluded that it was pronounced "Ge-NEE-sis," as if it rhymed with "pieces."

A year later when Opal was born, Oleta chose the word at the top of the next section of the Bible. She studied it, deciphered it as "Ex-O-dus," and laboriously inked the birth date and the name "Opal Exodus Mutt" in the Bible beneath Ruby's name.

Despite their "Bible names," Ruby and Opal were hellions who could get away with anything or, when it came to chores, with doing nothing. Over the years Cletis resigned himself to the fact that his spoiled, unruly sisters were the apples of his mother's eye. Although he was strong, hardworking, and patient, he was taciturn, not gifted with great mental quickness, and—to his eternal detriment—Oleta's son, and not a daughter.

3

Oleta had told her neighbor Zebbie that she wanted a girl from the placing out program, a girl who could help her with household duties and with her daughters. The reality was that Johanna—or Hannah, as the Mutts called her—did virtually all of the household tasks, most of the cooking, and even some barnyard chores.

Johanna learned it was easier and faster to hang out the wash and gather the eggs herself than to coerce the Mutt girls to do these jobs. When the girls hung out the laundry, the wet clothes ended up on the ground instead of the clothesline, and Johanna had to wash them over again. When Ruby and Opal collected eggs, a few were always broken, and Johanna was held responsible.

Johanna had been at the Mutts barely two weeks when she woke up one morning to discover that her hair had been smeared with molasses. She tied a cloth over her head so that Oleta would not know. During breakfast, she gave no indication to her two tormentors that anything was wrong. She spent part of the afternoon scrubbing the viscous brown liquid out of her hair. The soap smelled awful. She poured more water over her head and tousled her short hair with both hands. *It'll dry before Mrs. Mutt sees it.* Then she grinned because her next thought was, *It's a good thing I don't have long hair!* Johanna never mentioned the incident to Ruby or Opal. It left them more worried than if she had come after them with a stick.

Johanna discovered that her foster sisters' mischief was not limited to the pranks they played on her. They also seized any opportunity to get her in trouble with their mother. On a Saturday morning in autumn, when Oleta had gone to town and left Johanna to watch her daughters, Ruby and Opal snatched from the top of the chifforobe the hatbox that held their mother's precious, flower-bedecked hat. Removing it from its box, they took turns trying it on and strutting back and forth across the room.

Johanna cajoled, begged, pleaded. Nothing could entice them to put the hat back where it belonged. She knew that the hat could be destroyed in the struggle if she tried to take it away from them. She would be blamed. Oleta would scream at her, and when Oleta lost her temper, she incited Angus until he unleashed his wrath on Johanna as well.

Johanna abruptly changed tactics. "Here, let *me* try it on!"

She later castigated herself for being so naive. *I should have known something was wrong when Ruby let me have the hat!* Through the window, Ruby had seen her mother climbing down from the wagon and lumbering towards the door with her packages. No sooner had Johanna placed the hat on her head than Oleta opened the door.

Ruby screamed as if she were hysterical. "Mama! Mama! Hannah's been trying on your hat!"

Clutching the front of her dress in her hands, Opal joined in. "We tried to stop her, Mama! We know how much you love your hat!" Opal worked up a small, indignant crocodile tear.

Johanna stood paralyzed, the troublesome hat still atop her head.

A scarlet wave spread over Oleta's face. It rolled from the base of her neck to the top of her skull. For a moment, it made Johanna think of mercury rising in a thermometer. Oleta dropped her parcels. Then she charged Johanna like a bull. She grabbed the sides of the hat with both hands and ripped it off her head. Johanna did not have to wait long for the shouting to begin.

Ruby and Opal egged their mother on. "Did she hurt it any?" Ruby asked, feigning heartfelt concern for the piece of dilapidated millinery.

"Hope she didn't get no dirty, smudgy handprints on it," Opal chimed in, supplying her mother with another source of possible outrage. Oleta grabbed a broom and began jabbing at Johanna's feet as she railed at her.

While Oleta was spewing a torrent of angry words at Johanna, Ruby kicked a hole in a small sack that had fallen on the floor with the rest of the parcels. The chalky white substance scattered everywhere. Ruby groaned. "And she caused you to spill baking powder all over the floor!"

Oleta whirled around and grew even more enraged. She hurled the broom at Johanna's feet, screaming at her that she was "worthless" and "undeserving." She thrust the hat in Johanna's face. "Now put my hat away and clean up this mess!" she shrieked.

Johanna put the hat away, picked up the broom and started sweeping the floor that she had already cleaned once that morning. Oleta stood glowering at her, her hefty arms folded across her chest like a policeman's. Ruby and Opal stood behind their inflamed mother, grinning and making faces at Johanna.

Johanna knew that as soon as Angus came in for supper, the yelling would start all over again. She also knew that she would not receive any supper that night.

The yelling resumed, just as she predicted, but after a while, she could no longer hear Oleta's strident voice. She was listening to the defiant voice in her own head saying, *Just wait. Just you wait.*

4

Like other farm children, Johanna went to school six months a year, starting in early November. Cletis explained to her, "When the weather gets warm enough in the spring, Pa will need you part of the day to help with planting. In the summer, everyone helps with the farm work." *Everyone except Ruby and Opal,* he thought. *Those two don't do a lick.* During the few years he had attended school, Cletis had hated it. He intended for his words to reassure Johanna that she wouldn't have to endure school forever. She made no reply. She welcomed any reason to be away from Oleta.

On the opening day of school, Johanna realized that she had inherited from Cletis the formidable task of herding Ruby and Opal to the schoolhouse and back. They dawdled the entire way, knowing she would be blamed if they were late.

The first week of school Johanna learned to carry all three of their dinner pails because they set theirs down and "lost" them. A time-consuming hunt was required to find them. When Ruby offered to carry her pail, Johanna later discovered ants scurrying over the food.

In school Johanna listened and tried hard. She was happy simply to have the burden of Ruby and Opal shifted temporarily each day to Miss Cooper. The teacher was not unsympathetic to Johanna's situation. On the first day of school Ruby pointed out Johanna to her classmates and announced, "Ma and Pa got her off the train." By way of further introducing the newcomer, she offered the observation, "She talks funny."

"*Ja,* she does!" Opal giggled in complicity, twisting a braid around her finger and sucking on the end of it.

Miss Cooper observed that not only did Johanna have to contend with the incorrigible Mutt sisters, but that her accent and her curious arrival on a placing out train also made her the victim of teasing and cruel remarks by classmates. Even in Johanna's presence, the Mutt girls and other pupils talked about her as if she were not there.

When out of earshot of Miss Cooper, Franny Bains contemptuously referred to Johanna as *bestellt,* something ordered from a catalog, merchandise that could be returned if it proved defective.

Johanna knew Cletis had suffered Franny's barbs, and she wondered if Franny was one of the reasons Cletis decided he had had enough school. As the banker's daughter, Franny lorded her family's wealth over the others.

"Your parents didn't want you!" This was the taunt of Franny's that wounded Johanna most. *They loved me!* Johanna clenched her jaw and screamed in her head. *And they would never raise me to be a rude girl like you!* Johanna kept to herself and looked away whenever Franny ridiculed her.

A few weeks later, Franny was enraged when she opened her fancy school box. Every nib was crushed, every pen snapped in half. She held up a broken stub. "Hannah, you did this!"

Johanna merely shrugged. In her best German accent, she suggested, "Vhy you not order some more, Franny—from a catalog?"

5

Johanna fantasized constantly about finding her sisters. Twice she sneaked to the entrance of the farm and started down the road, only to become confused when the road forked. Which way led to town? When Oleta finally took her with her on a trip into town, Johanna tried to make a mental note of every turn, every landmark. On her third attempt to leave, she knew which fork to take, but after another hour of walking, she sat down beside the road in despair. She buried her face in her hands. *I have no money, no plan. I don't know anything about Texas or how to find my sisters.* After a while, she got up and began trudging back to the Mutts', scuffing up the dust with her shoes and kicking at rocks. Johanna let out a long sigh. *Wherever they ended up, please let them be happy and well.*

From that day on, at every chance she got, Johanna slipped out of the house and walked to the edge of the Mutts' westernmost field at sunset. She stood facing the horizon, stood watching the sun disappear, stood staring in the direction the train had taken her sisters, stood yearning.

EIGHT

1

As soon as the Jäegers arrived home from the depot, Albert carried Inga to their bed. While he telephoned the doctor, Anna filled a basin with cool water and began to bathe the child's feverish body.

Albert waved his hand in the air as he spoke in German into the telephone. "That's what I said: We got her off the train. She's very sick. You come *now*, Viktor. *Please.* I'll explain when you get here."

Within an hour, Dr. Schmidt arrived. He finished his examination and peered over his wire-rimmed spectacles at the listless child. "*Die Pneumonie,*" he announced. "And she is severely malnourished."

"Will she survive?" Anna asked in a whisper. Inga was dozing fitfully, laboring to breathe. Her sudden coughing spasms left her depleted of oxygen and blue in the face.

"She's past the worst of it, I think." The doctor extracted a brown bottle from his bag and instructed the Jäegers on the dosage. "How old is she? Six?"

"We were told eight," Albert replied.

"She's small for her age." The doctor closed his bag and finished giving the instructions for Inga's convalescence.

Albert walked his tall, bushy-bearded friend to the door. The doctor shook Albert's hand. "If she should take a turn for the worse, call me right away." Albert gave him a grateful nod, and then closed the door softly.

When he returned to Inga, Anna was helping her sip water from a blue glass. "Like cures like," said Anna with authority. "Inga has the blue cough. For the blue cough, a blue glass. Best not to take chances."

Although she said nothing more, Albert understood Anna was hoping that if Viktor Schmidt's medicine did not work, the homeopathic folk cure would.

2

Albert and Anna lavished care on Inga and were heartened daily by her improving health. By September, she had recovered her strength completely.

"She looks like a different child!" Anna rejoiced. A pink tinge had replaced the anemic pallor of Inga's cheeks, and exuberant childhood energy supplanted the torpor of sickness. Even so, Inga often hung back, peeking out shyly from behind a large chair or folds of the draperies. And she did not speak.

To keep Inga busy in the kitchen while she was fixing dinner, Anna sometimes gave her a piece of paper to draw on. Over and over again, Inga drew the same childish figures, two that were identical, and a third that was larger. Also in her pictures was a large, black mass with circular scribbles curling out of the top. When Anna would ask about the pictures, Inga would just look at her.

Gradually, though, Inga's confidence and curiosity began to bloom. Rather than hide, she fluttered throughout the house like a hummingbird. She explored every room, every drawer, every cupboard, every object. At first, she merely made small sounds of delight at her discoveries, but after three months, she began to speak.

The Jäegers' home was situated in the Little Rhine, or King William, district. The large limestone house, like the other early Victorian homes there, was adorned with iron cresting and flanked with spacious porches. Anna often took her daughter out on the porch and into the garden, chatting to her the whole time. "Look at our blue porch ceiling, Inga." Anna pointed upward. "Is like the sky." Albert had acquiesced and painted all of them blue. Anna insisted the color would keep wasps away, and he had learned long ago the tone she used whenever she was absolutely certain she was correct.

Their house was nestled between flower-filled gardens irrigated with water from the acequias. Leafy trees shaded the yard. The house had originally been illuminated with gas lights, but Albert had been among the first to convert to electricity. As a result, their home boasted lights in nearly every room and had freestanding stoves that produced steam heat.

In the hallway was a telephone whose sound thrilled Inga. "Make it ring, Papa!" she would beg, pulling him towards it.

Albert relished any chance to indulge his daughter. He would smile, call his neighbor and closest friend, Emil Braun. "Ring back, Emil, and put young Dieter on the telephone to talk to Inga."

Each bedroom at the Jäegers' featured the luxury of a faucet, from which flowed cold, artesian well water. Thick rugs and solid, heavy furniture—including a piano—distinguished the house as one of the finest in the area. The Jäegers were joyous at having a child to fill one of the four bedrooms.

Albert took his new daughter with him on strolls and to the park, and proudly showed her off. Anna read to Inga and played the piano and sang songs to her. At night, she tucked Inga into bed and sang her lullabies.

Anna's songs, in fact, had been the final key to unlocking Inga's tongue. Once Inga began singing along with Anna, she started to chatter happily and incessantly, releasing a river of words from behind some invisible emotional dam. She asked repeatedly for a lullaby whose words Anna did not know. Inga sang the lullaby to her dolls so often that Anna soon learned it.

Inga carried the same three dolls with her everywhere. "What are their names?" Anna had asked her.

Inga held up the bigger one. "Johanna." Next, a small one. "Helga." Finally, the other small one. "Inga," she said, pointing to herself. Anna walked over and picked up a picture Inga had drawn. "What are their names?" she asked. Inga gave the same answers. "Sisters?" Anna asked.

Inga nodded.

"And what is this?" Anna pointed to the large black object on one side of the drawing.

Inga looked up at Anna through long, black eyelashes. "The train."

That evening, Anna handed Albert several of Inga's pictures and told him how Inga had described the figures and the train. Suddenly she stopped mid-stitch and set her sewing in her lap, a look of surprise on her face. "Oh my. I think one of Inga's sisters is her twin."

Albert studied the pictures again. He sucked on his pipe, weighing the matter. Then he nodded. "*Ja.* I think this is so."

The next morning, they asked Inga if the dolls were sisters. "Sisters," she responded, pressing the three of them together in a tight knot and hugging them to her chest.

For several months, Inga continued to carry the dolls with her wherever she went. Anna sometimes found her sitting on the floor holding imaginary conversations with them or lying in bed at night singing a lullaby to them. Over time, though, her talk of her sisters began to fade. She put the dolls on a shelf beside her bed, insisting they remain there, where she could see them.

One evening, Anna asked her husband, "Do you think we could find Inga's sisters? Would it be wrong to try?" Before he could answer, Anna thought better of it. "Maybe her sisters are happy with other families. I know how I would feel if someone came asking about our Inga."

After several moments of mulling, Albert replied, "I think we should see what we can find out. We know her sisters left the train before she did, but we don't know where. I do not think the Aid Society would tell us. Still, I can look around and quietly ask questions. And even if we find out about her sisters, Anna, we do not have to act on the information. Someday, Inga will be old enough to know whatever we learn about them."

"If we could find them, I would take them," Anna ventured. She pretended to busy herself with her sewing, but she watched Albert out of the corner of her eye. "If they needed a home and wanted to come, of course." Anna tied a knot in a thread and clipped it with her scissors.

"I would take them, too," he replied. "We still have empty bedrooms."

3

Anna had carefully packed away the dress Inga arrived in. "I still have the dress I was wearing when *we* arrived in Texas, Albert," she said, explaining her actions to her husband. "The child has so little left of her past." Then she added, "I found this button in Inga's pocket." She held it up for him to see. "It doesn't match the dress."

"Inga," Albert scooped up his daughter and whirled her around, "where did this button come from?"

"Papa's button!" she exclaimed and reached for it.

The word "Papa" cut him like a blade. He already thought of himself as her Papa, as if no one else had ever occupied that role. "From Papa's coat. Johanna gave Helga one, too. Johanna said keep it forever."

"I see," Albert replied. "Well, we'll put it in the little box I carved for you." *There's room enough in her heart—and mine—for her to have two papas. I have everything her father did not: health, wealth, a home, work... even his daughter. And I'm alive to enjoy it all.* He made a silent promise to a man he never met, but who was now part of his life. *What I do, I do for both of us. I will take good care of our daughter.*

4

When it was time for Inga to start school, she grew tentative again. "Mama, will it be like it was at the Home?"

"No," Anna reassured her, "not like that at all." Anna recalled Inga's description of the bleak classroom and stark instruction in New York. "You will go to a fine school with nice teachers. It's called the German-English School. And your friends will be there." Anna was referring to the Braun children who lived next door. "You can walk to school together."

The next morning, Anna took Inga to see the school, a handsome stone structure on South Alamo Street. Dedicated to the memory of Friedrich Schiller, the school attracted pupils from all over Texas because of its curriculum, which was modeled after the German Gymnasium system, and its excellent faculty. "You will study both German and English," the director told Inga. "Also Spanish, history, poetry, writing, and mathematics. Girls learn singing and sewing, too." She explained that upon graduation, young men spent a year or two completing their education in Germany. Anna looked at her daughter and thought, *I'm glad she's a girl. I couldn't bear it if she left for a year.*

That evening, Anna told her husband, "I took Inga to see the school this morning." The Jäegers spent the evening chatting about Inga's education and her future. "So many decisions!" Anna declared. Her tone sounded put upon, but both she and Albert knew they took great pleasure in discussing their daughter.

Removing his pipe from his mouth, Albert chuckled, "I think we have many years before some of these decisions must be made!"

Anna smiled and held up the dainty dress she was making, inspecting it with a critical eye.

Gesturing to its small size, Albert said again, "Many years."

5

Preparation for Christmas started on December 1 with Advent. "This is for you," Albert declared when he surprised Inga with an Advent calendar after supper. "To make the twenty-four days before Christmas go faster. Now, go into the parlor to see what Mama has for you."

"Oooh!" cried Inga when she entered the parlor. "It's pretty." She bent low and sniffed. "And it smells pretty, too."

Anna had fashioned a wreath from cedar branches and anchored four candles in it. "There's one for each week before Christmas, Inga. Each Sunday afternoon, we will light a candle."

December 6, St. Nicholas' Day, was the children's favorite day, as Inga soon discovered. They hung up stockings to receive little gifts, trinkets, and toys, a tantalizing preview of the season.

"Tomorrow you help me prepare *Weihnachtsstollen*," Anna told Inga, referring to a Christmas bread rich with raisins, candied fruits and nuts, and topped with sugar icing. The house was still redolent of the anise cookies, peppermint cookies, and honey cakes they had baked earlier in the week.

The house's transformation thrilled Inga. Aromatic greenery, glowing candles, tempting odors from the oven, plates heaped with cookies. A child's delight.

"Inga, starting tonight we put candles in the windows and light them. It is our custom," Anna explained. "We do it so that if the Christ child is lost, if he is cold and wandering in the dark, he will see the candles and know he is welcome in our home." Anna looked at her adopted daughter. Her eyes filled with tears as she tenderly brushed Inga's bangs back from her small face. *A child, lost and wandering. This tradition never meant more to me than it does now.*

The week before Christmas, the Jäegers set up the crèche. "They're so small!" Inga marveled, handling with care each of the pieces Albert had meticulously carved. Each evening she would rearrange them ever so slightly as she recounted the Christmas story Albert and Anna had told her.

As was the custom, gifts were not wrapped, but instead laid on a *Gabentisch,* a table. Each person had a certain place on the table for his or her gifts. Anna explained to Inga, "A cover, a *Leinentuch,* must remain draped over the gifts until the day the gifts are unveiled." Inga circled the table each evening, gently touching the cover that rested over her part of the table and trying to guess what was under it.

The Jäegers, like all German parents, followed the tradition of decorating the Christmas tree the night before Christmas, and behind closed parlor doors. Soon the tree was laden with tin, straw, and paper ornaments, yarn dolls, and soft felt animals that Anna had sewn. Albert looped chains of popcorn and berries over the branches, added candles, and crowned the fragrant green tree with a star. "Perfect!" he declared.

Inga's delighted squeals on Christmas morning more than rewarded them for their efforts. She touched every ornament she could reach, chattering excitedly about each. Albert unveiled the presents and Inga raced over to them. There were toys and books, and a red coat and hat Anna had sewn for her. Inga tried them on, and then played with the toys. Afterwards, Albert and Inga joined Anna at the piano to sing with her while she played "Stille Nacht, Heilige Nacht" and "O Tannenbaum."

"Again! Play 'O Tannenbaum' again, Mama!"

Besides her new coat and hat, the two gifts that pleased Inga most were a game— a tseppli-board Albert crafted for her—and an odd-looking device whose name she could barely pronounce at first. "It's called a stereopticon," Albert told her, as he slipped a double-image print into the viewer. Inga was intrigued by its three-dimensional effect. She snuggled up beside him on the settee, and they viewed the stack of prints over and over. "We'll look at them again later," he promised. "Or maybe you can show them to Mama." He gave Anna a wink.

"I need some pictures for *my* new albums," Anna changed the subject. She treasured the pair of elaborate, plush-covered photograph albums from Albert. Like other Germans, they loved pictures. Both she and Albert knew that before long, the albums would be bulging with pictures of Inga, chronicling their adopted daughter's life. "I'm going to leave the first page blank," Anna told Albert later. "To remind us there was a part of her life before she came to us."

The celebration continued throughout the week. On New Year's Day the house was filled with pungent odors that emanated from the kitchen. To a candle-lit table, Anna brought savory pork and mouth-puckering sauerkraut ("to guarantee good luck") along with blackberry wine. She nodded and touched her daughter's shoulder. "Someday you will make this meal for a family of your own, Inga."

Albert smiled. He could always tell from Anna's tone when she felt absolutely certain of something.

NINE

1

Mr. Dunside had watched Danny's restlessness grow during the two years since the boy had arrived in San Antonio. He understood his need to search for his uncles, so Danny's decision to leave had come only as sad news rather than as a surprise.

Although Danny had set the date of his departure, neither he nor Mr. Dunside talked about how quickly it was approaching. Nor did Mrs. Bromley openly acknowledge that he would soon be going. Danny noticed, though, that supper more often concluded with his favorite desserts: hot, bubbly fruit pies; rich composition cake delicately flavored with rosewater; spice cake fragrant with ginger, cloves, and cinnamon.

From the moment Danny revealed his intention to go to Galveston, however, Mr. Dunside had spent considerable time explaining which rail lines to take and how to hop trains safely. "Here, take this." Mr. Dunside handed him an envelope with a folded paper inside. "It's an unofficial 'pass.' It may not be any good at all, or it may come in handy if you show it to another old railroad man. There's also the name of a mate I used to sail with. Seb still works for a shipping company on the Galveston wharf, as far as I know. He might be able to help you find your uncles." Mr. Dunside smoothed his mustache with the side of his finger. "Do you know the ship your uncles sailed on?"

Danny nodded. "The *Northern Cross.* I also know the date they sailed.*"* He paused. "Mr. Dunside, there's a friend I want to see on the way to Galveston. She's the one I told you about. Johanna. She was placed out in Sulphur Creek."

Mr. Dunside had his ear cocked, listening closely and straining to hear.

"She's about the only person I know in this part of the world who came from New York." In Danny's mind, the inhabitants of Mrs. Bromley's house, along with Johanna, constituted his loose-knit Texas family.

Mr. Dunside shouted at him and pointed to a map. "Getting to Sulphur Creek won't be no trick at all. It's not much out of the way if you're going to Galveston."

When the day of Danny's departure arrived, little was said at breakfast. Mrs. Bromley looked as if she was close to tears. Mr. Dunside looked stoic, holding his chin high. Only Dilue looked as calm as she always did.

After a bigger than normal breakfast, Danny picked up a small cloth sack in which he had stowed a change of clothes, the maps Mr. Dunside had given him, the little bit of money he had saved from working at Muehlenberg's beyond what he contributed for his room and board, and a few other items. Mrs. Bromley handed him dried beef and apples, biscuits, and cookies and gingerbread, each wrapped in paper and tied with string. Danny tucked them in his pack.

"Take this, too, son." Mr. Dunside pressed a folding knife into Danny's hand. "You never know when you might be needing a knife," he mumbled.

The unexpected sound of the word "son" touched Danny to the core. His throat felt tight, so he simply stood there, running his thumb back and forth over the finely etched scrimshaw on the knife's walrus tusk handle. His eyes glowed with pride at being entrusted with such a treasure. "It's beautiful," he whispered. Speaking louder so that Mr. Dunside could hear him, he repeated his words, "It's beautiful! I'll keep it with me always, Mr. Dunside. Promise me that someday you'll tell me the story behind it."

Mr. Dunside tipped his head in a slight nod. Danny shoved the knife deep in his pocket.

They walked out the front door together, except for Dilue, who remained inside. She had run her hands over Danny's face, as if fixing his image in her mind. "I hope you find what you're searching for," she told him. He studied her sightless, pale blue eyes, and exhaled slowly, recalling what they had seen when she was a child.

"Thank you, Dilue." Danny squeezed her strong, skillful hands. "You'll remember me, won't you? After I'm gone?" Danny had given her a bottle of rosewater cologne. He could detect the fragrance on her.

She nodded. He had also left with her a book with pictures of ships to give to Mr. Dunside after he had gone. He had waited two months for it to arrive at Muehlenberg's. And there were two pearlescent combs for Mrs. Bromley's billowy hair.

Mrs. Bromley hugged Danny. Tears flowed down her cheeks. "Lord, how I'm going to miss you, boy!" She wiped her eyes with the hem of her apron. "Who's going to eat all my peach pie? You take care of yourself. You know you always have a home with us here."

Danny gave the tiny, white-haired woman a long hug. "You make the best pie in the world! And I'm going to miss you, too, Mother Bromley." Danny's words surprised him.

Mrs. Bromley cupped his face in her hands and smiled up at him affectionately. Her eyes filled again, and she hurried back into the house.

Only Danny and Mr. Dunside remained on the porch. For a moment, they stood in silence. Neither seemed able to find the right words. Finally, Mr. Dunside extended his hand and shook hands with Danny. "You let me know how you're doing, you hear? You can always send word with any conductor who's on a train bound for San Antonio."

Danny nodded. "Mr. Dunside—" Still at a loss for words, Danny instead gave the old man an awkward hug. He spoke in a voice that Mr. Dunside could hear clearly, "You been like a father to me. I won't forget anything you've taught me." He grinned at the old sailor. "After all, the acorn doesn't fall very far from the tree."

Tears were now welling in the man's eyes. Danny could feel his own eyes starting to fill and his throat starting to constrict. Knowing that the longer he delayed, the harder it would be to leave, he picked up his pack, smiled at Mr. Dunside, and then started for the train station.

Mr. Dunside had arranged for Danny to ride to Sulphur Creek, but he didn't have the heart to see Danny leave on the train. "Tell Hank I'll be a little late this morning," Mr. Dunside called out to Danny. It would be the first time he had ever been late.

Danny strode off. After about twenty yards, he turned and waved again at his friend. He hoped Mr. Dunside couldn't see the tears in his eyes.

2

Danny felt strange boarding a train again. A flood of memories inundated him as he took a seat beside a window. It seemed as if a decade rather than two years had passed since he had climbed down from the train in San Antonio and gone home with the crusty old stationmaster.

Danny swallowed and cleared his throat, determined to think about the happy experiences that lay ahead: his trip to Galveston and seeing Johanna on the way. He played imaginary scenes in his mind. In all of them, she was shocked and thrilled to see him. Gazing out the train window, he took pleasure envisioning their reunion. He thought to himself, *She's probably as hungry as I am to see a familiar face from home.* The word "home" struck him as peculiar. Did it mean New York? The train west?

The scenery glided past the open window. *The train's no more comfortable now than it was the first time,* he mused. Although the Texas summer had not yet officially arrived, Danny's upper lip and forehead were peppered with beads of sweat. It ran in front of his ears and in tiny rivulets down the center of his chest and between his shoulder blades. To distract himself, he tore a square of gingerbread into small pieces and popped one spicy morsel after another into his mouth.

When the train rolled into Sulphur Creek that afternoon, Danny was elated. That night he unwrapped his one remaining biscuit and gulped it down. Then he lay down on a bench at the station, his pack beneath his head. For a split second, he could picture himself as a small, frightened boy sitting on a bench in the San Antonio depot, sneaking nervous glances at the old man Miss Darden was talking to. His lip curled involuntarily at the thought of her.

The next morning, a man picking up freight to deliver in town allowed Danny to ride with him after Danny helped him load boxes onto the wagon. On the way, Danny asked, "You know a man around here named Mutt, got one ear half bit-off?"

The driver thought a minute. "I seen somebody like that a couple of times in town, but I can't say as I've heard his name."

Danny felt encouraged at this news. He thanked the man, hopped off the wagon, and looked up and down the main street. He walked towards the bank. He was planning to ask more questions but decided against it, afraid he would be asked questions in return.

Instead, Danny entered Van Horn's Dry Goods. He pretended to examine the notions that were displayed on a well-worn counter. He milled around until the proprietor's wife was busy with a customer. At that point, Danny asked her where the school was. Still busy helping a woman select cloth, she pointed in the direction of the school. "Turn right at the corner, left at the undertaker's." In a distracted voice, she added, "It's about a mile and half to the school." She went back to unwinding bolts of cloth and extolling the virtues of each.

"School still going on?" he ventured.

She sensed a sale was imminent and prickled with irritation at Danny. She escorted him to the door, but as she closed the door behind him, he heard her say, "School ends next week."

Danny headed for the school. When he spotted the whitewashed building, he hid behind a tree and waited, eating his apple and watching. At noon the children, laughing and yelling, tumbled out the door to eat lunch.

Danny's spirits soared when he saw Johanna. *I bet it'll be just as easy to find my uncles,* he congratulated himself. Johanna was taller; she looked tired and thin, and she had braids again, but otherwise she looked the way he remembered her. She was trying in vain to make two younger girls settle down and eat.

Danny picked up a small rock and chunked it in her direction. On the second try, he landed one close enough to catch her attention. Looking in the direction of the sound, Johanna glimpsed his grinning face peeking out from behind the tree. Staring in disbelief, she let out a squeal. Danny ducked behind the tree again, but her shriek drew Ruby and Opal's attention, and they ran over to her.

"Didda ol' spider scare you, Hannah?" Ruby pestered her.

"Maybe she sat on a sharp rock," Opal joined in.

Johanna did not reply.

Although she did her best to get the girls to move away, they stuck close by, sensing that it annoyed her. Danny saw that she would not be able to come over to the tree. When she cast her eyes in his direction again, he pointed to the outhouse, and she nodded.

Ten minutes later, Miss Cooper rang the bell. She rounded up her reluctant pupils and shepherded them back into the schoolhouse. Johanna slid into her wooden desk near the center of the room, unable to concentrate on the arithmetic lesson. Over and over, her eyes gravitated to the open window. She waited impatiently for Miss Cooper to finish chalking arithmetic problems on the blackened section of the wall that served as a board.

Perhaps because Johanna looked so anxious when she raised her hand, Miss Cooper signaled her permission for the girl to be excused. In her eagerness to get outside, Johanna tripped over the coal bucket that stood empty beside the cold pot-bellied stove. The class erupted into laughter, but for once Johanna did not care.

"Her mother should have named her Grace," one of them hooted.

Franny Bains' voice dripped sarcasm. "Taking a little 'trip,' Hannah?" More laughter.

Miss Cooper brought the class back to order by eyeing a chair that faced the corner. Johanna scrambled out the door.

Johanna slipped around to the back of the outhouse, and Danny strolled over to her. "Hey, lass," he exclaimed, throwing his hands into the air, "I came to see you." He said it as casually as if she lived next door.

Johanna's mind was a jumble of joy and bewilderment. "Danny? How did you get here? Where did you come from? Do you know what happened to my sisters?"

Instead of responding, Danny asked her, "Are you happy? With the Mutts, I mean?"

"I have enough to eat. I get to go to school. But I'm not part of the family. They just wanted someone to do work. And their daughters are rotten." Her voice took on urgency as she returned to the one question she most wanted the answer to, the one Danny least wanted to be asked: "My sisters? What happened to them?" She looked expectantly at Danny and clutched the front of her skirt. As she searched his face, she could feel her heart start to race. He looked down for a second; it wasn't a good sign.

Johanna cast a nervous glance towards the schoolhouse. "I have to go back inside. You have to tell me what you know."

He began slowly. "One got placed out. I don't recall exactly where. I don't know about the other one, the one who was coughing."

Johanna moved a step closer. "Then they weren't placed out together?"

He shook his head.

"And you don't know where Inga got placed out?"

Danny felt his anxiety soar. He ran his hand through his hair. He hadn't wanted to talk about this. Not here. Not now. He felt caught.

"Danny! Tell me!" She clasped her hands together in front of her mouth as if in prayer.

He blurted out, "What I mean is, I don't know *if* she got placed out."

Johanna's mind reeled with confusion. "Well, if she didn't get placed out, what did hap—"

"Hannah!" Miss Cooper's voice rang out like a shot.

Johanna bit her lip. "Please. You have to tell me whatever you know."

"Hannah!" Miss Cooper's voice again, even more strident.

Johanna grabbed Danny's arm. "When can you come back?"

He realized there was no more time to talk. "Tell me where the Mutts live. I'll come there."

Johanna hurriedly told him how to get to the farm and how to identify it. She loudly banged the door of the outhouse, and before she started back to the schoolhouse, she warned him, "Stay out of sight. The Mutts aren't going to welcome anyone who's a friend of mine."

For the rest of the afternoon, she could think of nothing but Danny and her sisters. Every time she thought of Inga and Helga, her heart sank. She replayed her conversation with Danny over and over in her mind, trying to make sense of it. *He didn't know where Helga was placed out. He didn't know if Inga was placed out. If she didn't get placed out, then what happened to her?*

She finally succumbed to the thought she had been resisting. "Oh-h-h-h…" Her loud groan startled the sleepy classroom. She placed her head face down on her arms and sobbed.

"Hannah?" It was Miss Cooper. "What is it? Are you in pain?"

Johanna could not lift her head. She could only nod.

3

Danny had plenty of time to think as he walked to the Mutts' farm. He hadn't seen his uncles in years, and he might not find them anyway. He argued with himself,

What difference would a little more time make? Galveston will still be there. Finally, his mind was made up.

Danny knocked on the Mutts' back door. Oleta moved slowly, rising out of her chair at the kitchen table and padding to the door. She noticed his pack and eyed him suspiciously. "What do you want?" she demanded.

Danny took off his cap respectfully and held it to his chest. "Work." Thinking of his job at Muehlenberg's, he added, "I have some experience with farm equipment. I'll work for small wages and my keep—meals and a place to sleep."

Oleta started to send him away, but thought about the summer harvest and the work to be done in the fall. "Talk to my husband. Down in the field." She dipped her head to the right to indicate the direction of the field. She turned and eased herself back into her chair, and then resumed mending a rip in one of Ruby's faded dresses.

Danny walked to the field where Angus was examining some emerging sprouts and Cletis was chopping a tree stump. Cletis set down his ax and stared as Danny approached. Angus caught sight of him and stood up.

"My name's Danny O'Brien," Danny said, instantly wishing that he'd had the foresight to offer some name other than his own. "I'm looking for work in exchange for a little money and my keep. I have experience with farm tools," he half-lied, omitting the fact that his knowledge was limited to stocking them at Muehlenberg's.

Angus considered the matter for what seemed an interminable length of time. Then he said slowly, "Well, I *could* use some help… but we don't have no room." Angus was too proud to admit "or any money."

"It's warm. I'd be willing to sleep in the barn," Danny countered, discreetly studying Angus's crimped ear.

"Where's your family?" Angus asked, all of a sudden wondering why Danny wasn't working on his own family's farm.

Danny was blunt. "Don't have any kinfolk."

Angus considered this and concluded that it gave him an advantage. He spit tobacco juice on the ground. "This is a small farm. Can't give you nothing 'cept a place to sleep and meals. You sleep in the barn. Work six days a week, Sundays off. Take it or leave it." Then, as if to cinch the deal, he added, "You look a little puny, but I'm willing to give you a chance."

Danny felt his disgust rise. *No wonder Johanna can't stand these people.* He wanted to give Angus a smart reply, but he held his tongue. He thought about Johanna and he thought about Mr. Dunside. He could hear him saying, "You got to out-think that feller."

One of Mr. Dunside's adages popped into Danny's head. "Well, sir, I reckon that digging a hole is the only job where a man gets to start at the top. I'm willing to work my way up. When do I start?"

Angus was pleased with the boy's answer. He silently congratulated himself on his shrewdness as a negotiator. "Put your duds in the barn and get back down here. You can help him with that stump." He gestured to Cletis, but did not bother to mention his name.

Johanna arrived home from school, too downcast even to be bothered by Ruby and Opal's taunts of "Crybaby!" Then she saw something that brought a tiny smile to her face. Soaked with sweat, Danny was chopping away at the roots of a stump while

Cletis urged the mule to tug the rope looped around it.

At supper that night, Angus commented through a mouthful of food, "This here is Danny O'Riley. I'm giving him a try as a farmhand."

Afraid she would tip them off if she looked at Danny, Johanna focused on the cornbread and beans on her plate and went on eating.

Ruby and Opal giggled at their father's announcement. They stole glances in Danny's direction. They whispered secrets and poked each other. Soon they were competing for Danny's attention and pelting him with questions. He dodged their questions by answering them with questions.

After supper, Johanna cleared the dishes. As Danny walked out the kitchen door and headed for the barn, he called out over his shoulder, "Nice to meet you, Hannah." Then he glanced back and waved at his only friend in this part of the world from New York.

TEN

1

Danny's presence had crystallized Cletis's proprietary feelings towards his foster sister. Over time, Cletis's need to let Johanna know how he felt had welled up in him like dough on a warm hearth.

Seeking a breeze on the sultry summer evening, Johanna went outside at dusk. She was eager to escape Ruby and Opal's squawking and giggling and incessant demands. She strolled along a row of the cornfield. The tall stalks shrouded her from view, and she relished the solitude.

Cletis saw her slip out the door. He squared his shoulders, licked his palm and pressed his cowlick down, and followed her. As he approached, he stumbled and flattened a swath of cornstalks before he could recover his balance.

Johanna wheeled around and glared at him. She was thinking about her sisters and her parents, and she wanted to be alone. "What is it, Cletis?" Her tone was peevish.

"H-Hannah—," he stammered. He realized that he had no idea what to say.

Johanna's irritation flashed in her eyes.

"Well, I-I..." he began, but unable to find words, he grabbed her and tried to kiss her. She shoved her hand between their faces. Cletis found himself kissing her palm instead of her mouth.

"Let me go, you—you—you—*toad*!" she sputtered, unable to find a vile enough epithet. Her struggle inflamed Cletis further, and she was no match for him physically.

"Just one kiss!"

Rolling on the ground, Johanna pounded on Cletis whenever she could work a hand free. She hissed at him, "I'm gonna tell! Your father will take the strap to you!"

Cletis felt the familiar sting of rejection and humiliation. He felt foolish for not having expected it from her as well. "My father won't do nothing!" Cletis yelled. "You ain't family. You ain't *nothing*." He pinned her to the ground and was about to make good on his attempt at a kiss when he felt something tickle the back of his neck. He released Johanna's arm long enough to reach up and slap his neck.

A nonchalant voice announced, "There's still some daylight left, and there's still work to be done. You two oughtn't to be spending your time like this."

Cletis twisted around. He flushed with embarrassment and then hatred. Danny stood there smiling, dangling the corn silk he'd used to tickle Cletis's neck.

"Why, you little—" Cletis forgot about Johanna. He lurched to his feet and lunged at Danny. Danny turned sideways and dropped to his hands and knees. Cletis flew headlong over him. Danny watched in fascination as Cletis's face contorted with rage. He was out of control. He swung wildly, but Danny dodged him, staying clear of his erratic, inept punches and allowing Cletis to wear himself out. Johanna stood to the side, fuming at Danny, but thankful he had appeared when he did.

When Cletis had nearly exhausted himself, Danny punched him in the stomach. Cletis's eyes opened wide, registering the shock of the blow. A heavy groan seeped from his mouth. It sounded like air escaping from a blacksmith's bellows. He sank to his knees, clutching his belly.

"You damn Paddy!" Cletis spit out the words. "*You're* a nothing, too, just like her!"

Danny walked over and socked Cletis in the jaw, toppling him sideways. Cletis lay on the ground, still holding his middle and sucking in his breath. He kept his head tucked to his chest.

"Don't—bother—her—again." Danny barked out each word. It was a command, not a request.

Cletis looked defeated. He pulled himself to his feet and stumbled off. His shoulders sagged more than usual. He took the long way back to the house, circling the perimeter of the field. He kicked at clods of dirt and occasionally picked up a rock and flung it. Danny could see him stomping through the corn, swatting at random at stalks along the way.

Johanna ran back to the house and went inside. She felt confused by what had happened, and she was fearful of Cletis catching her alone again. Danny made it back well ahead of Cletis, but he waited until he saw Cletis walking towards the porch.

Angus sat there, chewing and spitting tobacco whittled.

At the last minute, Danny fell in beside Cletis so that they reached the porch at the same time. Cletis would not look at Danny. Angus glanced up at his son's disheveled clothes and hair and at the sweat that glistened on his face and arms. "What happened to you?" He flicked curls of wood off his lap.

Danny answered for him. "We had a race. Down by the cornfield."

Angus stopped brushing away the wood chips. He eyed both boys. "Who won?"

"He did." Danny made a matter-of-fact nod towards Cletis. And then, "Well, I reckon I'll call it a day." He headed for the barn, noticing out of the corner of his eye the puzzled expression on Cletis's face. Danny smiled. He could hear Mr. Dunside's voice saying, *Use your head, not your fists.*

ELEVEN

1

For several weeks after the fight in the cornfield, Danny and Johanna felt the tension between Cletis and themselves. Over time, the feeling faded, but Cletis no longer made eye contact with either of them. He spoke to them only when necessary.

Weeks later, when Danny and Johanna were working together in the fall vegetable garden, he told her, "You know, sooner or later, we got to figure out a way for you to leave here. You're obligated to them until you're seventeen, so we got to find a way where the Mutts can't stop you." He tugged at another weed. "And they can't know where you've gone."

Johanna reached down and pulled at a green carrot top. She glanced at the small, dirt-encrusted carrot that dangled from her hand, and for a split second, she saw the carrot doll she had made for her sisters in New York. Johanna stood up slowly. It hadn't occurred to her that there was any real possibility of leaving. "How? When? And where would I go?"

"We'll wait for the right time." Danny scratched his head. "I got to think on it. We'll just go on as usual until I reason it out."

School had begun again. The autumn air was crisp and invigorating, the fall colors glorious. Although Johanna still had to contend with Ruby and Opal, she welcomed the daily respite from Oleta and Cletis. *I'm glad Cletis doesn't go to school,* she thought. He hadn't attended since he was twelve, a decision Angus favored. There was more than enough work to be done on the farm. He needed Cletis's strong arms, legs, and back.

2

The winter was mild, and in the evenings, after firewood had been brought in and the animals tended, Johanna often sneaked out to the barn. She sat cross-legged, wrapped in one of Danny's blankets, spellbound as he regaled her with tales about Mr. Dunside, Mrs. Bromley, and eventually, Dilue. He described the seemingly endless array of items he stocked at Muehlenberg's—from dentifrice, pomade, shaving soap, and shoe gloss to lamps, suspenders, and corsets. Only once had she been allowed to accompany Oleta to the store in Sulphur Creek.

"I know all about farm tools," Danny began one night.

Johanna's face radiated skepticism.

"Enough to get me this job, I reckon."

She laughed and gave a reluctant nod.

"And I know about medicines, too." Danny began to rattle off names of the bottles he had so often stocked the shelves with. "Let's see, there's Moffat's Vegetable Pills, Dr. Hull's Worm Lozenges, Lee's Bilious Pills, Donley's Magical Pain Extractor Salve."

Johanna pursed her lips and shook her head in mock disgust at his bragging. Secretly, she longed to see the things Danny described, especially the gingham, bone buttons, ribbons, and lace. Sulphur Creek's store carried a small inventory of dry goods, but in spite of that, she had been so enthralled that Oleta had been forced to yell at her to make her leave.

Danny told her about his fights with Otto and about his classmates' jeers. He told her about a stout girl who stuttered.

In turn, Johanna recounted her clashes with Franny Bains and the Mutts, especially with Ruby and Opal. She told him tales of Oleta's pretentious aspirations for her daughters. "She wants to make *ladies* out of them! Have them wear fancy clothes! Learn fancy manners! Even gave them fancy 'Bible names'! *Those* two—can you imagine?" At other times, Johanna would mimic Oleta's high-tempered outbursts. In private, she and Danny referred to the Mutts by their first names or as "Angus and Anger."

One evening, she said to Danny, "It must have been hard to leave San Antonio. I would *never* have left if I had ended up there. At Mrs. Bromley's, I mean." Then she added, "Except to find my sisters, of course." She riveted her eyes on Danny's. He heard her suck in a deep breath. "Danny, do you know where Helga and Inga went? You never mentioned them again after that first day when you came to the school." She fidgeted with a piece of hay she was holding. "I've started to ask a hundred times, but I was too afraid." Her eyes filled with tears.

Danny had dreaded the question. He hoped against hope that it would never come up again. Confronted with Johanna's tears, he understood why weeping women reduced Mr. Dunside to applesauce. He wished desperately he could give Johanna the answer she wanted. He began slowly. "I only know what I told you before, that just one of them—the one that was sick—"

"Inga."

"Inga and I went back on the train after we were took to a church one night. It was just us two. All the others had been placed out."

Johanna's face fell. "If they'd only been able to stay together," she lamented. "And you don't have any idea where Helga was placed?"

"We'd been to so many towns by then. And we slept in lots of churches along the way." He was ashamed to tell her he'd hidden inside the pulpit podium and fallen asleep, and that by the time he woke up, Helga was gone. All he could do was reel off the names of towns between Sulphur Creek and San Antonio that he'd learned from Mr. Dunside's railroad maps. When he was through, he said softly, "It's got to be one of them along there. Might have been Franklin. Or it could have been Millard or Cartersville. Or maybe Squaw Bridge." He shook his head. "Sorry."

"I could go to each place. I could ask. I could—"

Danny cut her off. He couldn't bear to see her get her hopes up. In a low voice, he said, "Johanna, more than likely she's out on a farm somewhere. Once she left the train, she might never have been back in the town again. She might not even have the same name now. I heard the couple that took Märta—you remember her?—say to her that her new name was going to be Mary. Told her right on the spot. They hadn't even left the depot. Gave her a new last name, too, but I can't recall it." When Danny saw the expression on Johanna's face, he wished he hadn't told her about Märta.

Even though the Mutts called her "Hannah," it hadn't occurred to Johanna that her sisters might also have been given different names. She stared at her lap as she twisted the piece of hay around her finger. "Danny, what about Inga? You said you didn't know if she was placed out. If you were the last two, what happened to her?"

"Don't know," Danny mumbled. He cleared his throat and tried again. "Don't know if…"

Johanna dropped the piece of hay. "If *what*?"

She could barely hear his reply. "If she made it. I never saw her leave the train once we reached San Antonio. Miss Darden said she was bad off, that a man was going to take her to a doctor."

Johanna covered her mouth with her hands. She swallowed hard and closed her eyes. She bit her lower lip and choked back tears.

Danny was at a loss; he felt helpless to comfort her. "Maybe you can find 'em, Johanna," he offered weakly. He tried a different tack. "At the least, we can get *you* out of here. I told you during the summer that we'd find a way for you to leave. One of these days, I got to be on my way to Galveston again, but I don't want to leave you here by yourself." He was blurting a barrage of words, but they seemed to have the effect he hoped for.

Johanna managed a small, grateful smile. From the moment she had arrived at the Mutts' farm, she had wanted to leave, but even when Danny mentioned it, it never really seemed possible—at least not for a few years. *I'd be alone in a strange place. No money. Nowhere to go even if I had money,* she told herself. The realities of the situation overrode her hopes. "Danny, you know the Mutts would never agree. They might even come after me. Besides, just where would I go?"

"The Mutts don't have to agree because you ain't going to ask. And the answer to the second part is that they can't come after you if they don't know where you are. And the answer to the last part is 'Where I came from.'" He allowed her a moment. "Mrs. Bromley is old. Mr. Dunside is old. Dilue is blind. They need someone young." His idea was now clear to Johanna. He hopped to his feet. With a broad smile and a bow he had not used since his days on the streets of New York, he announced, "And I'm just the one who can take you there."

"How are you going to do that?" Johanna's expression mirrored her skepticism.

"We'll have to work that out," Danny conceded. "A few more months and spring will be here. Spring's a mighty good time to travel." His words kindled a spark of hope in her.

Danny knew he had part of the solution two days later when Oleta announced that in two weeks she, Angus, and their daughters would be attending an overnight "prayer meeting and baptism." She unfurled the broadside she had taken down from a tree on the outskirts of town. "Come behold God's miracles!" was emblazoned across the top of it. The camp meeting promised to be the biggest event in Sulphur Creek that year, and Oleta was determined she and her daughters would be there.

When they were by themselves on the porch after supper, Danny told Johanna, "I do believe the Lord may have provided an answer to our prayers, 'Hannah.'" And right away, he set to thinking about a plan that would enable him and Johanna to disappear. A miracle indeed!

3

"*We're* going to a re-vi-val! *We're* going to a re-vi-val!" Ruby crowed in a singsong voice.

Danny continued hauling feed sacks into the barn. Johanna sat shelling pecans, ignoring both Ruby and her sister.

"Going to be baptized," Opal chimed in with the same superior tone.

"Bet you *foreigners* ain't been baptized," sneered Ruby.

Johanna just looked at her, still not bothering to answer. But Danny set down a sack and shook his head with vehemence. "I wouldn't *want* to be! Too risky!"

Opal's eyes narrowed, but she persisted. "Mama says we're going to be 'saved.' We're going down to the river. We're going to have our sins washed away in the blood of the Lamb!" she proclaimed. Secretly, she was a little apprehensive about what role the blood played in all of it.

Danny tugged on the corners of a sack, dragging it inside the barn. When he emerged, he replied, "All that's fine and good, but how you gonna keep the sin from sticking *back* on you?"

The pair of sisters looked at each other and then stared blankly at him. Danny continued his work, pushing his way indifferently past Ruby.

"What do you mean?" demanded Ruby. She realized she was talking to the back of his head. She did not trust Danny, but she was starting to feel uneasy at the prospect of her upcoming immersion.

"Well," Danny began as he emerged again from the barn, "the Bible says your sins are gonna be washed away when you're baptized." He paused dramatically. "The Bible don't say those sins are going to *disappear.* It's not like sugar melting in water, you know."

Ruby was torn between her growing anxiety and her desire not to appear ignorant.

Danny raised his eyebrows. "Just exactly where do you think that sin *goes* when it's washed off? Have you ever thought about *that?*"

The sisters' eyes had grown large. Now confident of their attention, Danny expounded, "I heard that sin's like soap scum. It'll stick right back on you like glue." As he was giving the girls a minute to assimilate this, another thought popped into his head. "Where do you think pond scum comes from? And those foamy little swirls in the river?" He leaned towards the girls. In a solemn voice he answered his own question: "*S-I-N. Sin.*" Articulating each syllable clearly, he declared, "*Washed-away sin.*"

Now warming to his subject, Danny forgot about the sacks of feed. He grew more authoritative and expansive. "When people's baptized, their sins is washed off, but the sins don't dissolve. Nope. They just float on top of the water looking for something—or some*one*—to stick to." Ruby and Opal's eyes followed every movement of Danny's hands and arms. He extended his hands to his sides at waist level, palms down, fingers wide, and slowly lifted his outstretched arms to show the inexorable rise of sin beneath them. Then he sank back and crossed his arms over his chest. "And you can't wash it off either."

Despite herself, Opal gasped. "How *do* you get it off?"

"Can't. What you gotta do is to keep it from stickin' to you in the *first* place. You got to stir up the surface of the water to scatter the sin." Danny swirled his fingers and flailed his arms to show what needed to be done. "And once you been dunked by the preacher, you got to *keep* scattering the sin, so you best keep flapping." He pretended to turn his attention back to his chores, delighted with his inventiveness. Then he stopped in his tracks.

"Oh, and this is *real* important." Danny walked back over to them and divulged in a confidential tone: "Don't forget that at a baptizing, it's not just *your* sin that's comin' off in the water. It's the sins of *everybody* that's being dunked or ever has been dunked there. You better ask to go first 'cause if you don't, you'll be wading into a soup of sin of everyone that's been baptized ahead of you." He rolled his eyes ominously. "And there's no telling what *their* sins might be."

Afraid she would burst out laughing, Johanna kept her head down and began shelling pecans in earnest.

Another flash of inspiration hit Danny. He signaled his gullible audience to come nearer. "Up to now, it ain't mattered because your own sins are still stuck to you, but once you been dunked by the preacher and made it safely out of the water, for the rest of your life, you got to avoid being tainted *again*. Here's my point: You never know *where* a baptizing has taken place. Could be any river, any pond anywhere. So forever after when you go swimming, this is what you do: You rile up the water first with a stick or throw in a rock. Then jump in quick before the water smooths out and the sin settles back on the top. You got to keep moving, and when you're ready to get out, go beneath the surface and reach up with your hand. Splash it around over your head to break up the sin before you come up. Then hold your breath and *get out fast!*" Danny dusted his hands together as if he were brushing dirt off. "'Cause if you don't, that sin'll coat you like honey on a spoon."

The girls stood in slack-jawed silence, scarcely breathing.

Danny put one foot on a feed sack and tossed off a final suggestion. "Oh! It also helps if you shake like a wet dog when you get out of the water. Better remember that, too."

Later that afternoon, as Danny was reflecting with deep satisfaction on his story, it occurred to him that if what he'd said were true, every preacher in the country would be soaked in sin. He also concluded that if he had his way, it would take more than a preacher and a baptism to save Ruby and Opal.

TWELVE

1

"Damnation!" Gabriel jerked his hand out of the cloth sack that was slung over his shoulder and sucked the blood off his finger. Then he peered into the bag, extracted one of the sharp tacks, and hammered a notice to a tree.

Whenever Reverend Obediah Folsom planned to hold a camp meeting, he had his assistant, Gabriel Blower, paper the surrounding area with broadsides ahead of time. "COMING SOON! BEHOLD GOD'S MIRACLES! COME AND BE SAVED! PREACHING AND BAPTISM!" The flyers announced the dates and the location, and they featured a glorious account of Reverend Folsom's "considerable Bible training, preaching prowess, and healing powers."

Danny slipped away from the Mutts' farm one afternoon when he saw the boy tacking up notices nearby. He exchanged curious looks with the boy. Danny's eyes narrowed as he studied the boy's face. "The train?"

Gabriel's face lit up in recognition. "I'll be deuced! You were the one who was always acting up. Anybody ever take you?"

"At the last stop. San Antonio. The stationmaster." Danny quickly recapitulated the years since his arrival in San Antonio. "How'd you end up with—" Danny peered at the broadside the boy had just posted. "How'd you end up with Reverend Folsom?"

"People name of Bick took me from the train in Millard. I couldn't get along with them. When Reverend Folsom come through, I asked him if I could go with him. Told me no at first, but he changed his mind. Said he could use a helper. The Bicks was more than happy to see me leave. I been traveling with the reverend more than a year now."

Danny tried to imagine what kind of year it had been, living out of a wagon. "What's he like?"

Gabriel was blunt. "Crooked as a dog's hind-leg and a drunk to boot, but at least he ain't mean. And he pulls hisself together for the revivals. He figures he don't hurt nobody, and if they go away feeling better or behaving theirselves, he reckons he done some good." Gabriel slipped the sack of nails off his shoulder. It plopped on the dusty ground with a thud. He leaned back against the tree and rested the sole of one foot against the trunk for balance. It reminded Danny of a picture he had once seen of a stork. Gabriel scratched his armpit as a prelude to resuming his story. "The reverend used to be a drummer who sold patent medicines. I swear that man can sell *any*body *any*thing."

Danny detected a hint of admiration in his voice.

"He decided that peddling God was easier than lugging around a wagon full of bottles of snake oil. So ever since he's been peddlin' God and cheap Bibles. That's how he makes his living. And that's how he became the 'Reverend.'" Gabriel gave a mischievous grin. "The only bottles in the wagon now are whiskey bottles."

Danny made a wry face, as if he were expecting a bread-and-butter pickle but had bitten into a sour pickle instead. Then he went back to what interested him most: "Is he good to you?"

Gabriel shrugged. "We get along fine. I do my job—pasting and tacking these up before the revivals." He waved a handful of broadsides. "Then I work the crowds at the camp meetings, collect money, and clean up. And he sees to it that we have what we need."

"Tell me your name," Danny said, suddenly embarrassed at not having asked sooner. "I'm Danny O'Brien."

"Gabriel Blower."

Danny frowned and wrinkled his forehead.

"Arthur Boston," the boy amended his answer. "When I was left at the Aid Society Home, I was too young to know my last name, so they chose one for me. On the train everyone called me Arthur, and so did the Bicks. But Reverend Folsom figured we'd do better if I went by Gabriel." He grinned as he rolled his eyes heavenward, fluttered his eyelids, and flapped his imaginary wings.

Now Danny grinned. He recalled enough of his Bible lessons at the Home and at Mrs. Bromley's to know that the archangel Gabriel was the messenger for God. After a minute of silence, Danny began humming a few bars of the song he and Arthur had sung on the train about Miss Darden and Mr. Rice.

"K-I-S-S-I-N-G!" Arthur chimed in at the appropriate point and stamped his foot in delight. "Hoo-eee!" he hollered. Then he and Danny burst out laughing. "I can say in all truth, I ain't missed neither of them two!"

Danny nodded. He pursed his lips and his expression turned serious. "Say, you think you could help me with something, Arthur?"

Arthur shrugged. "Maybe."

"Do you remember a German girl on the train? Her name was Johanna and her twin sisters were with her."

Arthur thought a minute. "Yeah. One of 'em was sick?" He recalled Inga's jarring cough. Toward the end of the trip, it had kept him awake at night.

Danny bobbed his head. "I need a bottle of whiskey, Arthur—I can still call you Arthur, can't I? Johanna lives with a family here in Sulphur Creek. I need some whiskey to help her get away from them. Most of the Mutts will be coming to the prayer meeting. While they're gone there'll be a chance for her to run away and get a good head start. By the time they get back, she'll be *long* gone."

A troubled look crossed Arthur's face. Although he wasn't sure how a bottle of whiskey was going to help, he was glad to be of assistance. "They treat her bad?"

"Like unpaid help. *They* deserve something bad."

"What the devil! I'll do it!" Arthur slapped his thigh. "I sure as thunder *can* steal a bottle of his whiskey. I'll figure out a way, by damn." Danny was still marveling at Arthur's easy use of swear words when Arthur added, "The meeting'll be just outside of town, about two miles west of here. The old Hawthorne place. It's in a clearing near the river."

Danny beamed. "Can you also do a little something about Johanna's foster sisters? Their names is Ruby and Opal. Them two's terrible. They live to torment Johanna. They'll be at the revival with their mother and father. They're going to be baptized on Sunday."

The evangelist's helper was already warming to the challenge. Holding his sides and shaking with laughter, Arthur listened as Danny revealed Oleta's, Ruby's, and Opal's middle names. He convulsed with laughter when Danny told him the "baptismal sin" story he'd made up. Cackling and straining to catch his breath, Arthur croaked, "I can help. You bet your soul I can help!" And wiping away imaginary tears of laughter, he wheezed, "I passed a cemetery earlier today. I reckon it to be 'bout halfway 'tween here and the Hawthorne place. Meet me there tomorrow night. I'll have the whiskey for you." Then his tone became more serious. "But where will you and Johanna go?"

"San Antonio. We'll hop a train."

Arthur could feel a plan unfolding in his mind. "After this prayer meeting, Reverend Folsom and I are headed west to some more small towns. He likes small towns for revivals. Of course, he likes big towns for whiskey." He flashed a huge smile. "He'll start drinking as soon as the meeting is over, and I'll start cleaning up and packing the wagon. You and Johanna make your way outside of town, above the road, and come there. By the time you get there, the reverend will be dozing peacefully inside the wagon. I'll give you and her a ride to the next town. You two can hop the train to San Antonio after dark."

"You're an amazing lad, Arthur Gabriel Boston Blower!" Danny clapped him on the back. "You really are a 'Gabriel.' You can bet that Johanna and I'll be there!"

"And you can tell me how the whiskey worked."

"And you can tell *me* about the baptisms!"

The next night Danny crept out of the barn and made his way to the cemetery by the light of the moon. He stared at the headstones and shivered. *Where did they bury my mother?* It was a question he rarely let himself think about.

"Over here." The sound of Arthur's voice startled him. "This bone orchard make you jumpy?"

Danny nodded.

"Well, here's what you come for." Arthur held out the whiskey.

Danny accepted the bottle as solemnly and respectfully as if he had been handed the scepter of an empire. "Thanks, Arthur." He cradled the bottle in his hands. The memory of his father and uncles flickered across his mind. They were sitting around the broken-down table in the tenement, drinking and singing.

"Anything for an old friend." Arthur and Danny both liked the sound of the word "friend." "Gotta get back now." Arthur turned and strolled off whistling.

Later that night when Danny hid the whiskey in the barn, he realized he was again whistling the song from the train. *All I need now,* he thought, *is for Oleta, Angus, and their daughters to hurry up and leave for the revival.*

2

Oleta had been anticipating the camp meeting since the moment she saw the broadside. New notices had been posted throughout Sulphur Creek and the surrounding area to announce the preacher's imminent arrival. The flyer featured a likeness of the Reverend Obediah Folsom. Oleta asked the boy who had been nailing up the broadsides if she could have one to enclose in her Bible.

She had made up her mind the moment she learned the evangelist was coming: She, her daughters, and Angus were going, and despite his protests, she had not budged one inch. Furthermore, Ruby and Opal were going to be baptized at the culmination of the Sunday service.

The Mutts would leave Saturday morning with their daughters for a day and a half of "sermons, singing, swaying, sweating, and salvation." Cletis was to stay home and tend the farm. He would be the "man in charge," although his father had said it in a disparaging tone. Danny and Johanna were told to "do as he says." Still nursing a bruised ego and a grudge from the encounter in the cornfield, Cletis took pleasure at the prospect of ordering them around.

The week crawled by. Finally, it was Friday night. Oleta began issuing instructions: "Danny, fetch the tin tub from the barn." "Hannah, you start heatin' water for baths."

Oleta, Ruby, Opal, and Angus—despite his protests—took baths. Angus was the last to bathe. He spent only a few minutes in the dirty, soapy water, and then rinsed himself by pouring two buckets of water over his head. Oleta held up a pair of shears and pointed to his unruly hair. Angus squirmed miserably on a stool. "Take it easy, woman!" he shouted. "I already lost half an ear. I can't spare another one." Oleta finally gave up. She surveyed her handiwork and was not entirely satisfied with the outcome. She decided she could plaster down the uncooperative sprigs in the morning with a dab of cooking grease.

The next morning, Ruby and Opal looked no less silly after Oleta finished with them. She had painstakingly, and painfully, wound bunches of hair around strips of cloth, and then tied the ends of each strip together in a loop. She fervently hoped she would be unwinding curls by the time they arrived at the camp meeting. She intended to "fancify" their curls with colored ribbons right before the service began. She was determined that her daughters would resemble as closely as possible the stylish young girls and women whose pictures adorned her secondhand, well-thumbed issue of *Godey's Lady's Book*.

Years earlier, she had found the dusty magazine near the depot, accidentally dropped perhaps by a fashionable woman who had stepped outside for air during the train's stop in Sulphur Springs. Oleta could not read most of the words in the magazine, but she pored over illustrations of extravagant Paris gowns, dainty embroidered slippers, and fine furnishings. She often asked her daughters to read aloud from it because she was convinced it held important keys to gentility and social advancement for her daughters; indeed, that it could ultimately help them become ladies. "Pay attention," she chided them, "and someday you'll be fancy ladies, wearing fancy dresses, and everyone will call you ma'am."

Although their hair had dried overnight, Oleta refused to let Ruby and Opal remove the tight, hair-entwined strips of cloth the next morning. "Hurts," whined Ruby, tugging at a strip that dangled from her pink scalp.

Oleta slapped at Ruby's hand. "Leave it be! They got to stay just like they are 'til the last minute. I'll unwind them at the revival."

"But Mama, our hair's gonna get wet anyway." Ruby's protest fell on deaf ears.

Johanna went about her chores in amused silence. In the past, she had watched Oleta spend hours studying the illustrations in the magazine, teaching her daughters to make a curtsy of sorts, making them practice saying, "Pleased to meet you," and having them hold a fork and spoon as shown in the magazine. She even had them rehearse placing a napkin in their laps instead of tucking it in under their chins—"For a time when you might need to know how to do it," she'd explained. The well-attended revival would be her first opportunity to show her girls off.

In anticipation of the event, Oleta bought new cloth and added a few inches of length to the bottom of Ruby and Opal's outgrown "good dresses." From her magazine, she borrowed the idea of tacking a bit of lace at the neck of each dress. Surveying the results one last time, she felt satisfied. "Pack up the dresses and put them in the wagon, Hannah. And mind you, you be careful with them!"

Danny knocked on the kitchen door and came in. "Can I help?"

The normally slow-moving Oleta fluttered in and out of the kitchen in a dither. Under Oleta's critical eye, Johanna packed the dresses and began to wrap and pack a basket of treats earmarked for the revival: ham, corn, sweet potatoes, dried apples, bread, and molasses syrup. "What's taking you so long?" Oleta demanded irritably each time she came into the kitchen.

"She just wants to be sure everything is fixed exactly right," Danny reassured her. Then he mimicked Oleta's sour face for Johanna. When Oleta left the room, he pulled a small brown bottle from the back of the shelf, opened it and emptied it into the syrup. Johanna's eyebrows shot up in consternation. Noiselessly, he recapped the bottle, and replaced it on the shelf. He tapped the lid back tight on the syrup bucket.

Oleta swooped into the room again. "Hurry up, you good for nothing girl! You're slow as molasses."

At that instant, Johanna's look of consternation dissolved into a "serves-you-right" smirk. In silence, she carried the food to the wagon, then stowed blankets, a lantern, and other items that had been set out the night before.

Oleta debated about taking her Bible, but concluded that, as proud as she would feel showing it off, something might happen to it. Reluctantly, she put it back in the trunk. She pulled her best dress out and in a peevish tone muttered, "Well, wouldn't you know." She was soon fussing over a loose button on the collar. "Van Horn's must have sold me bad thread." She glowered at Johanna. "Or maybe you didn't sew it on good the first time."

Johanna couldn't recall ever seeing Oleta as worked up as she was over the revival. It was as if she saw it as the crowning moment of her life.

"Don't just stand there like a cow, Hannah! Get my hatbox. Put it in the wagon now," she snapped. "I don't want to forget my hat."

Johanna removed the hatbox from the top of the chifforobe and stood holding it, trying to dismiss the idea that kept forcing its way into her thoughts. "I've been around

Danny too long," she declared half-aloud. Giving in, she exhaled, "Why not." She glanced at Oleta. Oleta was squinting and stabbing a needle at a hole in the button of her dress. Johanna turned away, opened the hatbox, plucked out the hat, and after another furtive glance, stuffed it behind the wardrobe. She carefully replaced the lid and retied the frayed ribbon.

"Take care of the animals. Clean out the barn. Check the fence on the far side of the field." Danny could hear Angus reminding Cletis one last time what he was to do while they were gone.

Oleta called the girls, whose hair still made them look like silly rag dolls. Shouting and giggling, the two Medusas climbed into the wagon. Ruby began digging around in the basket. "Want some?" She held out a slice of dried apple to Opal, then popped it into her own mouth and sucked on it.

"Mama—" Opal tattled, but her mother ignored her. Oleta stood in the doorway, taking a final nervous look around and mentally checking off her list before closing the door.

Johanna walked over to the loaded wagon.

"You can't go," Ruby taunted her through a mouth full of apple.

"Wouldn't *want* to go after what Danny said about all that sin floating on the river."

Ruby's face darkened. She pulled the piece of apple out of her mouth and considered Johanna's words.

"But since you're going to be baptized anyway, you be sure to tell the preacher your Bible names," Johanna advised. "He'll ask you your name right before he dunks you." Johanna continued to talk as she smoothed a blanket in the wagon. "The preacher'll be impressed that you got Bible names. Not everyone has names like *that*." Ruby took it as a compliment.

Oleta, still mumbling and fretting, swept over to the wagon and climbed onto the seat. "Let's go!" she hollered to Angus. "We're wasting time!" As they pulled away, she turned and yelled at Johanna, "You put my hat in?"

With a guileless face, Johanna replied, "I put the hatbox in the wagon myself." Then she waved good-bye to them. She hoped it was forever.

3

Danny, Johanna, and Cletis watched the wagon disappear down the road. Cletis mustered an authoritative tone. "Let's get busy." He made incessant demands throughout the day. Johanna and Danny were cooperative, and he began to feel confident.

Johanna fixed an early supper for the three of them, tidied the kitchen, and excused herself for the evening. Danny and Cletis went outside and sat on the porch, where Cletis assumed his father's chair.

Danny began slowly. "Been thinking about that fight we had in the cornfield last summer, Cletis." He paused for several seconds. "I feel real bad about it."

Cletis shifted in his chair and then tilted it onto its back legs. He looked unconvinced. "So?"

"Well, your folks are gone. Hannah's not around and neither is nobody else. We work hard every day. Don't you think it's time we had a little fun? After all, we're both older now."

"Meaning?"

Danny edged forward in his chair. "I got me a bottle," he whispered.

Cletis sat motionless, hardly breathing. "Of what?" He spoke so softly that Danny almost couldn't hear him.

"Whiskey."

Cletis set the chair down hard on all four legs. He let out a low whistle. "Where'd you get it?"

"An Irishman can always find whiskey," replied Danny, dismissing his question. "What say we go to the barn and take a few swigs?" He tilted an imaginary bottle to his lips.

"Well, I guess…." *Pa left me in charge,* Cletis reasoned. *I can decide this for myself.* "I 'spose it'd be all right." *They went off and left me here.* A ripple of resentment coursed through him. *Ruby and Opal get to do something special.* Cletis nodded to Danny. "Let's go."

Once in the barn, Danny brought out the bottle of amber liquid. "You get the first draw." Cletis looked at the bottle uncertainly, then tipped it up and swallowed a huge gulp. He gasped as the liquid burned his throat and scorched his esophagus. He could feel it travel all the way to his stomach. He threw his head back and let out a whoop. He handed the bottle to Danny.

"Good, huh?" Danny put the bottle to his lips and tilted it upside down. However, he closed off the bottle with his tongue so that none of the liquid went into his mouth. He made a face and wiped his mouth with the back of his hand. "It's as good as I remember!" he declared, and handed the bottle back to Cletis.

Over the next two hours, Cletis drained most of the bottle, growing ever more convivial and exuberant. Danny half liked him. By eight o'clock, Cletis was out cold. Danny sprinkled what remained in the bottle on Cletis's clothes and on the straw on which he lay. Both Cletis and the barn reeked of cheap whiskey.

Danny went to fetch Johanna from the house. "It's done!" he boasted. "Come see!"

Cletis lay face down, sprawled like an oak that had been timbered. "What if he wakes up?" she asked anxiously.

"This lad won't wake up until Monday! I seen my father and my uncles put away a bottle hundreds of times. I can tell you this: You don't wake up for quite a while."

Danny pulled out the pair of scissors he had picked up when he went into the house. They were the scissors he'd seen Oleta use on Angus's hair.

"No!" shrieked Johanna. "Don't stab him!"

Danny silenced her with a disgusted look. "Calm down. I'm just going to spruce him up a bit."

Johanna sat on a pile of hay and watched Danny joyously chop random clumps of Cletis's hair. In spite of herself she began to laugh. She held up a wide space between her thumb and her fingers. "Maybe a little more off the right side."

Danny stood back and looked. Pleased with his first attempt at barbering, he sat down beside Johanna. "You got everything ready?"

"I've bundled together my other dress and some food, a blanket, a candle, and a few other things." *Including the button,* she thought to herself.

Danny walked over to one of the two stalls in the barn. "Watch this," he said. He shoved the feed trough to the side and scraped away the dirt beneath it. Johanna moved closer, peering at the box he was uncovering.

"What is it?"

"Cletis was good enough to tell his drinking companion"—Danny pointed his index finger at his own chest—"about a little money he's put away. Says whenever he goes into town to do some selling for Angus, he puts a cent or two of it aside. Been doing it for a few years."

Opening the lid on the box, Danny was impressed. Even though they were small coins, there were lots of them. Johanna looked unsure as Danny crammed the pennies and the one nickel into his pockets. "This is better than I hoped for!" he exclaimed.

"He's going to tell Angus, and Angus is going to come after us!" Johanna warned him.

"Can't," said Danny. "He can't tell his father he's been pocketing some of his money. That's the best part. He can't say *nothin'* to *nobody!*"

Once back to the house, they stayed up late going over their plan and exulting in their success up to this point. When the sun came up, Johanna and Danny nibbled on biscuits and jam and drank some buttermilk, but both were too nervous to taste the food. Johanna started to carry the dishes to the basin to rinse them, and then thought better of it. She left them on the table. Danny picked up their packs.

They were halfway to the front gate of the farm when Johanna stopped. "I forgot something." Although he was impatient to get under way, Danny followed her back to the house.

She marched straight to the chifforobe. She pulled Oleta's hat out from behind it and held it high in triumph. She swooped through the kitchen, grabbing a crock off a shelf. She tossed the hat on the porch and drenched it with molasses. She disappeared into the house again. When she returned, she dumped flour on the hat, but saved enough to coat the kitchen floor. Danny could hear her laughing. She pulled down the cover on Ruby and Opal's bed and poured ribbons of molasses across it. She pulled the cover up, lifted the pillows and pooled more of the sticky liquid beneath them. When she was done, she slid the empty molasses crock back on the shelf.

Danny hooted and gave her a round of applause. Then his expression changed. "I got to do something, too." He headed for the barn, where the newly shorn Cletis lay in the exact position they left him in earlier. Danny unearthed Cletis' moneybox again, put the coins back, and was reburying it when Johanna appeared. She said nothing, but she looked on in approval. During the night, Danny had dreamed over and over again of Mrs. Bromley sitting at her kitchen table counting out the coins to pay for the top, penknife, and candy he had pilfered.

They started again for the road. Johanna was calmer now, and her conscience began to nag at her. "The Mutts had it coming," she rationalized. She looked over at Danny. "But we're going to burn in the eternal fire for stealing whiskey from a preacher."

Danny shook his head in disbelief. "Johanna, it was *whiskey* that we stole from that so-called preacher. Not Bibles. Not money. *Whiskey.* Reverend Folsom is a flimflam man. Never saved anyone and never could," Danny snorted, "starting with himself."

"Well," said Johanna tongue-in-cheek, "maybe we'll be the *first* ones he ever saved. 'Course he'll never *know* it."

When they had gone a few miles, they spotted the Mutts' wagon returning home. Danny and Johanna darted from the road and hid in a grove of trees. As the wagon drew near, they could see Ruby and Opal laid out in the back, holding their bellies and moaning. Danny beamed. "Oleta and Angus don't look too good either," he announced.

He and Johanna could hear Oleta comforting her ailing daughters, "As soon as we get home, you're going straight to bed. And Mama's going to fix you each a soothing cup of tea with molasses."

4

When Danny and Johanna reached the deserted revival site, Arthur was burning the last of the trash and stowing banners in a wooden box. As soon as he spotted them, he waved and ran over. He stared at Johanna, and the recognition registered on his face. "I remember you! From the train!"

"This is Johanna Buehler," Danny introduced her. It was the first time she had heard someone say her full name, her true name, since Miss Darden told it to Angus Mutt nearly three years earlier. And to Johanna, he said, "This is Gabriel Blower—really Arthur Boston."

"Thank you for helping us, Arthur." Johanna gave him a shy smile.

"Glad to. I spent a year with a family who never saw me as nothin' except an outsider. Might as well have been a plow horse. I didn't exist, except to do chores, get slapped, and be yelled at."

Johanna gave a sympathetic nod. She stared at the side of the wagon. "Why is the writing so strange? Why does it have fresh paint in some places?"

Arthur pointed to the words "JE S U S SA VES." Spaces remained where some letters had been painted over with white paint. "It used to say 'Jessup's Salves.' That was the name of one of Mr. Folsom's patent medicines. And here, where it used to say 'Good Health,' he changed it into "GOd HeaLS." The "O" in "God" and "S" in "heals" were painted in big letters to take up the extra space created by the change in Mr. Folsom's vocation. Next to the slogan, the head and shoulders of a bearded man on a bottle of the salve had sprouted golden curls and wings. Where the outline of the bottle had been, rays of golden light had been painted in, framing the face with a celestial sunburst.

Johanna grimaced. Despite those alterations and new dabs of pink paint on the cheeks, the "angel" sported faint traces of dark eyebrows and a neatly trimmed goatee. She turned to Danny and Arthur. "Whatever that thing is, *it* needs healing."

Arthur walked them around to the other side of the wagon. It bore the countenance of a sleeping woman. The face was angled gently to the side, the back of one of the woman's hands draped serenely across her forehead. Johanna leaned closer to inspect the feathery wings, a recent embellishment. Arthur didn't even wait for them to ask. "Up there"—with his finger, he swept across the area above the face—"it used to say, 'Trust

Sleep Balm.' It was another snake oil Mr. Folsom peddled."

Johanna silently mouthing the words that now said, "Trust the SWeeT Balm," and the phrase "of Jesus" had been inserted beneath it. She turned to Arthur and drew in a breath as she rolled her eyes. He grinned and aimed his thumb below the sleeping face. "The Reverend didn't have to do nothin' to that part." Arthur repeated the slogan "Rest Assured" twice, once with the emphasis first word and then with the emphasis on "assured." "See what I mean?"

Danny stood there, shaking his head. "This beats all. He didn't even have to do much to change the wagon, did he?"

Arthur struck a pose, clasping his hands in an attitude of prayer, eyes heavenward. "The Lord works in mysterious ways."

Danny groaned. Then he suddenly glanced around. "Say, where *is* the reverend?"

Arthur tilted his head toward the wagon. "Inside. Sleeping like a newborn," he announced proudly. "I'm going to pour half a bottle of whiskey into the bottle he drank and tell him he drank two half-bottles. He won't remember, and he won't miss the bottle we borrowed." Arthur gave Danny a wry smile. "So how did it go with your bottle of whiskey?"

Soon they were laughing out loud. Danny told the story of Cletis's haircut several times. Johanna elaborated the details of Oleta's desecrated hat and the trail of molasses. Wave after wave of deep belly laughs left them barely able to talk. Johanna suddenly realized that until Danny had come to Sulphur Creek, she had not laughed since she arrived there. It felt wonderful.

With silly, complacent smirks and a silence punctuated by random, contagious guffaws, the trio sat and waited for the trash to finish burning. When Danny recovered from his last bout of laughter, he asked weakly, "What about the baptisms? The washing away of Ruby and Opal's sins?" His questions unleashed another torrent of hilarity.

Arthur doled out the delicious details. He took his time, as if he were ladling out a fine pudding, one rich spoonful at a time. "The girls were looking a might peaked Sunday morning—"

Danny interrupted him to explain about the Malto-Lax-fortified syrup. "I poured a whole bottle of it into the syrup," he hooted. Danny remembered Mr. Muehlenberg's comment about what a powerful "dose" it was for those in need of a good "spring tonic."

Arthur sprawled flat on his back on the ground and moaned. He laughed so much that he began to hiccup. When he was able, he continued his hiccup-riddled story. "Well, they come up to be baptized, acting real snooty, and I led them to the edge of the water. I said, 'Please say your *full* name,' and Reverend Folsom give me an irritated look. He just wants to know their first name—you know, 'So-and-so, servant of the Lord,'—'cause it's easier to remember. Anyhow, I whisper to the girls, 'Shout it loud and clear now so everyone can hear.' First Ruby yells, 'Ruby Gen-*E*-sis Mutt,' and then the other one hollers, 'Opal Ex-*O*-dus Mutt,' and I exclaim in a real loud voice, 'Bible names!' Folks begin to snicker in spite of it's being a solemn occasion and all. Reverend shoots me an if-looks-could-kill look, and the Mutt girls' eyes are big as pies. The missus looks as if someone opened the outhouse door on her without any warning, and the mister just stares at the ground. Then he reaches up and covers his bad ear."

Arthur paused a moment to allow Danny and Johanna to envision the scene he was painting. "Reverend Folsom motioned the girls to step into the water at the edge of the river. I leaned towards them and said, 'I'm sorry so many people has gone before you. You know how the sin floats in the water and all.' They began to simper, and they looked back at their ma. She just waved to them to go on. They looked at that water a-scared out of their wits. Finally, they waded in a little deeper, holding hands. They were terrified by the time Reverend Folsom pinched their stuck-up noses shut and dipped 'em backwards. Went board rigid with their arms crossed over their chests. After they were dunked, they looked happy just to have survived. Then they started waving their arms like crazy. They looked as if a hive of bees had stung 'em." He was chortling and shaking his head again. "They plain couldn't get out of that water fast enough! The second they climbed out of the river, I gasped and whispered to them, 'Oh, Lordy! There's sin stuck all over you!' They shook like wet hounds, and then they ran crying to their ma." Arthur grinned. "It was plumb wonderful!"

What he didn't tell Danny and Johanna was that he had been more than a little taken with Ruby despite, or perhaps because of, her haughtiness—and her bouncy ringlets.

5

While Gabriel stowed and battened the last few items, Danny hitched up the horse. One of the few things he had liked about being at the Mutts' farm was working with the team of horses. Danny had learned how to hitch and unhitch them and to care for them, and even though they were plow horses, he had sneaked more than a few rides on them.

"I'll drive the team, Arthur," offered Danny. "You tell us the story again."

Danny and Johanna listened to Arthur repeat parts of the baptism story three times. Each time, he added a detail or an embellishment that made it richer. Danny wasn't convinced all of it really happened, but after a point, it didn't really matter.

Obediah Folsom's horse, Zeke, had been rechristened Ezekial at the same time Mr. Folsom became Reverend Folsom and Arthur had become Gabriel. Throughout the afternoon and into the evening, the animal plodded along the road west.

Arthur forgot that he was not driving. "Giddyup, Ezekial," he droned out of habit.

The trio rode beneath the brilliant light of what Danny had heard Dilue call "a full Comanche moon." His thoughts turned to the newspaper story about Dilue's childhood. He shivered at the memory and pushed it from his thoughts.

When the town of Hokum came into sight, Arthur pointed to the sign on the depot and declared, "Well, this is about perfect!" Danny thought at first he was referring to the town's name and to Reverend Folsom's vocation. Then he realized that Arthur simply meant that it was the right spot for him and Johanna to get off.

Danny handed the reins to Arthur. "Thanks, Arthur—I mean Gabriel. Maybe we'll meet again."

"You never know where I might turn up." Arthur grinned, but he felt sad at seeing them leave. He raised his hand in farewell. "Good luck."

Danny and Johanna continued west on foot, skirting the depot, until they were a quarter mile past it. They had to wait only an hour before the train came through to drop off a mailbag in Hokum. As the train was struggling to break the bonds of inertia, Danny and Johanna loped along beside it. Danny tossed their packs on board, then leaped for the railing of the caboose steps and swung onto its platform.

"Jump! Jump!" he screamed to Johanna, extending his hand.

Terrified, Johanna lunged and grabbed his hand. Seconds later, she was still shaking, but she was on board. She was on her way to San Antonio.

<h2 style="text-align:center">6</h2>

"You can have Danny's bed in the attic, dear," Mrs. Bromley told Johanna as she patted her hand. "It will be nice to have a young person in the house again." She surveyed Danny, noticing how tall he had grown and going on about how he had "filled out." She smiled affectionately at him. "We grew rather accustomed to having someone young in the house."

Johanna felt as if she already knew Mrs. Bromley, and Artis Dunside's overly loud voice came as no surprise to her. "Mrs. Bromley and Mr. Dunside: prunes and proverbs" was how Danny had once described the pair, but the affection in his voice was obvious.

Danny had told Johanna about Dilue's appearance. Still, Johanna was not prepared for her first encounter with the disfigured woman. Johanna sucked in her breath and averted her eyes. "P-pleased to meet you," she stammered, knowing that her shock was obvious even to Dilue. Dilue said nothing, but she dipped her head slightly in acknowledgment.

Over the next three days, Danny told Mrs. Bromley, Mr. Dunside, and Dilue how he located Johanna, about his stint at the Mutts', and their "escape" to San Antonio. Mrs. Bromley made little "tsk" sounds and shook her head in disapproval when Danny told her about the whiskey he had used on Cletis, but he could tell that she was at least a little amused. He decided against telling Mrs. Bromley how Johanna "decorated" Oleta's hat and house with molasses and flour, and about the "dosing" he gave the Mutts. On the other hand, he knew Mr. Dunside would relish hearing about both events.

The old man's face glowed with pride when Danny recounted their hopping the train to San Antonio. "Wish I'd been there to see it!" he boomed.

Danny inhaled Mrs. Bromley's cooking. "How I've missed your corn cakes and pies, Mother Bromley! I'm going to hate to leave." Danny's lament was also his way of announcing that he would soon be departing again. Both Mr. Dunside and Mrs. Bromley had been expecting it.

"Will you be going to Galveston now?" Mr. Dunside inquired.

"Yes. This time *all* the way to Galveston."

"Do you still have the name I gave you? Of my friend, Seb? What about the map and the railroad information?"

Danny nodded. "I'm itchin' to get started. I want to set out midweek."

Three days later, Danny again bid farewell to his older friends. "Take good care of Johanna," he whispered loudly to Mr. Dunside and then to Mrs. Bromley as he embraced them and said good-bye.

Johanna was waiting for him on the porch. She stood staring at the rail, slowly running her fingers back and forth along it.

"Take good care of them, Johanna. I know they'll be good to you."

Johanna wanted to answer, but a flurry of feelings rendered her mute. She nodded her head.

Danny squeezed her shoulder, and yet again in their young lives, they parted.

As he walked away from the porch, Johanna called out, "I hope you find them, Danny."

He turned back to her and waved. His voice came like an echo. "And I hope you find *them*."

7

The foursome who now made up the Bromley household found it to be a happy arrangement. Like fresh spring rain, Johanna infused the others with her energy and enthusiasm. Mrs. Bromley welcomed her into her kitchen, her favorite room. The spry widow took pleasure in teaching Johanna how to bake. They spent hours talking as they kneaded bread, peeled fruit, rolled pie crusts, and lathered cakes with thick icing.

Johanna gradually took over many of the chores, happy to be able to help. She often found herself smiling. The same thought played over and over in her head like a refrain of a favorite song: *No more Mutts. No more Mutts.*

8

Mr. Dunside found as curious and appreciative an audience in Johanna as he had in Danny. One evening he handed Johanna an ornately carved wooden box. She ran her fingertip over the exotic-looking object. "This box will go to Danny someday," he told her. "Open it, and I'll tell you about what's inside."

One by one, Mr. Dunside extracted a few of the artifacts that summed up his life and explained their history. There were nautical pieces and railroad memorabilia. Most commanding, though, was a Colt .44. He lifted the gun gently and held it flat across his palms. "Danny's not ready for this yet. That's why I haven't showed it to him."

Johanna felt flattered that Mr. Dunside was sharing something with her that not even Danny knew about.

"There'll be a right time. When Danny's a man." He paused and looked straight at Johanna. "I want Danny to have this box if I… I mean when…" The word "die" intimidated him not at all, but he feared it might upset Johanna, or worse yet, cause her to cry.

Johanna knew what he meant and that he wanted to be sure there was someone else who could see that the box was given to Danny. Now she groped for the right words. "If *anything* keeps you from giving Danny this box yourself, I'll see to it that he gets it." Mrs. Bromley was further along in years than Mr. Dunside, and the old sailor was relieved to have the matter settled. Besides, he was certain that Mrs. Bromley did not approve of guns.

Johanna was soon so at ease with Dilue that she no longer thought about her appearance. Dilue tried to teach Johanna how to weave cane chair seats, but Johanna quickly realized that the work produced by her hands would never rival Dilue's. "I know what I'm good at—and what I'm *not* good at. You finish this chair, and I'll bake some gingerbread," Johanna often bargained.

Under Mrs. Bromley's tutelage, Johanna had become skilled at baking. When she returned home one day from doing errands, she mentioned, "I've been offered a job, Mother Bromley." Johanna was unsure what her reaction would be, so she tried to sound matter-of-fact. Still, her voice was tinged with excitement and pride.

The tiny, white-haired woman frowned. Dilue's swift hands ceased weaving.

Johanna hurried to explain. "Kirchner's Confectionery. They want to add pies and cakes. It's only for a few hours each morning. Frau Kirchner told me they need more help than their children can provide. When school starts, I'll work in the afternoons."

Mrs. Bromley was still frowning. It had been one thing for Danny to work at Muehlenberg's, but this was a different matter. Mrs. Bromley knew, however, that the Kirchner family was well thought of and that their candies had a reputation for quality. She studied Johanna's face and found it impossible to ignore the eyebrows that were raised so high in hopeful expectation.

"Well, I *suppose* if it's only for a few hours each day. And I suppose it would be good for you to be out of the house more and around others closer to your age." *Especially those of German descent*, thought Mrs. Bromley. She was confident of Johanna's baking and pastry abilities and had to admit to more than a modicum of pride in helping develop these skills. "I'll call on Mrs. Kirchner tomorrow, dear. I think it can be worked out."

9

Johanna began at Kirchner's the following week. It pleased her to be able to contribute money to the household. She could hardly wait to tell Danny.

Months passed, punctuated by occasional but eagerly awaited letters from Danny. It came as no surprise to them to receive letters from him from Galveston. It was where his subsequent letters were mailed from that came as a surprise.

THIRTEEN

1

Each day of Helga's life with the Dills was the same: hard work, poor food, wretched treatment. Her foster sisters, Lettie and Nita, went grimly and silently about their chores, seemingly oblivious to her. Although Althene rarely spoke when Stup was around, she spoke often and harshly to Helga when he wasn't within earshot. Whenever he felt like it, Mashburn pinched her, poked her, or pulled her hair. He would trip her and walk away, laughing and calling her clumsy. He watched for opportunities to leap out and startle her. Soon she wore the same frightened look as his sisters, "the Rabbits." Every tree, every corner, and every doorway represented a potential threat.

The lye soap Helga used to scrub the floor made her raw hands bleed. Her back and arms ached from carrying slops to the hogs. The summer sun reddened and peeled her fair skin. Her hair looked as clumped and dirty as the Rabbits'. She wore a tattered hand-me-down of Nita's. On her callused feet, she wore nothing.

Stup's temper compounded her misery. Whenever she, Althene, or the Rabbits failed to anticipate his needs or in any way displeased him, he slapped them with a force that often knocked them down. He raged at them, spewing threats and invective. Any nearby object might be hurled or kicked or smashed. Then he would storm off. At times, the recipient of his wrath could only guess at her transgression.

Helga understood why the Rabbits and Althene never spoke: They didn't want to draw Stup's attention. Invoking a child's magical thinking, Helga wanted to believe that if she closed her eyes tight enough and could not see Stup, she would be invisible to him. But even tightly clinched eyes could not save her.

In November, when the cool weather finally set in, it was hog butchering time. From the first day Helga was horrified at the sight near the barn. She covered her ears in a vain attempt to shut out the animals' terrible squeals of pain. Again and again, she clapped her hand over her nose and mouth. Her face ashen, she ran screaming from the pens and vomited. She sank to her knees, pressed her palms into her eyes to obliterate the bloody images, and rocked back and forth, moaning.

Althene came after her, jerked her to her feet and shook her with a fury. "You're lucky *I* came after you instead of *him*!" she said ferociously. Althene never called Stup by name. In fact, she never called him by any name to his face, and she never referred to him as anything other than "he" or "him." Stup remained in the pens where he and

Mash, wielding long, sharp knives, seemed to be enjoying their work. They were chatting and laughing, as if they were skewering inert bales of hay with pitchforks instead of slaughtering terrified pigs.

Althene led Helga back to the house and thrust a pail of food in her hands. "Take this to them." With unsteady legs, Helga retraced her steps to the pens. With each step, she fought the gag reflex that relentlessly pitted her empty stomach against her constricted throat.

Seemingly indifferent to the gore that surrounded her, Lettie went mutely about the tasks of sorting and removing various parts of the carcasses, placing them into separate bins, on racks, or on a refuse heap.

Each carcass was hoisted upside down by hooks through the tendons of the back ankles. Then it was lowered repeatedly into a vat of near-boiling water. Once the bristles were softened, Nita scraped them off.

Neither girl looked up when Helga came into view. When Stup and Mash saw her approach, they wiped their hands on the overalls beneath their leather aprons and sat down against the fence to eat. Grinning at Helga, Mash pulled off a gore-caked boot and emptied the blood out of it.

Helga was reeling, beginning to sway back and forth, when Althene materialized. She clamped her hand around the back of Helga's neck, and half held her upright as she hauled her back to the house. Mash snorted his disgust at the girl's squeamishness. He picked up some entrails that lay in the dirt nearby and flung them at Helga. "Sissy!"

Helga was actually relieved at the punishment of receiving no dinner that night. It was several more days before she could choke down food again, despite the fact that the hog butchering lasted only two days. Long afterward, she cried out in her sleep, seeing the awful spectacle over and over in her dreams. The nightmare ceased each night only because Althene would wake her with a kick and a warning to hush.

It was an even greater relief when Stup and Mash began taking the remaining pigs to the depot in Salt Box. Once there, the animals were goaded into a stock car headed for San Antonio. When they'd delivered the last wagonload to the depot, Stup sent Mash back to the farm and rode with the animals to the San Antonio stockyards.

Mash was surly at not being allowed to make the train trip, but even so, Helga found his single, unpleasant presence preferable to having both Mash and his father there.

2

It was coincidence that Stup saw Inga. Albert Jäeger had brought the eight-year-old with him to the stockyard. The sausage manufacturer stopped in front of Stup's hogs, pointed to them, and clucked to his daughter, "Not healthy, Inga. Look at their eyes." He shook his head and moved to the next group of animals.

Half hiding behind a post, Stup eyed Inga with incredulity. The resemblance was unmistakable, yet he could only remember the wheezing, feverish child he had shoved back at Miss Darden. Inga's pink-cheeked face was ringed with dark curls. They were held in check by a blue satin bow that matched her soft wool dress and coat. White stockings and black leather shoes completed her outfit. The overall impression was that an exquisite china doll had been brought to life.

Exclaiming with delight, Inga ran far ahead of her father. She giggled and chattered and pointed at the tightly packed pens.

"Say," Stup addressed Albert in a low, rough voice, keeping his head turned away from Inga. "That girl come off the train?"

Now it was Albert's turn to be incredulous. He stood transfixed, at a loss for words. Finally, he managed, "*Ja*! Why, yes! Yes!" He nodded vigorously to make sure that Stup understood. He searched Stup's eyes anxiously for some clue of what was coming next. Then he had a frightening thought: *Perhaps he intends to take my daughter away.*

"She had a sister looked just like her?"

Albert's face froze. In a more guarded voice, he replied, "*Ja. Ja.* We looked for her. Go on." Albert held his breath. Under no circumstances would he allow anyone to take Inga from him. *How does this man know about Inga's sister? What does he know about Inga?*

Stup considered asking him for money in exchange for Helga: The man was obviously well-to-do, and he seemed very interested. Stup hesitated. He had something else in mind for Helga.

"Her sister? You *know* her? Go on!" Albert insisted a second time.

"She got killed," Stup said bluntly.

Albert blinked. He felt pained, but also guilty relief that this fierce-looking man did not seem to want to take Inga away.

"Papa, come see!" Inga shouted to him as she leaned over the rail of a pen and touched a pig's curly tail.

Too preoccupied to hear her, he kept his gaze on Stup. "What? How it is you know this?" Albert demanded weakly. The anxiety fractured his English.

"Saw it happen. The child was the spittin' image of your girl. She was hit by a wagon and killed. Broke her neck."

Albert's face drained of all color. "Where? When?"

"*Papa!* Come *see!*" Inga implored, her voice brimming with exasperation.

"I'm coming," he said to her, speaking past Stup. He did not want Inga near this man. Then to Stup, "Stay. I come right back."

Shaken by what he had just heard, Albert hurried over to Inga and hugged her tight. "Show me!" he said gently. Inga pointed to different animals, prattling about their spots, their corkscrew tails, and their squeaky explosions of sound. "I see, I see," Albert cooed. Feelings of tenderness and protectiveness engulfed him. "Now, you be Papa's big girl and wait right here."

But when he turned to walk back to Stup, the man had vanished.

3

The minute Albert and Inga returned home, Anna looked at her husband and knew something was terribly wrong. She sent Inga to her room to play. "Albert, what is it?"

In a voice that cracked with emotion, Albert told her what he had learned in his strange encounter. Even though he had been given only fragments of information, he believed what the man had said: His knowledge of an identical twin and his correct speculation about Inga's arrival on the train couldn't be explained any other way.

"What do we say to Inga?" Anna's voice was as sad as Albert's face.

Albert tried to put out of his thoughts the image of his daughter's anguish upon learning what had happened to her twin. He slumped into a chair and rested his elbows on the kitchen table. "When she's old enough, we will have to tell her."

4

Stup returned to Salt Box in a good mood. He had made a little money from the sale of the hogs, and since he had not allowed the boy to go with him to San Antonio, he brought Mash a present: a knife.

Mash ran his finger along the side of the blade. He began flinging the knife at the wall, pulling it out, and flinging it again. Each time it struck, it registered a dull thud. Each time, Helga, Althene, and the Rabbits jumped.

"Hilda!" Stup bellowed. Helga walked over and stood in front of him. Her hands were shaking and she stared at the ground. "Your sister that looks like you—" Helga's eyes shot up to meet his, her fear momentarily dissolving at the mention of her sister. "She's dead." As Helga struggled to absorb his words, he continued in a flat tone, "Died of that sickness she had. Learnt it while I was in San Antonio. She was dead before the train even got there."

Stup turned and walked towards the door, signaling for Mash to follow and bring his new knife. "C'mon, boy. I'll tell you about San Antonio."

Helga stood biting her lip, tears streaming down her face. She could barely breathe because of the sharp pain in her chest. It felt as if Stup had lodged Mash's new knife in her heart.

Then Helga heard Althene murmur in a defeated, half-sympathetic voice, "If you'd been lucky, you'd have died, too."

5

The ensuing months bore out the truth of Althene's words.

"Hilda! Hey!" Mash yelled across the barnyard and hurled a rock at her.

She cringed and turned away, raising her arm to fend off the rock, but not in time. "Ow!" Her heart was racing, triggered by Mash's thunderous voice and the pain of the rock hitting the side of her head a split-second later.

She touched the tender knot that was now swelling beside her forehead. She immediately resumed feeding the chickens. She hoped her startled reaction and yelp of pain would satisfy Mash and that he would leave her alone.

"Hey! Look at this." Mash dangled a wiggling rabbit by its ears. Helga looked away. She didn't want to see any more. "I said LOOK!" he bellowed.

Mash pulled out his knife and began cutting on the terrified animal. Dizzy and nauseated, Helga closed her eyes. *I'm not here. I'm on the train. I'm not here. I'm on the train. On the train. On the train.* She repeated it over and over. It was a trick she had taught herself. Sometimes she could almost convince herself for a moment or two that she was back on the train, with the clatter of the wheels drowning out everything, and that the train had never stopped in Salt Box, and that she had never met the Dills.

Even though she tried to focus on the litany that ran through in her head, she couldn't shut out Mash's cruel voice. It forced its way into her consciousness again: "...rabbits don't make no sound. Can't. Except when they're dying." Helga clamped her hands over her ears to block out the rabbit's hideous keening. Mash held the rabbit's hind legs under his rough boots. He was stripping away the skin of the frantic, thrashing animal.

Then Mash tired of the game and slit the rabbit's throat. He kicked the carcass away from him. Its jerky reflexes caused it to flop around for another moment or two. Mash wiped his knife on his pants leg. "That shoulda been you," he snarled.

Helga sagged against a creaking fence post, clammy and cold at the horror she had seen and at Mash's words. She was afraid that someday it *would* be her.

6

"Aaaighh!" Helga yelped and jumped away from the barn door as Mash's knife bit into the wood beside her. It made a loud, ominous thunk.

He walked over, laughing, and pried it loose. Helga trembled, but said nothing. She never knew whether to look at him or to look away—whichever one she chose, it angered him. Afraid to move, she made the decision to look past him. *Please! Not again,* she pleaded silently. She stood rigid as Mash circled her, fingering the blade. Without warning, he grabbed her hair, twisted it violently and jerked her head back. Helga inhaled sharply, struggling not to make a sound. Still, an involuntary moan escaped her lips. *That's what you wanted, isn't it, you snake!* she thought. Then Helga was shocked to hear her own angry voice screaming, "You snake! You filthy snake!"

Mash's face flushed. His expression hardened, his jaw set with a look of sick pleasure. He ran the point of his knife blade across Helga's exposed neck, pressing just enough in one place to draw a trickle of blood. Mash held the red-tipped blade up before her eyes. She gasped, groaned, and crumpled to her knees suspended by the hank of hair Mash still held. With hacking motions, he slashed through it. Cut loose, Helga fell face forward to the ground, sobbing. With one hand, she clasped her throat; with the other, she covered her head. Mash flung the clump of hair at her and stomped off. "Stupid sow! I'll teach you what a snake is!"

7

Helga faced each day with deepening dread; she knew Mash would make good on his threat. It took less than a week.

"Get into the corncrib!" he ordered her one afternoon. He kicked at her to frighten her into moving closer to it. When she cowered and tried to back away, he thrust his knife at her. "I said get in! I ain't gonna tell you again."

As Helga edged towards the corncrib, she noticed the feed sack Mash held in his other hand. She thought she saw something in it move, and her terror began to mount. "Please, Mash. Please!" Helga was desperate, begging and sobbing. "I'm sorry I called you a name. I didn't mean it. *Please!*"

Mash liked the fear in her voice. "Get in." His tone was icy and threatening. He spit out the words as if he were hurling clubs at her. He gestured towards the corncrib with his knife. "Now."

She realized the futility of her pleas. She whimpered as she climbed the crude ladder and looked back in hopes that he might still change his mind. She placed one foot and then the other over the top edge of the crib and then slid to the bottom of the steep V-shaped bin that angled against the barn wall. She huddled there, wedged between its splintery, sloping side and the rough boards of the wall. Dust and particles of dried corn danced in the dim beams of light that fanned through the narrow spaces between the boards. Her nostrils stung. She felt as if she had straw in her throat.

Helga waited, barely breathing, for whatever terrible thing Mash was going to do. But nothing happened. In fact, there was no sound at all. She strained to hear, but there was only silence. *It's all right,* she told herself. She felt a giddy euphoria and chided herself, *He just wants to scare me.* She had to fight the impulse to laugh out loud at her own foolishness.

However, once it grew dark, Helga struggled to fight off panic. The sides of the crib were too steep and splintery to climb. She wasn't strong enough to pull herself over the edge even if she could have reached it. Her cramped legs were stiff and sore. She felt woozy from hunger. Her mouth and throat were parched.

Then she heard a sound. In a tremulous voice, she called out in the dark. "Mash? Please, let me out. I said I was sorry. Please."

No one answered even though she heard another sound outside the bin. A feeling of dread flooded through her. Then she realized in horror what was happening. "Oh, *please—NO*!!" she screamed. A long snake slithered over her shoulder and down her back. She couldn't see anything in the blackness, but she could feel the snake sliding over her. She froze, paralyzed with fear.

"Shut up," Mash ordered, "or I'll never let you out! No one would miss you anyway."

Helga eased her hand towards her shoulder, hoping not to touch the snake again. Then she pressed her forearm against her mouth to stifle her cries. She was shaking violently.

She felt another snake descend on her head, then another, and another and another. Large ones and small ones. She bit her arm to silence her screams, but she could no longer stand the agony. She flailed her arms uncontrollably, trying to knock the snakes off of her and away from her. Her hands and arms scraped against the sides of the wooden bin. In a matter of minutes, they were raw and peppered with splinters. There were too many snakes. Exhausted, she ceased her useless thrashing and simply covered her head with shaking arms. She kept her eyes closed and tried not to move. She could feel the snakes on her feet and ankles.

"That's what a *snake* is, Hilda. You remember that, or I'll have to teach you again."

"Mash, please…" The words came in a hoarse whisper. Helga could feel a snake coiling around her calf.

"I bet those snakes are hungry."

Helga tried to imagine what was coming next. She began sobbing and hitting on the sides of the bin. *"Mash!"*

"I said shut up!" he roared.

A shower of mice and rats descended on Helga as he emptied a second sack over the top of the bin. She again thrashed wildly, trying to knock the frenzied rodents away. They scurried crazily, crawling over her, biting her, trying to escape the snakes. The snakes writhed and twisted to get at the small animals. Helga could feel creatures crawling on her scalp, her shoulders, her feet. *I'm not here, not here, not here…* She pressed herself flat against one side of the bin. Her breathing became rapid and shallow. She heard Mash slam the rickety barn door behind him. Then she passed out.

It was still dark when she came to, but she realized someone had taken her out of the corncrib and left her on the barn floor. Even before she gently touched her face and her arms, she could tell they were covered with splinters, scrapes, and bites.

8

Althene was right. I would have been better off if I'd died like Inga. It couldn't be worse to be dead. Helga thought those same thoughts every night as she lay on her rough pallet. She never escaped the exhaustion spawned by overwork and malnutrition. Scrawny, overwrought Althene struggled with chronic stomach problems. "Lord, give me good digestion," she invoked some unseen entity under her breath each night before supper. With hunger gnawing at her own empty stomach, Helga always added silently, "Lord, give me something to *digest."*

Despite her meager, unvarying diet, Helga's pitifully thin frame began to fill out, a testament to the inexorable power of adolescence. Although she did not understand the changes occurring in her, she was not frightened by them. It seemed to be one more way her body, like her bleeding hands or a bleeding nose, reacted to the harshness of her circumstances. Althene offered no explanation, only, "It will happen again."

As Helga went through each day, she told herself, *At least it can't get any worse.* She found solace in that thought. Mash's cruelty never grew less terrifying, but she expected it. She expected Stup's harsh treatment and high temper. She expected Althene's remoteness and hostility. She expected the Rabbits' blank looks and mute mouths.

Helga learned that summer, however, that she was wrong: her life *could* become worse. Inexplicably, Stup announced one night, "The house is too crowded. You're moving to the barn, Hilda." Confused, but even more frightened of Stup, Helga quickly gathered up her pallet and her few articles of clothing and carried them to the ramshackle barn.

The first night, she lay awake the entire time. She placed her pallet as far as possible from the ominous corncrib. Each unfamiliar noise seemed threatening. Besides the sounds of the animals in the barn, there were sounds outside as well. In the blackness, she imagined there loomed hideous monsters, sinister snakes, dangerous intruders, and wild creatures with teeth that tore and ripped. At the slightest sound, she held her breath and strained to hear. Moreover, she hoped that if she made no sound—not even breathing—none of these fiends would detect her presence.

After several nights, she began to feel less uneasy. The waxing moon, as it eased towards fullness, cast a comforting glow.

The first time it happened, Helga was almost asleep. A filthy hand clamped over her mouth, shocking her into a state of wide-awake panic. In the moonlight that filtered through the slats of the barn, she could see Stup's bulging eyes and contorted face. His rank breath made her gag. Helga felt his weight sink down on her. Then she felt a stab of pain as if she were being split apart. She tried to scream, but his truncated fingers muffled her cries. When it finally ended, and he uncovered her mouth, Helga sobbed hysterically.

Stup slapped her so hard that the shape of his four equal-length fingers left a flaming red outline on her cheek. She lay whimpering and snuffling, her face turned to the wall. Her entire body burned and throbbed with pain. Stup stood, yanked his pants up, and growled at Helga, "I'll be back."

The next day, when Helga looked at Althene, Althene hunched her head farther down than usual between her thin shoulders and turned away. The realization exploded in Helga's head: *She knows! She knows, and she isn't going to do anything to help!* Then Helga looked at the Rabbits, and a further realization burst upon her: *I'm not the only one.* Then it occurred to her, *Maybe even Althene. Maybe he hurts her that way, too.* A profusion of angry, jumbled thoughts exploded in Helga's head. She flung the door open and stormed out. For once, Althene did not come after her.

Stup gave no indication that anything out of the ordinary had happened. At night, he appeared in the barn regularly. Helga lay there, her dread increasing with every approaching footstep.

She no longer cried. She turned her head towards the wall and stared out through the cracks between the boards, slowly twisting a lock of hair. Then she began her silent litany. *I'm not here. I'm on the train.* By concentrating on the traces of moonlight, she could put herself back on the train again with her sisters, before she ever met the Dills.

The rhythmic motion became the lurching of the passenger car. She could hear the clacking of the wheels in her head. The openings between the crumbling boards of the barn became the windows of the train. Helga stared out the windows in the dark, listening to the rumble of the train and watching the countryside click by.

9

For nearly two years, Helga's situation remained the same. She moved through the days and nights in numb detachment, beyond despair.

Then she began to feel ill all the time. Althene scolded her relentlessly for her laziness. Helga accepted Althene's shrill bleating, too exhausted to do otherwise or to do the tasks Althene was demanding. It seemed as if she fell asleep whenever she sat down.

When Althene learned that Helga had been vomiting in the mornings, she realized Helga's condition. "It was only a matter of time," she said in disgust to Helga, but Helga did not understand. Althene dared not mention it to Stup. *It'll become obvious soon enough,* she silently lamented. She dreaded that moment.

Stup was furious the night he finally noticed the change in Helga's gaunt profile. He jerked her to her feet, cursing her and slapping her. He picked up her dress and threw it at her. "Put it on!" She scrambled to pull it over her head as he shoved her out of the barn and towards the gate of the farm. Stup railed at her, shouting vile epithets and ordering her to get out.

In a daze, Helga stumbled down the rutted wagon path that led to the road. Stup followed behind, shoving and pushing her, sometimes causing her to fall. Stup's rage fed on itself. When they got to the road, he hit her repeatedly. He blackened her eyes and bloodied her mouth. He slammed her again and again in the belly, the focal point of his rage.

Stup left her lying in the road, doubled up and groaning. Helga crawled to the side of the road and staggered to her feet. *I feel like a sack of broken bones.* Fear that Stup might return to inflict more harm—this time with a knife or a gun—spurred her on despite her pain.

With only scant moonlight, Helga was unable to see clearly where she was stepping. Each time she stumbled, she bruised or cut herself. Fear of pursuit kept her moving until the exhaustion and pain took their toll. Finally, Helga could go no farther. She sank to her knees; the dirt and gravel stung the raw, scraped areas. *Althene was right: If I'd been lucky, I'd have already died.*

No longer caring whether she lived or died, Helga lay down beside the road. She clutched the hem of her dress. Through the ragged cloth she could feel the button she had stitched there. Then she lapsed into merciful unconsciousness.

FOURTEEN

1

Danny stared out the train window. *It was harder to leave San Antonio this time,* he thought, *but I'm glad Johanna is there.* He set his jaw. *This time I'm going to find Uncle Shamus and Uncle Aidan.*

Before Danny had set out the first time, Mr. Dunside had told him, "If you need help or a place to stay, look for a four-room house out in the middle of nowhere." The old stationmaster explained, "It'll be a section house, a house where a railroad foreman and his family live. There might be a two-room bunkhouse for the section crew. A tool house. A well or cistern. Nothin' more."

Danny tried to recall the other things Mr. Dunside had told him about the forlorn-looking dwellings that dotted lonely stretches of track. He could hear the old man's voice: "Each crew is responsible for ten to thirty miles of track. If you get stranded, walk along the tracks until you come to one of these. You'll be able to get water there, and chances are they'll be so glad for company that they'll give you something to eat just to coax you to stay for a visit."

As the train rolled past an occasional section house, Danny wondered what kinds of people were drawn to so solitary a life. Although he saw several of these isolated posts, he had no need to sample their hospitality. He was able to hop a series of trains that kept him moving steadily towards his destination. He had waved at a few of the section house occupants, and he felt a pang of regret at not discovering for himself the nature of these self-sufficient souls. *What do their children do all day long? Do they grow up to be loners? Do they end up overly attached to their families, or eager to get away?* He thought about his own family and how he desperately longed to see any of them again.

2

It took Danny only two days to get to Galveston. As soon as he got off the train, he asked for directions to the docks. He stood for a long time looking out at the sea and inhaling the sharp, salty air. When he closed his eyes, memories of the crossing from Ireland swept through his head. Opening his eyes, he stared at the ships. *Where did Shamus and Aidan's voyage take them? Did they ever set foot on Galveston beach? On Texas soil? On land?*

It took Danny the rest of the day to locate Seb Pendleton, Mr. Dunside's former shipmate. "All of us old scalawags is landlubbers now! So Artis is working for the railroad, is he?" Seb was practically shouting. Danny wondered if all sailors developed booming voices.

Seb sported a grizzled gray beard that glinted with traces of the rust-colored hair of his youth. Danny found himself thinking that despite Seb's hunched shoulders and weathered countenance, he must have once been handsome.

Danny ate supper that night with Seb in his small quarters. Seb gestured to a space on the floor and tossed Danny a blanket. "Make yourself at home—such as it is." He gave Danny an ironic smile. "Sailors get used to living in a small space."

Danny told Seb about Mr. Dunside and their life in San Antonio.

The old sailor regaled Danny with only a few colorful stories of adventures he and Artis had shared at sea before he drifted off to sleep mid-sentence and began snoring loudly. Danny was wishing Seb had told him more tales of his life at sea when he realized that his own eyelids were growing heavy.

Before sunrise, Danny was awakened by Seb's stirrings. Danny felt groggy and stiff from sleeping on the floor. He stood up and rubbed his backside while he sipped a mug of black coffee to clear his head. He asked Seb how to find out the information he most wanted to know: what had happened to the ship his uncles had sailed on.

Seb scratched his head and then his beard. "Gimme a couple of days, boy. Let me see if I can find anything." Danny supplied him with the few details he knew.

Danny spent the day at the docks doing odd jobs in exchange for food. That night, Seb asked Danny questions while he showed the boy a fancy sailor knot he'd never seen before.

After a silence of several minutes, Seb began to talk again. He started slowly and untied the complicated knot as he spoke. "I found a little information about the ship your kinfolk was on."

Danny felt his heart stop, and his eyes locked on the old sailor. He hadn't expected Seb to learn anything so soon, if at all.

"According to the company's logs, the *Northern Cross* never arrived in Galveston." Danny sat motionless, not even blinking as Seb went on. "They speculate a storm blowed the ship off course. From reports that trickled back, it 'pears she overshot Galveston and broke up off the coast."

"The coast? Where?"

"Down near the south-most tip of the state. Near Mexico."

"Mexico?" Danny stood there shaking his head no. The small, but perceptible movement did not escape Seb's eye. "But what about survivors? Were there any survivors?"

"No one knows. There was rumors that some of 'em held onto debris from the ship and was washed ashore." Seb twisted one corner of his beard between his thumb and his forefinger.

"What happened to them? The ones that might have washed ashore?" The pitch of Danny's voice was rising.

Seb shrugged helplessly. "Coulda stayed there in south Texas. Coulda tried to make it back to Galveston. Coulda gone anywhere." His voice trailed off, and he shrugged again.

Danny struggled to visualize Mr. Dunside's maps in his mind's eye. He wondered if his uncles could have even figured out which direction to go if they had reached shore. "So if they made it to shore, they would have headed north?"

"More 'n likely—if they made it that far." Seb could see Danny's optimism beginning to rise, so he instantly added, "Now don't get it in your head that you can just take out for the border and find the pair of 'em strolling along waiting for you. Besides, it's hotter 'n Hades now in those parts."

But Danny wasn't listening to him. He was on his feet. "If they're there, I know I can find them, Seb."

Seb stroked his beard with the back of his gnarled hand. He glanced at Danny and could see that an idea was forming in the boy's mind. Seb considered Danny briefly, then shook his head as if to dismiss Danny's extravagant claim. This time the old sailor was blunt. "More 'n likely, boy, they're not alive. Even if they are, that ship broke up years ago. They could be anywhere. And you're going to take off half-cocked, are you? How you going to eat? What if the trains don't run to where you're wantin' to go? You got any money? What if you don't find anything once you get there?" Seb's eyes fixed on the worn cap that hung limply from Danny's pocket. "Why, you don't even own a proper hat. The sun can be a scorcher out there." Like any sailor, Seb knew firsthand about weather and respected it.

Danny reacted with frustration and then anger at the flood of unwanted questions. He snapped at Seb, "Look, I just want to find my uncles!" He collapsed into a chair, miserable. His plan had been simple, and he didn't want to hear about complications, much less think about them.

Seb allowed Danny a minute to collect himself. He understood. Then he began again, but in a quieter voice. "I was a brash, impatient young man myself, just like you." He explained that he'd impetuously left the farm and the fields to go to sea. "Got sick of planting and harvesting, planting and harvesting. And all that ever come of it was disappointing crops. Barely enough to feed the family." He scratched his whiskers. "One day I had a bad argument with my father. He cuffed me hard on the side of the head and told me I could leave for once and for all if I was so sure there was something better out there."

"What did you do?"

Seb combed his beard with his fingers. "I was sixteen and hotheaded. I ran away that very night." There was a long pause. "I never saw my family again."

Danny studied the old man's face. "Are you sorry you left?"

Seb sidestepped the question. "I've thought about that many a time over the years. I enjoyed my life as a sailor, but that spur-of-the-moment decision changed my life in every way." Seb looked Danny square in the eye. "What I'm saying, boy, is that there's a right time for everything. And at this point in your life, there's still plenty of time for everything." Seb settled back in his chair and said in a low voice, "Nothing's as easy as it seems, boy. You can save yourself an ocean of frustration by not jumping into something with your eyes closed. Besides, *wanting* something don't always make it happen."

Danny still felt angry and overwhelmed, but Seb's words caused a shift in his thinking. *Of course he's right. Didn't Mr. Dunside try to tell me the same thing? I'm not going to just stumble across my uncles. In fact, I might not ever find them. There ain't no reason to think otherwise. I might as well just be a man and face it.* Reluctantly, he acknowledged to himself the reality of the situation. Then he made a vow to himself: *I'll do what I can to find them, but from now on, I'll go about it with more thought—and more patience.*

3

In a letter to Mr. Dunside, Danny wrote: "I figure to stay in Galveston for several months. I plan to work and learn what I can and try to put a little money back. After next winter, I plan to go to West Texas."

Mr. Dunside was puzzled, but he was even more puzzled by Danny's final sentence: "Once I get there, I will be heading for the Mexican border."

4

The summer passed quickly. Danny worked on the docks loading and unloading freight. The physical labor, along with the salt air, piqued his appetite. He grew tan and sturdy, and by year's end, he resembled a man instead of a boy. Seb could see that Danny had developed not only his muscles, but his confidence.

Mr. Dunside sensed in Danny's letters his growing maturity. *Perhaps it's time,* he thought. After prolonged deliberation, he carefully packed his Colt .44 in a wooden box and shipped it to Danny.

"Danny, you might need this," his note read. "Learn how to use it properly. Treat it with respect. Only a fool shoots off his mouth or his gun without a reason." Danny smiled when he read the last line; he could hear Mr. Dunside saying it. He ran his fingertips over the smooth barrel, thinking that he would have been disappointed if Mr. Dunside had missed an opportunity to offer a bit of advice.

When Danny prepared to leave Galveston in February, he tucked the treasured knife and the Colt in the center of his pack. He slung it over his shoulder and shook hands with Seb. As he walked away, Danny reached up and patted the roll.

He felt ready for whatever the future held.

5

Danny hopped off the train and waved thanks to the conductor. Mr. Dunside's letter had come in handy more than once as he'd hopped train after train. The tracks led west, but the focus of Danny's interest lay farther south, towards the Mexican border. The conductor waved back. "Flint's about six miles due south," he shouted.

Danny began walking in the direction the man pointed toward.

The weather was unseasonably cold. Nevertheless, Danny was coated with a film of nervous sweat, and his mouth felt as dry as if he had eaten sand. A swirl of thoughts filled his head. *Would Shamus and Aidan have survived in this part of the country, even if they had made it up from the border? Would people remember them because of their Irish brogue? Or were there so many Irish now that no one would remember the two men?*

The wind swept over the barren ground as Danny tramped towards town. He was again aware of how parched his mouth and throat had become. *What's this place like in summer?* he wondered.

The town of Flint was as hard and dry as its name. A livery stable, a one-teller-window bank, a sheriff's office, a saloon, and a small dry goods store flanked its one street, and that was the town.

Danny heard tinny piano music wafting from the saloon. In a virtually deserted town in the middle of the day, it sounded as ludicrous as a vaudeville performer at a funeral. Danny walked towards the saloon. The hand-lettered sign outside the door invited all passersby:

> Whiskey sold here.
> If it won't cure what you got,
> there ain't no cure.

A small, baldheaded man looked up from the piano and stopped playing. "Where'd you come from?" he asked, pushing up the red elastic bands that held his rolled shirtsleeves around his biceps.

Danny stood close to the grate of the potbelly stove and gulped a welcome glass of water. When he finished, he explained who he was looking for.

The piano player minced no words: "Nope. Haven't heard of anyone like that in these here parts." He turned back to the piano and half-heartedly plunked out a few more bars. Over his shoulder, he added, "Not a lot of folks come through here, though. Most of our regulars are ranch hands from nearby. Talk with some of them cowboys. Bunches of 'em were in after the fall roundup. They swap yarns and news with each other."

He swiveled on his piano stool to face Danny. "It's going to take you some time to find your kin—*if* you find them. It's a big place out here." He turned back to the piano. "Can you ride?"

"Ride?" All Danny could think of was the countless trains he'd ridden the last few days.

"*Horses.* Can you ride horses?"

"I done some riding when I worked on a farm. I know how to saddle and hitch horses."

He sniffed at Danny's answer, making it clear that such meager experience counted for nothing. "I don't suppose you ever worked with cattle?"

The Mutts' single cow constituted Danny's total experience with beef on the hoof. "A bit," Danny replied cautiously, not sure where the conversation was heading.

"I see," said the musician, unimpressed. "Well, you might *try* to hire on at the YT Ranch. Seems I heard they need a cook's helper. Their cook ain't been exactly right"—he tapped the side of his head with an index finger—"since his wife died." The way he said "cook's helper" indicated it was a job that required no skill at all and, therefore, might be one for which Danny was qualified. He resumed his playing and talked over the out-of-tune song. "It would give you a way to feed yourself while you try to find out something. I think their cook is Irish. Scotch or Irish. I can never tell. They seem the same to me."

Danny lowered his water glass as he felt his lips compress in disgust at such ignorance.

Oblivious, the piano player went on, "Some of the YT hands will be in town tomorrow night. Friday's payday, and things are slow on a ranch during the colder months." He smiled, anticipating the revenue and the respite the rowdy evening would bring from the humdrum weekdays.

"By the way," the piano player stopped mid-chord, "you might want to do something about them clothes."

Danny looked down at his outfit and then looked up at the piano player again as if to ask, "What?"

"The hat!" the little man sputtered. "Them shoes! If you're planning to pass for a cowboy, you better buy you some boots and a hat. Try Wilkins' Dry Goods. Down the street." He spun back to the piano and began thumping out the same tune.

6

By the next evening, Danny had found out where the YT was and verified that they indeed needed a cook's helper. *I know I can convince them to take me on. All I need is a horse to get there. I sure ain't going to walk that far!* He refused to admit to himself that it was the humiliation of arriving on foot that troubled him most.

"Yessir. I got me a job waiting. Just need a way to get there," Danny lied to the owner of the livery. "I'll return the horse to you next week, along with the rest of the money I owe you."

In a humorless tone, the man warned him, "We take horses serious out here. You don't bring my horse back, I'll track you down and kill you."

As Danny plodded out of town on his newly rented mount, he muttered to himself, "Then the YT better still need a cook's helper."

FIFTEEN

1

Danny slowed his horse and stopped in front of the wide wooden gate. The massive carved sign that arched over it announced to visitors they were entering the YT, a cattle ranch that sprawled over three-quarters of a million acres of south Texas. To Danny, it represented the Promised Land.

He had ridden for two hours; he was tired and dirty. He hoped that his boots and hat, which looked both new and cheap, might nevertheless give him the semblance of a cowboy. He reached back and touched his saddlebag for luck. Packed inside was the long-barreled Colt .44 Mr. Dunside had sent him.

Danny passed through the gate and scanned the vista. In the distance, he could make out the figure of someone working on a stretch of fence. As he drew closer, he saw a leather-faced, sun-baked scarecrow of a man hammering wire to a fence post. Twigs Callahan stopped his work, shoved the brim of his hat back, and surveyed Danny from the tips of his unscuffed boots to the top of his store-fresh hat. Twigs was working as a pliers man that day, inspecting the barbwire fence. On the ground beside him lay a pouch full of staples and a spare roll of wire. He considered working with cattle his rightful role; it only added to his irritation to be caught at this demeaning off-season duty.

Equally irritated by Twigs's blatant, disapproving assessment of him, Danny struggled to return a level gaze, but then folded. His words tumbled out in a rush. "Can you tell me where I can find the foreman?"

"Reckon I could." Twigs's tone was noncommittal. He smoothed one end of his droopy white mustache and ran his finger around the bandanna that encircled his scrawny neck. "I s'pose you're wantin' to hire on." He sounded as if he'd had to deal with an endless stream of applicants all day long.

Annoyed further, Danny tried to sound indifferent. "I heard the YT might need a cook's helper." He suddenly felt foolish, so he added, "'Course I'd rather work as a hand."

Twigs sized up Danny. It was clear to Danny that the man had concluded that cook's helper was the more likely job. Twigs volunteered in a nasal monotone, "Cook can use some help. His biscuits would make a buzzard gag. Dry as dust and hard as rocks." He sighed and waved his hammer in the direction Danny was facing. "North range. Tom Bartlett." Twigs turned his back on Danny and resumed nailing barbwire to the post.

2

The sheer size of the ranch awed Danny. He shook his head and exhaled. *One man. One man owns this.* After another two miles, he came over a rise and found himself staring at a sea of cattle. They lowed as they meandered over the range grazing on the sparse grass and vegetation. The wind changed, and the odor of dust and dung stung Danny's nostrils and throat. His stomach rolled and he fought the urge to gag. His hand was halfway to his mouth when he realized that he couldn't afford to look as if he were affected by the stench.

He was surprised that only a handful of cowboys managed the flowing herd. He trotted towards an oak brown cowhand and his similarly-colored horse. They looked as if they'd been carved out of the same block of wood. When Danny drew closer, he was surprised again. *He ain't much more than a kid.* The boy stared impassively at Danny as if he had been expecting him.

"Tom Bartlett? The foreman?" Danny asked.

The cowboy shifted his weight, spat, and pointed at two men fifty yards away who talked from astride their horses. "The palomino."

"Palomino?"

The cowhand turned back to Danny. He studied him a minute, shook his head, and spat again. He spoke slowly, as if he were talking to a half-wit: "Mr. Bartlett's the one on the palomino. Pal-o-mi-no. The—big—gold—horse. White mane, tail, and stockings." He paused. "You do know what a mane is, don't you?"

Danny lowered his eyes, ducked his head, and reined his horse in Bartlett's direction. He was relieved to see the other man ride off, leaving no one to hear his conversation with the foreman.

Tom Bartlett was an imposing man. He sat tall in the saddle, his gloved hands draped over the pommel as if they were molded to it. Danny had been unsettled when Bartlett turned and looked at him long before Danny thought he was close enough to be heard. Bartlett's face was tanned an adobe color despite the broad brim of a stained, gray hat that shaded his face from the late winter sun. Like gulches cut through a canyon, deep creases traversed his cheeks. Neatly and deliberately, he rolled a cigarette. He struck a match and lit the cigarette in one continuous motion.

Danny drew his horse up beside the foreman's and nodded in greeting.

Bartlett took a drag on his cigarette and gazed out at the herd. A minute passed and Bartlett still had not said anything, so Danny directed his own eyes at the enormous horse, admiring its tawny body and its creamy mane, tail, and stockings. Embarrassed finally by the prolonged silence and his gawking, he blurted, "I heard the YT might need a cook's helper, that you might be needing a man."

Bartlett studied Danny and then returned his gaze to the shifting herd. He exhaled a stream of white smoke and considered the matter. After a minute, he replied, "If you can haul wood, carry water, wash dishes, and make enough sense out of what Brody McCorkle's saying to follow his instructions, you got the job. Pays fifteen dollars a month plus chuck."

Danny nodded, even though he wasn't sure what "chuck" was.

"Stow your belongings in the bunkhouse"—he flipped the ends of the reins in the direction Danny had come from—"then go find Brody in the cook shack."

3

Danny was too green to appreciate his luck: the YT was large enough to *have* a bunkhouse. Before his eyes could adjust to the darkness inside, the bunkhouse's pungent smell assailed his nostrils. It was a peculiar and unforgettable blend: sweat, dried cow manure, work boots, coal oil, and an odor he remembered from Muehlenberg's, the licorice that permeated plugs of chewing tobacco.

The bunkhouse was little more than a shack made of cottonwood logs, better than some because it had a wood floor and a faded coat of whitewash. The walls were pasted with tattered pages from catalogs, newspapers, and picture magazines. A toppled stack of worn magazines was strewn in one corner, along with dominoes and decks of grimy cards. Danny would soon discover that bedbugs and lice also inhabited the bunkhouse, as well as occasional mice, rats, and rattlesnakes. He stashed his gear against a wall and set out for the cook shack.

Brody was dumping water into a simmering pot of beans. He was either unaware of Danny's presence, or else he was ignoring him. Danny wasn't sure which. A short, intense, barrel-chested man, Brody seemed not only to be in perpetual motion, but also engaged in a nonstop conversation with himself. He continued moving among steaming cast-iron kettles and smoking skillets. Muttering constantly, he stirred a kettle with a large spoon. He poked something in the skillet with a fork and sampled it twice, fussing aloud the entire time.

Danny walked over and cleared his throat. "I'm your new helper. Danny O'Brien." He held out his hand.

Brody stopped talking to himself and straightened up. He plopped the spoon in Danny's outstretched hand. "Stir this." He went to a shelf to get some pepper. "Menu don't change much. Beef. Beans. Sourdough or cornpone. Sometimes canned vegetables. Every now and then, dried fruit."

Danny nodded and began stirring the salt pork into the beans.

4

At supper Twigs held a biscuit aloft and chided Danny, "Thought you was going to do something about Brody's sourdough bullets." He scowled. "Cow chips would be more tempting than these." Now that Brody had a helper, Twigs felt even freer to complain. On ranches, the rule was that any man who complained about the food ended up spending a day as the cook's helper—or even as the cook.

After sampling a biscuit, Danny wished that sometime at Mrs. Bromley's, he'd asked her how she made biscuits. Brody glowered in Twigs's direction and hurled an unintelligible curse at him.

"Brody, I can't tell when you're cussin' me and when you're complimentin' me,"

Twigs went on. "That's what comes of havin' a Scotch mother and an Irish pa. Hell, you can't even laugh in English."

Brody frowned again. He dismissed Twigs's jibe with a sweep of a ladle and resumed a stream of barely audible chatter beneath his breath.

"That man's mouth flaps like a runaway winder shade," Twigs proclaimed. He held up a slab of beef he'd speared with his fork. It was so undercooked that it dripped red juices. He shook his head in disgust. "Brody," he hollered, "I seen a cow *cut* worse than this get well. You should serve it with liniment." The others laughed, and a few nodded their agreement.

Brody ignored them, but his muttering grew louder.

Twigs called out to Danny, who was putting a lid on a large pot of beans, "Stewpot, leave them whistle-berries be and come meet the boys." Not wanting Twigs's barbs directed at him, Danny did as he was told. He approached the cowhands who sat or squatted silently on their haunches, finishing their evening meal. Danny was surprised at how young they were. Most were only a few years older than he was.

Twigs proceeded with the introductions. He pointed first to a ranch hand who seemed little more than a boy. "This here's California. He's our jingler—our wrangler. He can educate you about them broomtails. We call him California 'cause he's always chinnin' 'bout how he's going there one day." Twigs scoffed. "Yup. Cal's all talk. He ain't never even made it as far west as El Paso." The others hooted. The shy, blond adolescent raised a couple of fingers in embarrassed greeting to Danny.

Another voice chimed in, "Hell, Cal ain't made it as far as the west range of the YT." Danny would soon learn that the job of wrangler was considered the most menial one and that wranglers were the butt of most jokes. The wrangler also rode the sorriest horse. The trade-off was the experience: it usually led to becoming a cowhand.

Twigs turned his attention to the speaker. "That there's Ples. Rumor has it that it's short for Pleasant, but don't put no stock in it." Ples glanced up from his tin plate, grunted, and continued shoveling beans into his mouth. "We speculate that as a baby, Ples musta been baptized in vinegar."

Turning in the other direction, Twigs pointed to a sturdy, weather-beaten old cowpuncher whose lips smacked as he ate. "That there's Bum." Twigs called out, "Hey, Bum, you met Stewpot yet?"

Bum, who had passed Danny earlier when Danny was on his way to the bunkhouse, set down his spoon and stroked his snowy whiskers. "We howdied, but we ain't shook yet." He gave Danny a half-toothless grin and extended his hand.

Twigs continued, "Bum's done lost so many teeth that he echoes when he talks. The old buzzard's been a cowpunch a long time. Since after the War." More than two decades ago, Bum and Twigs had discovered, as had other Texans returning home from the War Between the States, that cowboying was about the only work available.

Twigs introduced the rest of the waddies—Jot, Wash, Harper, and Cy—and concluded his introductions with Squint, a peculiar looking man with an abnormally small head and unusually close-set eyes. "'Squint' needs no explainin'. He can look through a keyhole with both eyes at the same time."

Danny thought he detected a note of pride in Twigs's voice, the same sort a child might have at showing off a two-headed toad. To deny Twigs any satisfaction and to deprive Danny of having his curiosity satisfied, the flounder-eyed Squint kept eating without looking up.

To everyone, Twigs announced, "And this here greener is Danny O'Brien. I reckon we'll call him 'Stewpot,' seein' as how he seems to have found his calling as a belly-cheater." Referring to Danny's brogue, Twigs needled, "This feller wears his brand on his tongue, just like Brody." Twigs moved towards Danny. "Here. Take a plate of chuck and join us."

Just as Danny started to smile at the invitation, he realized Twigs had handed him not a plate, but a dried cow chip with beans ladled on it. Danny quickly dropped it, turning his head in disgust. The boys hooted.

Danny wiped his hands on his pants legs. A huge grin spread across his face. "Twigs, you been complainin' about the chuck, but the problem ain't the food—it's the plates."

The others laughed, surprised by his good-natured response. They respected any greener who could take a ribbing, especially one from Twigs. Even Twigs found himself smiling.

After supper Twigs told Danny, "There ain't enough room in the bunkhouse for a shadow. You'll have to sleep on the floor." Danny shrugged nonchalantly, hoping to show that he was willing to work his way up.

Cal volunteered, "It'll turn warm before long. Most of us sleep outside then. In fact—"

Twigs interrupted, "You best get busy with that pile of dishes, Stewpot. You can't plow a field by turning it over in your mind." Then he winked and added, "You can join us for a chew when you're through helping Brody." Twigs made a clicking sound with his tongue and his teeth, and strolled off into the darkness.

5

It was then, as the others were dispersing, that Danny noticed Janie. Since he hadn't seen her walk up, he thought at first he imagined her. What was a slip of a young woman with a mass of flaming red hair doing here on the YT? And yet there she stood, her back to him, washing and rinsing stacks of tin plates and enamel cups in kettles of soapy and clean water. When she turned to get more hot water, she glanced up and saw Danny watching her. She ignored him as completely as if he were a fence post. The cowhands seemed to take her for granted, and Brody acted as if her presence was routine.

As Danny scraped burned beans off the bottom of a pot, he continued to sneak glances at her. *She's pretty*, he thought. *And a whole lot prettier than anybody else around here.* He looked down at the pan he was cleaning and grinned. The plain, oatmeal-colored dress she wore did not obscure the faint curves beneath it. By the time he made up his mind to ask her who she was, she had doffed her apron and disappeared.

Rejoining Twigs and the others, Danny had a wagonload of questions. But first he wanted to know who the redheaded girl was.

"Janie McCorkle. Brody's daughter," Twigs's tone made it sound like an ominous warning. "Brody's missus died a year ago. Janie mostly works in the Big House now. We've been short a cook's helper, so she's been pitchin' in to help Brody when she ain't needed in the house. And when she ain't doing either of those, she's like as not got her nose stuck in a book."

One of the others added, "She wants to leave the ranch and move to town, but Brody won't hear it. Says it ain't proper for a young lady of sixteen to be livin' on her own."

Twigs went on, "By the way, Brody done made it clear: he don't want no sorry cowpokes triflin' with his daughter." Chewing his tobacco thoughtfully, Twigs pulled his coat tighter around him and leaned against the side of the bunkhouse. "Young Cal once was smitten with a case of calico fever and had a notion of courtin' her. He found hisself in a two-hit fight: Brody hit him and Cal hit the ground." Everyone except the lanky wrangler laughed. Cal's hat rested in his lap. He stared at it as if he were trying to memorize a treasure map. Over and over again, he ran his fingers along the soft crease.

To change the subject, Danny asked about Tom Bartlett. Twigs, who by now seemed to Danny to be the official spokesman, answered. "Pretty much stays to hisself. He's steady, though. Real steady. Sober as a corpse, but the kinda man you'd want around in a pinch. Can ride anything with hair on it and shoot dead-on. Fearless, too. He'd take on hell with a bucket of water." Twigs reflected a moment, still mentally inventorying Bartlett's qualities. "That man can hear the sun rise and the moon set. Not much catches him unawares." He added admiringly, "And what Tom Bartlett don't know about cattle"—Twigs spat tobacco juice on the ground for emphasis— "ain't worth knowin'."

6

Danny's favorite part of the day soon became after the work was done, after the evening meal was finished, when the cowboys sat around the campfire, smoked, and talked. He discovered this was when he learned the most from the other men.

One night, a few weeks after he arrived at the YT, he lay on the ground on his bedroll, his hands crossed behind his head. He gazed at the dusky sky and inhaled the clean perfume of earth coming into bloom. His muscles ached from lugging buckets of water and firewood earlier that afternoon. Cal walked over and dropped his saddle and bedroll near Danny. Danny wished that he rode herd and that he had a saddle to use as a pillow. Cal pulled off his boots, rolled a cigarette, and stretched out full length on his blanket. He rested his head on his saddle and smoked.

"Horses all squared away?" Danny asked.

"Um-hmm."

"Who owns the best horse, Cal?"

"It's flat out amazing how much you don't know," Cal marveled, but his tone was good-natured. "Horses belong to the ranches. Cowboys just use 'em. So if you ever get to ride, don't go and get yourself too attached to any broomtail in particular."

So that he could hear better, Danny rolled over on his side. He raised up on one elbow and propped his head on his hand. Pleased by Danny's interest, Cal went on. "I had this friend by the name of Hamp. Had him the finest little cuttin' horse that he'd been training for four years. Somebody made a good offer for it to the top screw—the ranch owner. He sold that critter right out from under Hamp." Cal flicked the glowing stub of his cigarette into the dirt. "After that, Hamp never again let hisself get too interested in someone else's horse."

"It takes four years to train a horse?"

"Hell, it takes four years just to get 'em *broke* good. The critters *start* bein' good cow horses at six years. It's ten years before a cow horse hits his prime."

Cal spit out a bit of tobacco. "Twigs says cigarettes got fire at one end and a fool at the other. Prob'ly right." He fished in his vest pocket for his tobacco pouch and another paper. "Takes longer to roll 'em than to smoke 'em. They don't last no time at all."

Danny nodded. He'd noticed how quickly the fire moved up the crude cigarettes. He now sat cross-legged and wide-awake. "What do cowboys do with their horses out on the range? I mean, what do you tie 'em to? Twigs says there's so few trees that birds build their nests out of barbed wire."

"Hobble 'em when we're on the open range, but a good horse'll stand without hitchin'. A horse that'll wander off ain't no use to a cowboy."

Cal licked the cigarette paper to seal it around a thin line of loose tobacco and shoved the makings back into his pocket. He enjoyed being an authority, and Danny was an ardent pupil. Danny was glad to have someone he could ask questions without feeling foolish.

Cal fingered the flimsy cigarette and started talking again. "Horse goes into the remuda when it's about four years old." He noticed Danny's puzzled look and explained, "Remuda is all the horses the cowboys use. When we're riding herd, each cowboy needs a string of five to ten each day. Only geldings go into the remuda—" Cal flicked another piece of tobacco off the tip of his tongue, then grinned. In a patient voice, he began, "Now a gelding—"

Danny held up his hands and laughed. "I know, I know."

"The reason for having only geldings is that a stallion'll fight with other horses, and lady horses sometimes just get it in their head to up and go home. And there's usually some gentleman horse interested in escorting one of them bunch-quitters home."

"If it takes that long to train them, how long can a cow horse work before it's used up?"

Cal popped a match with his fingernail. It produced a bright yellow burst, and he lit his cigarette. "Well, like I said, it takes until about the age of ten to get some real use out of 'em. Then they're good for several years—if they don't get hurt." Cal inhaled again, causing the crude cigarette to glow brightly and unevenly. "At the end of each fall, old horses are culled. Ones that done good by us get to spend the rest of their lives grazing. Poor ones is sold for farm work."

"And the rest? The ones that are still good?"

"Turn 'em out on the range. Let 'em graze and rest up. We keep a few for winter work, but we grain feed 'em." Danny settled back on his bedroll. Cal was deeply engrossed in the topic now. "Each cowboy is responsible for his own string. A man who don't take care of his horses don't last very long. With this outfit or any other."

"Cal, will you show me how to ride? Ride good, I mean."

"Sure." Cal tossed aside the remnant of his cigarette and watched as it flickered and died out. He was embarrassed by the compliment and could think of nothing more to say in reply. Instead he told Danny, "If you want to see something interesting, watch horses cross a river. Mares always swim with their colts on the downstream side. I reckon to block the current with their body. Gives the colt stiller water to swim in." Cal's voice had become drowsy. He yawned, placed his hat over his face, and within minutes, was fast asleep.

7

Ples sauntered up and took over Cal's end of the conversation. "What he said about horses—it's not that way with cattle." He put his saddle on the ground and squared it to his satisfaction. With a snap of his wrists, he unfurled his blanket and draped it over the ground. He groaned and pressed his thigh as he lowered himself. "Pulled muscle," he explained. "Now about crossin' rivers. When mama cows is bein' taken across, they nudge their babies to the *upstream* side so the calves can rest against 'em." The steady sound of Cal's snoring punctuated the cool night air.

Ples told Danny more new things: Thirsty cattle stampede when they catch the scent of water. A cow can drink upwards of thirty gallons a day. Ten miles is as far as a cow can walk to get to water.

Other cowboys began to bed down. Twigs wandered over and stood scratching his armpits. He squirted tobacco juice through his yellow and brown teeth. "You know the difference between a bull and a steer, Stewpot?" Without waiting for Danny to reply, Twigs answered his own question: "A bull has his work cut out for him; a steer has his works cut out."

Danny laughed out loud. He had begun to feel like one of the boys.

Twigs refrained from telling him quite yet about the tradition of eating "calf fries" during the spring roundup. As the yearlings were branded and castrated, some of the just-removed testicles were sizzled in a skillet of hot fat. Everyone was expected to partake. Instead, Twigs advised Danny, "If'n a bull is ever charging you, Stewpot, you fall to the ground and roll towards him. That critter will jump clean over you." Danny was just about to express relief when Twigs added, "Then get up and run like hell."

Bum had been listening. He was picking his few teeth with a toothpick he had whittled. "You see them Longhorns out on the south range last week, Stewpot?"

"Yup. When I carried supplies out to Mr. Bartlett." There weren't many Longhorns, but the sharp six-to-eight-foot racks of horns that crowned the animals' narrow skulls had made a sobering impression on Danny. "Cal said they sometimes dehorn 'em. I can see why."

Bum continued in his hissing, sibilant fashion, "Longhorns is tough, ugly, and mean-tempered. Any cow will defend its calf something fierce, but a Longhorn can fight off a wolf. And it will. Ranchers used to favor the Longhorn. They can survive freezing winters and summers hot enough to melt the shoes off the horses. Why, we made some drives that…" Bum sighed, and his voice faded "It's all changed now." His voice was tinged with nostalgia.

"That was something, all right," Twigs chimed in. "Like to got myself killed more than once. Longhorns got tall legs and light bodies. They can travel long distances." Twigs had peeled off his shirt so he could scratch his chest through a hole in his long johns. "I don't suppose you know anything about trail drives, do you, Stewpot?" Twigs knew the answer before he asked, so he went right on. "Well then, you probably don't know that cattle can get strung out half a mile or more on the trail. And that a trail can be fifty miles wide in places."

Danny's eyebrows shot up as he murmured his surprise.

"Fortunately, cattle are followin' animals. They like to follow a lead steer." Twigs cut a fresh plug of tobacco and shoved it in his mouth.

Ples had been lying with his arms folded across his chest and his hat over his face, listening. He shoved his hat back, succumbing to the urge to add his two cents' worth. "Stewpot, you ever hear of Charles Goodnight's Old Blue? That critter made the big trail drive twice a year for eight years—probably more than most drovers. Shoot, after a while he coulda took the herd by hisself. They stuck a bell on him. Muffled it at night, of course. Come sunrise, Old Blue was at the fore of the herd, ready to go." Then Ples actually laughed. "Spoiled, though. I heard tell that old bull slept with the horses in the remuda and demanded handouts from the chuck wagon. Had a right nice old age. Lived out the rest of his years at the ranch."

Twigs commandeered the conversation again. "Some Longhorns were so wild that they sewed their eyelids shut. By the time the gut thread dissolved, the critter was likely to have become herd broke and settled in without causing any more turmoil."

Danny grimaced. "What about Longhorns that never settled down?"

Twigs pantomimed cutting meat with a knife and fork and then patted his belly. "Dinner." He scratched his whiskers and rubbed his eyes with leathery, scarred hands. "If any of us is gonna live to a right nice old age, we'd best stop waggin' our chins. Sun'll be up 'fore you can blink."

8

Danny continued to learn more each day. He learned that the YT, like other ranches, now ran mostly shorthorns, Herefords, and Angus, cattle bred to overcome some of the Longhorns' less desirable characteristics. Bum told him, "Longhorns can run like crazy. It's a terrible thing if a herd of 'em goes on a stomp, and night stomps is the most dangerous. Now your Herefords is the easiest kind of critters to handle in a stomp. They can't even run fast enough to make a horse followin' 'em get warm."

When Danny handed Bum a cup of strong, black coffee one morning, he asked, "Bum, you think I'll ever see a stomp?" The thought both thrilled and frightened Danny.

The grizzled old cowboy wiped the back of his sleeve across his mouth. "Not if you're lucky."

Later, Danny picked up some biscuits and bacon and sat down beside Bum. "Why aren't there big trail drives anymore?"

Bits of biscuit flecked Bum's whiskers. Through a full mouth, he mumbled, "Railroads. Railroads ended 'em. Ranches still hold roundups twice a year, but afterwards we deliver the herds to nearby railway cattle lots. That, or pay drovers to take 'em. The railroads came to the ranchers. In the old days, it was the other way around." With a sucking sound, Bum drained the rest of the coffee from his cup.

Danny set the hard biscuit down. He felt disappointed. Many nights, he had lain in the dark envisioning himself on a spirited horse, dashing about a lively herd, shouting and waving his hat. Cal had been teaching him to ride. Danny had taken to it quickly and was already beginning to ride like a seasoned cowboy. He ate the rest of his breakfast in silence until Twigs walked over. "Tomorrow's payday, Stewpot. We're going into Flint tomorrow night to blow off a little steam. Don't suppose you'd like to come along?"

Danny brightened. "You bet!"

9

At the saloon in Flint the YT cowboys sat around a table drinking and swapping tales. Danny took a long pull from a glass of warm beer. He closed his eyes as the foamy liquid rolled down his throat, trying to act as if he'd drunk beer all his life.

He realized that the presence of a new man was a good excuse for the others to retell all of their favorite stories. Cal downed a healthy slug of beer and turned to him. "Stewpot, did I ever tell you about the dupe that bought the same herd twice?"

"No, but I reckon you're fixin' to tell him," observed Twigs.

Cal explained with a flourish: "The seller drove them steers around a hill, and damned if he didn't sell that fool the same cows a second time!"

Danny laughed, and in spite of himself, Twigs did too.

"Hell, I can top that!" It was Ples. "I heard tell of an Easterner who come out West and a rancher sold him javelinas!"

The others snorted in derision, but Danny's face remained blank.

"Stewpot, I swear, you're as ignorant as that Yankee I'm telling you about. Javelinas are mean, ugly, wild pigs. Bristly with one big tusk. Look like a hairball with a butcher knife sticking out of it. Ain't good for nothin'—including eating." Ples turned back to the group and swirled the frothy beer in his glass. "Well, this Eastern dude don't know that javelinas ain't got no tails. So the rancher tells him they're hogs and that the way he marks his hogs is by chopping off their tails! Sold 'em to that dandy for two dollars a head!" Ples hooted and shook his head, "Hooey! I bet he was riled when he found out he paid good money for a varmint and a pest!" Ples finished his beer and waved for another, and then borrowed enough tobacco from Cal to make a cigarette.

Twigs rocked back on two chair legs, aimed at a spittoon, and hit it.

"He could spit tobacco into the neck of a swingin' bottle," marveled Cal.

Twigs took the compliment in stride and then spoke up. "That Yank must've been the same sorry dude that these horse traders sold a blind horse. That fool come around the next day screaming, 'You hoodwinked me! You sold me a blind horse. Gimme my money back!' And one of the horse traders he says, 'Well, I told you before you bought him that he was big and fast, even though *he don't look too good*." Twigs sipped his whiskey and, despite groans from the others, cheerfully repeated the words, "even though he don't *look* too good."

Then it was Bum's turn. "That's nothin'. I heard tell of a waddy up in the mountain country that wagered twenty-five dollars that he could rope a grizzle bear and bring that critter under his control. Now they knowed he could rope good, but they also knowed it took leastways half a dozen men to bring a grizzle bear under control. They reckoned there was a trick, but they couldn't figure out what it was. Finally, they took his bet. Well, it didn't take long before they come across a bear and, sure enough, the feller throws a loop on it. 'Course, he can't set the horse because the bear woulda pulled the horse instead of the other way around. That bear rears up, ready for supper. Them other cowboys is saying, 'That waddy's on his way to the eternal range for sure.' But the waddy pulls out his .44 and puts two shots smack between the bear's eyes. Shoots him dead. Then he turns to the others and says, 'Gents, as you can see, that bear is roped and under my control.'" Bum concluded his tale, "They paid up, but they never bet with him again."

The others raised their glasses and gave grunts of approval: "I bet they didn't!" and "Right smart, that one."

Feeling his whiskey, Bum announced, "Hell, I woulda seen right through that. No sir, he couldna tricked me."

A thought that hadn't occurred to Danny since he was a child in New York nudged its way into his mind, and he grinned. All of a sudden, he heard himself saying, "Say, Bum, I bet you a dollar I can tell where you got your boots…"

Danny's standing rose considerably after he bamboozled Bum out of a dollar that evening.

Although Danny soaked up tales and information of every sort, he felt deep sorrow that he could not learn the one thing he most wanted to know, the fate of his uncles. None of the YT ranch hands knew anything of Shamus or Aidan O'Brien. Sensing Danny's disappointment and discouragement, Ples told him, "Cowboys drift from one outfit to another. Keep your ears open. You might yet run across somebody who knows of 'em."

Each night, Danny was both saddened and consoled by the sound of Brody's lonesome Irish ballads that wafted to the bunkhouse. Before a full moon had passed, Danny knew all the songs by heart.

SIXTEEN

1

At the YT Danny grew accustomed to the daily routine. His work started well before sunrise and was often tedious, but it was punctuated with small amounts of free time that he cherished. Whenever he could, he used this time to ride or, in Twigs's derisive words, "to polish a saddle with his backside."

Danny's previous riding had been confined to plodding around on the Mutts' farm. Now he had the open range—with its grasses, brush, prickly pear and other cacti—and space to roam, new territory to explore. In exchange for writing some letters for Cal, Danny learned from the wiry, bowlegged young wrangler how to mount and dismount a horse with easy grace and how to ride with skill. Cal had even taught him the basics of breaking horses. According to Twigs, there was no better teacher. Normally stingy with compliments, Twigs said flat out that Cal was "born to the saddle."

Danny viewed Cal's worn leather leggin's, chaps, as proof he was an accomplished rider, and he admired Cal's spurs. In particular, Danny liked the jinglebobs on his spurs. The first time Danny noticed them, he picked up one of Cal's boots off the bunkhouse floor. He flicked the small metal attachment and listened to its music. "What are they for?" he asked Cal.

"Nothing."

"I mean, what do they do?"

"They don't do nothing. Just make a nice sound."

Indeed, they served no other purpose than to produce a merry, attention-getting jingle that was not unlike the pleasurable sound of a handful of silver coins in a pocket. When Cal fastened his spurs on the loosest setting, the "town notch," his spurs clicked against the ground, setting off a chorus of jingling. "You file the points off the rowels so you don't hurt the horse," he explained. "And it might not look like it, but bigger spurs are kinder than small, sharp ones."

Cal showed Danny a dog-eared R. T. Frazier catalog, the cowboy bible. He had already picked out the new saddle he wanted. "Thirty dollars," Cal whistled and shook his head. "Worth it, though. A man might be afoot—not own a horse—but every self-respectin' cowpuncher owns a saddle. If he don't, he gets assigned ground chores."

Cal flipped to a page of cowboy hats and thumped on a drawing of high-crowned, ten-gallon one. "You can tell where a cowboy is from by the shape and size of his hat.

John B's are favored in the Southwest." Danny looked blank. "John B. *Stetson*. Philadelphia hat maker. A 'John B' is a cowboy hat," Cal explained. "Top-notch." He circled the image with his finger. "I want me one made of beaver." He sighed. "Take a month's pay or better."

It was Cal who was responsible for the outfit's remuda. Although the position of wrangler was a lowly one, it was crucial. Each range hands used several horses every day. Moreover, cowboys looking for work often judged a ranch by the quality and care of its horses. Cal told Danny, "I hired on a year ago when I was a young shaver, barely fourteen. Started as a 'night hawk,' taking care of the remuda at night. Pret' soon, I got made the outfit's wrangler." He looked up at Danny. "But I'd still rather be a leather pounder. A cowboy." Cal was aware he was the youngest man at the YT. "Just got to pay my dues. Bide my time."

Whenever he had a chance, Danny hung around Cal. He was glad for the company of someone near his own age, and he liked to hear Cal talk about horses. "On a drive with 3,000 cows, it takes at least ten men to handle the day shift," the wrangler explained. "Come late afternoon, the cattle are rode down—gathered—and moved half a mile or so off the main trail."

"So they can graze?" Danny asked.

Cal nodded. "At dusk they're bedded down in an open area. In an open area, there are fewer things around that might frighten them." He picked up a hackamore to inspect it. "At night, there are four night shifts of four men each. On night watch, a pair of hands rides slowly around the herd, going opposite ways. They serenade them doggies with lullabies to keep 'em calm." He continued to talk while he repaired the rope bridle. "On a trail drive, each cowboy's responsible for his own string of horses. That's usually somewheres between seven and ten mounts. The boys check their horses every day and count 'em out to me. Throughout the day, when a hand needs a partic'lar horse of his, I cut that one out of the remuda." Cal gave the hackamore a tug. Satisfied that it was fixed, he placed it on a peg with the other bridles and halters.

Cal described the types of horses. Danny learned there were rope horses for lassoing cattle, night horses that could work in the dark, running and branding horses, and even ones adept at herding cattle across rivers and streams. Most prized was the cutting horse. It could single out a cow by using its ability to anticipate the cow's moves, and spin and turn to block the animal's attempt to return to the herd. A fine cutting horse was the pride of an outfit: a horse had to be born with the aptitude, and even so, it took years of training and experience to develop it. It took an equally expert rider to anticipate the horse's quick actions and stay aboard.

Over time, Bartlett noticed Danny's eagerness to learn to all Cal had to offer about horses. He watched Danny's continual, self-imposed practice and the dramatic improvement in his horsemanship. He was impressed with Danny's endless questions and boundless curiosity. He also knew the rarity and value of a literate ranch hand.

2

After supper each night, Danny cajoled and flattered Ples, the best roper among them, into teaching him how to handle a rope. In Ples's rough hands, lengths of recalcitrant rope were transformed into fantastic knots of every sort. "Each one's different, serves a different purpose. You need to know how to tie 'em. You need to know when to use 'em."

Before long, Danny could tie every knot that Ples could, and almost as fast. Danny didn't mention that he had already learned from Mr. Dunside how to tie countless knots, and that Seb had added a few more. Although Ples was astounded by the speed with which Danny seemed to learn, he attributed it to his skill as a teacher.

Danny's progress with the lariat was more erratic. *La reata*, Ples told him, as he adroitly twisted the rope to form an adjustable loop. Holding up the finished product, Ples explained, "Spanish for lariat, Stewpot. A rope with a running noose. A cowhand named Gonzales taught me how to use one. Best damn roper I ever knew."

Danny rewound the rope and tried to lasso a fence post. He missed. After twenty frustrating minutes of futile tries, he came close.

You're holding it too tight," Ples called out from a distance.

After another fifteen minutes, Danny succeeded. He let out a whoop and waved to Ples.

Ples walked over to him. "Well, I'll give you this much, Stewpot. You're a persistent son-of-a-gun."

"I reckon I am, Ples. I reckon I am." Danny's amused smile was imperceptible. In his head, he could still hear Mr. Dunside exhorting him as a young boy, "If something is difficult or boring after five minutes, then spend ten minutes on it. And if it's still hard or boring after ten minutes, then spend twenty minutes on it. And if it's still that way, spend half an hour on it, and then an hour. Sooner or later, it will become interesting—and easier."

At idle moments, Danny could be found roping fence posts, saddle horns, tree stumps, and an occasional unsuspecting calf. Ples warned him that a cowhand could be fired for trying trick roping during the workday. "There's two catches a cowboy's absolutely got to know. That and the knack of using the rope to turn a steer that's trying to break away from the herd. You do it wrong, and you can break the steer's neck when you flip him. That's a no-count way for a rancher to lose profit. They don't look kindly on it."

In front of the others, Twigs continued to patronize and tease Danny. But when it was just the two of them, he explained to Danny how to shift the coil of a lariat from one hand to another to tally every hundred head of beef out on the range. He counseled Danny that roping was the most dangerous part of a roundup: It only took a split second of carelessness—a line sloppily dallied around the saddle horn with a steer straining at the other end—and a man could have his thumb or fingers severed by a rope.

3

Although the other range hands owned six-shooters, Danny never asked for anyone's help in using his pistol. It was Bartlett who heard the sound of Danny's Colt .44 in the distance and rode out to where he was shooting at stationary targets. Given the cost of cartridges, Danny had rationed himself only a few shots each day, trying to learn as much as possible from each round.

So intent was Danny that he wasn't aware of Bartlett for several minutes. Bartlett watched silently from atop his horse, then dismounted. A man of few words, Bartlett advised, "Keep both eyes open. Squeeze the trigger gently. Don't pull it." He kept his own eyes focused on a dented tin cup that served as Danny's target.

Danny fired and missed. He handed Bartlett the .44, wanting to observe. Bartlett leveled the gun and gently squeezed the trigger. A shot cracked through the air. The cup quivered but didn't fall from the piece of fence post on which it rested. Danny looked back at Bartlett in confusion and embarrassment.

Bartlett lowered the gun slowly and handed it to Danny. Then he mounted his massive golden horse and pointed to the cup. "Through the handle." He touched the brim of his hat and trotted off.

Danny walked to the stump and poked his finger through the opening of the cup handle. He could feel a slug embedded in the tree behind it.

After that day, when Bartlett was moving from herd to herd, he would sometimes appear at free moments and give Danny pointers on how to improve his marksmanship. When Danny was proficient enough to nail even small stationary objects, Bartlett showed him how to draw rapidly and fire at objects on the fly. Bartlett was patient and never taught Danny how to do anything new until he was satisfied that Danny had mastered what he had already shown him. Danny took it as a sign of progress whenever Bartlett volunteered new information.

Months went by. As Bartlett mounted his horse to ride off one afternoon, he said over his shoulder, "One of these days, O'Brien, they're going to start calling you 'Sure Shot' instead of 'Stewpot.'"

"Yessir!" Danny beamed in spite of himself. His next thought was, *I wish you'd teach me how you move so quiet and how to hear things before everyone else does.* Dilue was the only other person he knew who possessed that ability, but she was blind. *Maybe he's the kind of man Mr. Dunside talked about, one that uses in proper proportion the one mouth and two ears the good Lord gave him.*

4

At supper the following week, Bartlett asked, "O'Brien, you want a chance to ride?" The others stopped talking and listened.

"He ain't no cowboy. He wouldn't even make a good drag man," drawled Bum, referring to the two or three cowboys who held the dusty position at the rear of the herd and prodded the slower animals along. "Not enough gravel in his gizzard." As one of the most senior members of the outfit, Bum, like Twigs, felt free to offer his opinions. He knew Bartlett would give them consideration. "Stewpot ought to stick to lassoin' frying pans and ridin' ponies," he whistled through his missing teeth.

"Let him break one of the new horses, the one we been callin' Diablo," chimed in Squint, cocking his head to the side, as if to see better. "He rides him, he rides the herd with us. If he don't, he keeps ridin' the chuck wagon." Squint's beard was studded with traces of bread and dried beans.

In response to Squint's proposal, a murmur of consensus rippled among the hands. Bartlett remained impassive. He knew the men liked having a say, and unless it was a critical matter, he didn't intervene. When no one offered any opposition to his idea, Squint declared, "Well, then, it's done. We'll do it one morning before breakfast." And as if to explain the timing—and the outcome he expected—he added, "We'll do it early so Stewpot won't be late to help Brody."

There were hoots and hollers. "That bronco is a real cinch buster!"

"A fire-eater!"

"You'll be throwed off in less time than it takes to tell it!"

"Might as well try to ride a cyclone, Stewpot!"

Later that night, Danny sought out Twigs and Cal. Twigs could see he was scared. "Don't let 'em spook you with all that talk. Thunder ain't rain," Twigs reminded him. "There ain't never been a horse that can't be rode." Then he chuckled. "Nor for that matter, a cowboy that can't be throwed."

At first Cal was angry that Danny might have a chance to ride the herd before he would, but he consoled himself that a cook's helper was much more easily replaced than a wrangler. Besides, he liked Danny.

The soft-spoken wrangler reassured him, "You're already a good rider. These here horses are mustangs, wild horses from out on the plains, but they can be rode. You just got to punish 'em bad every time they fight you. Use a quirt in one hand, and with the other, hang on tight as… as…"

Twigs finished Cal's sentence, "…a tick on a pup's ear. You're gonna feel like a snake being shook by a hound, but you just stick to that saddle like paper to a wall, you hear? Boze'll be here in six days. You watch him close and learn what you can."

Danny knew that many of the YT's mustangs still bucked the first time they were mounted each day, even ones that had been in the remuda for years. "They's jus' limbering up," Cal had commented. Tonight he volunteered, "I know one old outlaw horse that sunperched about a quarter of a mile every time he was mounted. I was told he done it all his life. Pitchingest critter I ever seen. We broke him, but never could gentle him."

Danny listened solemnly. He was aware that a knot had formed in his stomach.

"'Course it wouldn't be a bad idear to spend a few minutes in the amen corner the night before you and Diablo square off," Twigs advised.

Before Danny had a chance to respond or to ask who "Boze" was, Twigs slicked back his sparse hair, secured his hat on his bony head, and sauntered off. He was whistling "Amazing Grace."

SEVENTEEN

1

The following week "Boze" Lanham arrived at the YT, just as he had every spring for years. The black cowboy's nickname came from his early days spent on the Bozeman Trail in Montana. Ranchers now knew him one of the best broncobusters in the business and willingly paid him five dollars a head to break wild horses.

When Boze rode up, Cal tossed aside the bridle he was repairing and strode out to meet him. "Howdy, Boze!" Danny scrambled to go with him.

Boze waved a greeting. He slid off his horse and handed Cal the reins.

Cal turned to Danny. "You're lookin' at the best broncobuster there is. Ain't *no* one better at bustin' hosses than this man. I once seen Boze bust six in a single morning."

"Six?" Danny whistled at the number. He had an appreciation of what that meant; Cal had been letting him get experience on partially broken horses. Danny extended his hand towards Boze. "I'm mighty glad to make your acquaintance. I'm hopin' I can learn a lot from you in short order."

The talk that evening was all of Boze. Everyone anticipated his arrival each year and looked forward to watching him do what he did best. Standing around the campfire after supper, Ples told Danny, "Rumor has it that an uppity cowboy once sneered at Boze when he was gettin' ready to bust a fierce horse. He says to Boze, 'I think you might justa met your master in that one, boy.' Well, Boze looks him dead-level in the eye and says, 'First, I ain't a boy, and second, the son of a bitch that's my *master* ain't been *born* yet.'"

Danny gave a broad smile. "From what I hear, he was tellin' the truth."

"You can count on it." Ples slurped down the rest of his coffee, then shook the remaining drops out of the cup into the dirt. "But you can see for yourself in the morning."

2

During the next few days, Boze worked his way through horse after horse. Danny studied his every move, wincing the few times Boze got slammed into a corral post or was thrown by an intractable mustang. As Boze prepared to mount a particularly wild mustang, he called out to Danny, "Mos' cowboys what gets pitched gets frowed fo' they ever gets on. The biggest part of breakin' a hoss happens here." Boze tapped his glistening forehead with his index finger.

"That's a fact," Cal seconded.

Boze twisted a mustang's ear and was instantly in the saddle.

As they watched Boze, Cal gave Danny pointers. "There's names for different types of pitchin'. Now the worst ones is 'wigglers.' That's what that last one was. Toughest pitchers there is. They come forward and up. Land on their front feet with their rear ends in the air." Cal made an arcing movement with his cupped hand to show the horse's motion. "Then they wiggle their back ends when they're upright like that. Ain't too many men can stay on a wiggler." Cal looked admiringly at Boze, and then continued his descriptions. "There's also what they call a 'fence rower.' Jumps first to one side then the other. One that jumps only to the side is what's knowed as a 'sunpercher.' Them that jumps straight ahead is your 'pigeon wingers.'"

Danny nodded. He stood on a rail of the corral and gripped the top of a corral post with both hands. He had begun swaying in an unconscious attempt to help Boze. In a distracted voice Danny asked, "What's cayusein' mean, Cal? I hear Boze say it."

"Boze says cayusein' means the same thing there and in South Texas as pitchin' does elsewheres in Texas, or buckin' does somewheres else. Cayusein', pitchin', buckin.' All the same. Boze says he heard it's called that on account of the Cayuse Injuns, that they were an Oregon tribe. Good riders."

Regardless of the word, Danny felt trepidation about his impending ride.

3

Early the next morning, the entire outfit flanked the corral, jostling each other for space around the rails. Bartlett instructed Boze, "Saddle and bridle Diablo, then leave him be."

Danny stood to the side, trying to look calm, but inwardly struggling to stave off feelings of panic and dread.

"Two bits says Stewpot don't last a minute," bellowed Ples.

Bets were instantly placed, an exception having been made to the ranch's rule against gambling. Then Ples jibed, "Horse sense is what keeps the horse from bettin' on a man, Stewpot."

Cal had lent Danny his dress spurs because the rowels on them were sharper than the gently curving, star-shaped ones on his working spurs. He'd also let Danny use his chaps, a pair of batwings that buckled at the waist with leggings that fastened in the back. Danny knew they offered protection from cactus and thorns out on the South Texas plains. Cal didn't bolster Danny's confidence when he added, "They also protect against rope burns, hits against the corral post, and horse bites." Cal handed Danny his gloves, which flared back into gauntlets. "You may as well take these. The more you're covered, the less there is to get bunged up."

Earlier, as Danny put on his boots, he recalled Cal's reminding him, "Being dragged by a horse is the cause of most cowboys' dying. That's why you need boots with pointed toes and undercut heels. They slip out of the stirrups easy." Danny nodded as he reached down and gave one last tug to the "mule ears," the floppy grips on either side of the boot tops.

Once again, Danny became aware of the voices around him. "Never agree to ride any horse named Loco, Widow Maker, Bone Crusher—or Diablo." Bum's advice was delivered in a loud voice.

"Might just as well try to ride an ocelot. Or a jaguarundi," someone else volunteered. "Maybe you should start with wild turkeys and deer."

Squint called out, "You're a fool, Stewpot. You'd jump in the river to get out of the rain!"

It had taken Boze several minutes to rope the high-strung horse, snub him to a post, and get a bridle on him. He used grass-rope to cross-hobble the horse, linking a foreleg just above the pastern joint to the opposite hind leg. Then he worked a saddle blanket on him and finally, a forty-pound saddle. The wild-eyed horse bucked at each notching of the cinch. This much accomplished, Boze signaled to Danny. Standing outside the corral, Danny tightened the knot on his bandanna. He took a deep breath and stepped forward. *Guess I'm ready as I'll ever be.*

Cal had been watching Boze saddle Diablo. When Danny approached the bronco, he heard Cal trying to help him. "Look out! He's a wiggler!" Danny felt another current of fear electrify his groin.

Boze handed his quirt to Danny. Danny slipped the loop over his wrist and clenched the braided rawhide whip so tightly that his knuckles turned white. "Ear down," Boze advised in a low voice.

Danny took another deep breath, and then doing as he had seen Boze do, he twisted the horse's ear. He was counting on the pain to distract the horse as he swung unsteadily into the saddle. Danny had also seen Boze fan the sensitive tips of a mustang's ears while he was breaking him. "The horse'll finally quit bucking just to stop the pain," he had explained.

No longer tethered, the huge, skittish horse launched into action, snorting and thrashing, trying to dislodge both Danny and the hated saddle. Danny spurred Diablo and applied the quirt every time the horse kicked or bucked. With his other hand, Danny gripped the saddle horn. He clutched it as tightly as if he were suspended over a mountain ledge, clinging to a small branch for his life. He could feel cold, clammy sweat spreading beneath his armpits. He tried to swallow, but his throat was too dry. He tried to let the motion ripple through him, but his teeth gnashed each time Diablo's front hooves hit the dusty ground.

Danny's head jerked up as the horse flung itself in furious arcs. At that moment, two flickering images registered in Danny's mind: the faces of Tom Bartlett and Janie McCorkle.

Diablo pitched all over the large corral, bucking and twisting without pause. He rocketed forward, simultaneously punching the air with his hind legs. Danny clung with his knees to try to avoid being pitched over the horse's head. Pain riveted Danny's hand and arm as both his hand and the reins ripped loose from saddle horn. There was a din of hollering and yelling in Danny's ears. All he could see was a blur of faces, but in his mind's eye, he kept seeing only two, Bartlett's and Janie's. It made him determined not to be thrown from this lightning bolt of a horse.

No sooner had he strengthened his resolve than he crashed to the ground, landing on his shoulder first, then hitting his face on the packed soil.

"Eatin' a little dirt, are you, Stewpot? Plowin' with your face?" It was Bum's rusty voice rising above the chorus of hisses, jeers, and catcalls.

Slightly dazed, humiliated, but still cognizant enough to realize that he needed to get clear of Diablo's hooves, Danny rolled sideways and staggered to his feet. He was still clutching Boze's leather quirt. Bum's goading continued, "You couldn't ride a charley horse!"

From anger, humiliation, or both, Danny abruptly ran at the pacing, snorting horse. Advancing from an oblique angle and using a trick mount that Cal had taught him, he flung himself onto the startled horse and clamped onto the saddle horn. Although he was flipped into the air more than once, he hung on ferociously. After several fruitless attempts, he was finally able to work his feet, one at a time, into the stirrups. He applied the spurs and quirt to counter the horse's every attempt at resistance. Danny hunkered down, lashing at Diablo's ears with the rawhide strips of the quirt, and continued to ride out the storm.

Eventually Danny realized that he and the horse were moving together rather than at odds. Without warning, Diablo, foam spewing from his mouth, simply ceased his struggle. Snorting, tossing his head high and slinging foam, the heaving black horse began to canter restlessly in immense circles. Danny didn't fight the horse, but let Diablo slow to a stop when he was ready. Boze approached Diablo and took the reins as Danny slid off the horse. Trying to sound as if breaking broncs was the kind of thing he did every day, Danny handed Boze his quirt and announced with all the dignity he could muster, "I'm much obliged."

"I thought it was O'Brien. But I tell you what, Mr. O'Bliged," said Boze, drawing out the "O" and grinning, "I think we got us a new cowboy here."

Appreciative whistles and shouts replaced the jeers. "Dogie, you got more sand in your gizzard than what I give you credit for," Bum conceded.

Exhausted and caked with dirt, Danny walked stiffly to the side of the corral. Some of the spectators had already begun arguing over their wagers, trying to determine how being thrown but getting back on should figure into the matter. The excitement over, Boze went back to work. He mounted Diablo and began flicking his slicker in the horse's face to teach him to ignore sudden, unexpected movements and noises.

The sound of Tom Bartlett's voice silenced the men. "A new cook—a new cook's *helper*," he quickly corrected himself, "is coming next week. After he gets here, O'Brien, you can ride herd."

Danny appreciated the significance of this: roundup was imminent. While Bartlett was speaking, Danny noticed that for the first time, Janie was looking directly at him. For the first time, he saw what intensely green eyes she had. For the first time, she smiled at him. As she turned and walked back to the Big House, the other cowhands leaped into the corral, pumping Danny's hand and slapping his back in congratulations.

Only after the excitement subsided did he realize two things. One was that Tom Bartlett had assumed he would succeed. The other was that he hurt all over.

EIGHTEEN

1

"Hold still, now." Janie applied the poultice to the deep bruise that bloomed like a gargantuan purple flower over Danny's shoulder. Danny sighed with contentment from the warmth of the poultice and the attention from Janie.

He could gladly have kissed Twigs for suggesting that she treat his injury. "Her mama used to doctor the ranch hands. Why, Maggie McCorkle could poultice a hump off a buffalo!" Twigs reminisced. "Maybe the girl knows about doctorin', too." He gave Danny a sly wink.

Danny was grateful for any pretext that allowed him to go to the Big House and study both Janie and the house at close range. The kitchen was large and pleasingly redolent of cooking odors, scoured floors, and now, boiled mesquite leaves. Janie herself smelled of soap and a hint of lilac, a welcome contrast to the dust, sweat, livestock smells, and tobacco odors that clung to the cowhands.

Danny sat with his shoulder swathed in muslin strips that held the steamy, sodden leaves against his injured shoulder. "Comfrey makes good poultices, too," Janie told him. "So good, they call it knit-bone. But mesquite's more plentiful here. Boiled mesquite root can also quell your stomach and heal a wound." And as if alluding to his bronco busting, she finished her tutorial with, "A boiled onion poultice will ease soreness, too." She eyed his blotchy shoulder and chest. "You look as if you need to steep in a pot of boiled onions." To Danny's disappointment, she seemed to be all business.

When the poultice began to cool, she applied another one and replaced the muslin cloths. "It needs to stay on at least an hour. Longer is better."

Danny was thrilled. He used the time to look around the kitchen. Near the sink he spotted a pan with a blue checked cloth draped over it. "Seems poultices can also make you hungry," Danny ventured.

"I reckon they can." She lifted the checked cloth and offered him some shortbread. He thought he saw her smile.

Danny returned every day that week for a poultice. Gradually the conversation shifted from poultices and cures to their own lives. Other than Cal, Janie was the one closest to Danny's age.

2

Janie recounted her family's life at the YT. To Danny, the musical quality of her voice, even more than Johanna's singsong tone, imbued every word with poignancy and charm. "I've been at the ranch since I was seven," she told him. "When I was nine, my baby brother died. He's buried beneath the mesquite tree." Danny had noticed the small, enclosed cemetery the first day he arrived at the YT.

Janie saturated a cloth in hot water and wrung it out. "We lived in a small house except when my father went with the outfit on a cattle drive. But they don't take the herds north nowadays." She changed out the cloth on Danny's shoulder. "While he was gone, my mother and I kept on with our cooking and cleaning duties, but we'd move into the Big House. Last year, after my mother died—" Janie's voice broke slightly. She turned away and walked back over to the stove. "After my mother died, I moved into the Big House. I cook and take care of it, but I still help my father when the Wyatts are gone, or when all the cowboys come in from the range for branding time, or when I'm not needed at the Big House." Her eyes suddenly took on a spark of amusement. "Or when there's no cook's helper."

Danny learned that Maggie McCorkle was buried near her infant son. It was to the tiny cemetery late at night that Brody often wandered to sing his doleful ballads.

The ranch hands had liked the good-natured Maggie, and they told Danny that although they missed the petite, energetic woman's doctoring skills, they missed her baking skills most of all. "She always done the fancy baking," Ples explained. "After her death, Brody lost any heart he had for baking. Even for making biscuits." It somehow seemed to Brody fitting that Maggie's culinary secrets should be buried with her.

3

One day Danny took his gaze off Janie long enough to peer past the kitchen door into the rest of the house. In a whisper, he asked, "What are they like—the people who live here?"

Janie told him about Logan and Aldonza Wyatt, he the crusty, stalwart ranch owner and she, a Mexican beauty half his age. "Mrs. Wyatt, his wife of twenty years, died."

Danny remembered an ornate marker in the cemetery that stood at the foot of a towering oak. It was inscribed "Abigail Gladstone Wyatt," and below that, "Loving Wife."

Janie leaned forward and spoke in a lower voice. "Not long afterwards, Mr. Wyatt disappeared from the ranch. Just took off and left Tom Bartlett in charge. He was gone for several weeks. Then, as abruptly as he left, Mr. Wyatt reappeared. With Aldonza at his side. He never offered any explanation, and no one ever asked. I think he liked being married and just didn't know what to do without a wife. Everyone calls the new Mrs. Wyatt 'Miss Aldonza.' Felt too strange calling her 'Mrs. Wyatt.'"

Janie leaned back in her chair. "Mr. Wyatt and Miss Aldonza are an odd pair. Most people wouldn't have bet it would last, but they seem happy. Miss Aldonza takes almost as much interest in the day-to-day of the ranch as Mr. Wyatt. Except her passion is horses. His is cattle."

"I once thought I saw a dark-haired woman out riding alone on the range," Danny said. Now he realized who it was.

Janie nodded as she took plates from a shelf to set the table for supper. "Miss Aldonza sometimes goes to Mexico to visit her family. She just came back from there."

At the sound of the word "Mexico," Danny suddenly sat up straight. *Perhaps she could tell me exactly how far it is to the Texas border. Maybe she'd know what kind of terrain Aidan and Shamus would have met with if they had made it ashore and started walking north, farther into Texas.*

Janie folded cloth napkins. She began talking again as she set the napkins and silverware beside the plates. "Mrs. Wyatt—the first Mrs. Wyatt that died—she taught me to read and write and do numbers."

Janie stood with her hands on her hips and surveyed the table. She seemed satisfied. Then she crooked her finger at Danny. "Come look." She led him through the house to the parlor. "There," she said, pointing to a glass-doored bookcase. "Mrs. Wyatt and I used to take turns reading. When she got so sick she had to stay in bed, I read to her every day. For hours." Janie opened the cabinet door.

Danny was only half-listening. As he had squatted down to see better, he noticed the faintly musty, but pleasantly rich odor of the books. He started to run his hand over the handsome volumes but hesitated a few inches from their spines. "Leather." He said the word with reverence.

"It's all right," Janie said. "Before she died, Mrs. Wyatt said I could read them whenever I want. She told Mr. Wyatt that, too. He doesn't have any interest in them."

Danny touched the fine, soft leather and the gold lettering that embellished several of them. "There are so many," he marveled.

"*That* one!" Janie called out as his fingers passed over Cooper's *Last of the Mohicans.* "It's wonderful! It's about the French and Indian War, and a scout named Hawkeye and the Mohican chief Chingachgook and his son, Uncas, and Colonel Munro's daughters, Cora and Alice." Seeing his bewildered expression, she shrugged. "There's too much to explain. You'll have to read it."

Danny's curiosity was piqued. "And this one?" He pointed to a rich green volume embossed *Jane Eyre.* Never removing his hand from the book spines, he settled himself cross-legged on the floor in front of the bookcase.

Janie knelt beside him, tilted her head, and looked at the title. "Oh. That one's about an orphan girl who has a wretched life and is sent to live in a charity home. She and Mr. Rochester finally are happy," Janie announced, jumping to the end of the story.

Danny continued to walk his fingers over the smooth spines of the books. When he touched a rich ruby red one, Janie told him, "That's the last one we read before Mrs. Wyatt died. It's a more recent book. It has some pen and ink drawings in it. Pull it out if you like."

Danny slipped the volume from the shelf and turned the pages.

161

"There," Janie pointed. "That's a picture of Huck Finn. He's an orphan boy who lives with the Widow Douglas and her sister, Miss Watson, and they try to reform him." She flipped some pages. "And there's the king and the Duke—they get tarred and feathered and run out of town on a rail." Janie was laughing now. "I guess I don't have to try to tell the whole story in one breath now, do I?"

"I didn't know there were so many stories about orphans," Danny said. He suddenly felt embarrassed at having blurted out the word "orphan."

Janie felt embarrassed as well. "Neither did I. 'Til you mentioned it, I mean. But it's okay." To cover the awkwardness, she moved on. "See the tan book?" Danny replaced *Huckleberry Finn* on the shelf and extracted the one next to it. "It's *Great Expectations*. It's kind of a gloomy story about an orphan boy named Pip and his mean sister and Miss Havisham and the beautiful Estella." She flushed at the mention of yet another orphan and quickly added, "But it ends on a good note." She looked at Danny and smiled. "And I hope *your* story will have a happy ending, too."

Danny felt both pleased and flustered by her kind words. He cleared his throat. "You think Mr. Wyatt might let me read some of these?" He was aware of how tentative he sounded. Just being in the parlor with its heavily carved furniture and luxurious, thick draperies made him feel as if he'd trespassed. "I'd be careful."

"Why don't you ask Tom Bartlett? Mr. Wyatt would let you if Mr. Bartlett asked him."

Within the week, Danny was reading the books. He was not allowed to remove any books from the house, but Mr. Wyatt agreed that when he wasn't out with the herd, he could read at the kitchen table for a while each evening.

That suited Danny just fine.

4

After another two days of applying poultices, Janie announced to Danny, "The soreness in your shoulder should be about faded by now." Indeed, the swelling had dissipated, the deep bruise was fading to yellow, and the torn muscle had begun to heal. "You're lucky you're working in the cook shack," she teased. "If you were out on the range, you'd just have to make do as best you could."

"I'd hurt my shoulder all over again if it meant I could keep seeing you."

Janie pretended to be unaffected by his compliment, but her face flushed. "Careful," she teased. "Gossip travels faster on the ranch than in a one-horse town." With mock sternness, she added, "You'll live, and anyway, once roundup starts, you'll be too busy to think about anything else."

Danny was indeed impatient to participate in his first roundup. He had hoped to gain experience cutting yearlings out of the herd, but Bartlett informed him that although he could work with the men to round up cattle, he'd be working as the tallyman after the cattle were brought in. Bartlett explained, "The tallyman records the number of various animals. He notes the brands of strays that have mingled with the YT herd on the range."

Danny was disappointed, but he held his tongue. He knew that roundup wasn't the time for a green cowboy to learn his trade. He told himself, *Just 'cause I broke one mustang don't mean I got the skill of an experienced cowman or cutter.*

5

On the south range the first morning of the roundup, Danny trotted alongside Bartlett, listening to him describe the procedure. "In the mornings, we fan out in large circles. We drift the animals back together into a herd. In the afternoons, we brand what we've rounded up. For the next several days, we'll be rounding up the herd from different ranges." Bartlett pulled his horse up short and scanned the vista. "Keep a watch for strays that have wandered into creek beds, ravines, and remote areas." Then he loped off to talk with Twigs.

Danny was soon soaked with sweat, covered with dust, and hoarse from shouting at the cattle. His shoulder had begun to ache again, and his mouth felt as dry as if he'd sucked on a cotton boll. Two bright red scratches ran in parallel streaks across his cheek and neck. So intent was he on getting to a cow he had spotted in a ravine that he failed to see an overhanging branch. Like a cat, it seemed to reach out and claw the surprised young cowboy. *Twigs warned me to keep my head down,* Danny scolded himself. He touched his cheek and pulled his hat lower on his brow.

As he worked the cow back towards the herd, Danny listened to the men's shouts and the sharp whistling sounds they made through their teeth. In particular, he admired Ples' ear-splitting whistle, something he was never able to learn. His attempts came out sounding puny and absurd. He was still thinking about that when a hawk circling high above screeched and suddenly descended on a rabbit. *Even that bird can whistle better than I can.*

By midday, scores of animals had been rounded up. Danny liked being one of the hands, and he liked being out in the open. For a split second, the image of the dark, suffocating tenement in Five Points and its filthy, crowded streets inexplicably flashed through his mind. *I'd rather be picking my way through the brush,* he thought. *The land of thorns.* He had no chaps, and whenever he had to dismount, he was careful to dodge the prickly pear, yucca, and catclaw. Mesquite thorns were a menacing inch long. Danny noticed a thorny shrub with white flowers. *Guajillo?* Yes, that was what Brody had called it. He said guajillo gave the best honey in the world. "Heap of trouble to get to it, though," Brody had grumbled to himself.

Clumps of chaparral, vines, and grasses dotted the landscape. Tucked in between the brush were spring wildflowers. The profusion of colors created a brilliant patchwork. In spite of his scratched legs and face, Danny had to admit the land, though unforgiving, possessed a certain beauty.

In the afternoons, the men separated bawling yearlings from their equally vocal mothers. Danny watched Ples deftly cut one young animal after another from the herd, rope it, and take it down for branding. Ples had once told him, "Good cutting horses are born that way. They either got herd sense or they don't. Can't be learnt." Now Danny understood. Ples's horse seemed to anticipate a calf's every move, spinning to counter the dodging animal. Danny also understood what Cal meant when he said that there were different types of horses. Cutting horses. Branding horses. Rope horses that were used when lassoing was being done. Night horses that could work in the dark. Even horses trained to herd cattle across rivers.

The sound of Twigs's voice brought Danny back to the task at hand. "We heat the irons only to dull red. Hotter burns too deep and sets their hair on fire." The acrid odor of burning hide hung in the air, causing Danny to choke back his midday meal and say a silent thank you to Tom Bartlett that he had made him a tallyman.

"Pay attention," Twigs hollered at Danny, who was counting the number of mature beeves that would be sold to drovers to take to market. A wild-eyed cow was bawling hysterically as her lassoed calf struggled under the grip and the knees of two men. "Them cows loves their babies," Twigs shouted. "The mama always identifies her calf by its bawling. We use the mama's brand to tell what the yearling's should be. You markin' them brands careful-like in your book? Ain't no help at all if they're wrong."

Danny nodded. It was a simple, clever way of double-checking ownership; the cows did the work. The talleyman looked at the brand on the bellowing cow. It was obvious which calf belonged to the mama cow. If they belonged to a neighboring ranch, the proper brand was applied and they were returned to the owner. It was a courtesy ranchers had extended to each other from the time when there were no fences to prevent the mingling of grazing herds.

Over the bellowing of a cow, Twigs shouted, "When we're done, critters from other herds'll be separated from ours and driven home." Twigs pointed to the cow's flank. "Mark it down now." In his book Danny penciled a combined notation of a brand and its placement on the animals: right or left, flank or shoulder.

"Don't forget, Stewpot, you read the brand from left to right, top to bottom, and from the outside in." Twigs sounded like a schoolmarm who was explaining to a five-year-old how to hold a book, open it, and turn the pages. It was deliberate; his comment was intended to remind Danny how green he was. The first thing any cowboy learned was how to read brands—and Danny had been soaking up knowledge about brands since the day he arrived at the YT. He liked them as much as he did the emblems of the various railroads, and he had often filled odd moments drawing brands. He'd even created the brand he'd use if he ever owned a cattle ranch.

The calf made a piteous sound as the glowing brand was pressed into its flank, and this was followed by swift, unceremonious castration. Danny winced and instinctively dropped his hand in front of his own crotch.

The sorting and branding continued throughout the afternoon. The ears of YT stock were notched, ailing cattle were doctored, and when necessary, steers were dehorned. By the end of the day, more than two hundred and fifty animals had passed through the exhausted cowboys' hands. The men emerged filthy, tired, and ravenous. The same process began all over again at sunrise the next day on another range.

Bartlett had grown increasingly concerned over Brody's eccentric behavior. He knew that no ranch could keep its hands, much less its best hands, without a good cook. So he was more than a little relieved that the cook's new "helper," Jefferson Dooley, had arrived just before the roundup began.

6

Dooley was an enormous black man of indeterminate age who sported a full set of lavish white whiskers. His appearance brought to mind mounds of chocolate pudding topped with fluffy cream. His faded, red suspenders were taxed to their limit and threatened at any moment to slide off his massive belly to his sides. Twigs quickly dubbed him "Rounder" because of his considerable girth.

Dooley told them he'd worked on some sizable ranches before the YT. Although they were competing ranches, none was as expansive as the sprawling YT.

"All them other ranches is just two-bit, cocklebur outfits," Squint scoffed.

"Shirttail outfits that don't run enough cattle to hold a decent cookout," Ples needled, then spat for emphasis. Danny didn't join in, but he was pleased not to be the new man on the receiving end of their jibes.

Dooley listened patiently, never mentioning that he himself had been a working cowhand for almost two decades before a damaged knee and age finally caused him to "sell his saddle," to end his days on horseback. Nor did he mention that he had spent time as a young man fighting Indians. He did not tell them that he had been one of the fierce black soldiers the Indians dubbed Buffalo Soldiers. He did not tell them that when his fighting days were over, he had "retired" to the position of cook—not cook's helper—at the mighty Coronado Ranch, and that on trail drives he had been second in command only to the powerful trail bosses.

Like other range "cookies," Dooley had held considerable authority and responsibility: feeding the drovers, selecting campsites near water, doctoring the men, repairing equipment, and burying the dead. Cookies took care of the cowboys' bedrolls and dry clothes, as well as the corral ropes, branding irons, hobbles, and other gear stowed in the "bed wagon," or hoodlum wagon, that always followed the chuck wagon. Dooley knew problems with food or mistakes with water or equipment could mean disaster on the trail. And without a good cook, a ranch's cowhands quickly disappeared in search of an outfit that had one.

In truth, Dooley had more experience on the trail than most of the hands at the YT and more experience as a cook than Brody had. Dooley knew it and Bartlett knew it, yet out of regard for Brody's years of service, neither man ever mentioned it. Bartlett wanted a solid backup for Brody before roundup and the hectic summer months began. Cooks usually earned fifty dollars a month—twenty more than the cowhands—but he saw to it that Dooley was compensated beyond the regular pay.

Dooley took the cowhands' ribbing in stride. On trail drives, he had lived through attacks by Indians and rustlers. He'd survived Longhorn stampedes and had watched men trampled to death beneath the hooves of a spooked herd. He'd watched men drown trying to guide herds across treacherous, rain-swollen rivers.

Over the years, Dooley had been a witness as towns, farmers, and barbed wire encroached on the open range, and the cattle trails had been pushed farther and farther west: the Sedalia Trail that ended in the city of the same name in Missouri; west of it, the Chisholm Trail that led to Abilene and Ellsworth, Kansas, depending on which of the final north forks one chose; and the Western Trail that offered Dodge City as the payoff. Dooley had moved cattle on all of them. The only one he had missed was the Goodnight-Loving trail that swooped from near Ft. Worth west to Ft. Sumner, New Mexico, crossing the Colorado and Pecos Rivers and dipping south towards the colossal Kokernot Ranch.

Dooley knew firsthand of Abilene, Dodge City, and other cow towns at the end of the trail, wild places rife with saloons, dance halls, and other hold-em and hit-em joints. "We was sally-hootin' in the sally-joints and celebratin' with the lid off!" as Dooley would later describe it to Danny. "There were poker players, card sharks, con men, and fancy women. All of 'em just itchin' to relieve weary cowboys of their hard-earned wages." Dooley instinctively knew—and lamented—that the last great trail drives had occurred during the Eighties, their demise hastened by the advent of the now ubiquitous barbed wire and the expansion of the rail lines. He took deep satisfaction in knowing he'd been part of monumental drives, the likes of which no current cowboy would ever experience.

7

The first evening Dooley arrived at the YT, his initiation had begun. "Those ranches you worked on mighta been small, Rounder, but you ain't. Maybe you just outgrowed 'em," Twigs speculated.

Ples finished rolling a cigarette. "I don't believe you could sit down in a number three wash tub. In fact, I reckon you sit down in *shifts*." The others guffawed, but Dooley was unfazed. Ples exhaled a stream of smoke. "Yessir, I bet Rounder's looked upon as the po-litest cowboy in these parts 'cause when he stands up, *three* ladies can sit down!"

Dooley continued kneading flour into a sizable, shapeless mound of dough.

Encouraged by the others' laughter, Ples kept on. "Hey, Rounder, you take care not to fall down. You might rock yourself to sleep before you could get up!" He slapped his knee on that one and shook his head as if he might just choke on his own laughter.

Then they heard Dooley's low, husky voice. "Jus' wait 'til you taste my biscuits," he said gently. The ranch hands grew quiet. The main requirement for any cook was not to be able to cook, but to drive a team of mules. Brody was good at driving a wagon's team. Dooley had heard about Brody's biscuits. Folding his thick arms across his chest, he closed his eyes and compressed his lips as if just the thought of his own biscuits transported him. With supreme confidence, he announced, "Yessir, I make about the best biscuits in these here parts. Tender as your grandmother's bosom." With his thick eyelids still closed, he smacked his lips. "You sop these biscuits in red-eye gravy or molasses… mmm-mmm-*mmm*. They'll tickle your tonsils, I guarantee."

A few of the men involuntarily licked their lips, and several found their mouths watering at the prospect of these flaky clouds. Dooley opened his eyes and slowly scanned the cowhands. A silence lingered until Ples extended his hand towards the new cook's floury one. In a respectful voice, he said, "Welcome to the YT, Mr. Dooley."

NINETEEN

1

Although his biscuits alone would have done the trick, Dooley assured his place at the YT when he ambled over to the hatchet-faced Squint and handed him some money. "Here's yo' dollar."

Squint cocked his head to the side and eyed Dooley suspiciously. "Ain't mine."

"Sho is. Man give it to me five years ago. Tol' me to give it to the next feller I met who was uglier than me." When the hoots of the cowhands subsided enough for him to be heard again, Dooley told him, "You ever meet a feller uglier 'n you, you give it to *him*."

Even Squint smiled.

From then on, Jefferson Dooley was simply called Dooley. He did, indeed, produce biscuits that lived up to his ethereal description. Brody still chattered to himself but seemed less agitated now that the cowboys' steady stream of complaints about the food had ceased. "Dooley's dumplings" were an instant hit. And given some dried fruit, Dooley could turn out a highly respectable cobbler as well. With rice and raisins, he could produce spotted pup, a favorite dessert. But what cinched his place was a dish that contained neither flour, sugar, or fruit: a fiery concoction of red peppers and meat stewed together.

Weeks later, when a cowhand turned up seeking work, Ples boasted to him, "I can understand a man wantin' to sign on. I reckon you done heard about our cattle, our horses, and what a top-notch outfit the YT is."

"Naw," came the stranger's reply. "What I heard is that the YT got that cookie with the name of Dooley."

That cinched Dooley's reputation at the YT.

2

For the YT, Dooley's arrival had also meant a fresh source of stories, news, gossip, and speculation. Danny in particular plied Dooley with questions. The ebony Goliath peeled off tales of his earlier life like layers of an onion. In a leisurely fashion, he doled out one fascinating story after another. Danny was as spellbound as he had been by Mr. Dunside's tales of life at sea.

One night, as Dooley was tossing out a pan of greasy dishwater, Danny asked him, "Do you ever begrudge havin' to give up cowboying? Musta been hard to leave it and become a cookie."

Dooley lifted another pan and heaved the water from it. The liquid made a silvery arc that glinted with iridescent sparkles and landed with a splat. "Nosir, but I loved cowboyin', I can tell you that for sure. What you got to remember is this: You can't always do what you like, but you can always like what you do. That's the secret." The cook shot Danny a huge smile. "Now suppose you help me round up them pots and pans and stow them."

Danny began gathering the clean cooking utensils, the price of hearing Dooley continue his tales.

"Yessir. I seen a whole heap o' things in my lifetime." Dooley drifted a moment, enjoying a memory known only to him. Danny had already wheedled from Dooley yarns of trail drives and the sinful cities at their ends. "Yessir," Dooley repeated with his mouth still bowed in a toothy smile, "a whole *heap* o' things."

"What kind of things?" Danny tried not to sound too eager.

Dooley began to talk of his buffalo soldier days. "There was two Negro cavalry units, the Ninth and the Tenth, and two infantry, the Twenty-Fourth and the Twenty-Fifth. This was before 1880, mind you. The Tenth was sent to Kansas with Colonel Ben Grierson. Now the Ninth, my unit, came to Texas with Colonel Edward Hatch." In his mind, Dooley could still see the colonel, a recent war hero, dressed in the Army's deep blue uniform trimmed with gold braid and brass buttons. Danny waited for him to finish his private reminiscing.

"In West Texas, Stewpot, it was so hot men fell over from sunstroke, and in the winter, it was so cold that the water flat froze in our canteens. On top of that, the Army give us the worst of everything. The worst equipment. The worst horses. The worst food. I swore I wouldn't never again eat food that bad. And I ain't." He patted his belly and smiled. "But the gov'ment did pay us thirteen dollars a month, outside of givin' us room and board—if you could call it that." Dooley stood with his hands planted on his hips. "In white units, near a third of the men jus' up and quit. The Negro units had the lowest desertion rates in the country. Why, there wasn't hardly a man what quit his unit."

"Was Colonel Hatch a Negro?"

Dooley let out a huge guffaw. "Sakes no! Officers was white. Lots of them refused to serve with Negro troops. That pretty 'boy general'—what *was* his name?" Dooley scratched his woolly head, as if to jar loose the recollection. "Custard, I believe it was. Turned the Ninth down flat. Refused to have anything to do with our unit and joined the new Seventh Cavalry instead." Then Dooley reported with a trace of satisfaction, "Got hisself slaughtered. That was up in Montana at Little Bighorn in '76." His eyes narrowed and clouded. He stopped stacking frying pans and in a quieter voice added, "Got ever last one of his men killed, too. Never had no chance against Sitting Bull. Cheyenne warriors showed up to help the Sioux. Nosir, the Seventh never had *no* chance." He shook his head in disgust.

Danny was quiet for a minute, too. "Tell me about the Ninth, Dooley. Tell me about your unit."

Dooley resumed stowing the pots and pans. "Well, down near the border, we tangled with Meskin bandits and down-and-out war veterans. Out-to-pasture vets who couldn't find no work took it into their heads to roam around out West plunderin' whatever they wanted. Then there was the Injuns. Kiowas and Comanches comin' down from the North, and Kickapoos ridin' up across the Rio Grande from Mexico. It was somethin'!"

"You ever do battle with them? Head on, I mean?" Danny tried to envision a younger Dooley on horseback, hollering and shooting a rifle, but he couldn't imagine Dooley with any less girth than he had now.

"You know it! In '74 and '75, I fought in the Red River War. Kiowas and Comanches didn't take kindly to President Grant's puttin' 'em on reservations. March, fight, march, fight. We plumb wore 'em out." Dooley pulled the leg of his pants up to reveal a chalky scar that ran the length of his calf. He traced it with his finger. "Arrow," he said. "Had to cut it out."

Danny felt a sympathetic twinge in his own calf and grimaced.

Dooley lowered his pants leg and leaned towards Danny. "You ever hear of Geronimo?"

"Hear of him! Why, I practically *seen* him! With my own eyes."

Dooley raised his bushy white eyebrows and gave Danny a skeptical look. "Where? When *you* ever seen Geronimo?"

"I said I *almost* seen him." Danny's face flushed slightly, and he backed down from a claim that now seemed extravagant and foolish even to him. "Well, I personally know a *man* who saw him up real close." He felt like a bigger idiot and burbled on. "In San Antonio. At the depot. He was sent through on his way to Florida."

It was clear from Dooley's arched eyebrows and pursed lips that he was not impressed by what Danny was telling him.

Danny continued to spill out words in an embarrassed tumble. He was eager to convince Dooley of his brush with the great chief, no matter how indirect it might have been. "Him and his braves was bein' escorted by—"

"—by the U.S. Army."

Danny nodded vigorously, feeling at last that he was making progress.

"And just *who* do you s'pose surrounded and captured that renegade Injun?" Dooley leaned back and crossed his slabs of arms across the top of his belly.

Now Danny's eyebrows shot up. He grinned, proud to know a man who had helped capture Geronimo. It thrilled him that in some way, both he and Dooley shared a connection with the famous Chiricahua Apache leader.

"I might not a' liked them Injuns, but I always had respect for 'em. Once, we chased down a band of 'em. We'd killed all of 'em 'cept one. We chased him out onto the open prairie and surrounded him. Yessir, we tightened like a noose around that Injun." Dooley touched his mammoth thumbs and fingertips together in a gesture that suggested choking. "He'd already been shot a heap o' times. All of a sudden, he just stops and slides off his horse. Stands there with his arms a-folded 'cross his chest. Why, he was bleedin' like a stuck pig from his shoulder, his side, his leg. But he stands straight and tall like some kind of a king. Looks right past us like we wasn't even there. Flat out ignores us. Then he starts a-singing his tribe's death chant as if it was the onliest thing in the world on his mind. Well, sir, we dismounts, not making a sound.

We stands in a circle around him, hushed and stayin' at a respectful distance. That Injun's eyes never blinked, and his voice didn't never quaver. When he's done with his song, he stands ramrod still for a piece. Then he sways and sinks to the ground, dead."

For several minutes, Danny sat in silence, his eyes wide. In a subdued voice, he said, "I hope when my time comes, I die with courage and dignity."

Dooley nodded. "I think most people dies pretty much the same way they lives."

3

After supper one night, slurping stout black coffee that dripped down his mustache, Twigs asked Dooley the details about where he'd worked in years past. The more Dooley talked, the more Danny realized that Dooley might have been around South Texas long enough to have run across his uncles. He had resigned himself to the fact that his uncles were probably dead, and that even if they weren't, he would never find them. But the thought passed through his mind that, along with his biscuits, Dooley himself might be manna from heaven.

Danny interrupted Dooley. "Did you ever know any Irishmen that cowboyed? Shamus and Aidan O'Brien? It would have been several years ago."

Dooley stopped his work and stroked his whiskers. "There's a passel o' Irish down south now. San Patricio is pret' near all Irish. 'Course, you Irish ain't exactly famous for your cowboying skill." Dooley's voice trailed off. After a few seconds, he brightened. "But I knowed another Negro cowboy, though. Hell of a scout. Rode on one trail drive with a former Texas Ranger who'd once been an Indian scout. They got on real good." Dooley sucked down a mouthful of coffee. "Cattle rustlers is the reason the rancher hired him. The ranger, I mean. He helped get the whole damn herd all the way north. That's where them steers was put in railroad cars and shipped 'em out. Didn't lose a one to rustlers." Dooley shook his head at some unspoken recollection. "There was lots of tales told about that trail drive. Can't call the ranger's name, but I heard tell he was a character."

Danny, not connecting Dooley's response with his question, looked quizzically at him. Dooley saw the furrow in Danny's brow and got to the point. "My friend told me about a young Irish feller on that drive who—"

"Who *what?*" Danny leaned closer to Dooley.

"You kin to them folks you askin' about?"

Danny nodded. "My uncles. What happened to the Irishman?"

Dooley hesitated, then said in a lower voice, "One got snake-bit to death before they reached the Pecos River. A rattler, if I rememberin' right. There was stories about the drive bein' hexed from the get-go."

Danny blinked and a shudder passed through him. "Dooley, I had two uncles. Was there another Irishman on that drive? Besides the one that died? Danny's voice was barely audible.

The cook again shook his head. "Sorry, young feller. I don't know nothin' more than that."

"Then what about the old ranger? If he's still alive, he might know."

"Far as I know, he's still alive. Leastways that's what I heard tell. I can't say for sure as to his whereabouts. Could be living out on the land. Could be in the little town near where their spread was. I may have misremembered, but I can tell you the general vicinity." Dooley described to Danny where he thought it was, but then he cautioned, "Don't be settin' your hopes too high. You may not find him. You may not find *anything*."

"I know, Dooley, but I got to try, even if it don't make sense." Danny stared at the fire.

Dooley picked up a stick, poked at the fire, and listened to the crackling sound as the embers flew up. He tossed the stick on the renewed blaze and murmured, "Always seems like the greater a man's itch, the shorter his reach." He looked up at Danny. "But I was a young man once. I know how it is. So you do what you got to do, you hear?"

4

Aware now that his uncles might have been on a trail drive, Danny pestered Dooley for information about the long treks. "Dooley, my uncles would have come to Texas around the end of '85." Danny touched his fingertips in turn, silently counting. "But it could have been in the spring of '86."

Dooley shook his head. "Hmmm. Mighty bad year in Texas in '85. Mighty bad. The president—let's see, that woulda been Cleveland—ordered the cattle out of the Indian Territory. Texas grazing land was already crowded. Wasn't no room for the near half million more critters that done come our way. Then there was a prairie fire that fall. Burned up thousands of acres in the Panhandle like they was kindling. Yessir, it did. I lost some friends in that one."

Danny's stomach gripped. He saw mental images of his uncles and thousands of panicked, bellowing cattle perishing in the conflagration. "Must have been awful."

Dooley dipped into a kettle, sampled some fragrant beans, and then clanged the lid down. "And I tell you what, '86 wasn't no better. In January there come an ice storm that killed 150,000 head. Flat froze 'em to death. I heard tell it was so bad that Galveston Bay froze." Dooley frowned. "Yessir, them was two of the coldest winters ever, '86 and '87. Blizzards blowed cattle up against fences and froze 'em where they stood. They say when them cows exhaled, their breath froze into a solid block so heavy they couldn't raise their heads. Terrible droughts in '86 and '87, too. Lordy! Them uncles of yours chose a mighty pitiful time to come to Texas." He shook his head. "*Mighty* pitiful."

Danny nodded gloomily and sighed. *Sounds like the O'Brien luck.* Even he remembered the great winter storm of '86. It hit the entire country, leaving New York so bone-numbingly cold that he'd almost been glad he was at the Aid Society Home and not living in the tenement or on the street. An ironic thought crossed his mind: at the time, he had envied Uncle Shamus and Uncle Aidan for escaping the storm, for sailing to Texas where it was warm.

Dooley took note of Danny's desolate expression. "Here. Taste this," he insisted, and shoved a spoon in Danny's direction. It pained him to see the boy look so low. "I done always talked too much," he said.

"No. It's fine, Dooley. I asked." Danny licked the spoon. "Good," he said, trying to muster some enthusiasm. He handed the spoon back and changed the subject. "Dooley, tell me about stampedes." He knew that stampedes sometimes occurred on the YT.

The portly cook was more than glad for a new topic. "Lordy!" Dooley wiped his hands down the sides of his apron. "Stampedes—stompedes is what we call 'em— happen mostly on stormy nights, but *anything* can set off a herd at any time!" Dooley rolled his chocolate brown eyes. "A clap of thunder, a flapping rain slicker, a jackrabbit, the clatter of a tin cup, even a loud sneeze… and a herd that's stomped once or twice is likely to break again and again. All it takes is one or two animals being scared. It spreads through the herd like 'lectricity. Takes days to settle 'em down again. And even longer to round 'em up. Sometimes you never do find 'em all."

Dooley dumped some salt in another pot, tasted the stew, and then added some more. A rich, meaty aroma filled the air. "Say, did you know stampedin' cattle don't make no sound?"

Danny's skeptical look prompted him to explain.

"The ground thunders and rumbles like a train, but the animals themselves don't make no sound. And a stampedin' herd gives off mountains of dust and enough heat to blister a cowboy's face. Lord, it's dangerous! I seen *steers* get injured. Seen 'em get crippled. Even seen 'em get crushed by a spooked herd. The best riders tries to get ahead of the stomp so's they can slow the herd and turn it. Might use their slickers or even fire their guns. There's some, o' course, that holds that guns just spooks 'em more. Well, after three or four miles, them cattle begins to circle. Then they start to milling. A four-mile stomp in the heat can take fifty pounds off a steer. Yessir, I seen more than one rancher's profits run flat into the ground, like *that.*" Dooley snapped his fleshy fingers to show how fast a profit could disappear.

"But then it's safe? Once the herd starts milling?"

"Not hardly! That's when the real danger *begins*. You got scared animals packed together. Any cowboy gets jostled from his horse won't live to tell about it. Make a sieve outta him or turn him into buzzard food. Cowboys workin' in pairs keep talkin' or singin' to each other during a stomp. Soothing songs can help calm them critters. Hymns is a popular choice." Dooley grinned. "Anyway, that's how the hands knows they's both there. If there's silence or a riderless horse, it's a terrible bad sign." He raised his bushy white brows, and Danny leaned forward again to hear what was coming next. "I seen it happen once. On a drive up the Sedalia. When the dust settled, we knowed we was missing a man. Well, sir, when them critters separated out, all that was left of Ollie was the butt of his gun. He'd been ground to dust. Weren't even no clothes left. Dust to dust." Dooley exhaled heavily. He brushed his hands together as if removing dust from them. "Flat wouldna b'lieved it if I hadn't a-seen it with my own two eyes."

Danny fell back and let out what would have been a whistle, if any sound had come from his mouth.

5

Dooley told Danny tales of other stampedes, of successful and unsuccessful attempts to rescue animals from quicksand and bog holes, of men thrown and kicked by horses and charged by angry steers. He told Danny that the average trail drive had 1,500 to 3,000 head of cattle, with one cowboy for every 175 to 300 head of cattle. He explained that herds were no larger than 3,000 animals because that's how many could drink from a stream at the same time, and it took almost a mile of stream frontage for that many cows to drink side by side. It was important, he said, because thirsty cattle at the back would fight or injure the other animals to try to get to the water. Dooley recounted stories of men punished by the wind, the rain, and even, like the animals, frozen to death in blizzards. He described "days hotter than furnaces" that made it necessary to cool the horses' bits in water so the metal wouldn't burn their mouths.

"I ever tell you 'bout that prairie fire on the Goodnight Ranch?" Dooley asked, knowing full well that he hadn't. Before Danny could say no, Dooley held up both hands and chuckled. "Well, now, don't stop me if I have, 'cause *I* wants to hear the story again."

Danny grinned back and shook his head in mock disgust. He recalled hearing Bartlett order Cal, Ples, and other ranch hands to plow fire breaks on the ranges. It was a task they hated. They had to plow furrows in the stubborn ground in parallel rows seventy-five to two-hundred feet apart, and then burn the scrub and grass between them. Bartlett knew that if a fire broke out—and lightning could instantly set the terrain ablaze during a dry summer—there was at least a chance of saving the stock.

Dooley lodged his bulbous thumbs under his suspenders and began his story. "The Goodnight is a spread up in the Panhandle—you done already heard how huge it is. Well, one day a fire breaks out. Two waddies attacked it with slickers, wet gunnysacks, whatever they was in reach of. That pair was desperate to stop the fire from spreadin', but there wasn't no water in sight. So you know what they done did?" Danny waited, confident Dooley would answer his own question. "Shot the biggest steer and skinned him on one side. Tied ropes to two of its legs and dragged that bloody carcass on either side of the fire line 'til they quenched the flames. Yessir, those riders had to keep switchin' sides so they didn't scorch their horses' hooves. It stopped the fire, I hear. Like erasin' a slate." Dooley yawned, snapped his suspenders, and stretched his heavy arms. "Yessir, that's what I heard."

Danny mulled what Dooley had said, trying to decide if the story might be true, and if it was, if he could have handled the crisis with such presence of mind. *The cowboy's life. Endless eighteen- and twenty-hour days… days of black coffee and beans… with too little sleep… rubbing tobacco in your eyes to stay awake… too many punishing hours in the saddle… with unexpected crises thrown in for good measure. It's a hell of a life,* Danny thought. Then he realized, *Those who choose it wouldn't have it any other way.* He could see that in the men around him. Danny stared off in the distance. *Mr. Dunside felt that way about his life at sea and later about the railroad. Maybe it has to do with being part of something bigger than yourself.* His next thought was, *Will I ever feel like that?*

Danny glanced over at Dooley. His heavy eyelids had closed. His hands were clasped over his belly, and he was snoring peacefully. "Sleep," Danny said softly. "You've earned it, my friend."

TWENTY

1

The next night, Dooley stowed the last of the food and utensils, except for the coffee pot. He filled a blue enamel cup with the steaming liquid and grunted as he eased his large frame down beside the fire. Danny wandered over, hoping Dooley would share a story with him. He marveled that once Dooley settled in by the campfire, the coffee pot never seemed to run low.

Knowing what Danny wanted, and always ready for an attentive ear, the jovial Dooley patted the ground beside him and motioned for Danny to join him. "Say, you want to hear tell a story Boze once told me?"

Danny stretched out on the ground facing Dooley and leaned back on his elbows to listen.

"Boze once told me 'bout a feller name of Lemmons. He was a mustanger. He was black as Boze, but not like any mustanger you ever heard of. Lemmons mustanged by hisself, never with no one else."

"By himself?" Danny looked surprised. "Dooley, it ain't possible for one man to round up a herd." Danny knew that mustangs were not only wild, but they were sure-footed and had great stamina. It was those qualities that made the wiry, compact animals difficult to capture.

Dooley gingerly sucked in a mouthful of strong, hot coffee. "Yessir, Boze told me Bob Lemmons could tell the herd he was trackin' by its droppings! Didn't matter even if the manada was out of sight. A manada is what you call one of those there bands of wild horses. You want to know how well Lemmons knew the tracks of a manada he was followin'?" As was his habit, Dooley answered his own question without waiting for a response. "Well, sir, he could pick out them hoof prints even when they was mingled with another herd's! Even when the manada's tracks was crossed by the tracks of another manada."

Danny let out a low whistle, but then grinned. "You're lyin', Dooley!"

The cook shook his head. He appreciated a challenging audience. "Nosir! That man made them mustangs he was trackin' think he was one of 'em. Made hisself *into* a mustang. He rode the same horse the whole damn time. Wore the same clothes. Even stowed his victuals up in a tree 'til the smell of human had wore off. Then he went to work."

Dooley kept Danny waiting while he poured himself another cup of thick coffee.

The pungent odor was pleasing to Danny. "Nosir, Lemmons wasn't in no hurry. Boze said Lemmons would git closer 'n closer to the herd each day 'til finally he just made hisself part of it. Inside of another week, Lemmons would run off the stallion and take over. Then *he* was the stallion who was leading the mares. If another stallion tried to challenge him for the herd, why, he flat run 'em off. Then he set his sights on gainin' the trust of the lady hosses. He'd lead the herd to water and then take them to new ranges, just to see would they follow him."

"You sure Boze wasn't tryin' to put one over you on, Dooley? Mustangs following a man they think is a *horse? A stallion?*"

"That's the way I heared Boze tell it, and Boze always tell it straight. He said after Lemmons walked 'em down, he would begin slowly takin' the herd in the direction of home." Dooley moved his free hand in a slow arc in front of him. "Then when he gets close enough, the cowboys would open the gates of a make-do corral. Lemmons would break into a dead run. His herd would follow him right into the corral, just as pretty as you please!" Dooley snatched a handful of air to illustrate the animals' sudden capture. He shifted his bulk and settled back to sip more coffee. "Then, of course, it was up to Boze and other broncobusters to do the breakin'." Dooley reflected a moment. "Think about it," he said. "One man bringin' in a whole herd of wild horses all by hisself. Horses in as perfect a shape as when Lemmons first started trackin' 'em."

2

Danny lay in his bedroll that night staring at the stars and thinking about what Dooley had described. He closed his eyes, trying to envision Bob Lemmons transforming himself into a mustang so completely that the horses in the herd accepted him as their leader—even to the point of following him into captivity. *What did Lemmons's peculiar approach say about patience? About the ability to blend in?* Danny wondered. *What did it, along with Lemmons's uncanny ability to read the mingled tracks and droppings of a herd no longer in sight, say about paying attention to the smallest of details? And what about the other horses' willingness to follow an impostor into captivity just because that impostor had gradually worked himself into the group and gained their trust?* Danny sensed there was a lesson there, too. He drifted off to sleep thinking that there were lots of lessons in what Dooley had told him.

That night, Danny dreamed he was a mustang. But when he awoke, he wasn't sure whether he had been the stallion or simply one of the herd.

TWENTY-ONE

1

Danny thrived at the YT. He honed his abilities to ride and to handle a gun, and he learned about cattle and human nature. He learned from the books Mr. Wyatt let him read in the Big House. From the range hands he worked with, ate with, and lived with twenty-four hours a day, he learned the camaraderie that develops among men whose work binds them in common purpose. He luxuriated in the sense of security and comfort it brought him. He had earned their respect and friendship. They had earned his.

It was with an ache of regret that he approached the foreman after dinner one night. He doffed his hat and stood there, struggling with how to begin. Finally, he just plunged in. "Mr. Bartlett, I'll be leaving soon. The season's about over. And, well, Dooley told me about a man who might know something about my uncles—" Danny amended it softly, "—or uncle. I got to try again to find 'em. I plan to leave at the end of the month."

Bartlett knew that Danny queried every new hand and everyone who passed through the YT about his uncles. "If I was you, I reckon I'd do the same."

2

Something happened the week before Danny planned to leave that caused him to postpone his departure. It was a Saturday, in the early hours of the morning. Danny and three other cowboys were tending the herd, watching over the shifting sea of brown hides and pearlescent horns, and waiting for their replacements to arrive.

Bum was the first to become alarmed. Galloping over to Ples and then to Danny, the grizzled little man shouted through snaggled, yellow teeth: "Rain!" Pointing to cows and calves grazing complacently in a dried riverbed nearby, he screamed orders: "Get them outta there or they'll drown! Get 'em out *now!*" Then he bolted off to warn the other cowhands who were spaced around the periphery of the herd.

"Rain?" Danny shouted to Ples. Danny was puzzled. He noticed that the air had changed slightly and the clouds seemed to be moving a little faster, but other than that, there was no indication of anything out of the ordinary.

Ples spit tobacco juice and swore as he abruptly reined his horse and spurred it towards the cattle in the riverbed. "*Bad* rain!" Ples yelled back over his shoulder and signaled for Danny to follow him.

As they worked to move the stray cattle back toward the herd, Ples shouted, "Only fools or strangers try to predict the weather in Texas, but Bum's hardly never wrong. He senses change 'bout as fast as the animals do, way ahead of the rest of us. If he's right, what's comin' is a gully-washer. A sonofabitch that'd float an anvil. It can turn a dry riverbed back into a river in a matter of minutes. Makes the herd spooky." Ples circled behind a few errant animals, cracking a rawhide lariat to hasten them towards higher ground.

"Tighten your bandanna," he yelled to Danny, pointing to his neck. "Keeps the rain from going down your neck."

Danny was thinking *What rain?* when he felt the gusts of wind. Looking skyward he was stunned to see dark clouds rolling in from nowhere. They were amassing at a fearsome rate. Within minutes the temperature plummeted. The animals began shuffling uneasily and complaining loudly.

Then it began. Torrents of rain were unleashed from the sky. Spectacular lightning flashes were followed by deafening, staccato thunderclaps that caused the cattle to bellow in fear and threatened to set them into frenzied motion.

At the first lightning flash, the hands began stripping off their guns and metal spurs, and they covered their knives. As Ples divested himself of his spurs and his gun, he motioned for Danny to do the same. Despite their own agitation, the men scrupulously observed the cowboy custom of not swearing during a storm.

All the while, Ples kept moving, scanning the drenched and skittish animals, and trying to hold the herd together. He twisted in his saddle, trying to watch in every direction at once. Suddenly he raced towards the riverbed, which had now become a raging stream. Rain cascaded from the brim of his hat like a miniature waterfall, making it hard for him to see. On the third try, he managed to lasso a bawling, wild-eyed calf that had slid down the bank and was in danger of being washed away.

Just as Danny was thinking things couldn't be any worse, the hail began. Hailstones bounced and ricocheted off the ground like drops of water popping in one of Dooley's hot skillets. The pellets stung Danny wherever they hit. He angled his hat farther over his face. Still, it sounded to him as if a drummer were pounding on it. "The hail is worse than the cow splat that's been raining down on us!" he shouted to no one in particular. His words were lost in the din.

He had barely finished his sentence when the storm ceased almost as suddenly as it had begun. The wind calmed, and rays of shimmering sunlight pierced the leaden sky.

Twigs pointed upward and shouted, "Sundog!" In its wake, the storm had left a half rainbow. He shouted to Danny, "Folklore has it that there's turquoise in the wet ground at the end of it."

Danny and the others were too tired to respond, and there was still work to be done.

3

Other cowhands arrived to help, and within two hours, most of the strays had been rounded up and reunited with the herd. "We were plumb lucky," Twigs declared.

"If that thunder and sky-fire had commenced at night, it would have set off a stomp for sure. It would have took us a week to round them critters up again."

Mud-splattered, weary, and sodden, Bum, Ples, Danny, Cal, and Twigs turned their tired horses towards the corral.

"Never seen anything like that," Danny said half-aloud.

Ples didn't know whether he was referring to the storm or the rainbow. "I only seen it once before. It's scary, all right." They plodded on. "Did you know it's the number of flashes tells you it's a bad storm? Lots of folks think it's how bright the flashes are. But that don't mean nothing."

"The whole sky was lit up!" Danny shook his head, still in disbelief at what he had seen.

"Yup. You *know* it's a bad rain when the animals start linin' up by twos!" Twigs tipped his hat to pour the rainwater off. "I'm ready for dry clothes and hot grub."

As they drew closer to the bunkhouse and the cookhouse, Cal pointed to the chimney and frowned. "No smoke." It was a bad sign: it meant no supper was under way.

4

As they drew closer, it was apparent that something far more was wrong. Outside the kitchen door of the Big House, Bartlett's palomino stood with its reins down. The five cowhands loped over, although it was Twigs, the most senior man among them, who dismounted and walked to the door.

Dooley opened it. Behind him they could see Brody laid out on the kitchen table. Janie was sobbing. Aldonza had her arm around her, trying to comfort her. Bartlett stood to the side in quiet conversation with Logan Wyatt.

Danny slid off his horse and removed his hat. He walked to the door to wait for Twigs to emerge.

A few minutes later Twigs came out and closed the door softly behind him. "Lightning. Brody saw the sky start to darken. Ran to warn the Big House with the dinner bell and to get dry firewood."

Twigs told Danny and the others the rest of it. Janie heard the bell clanging and dashed out to gather clothes off the line. Aldonza began shutting and fastening the windows. Dooley headed for the barn to secure the milk cows and shoo the chickens inside the roost. With a load of wood in his left arm, Brody raised a metal bar in his other hand to strike the metal triangle one last time. At that instant Janie saw her father illuminated by lightning that arced from the ashen sky to the tip of the rod. She heard a crackling sound. Her father's hair stood on end.

What she could only imagine was the excruciating pain as the electrical current roared through his nerves, his arteries, his spine, his skin. How his heart had pounded in wild, erratic beats that were abruptly halted by paralysis.

The load of wood was flung to the ground as Brody's left arm went rigid. Janie saw the startled expression frozen on her father's face. After a few terrible seconds during which he appeared to be an apparition, he fell to the ground, bleeding. His wide-eyed gaze was unfocused and unseeing. When they opened the fingers of his other hand, which were clamped around the metal bar, they saw his palm bore a deep wound and was slashed with a bright crimson-and-black stripe of burned flesh. One shoe had exploded off; the other still clung to his foot but was shredded and singed.

Aldonza told Twigs that she had seen Janie struggle to make her legs move, but the girl had stood in the deluge, draped with wet laundry, transfixed by the sight of her father. Aldonza's screams brought Dooley running from the barn. She shoved Janie towards the house and held open the door as Dooley carried in Brody's body.

5

That evening, Brody was laid out in his small cook shack. Danny placed candles around him for a wake of sorts. The other cowhands doffed their hats, went in to pay their respects, and filed back outside.

"In honor of Brody, I done made sonofabitch stew for supper," Dooley announced. "He'd a-liked that, I think."

"What is it?" Danny had never heard of it.

"Well, sir, it's what you call a gen-u-ine delicacy: beef stew, but made with tongue, liver, testicles, and sweetbreads. Flavored up with hot sauce and marrow gut."

Danny blanched. "Testicles? Marrow gut? What's marrow gut?"

"Now you taste it 'fore you go decidin' it ain't no good." Dooley thought it better not to explain that the marrow gut was the half-digested food in the gut that connected the young steer's stomachs. "Yessir, I believe Brody woulda liked it," he repeated. "And I done cooked up cowboy beans, biscuits, and vinegar pie to finish it out."

Danny had to admit that the stew was better than he expected. "If I didn't know what was in this, Dooley, I'd say it was downright tasty."

Mr. Wyatt donated a bottle of whiskey, and after supper the hands downed a glass in Brody's name. Warmed by the alcohol and feeling maudlin, Danny sang Brody's favorite, plaintive songs. The others finished the evening with good-natured stories about Brody.

They buried Brody the next morning in the small YT cemetery. Logan Wyatt and Tom Bartlett spoke a few words, and then Mr. Wyatt directed Twigs, Squint, Danny, and Ples to lower the wooden box. Janie watched as her father was laid to rest alongside her mother and brother. Aldonza held Janie by the arm to steady her. Throughout the funeral, Danny watched her and shared her grief. He knew what it was like to lose both parents from your life.

6

Janie continued to look pale and drawn. She ate little and said almost nothing during the days that followed. Such grieving was to be expected, but it came as a surprise to the Wyatts when she told them, "I've made a decision. I'm grateful to you both, but I'm leaving the YT. Next week."

Logan and Aldonza Wyatt tried to dissuade her, but she was adamant. "I can't stay. There's too much sadness for me here."

The Wyatts realized they weren't going to talk her out of it, and acquiesced. Aldonza placed her hand on her heart. "If you change your mind, niña, you know you can always come back."

Janie nodded and thanked them.

She had a bit of money she had saved, as well as some Brody had set aside. The Wyatts gave her the pay they owed Brody, along with the use of a horse and saddle. Mr. Wyatt invited her to select any volumes she wanted from his first wife's collection. "No one else will be needing them, and I'll always be grateful for the hours you spent reading to Abigail. It was a great comfort to her."

Like the Wyatts, Danny had been shocked by Janie's decision. It was agreed that he would escort Janie as far as Anuncio, a day-and-a-half ride.

The next day, Mr. Wyatt beckoned to Danny. "O'Brien, you're going to be needing a horse, too. When you go to Anuncio, I mean."

Danny removed his hat. "Yes, sir." He had hoped that the ranch owner might lend him a horse for the trip.

The man stared at Danny for a long minute as if trying to make up his mind. Then he said, "You saddle up Diablo when it's time to for you to leave."

"Thank you, sir! I'm mighty grateful. I'll be real careful with him. And I'll tell the livery in Anuncio to take good care of him until he can be returned to the ranch."

Wyatt did not reply. He looked at Danny for another minute, then turned and rode off.

Two days later, Janie and Danny headed for the gate of the YT, the same gate that had greeted Danny in what now seemed a lifetime ago. Bartlett rode part of the way with them. "Keep moving due south," he told them. "Janie…" he started, but finding no words, he simply touched the brim of his hat instead.

She understood that he wished her well. "Thank you, Mr. Bartlett."

The foreman trotted his horse closer to Danny's. He lowered his voice. "The horse is yours, O'Brien. Compliments of Mr. Wyatt, with the understanding that you're not to say anything about it to anyone."

"But why—"

Bartlett held up a leather-gloved hand to silence him.

"He said that horse was as mean as they come, and it takes courage to break a horse like that." Then Bartlett repeated the first advice he had ever given Danny: "Keep both eyes open, O'Brien."

Danny nodded, barely able to comprehend the gift he'd just been given. "Yes! I will! Thank you! I mean, thank Mr. Wy—"

But Tom Bartlett had already turned his horse and was loping away.

7

Janie and Danny guided their horses through the chaparral, weaving their way among evergreen oaks, bramble bushes, and other thorny shrubs. A peregrine falcon soared in large, graceful loops in the brilliant blue sky. Only the squawking of some chochalacos interrupted the silence. Danny inhaled the clean, fragrant air. For the first time in months, there was no odor of cattle.

He waited for Janie to initiate conversation, and after several miles of silence, she began to talk. "Maybe things will be better in Anuncio."

"You scared?"

"Yes. But more scared of staying at the YT and spending my whole life there."

"What will you do in town? How will you live?"

Janie shrugged. Danny noticed that she was biting her lip. "Don't know. Live on the money I have until I can find work." She looked up at Danny. "What about you?"

"I'm going to try to find out what happened to my uncles. Dooley told me about a man and his brother that had some Irishmen on the trail drive they led after they quit their days as Texas Rangers. Only one brother's still alive, and he's old. Dooley thought he might know something."

When nightfall approached, Danny gathered kindling and built a fire beside a trickle of a stream. He chucked a stick at a lizard sleeping on a warm rock and it scurried off. A white-winged dove, sounding lonesome and forlorn, cooed in the distance.

Danny tried to make small talk. "Coyotes will be out soon," he said. He worried that he might have frightened her, so he volunteered, "At least they're not as mean as javelinas." They had been startled earlier by the appearance of several of the sharp-tusked animals. Danny continued to ramble, filling the strained silence. "They're as bad-tempered and mean as they look. They even graze on prickly pear." He glanced at Janie. *Why did I say that?* He saw her expression and castigated himself for his thoughtless chatter. "We'll be fine, of course."

They ate a simple meal and sat staring at the fire. After a while, Janie began to talk about her father's senseless death. Tears rolled down her cheeks. Then she dissolved into great, grief-stricken sobs. *"Why?"* she asked. "He was all I had left."

Danny thought about his own shattered family and his futile search for his uncles. "I don't think we ever find out why." He wanted desperately to give her what she needed but was unable to assuage her grief. "Janie, you got to try to just accept things. Even if you don't understand 'em." The words he offered sounded empty even to him. *I haven't accepted what's happened to my own family.*

Janie's sadness seemed unbearable to him. He drew her close and stroked her hair. It had the same faint lilac fragrance he remembered from the first day in the Big House kitchen.

Janie leaned closer to him. *He's suffered losses, too,* she thought. *Ones worse than mine. At least I know what happened to my family*—and with a twinge of bitterness and regret—*even if it only means knowing where they're buried.*

In an action that surprised even him, Danny turned Janie's face towards his and kissed her. She withdrew but gazed at him and studied his face with earnest curiosity. He felt the heat of passion flow through him, but the sorrow in her eyes tempered it. He pulled her close to him again, and she laid her head against his chest. He wanted to kiss her once more, but knew the moment was wrong. She had said it when they left the YT: "too much sadness."

The moon cast a glow over the South Texas plains, smoothing the rugged clumps of chaparral into soft, indistinct silhouettes. Janie leaned back against Danny, crossing her arms over his, and they sat in silence staring at the stars. The stillness was broken only by the soothing sound of the wind blowing through the brush.

Danny finally spoke. "My father... my uncles... my sister. Wherever they are, they look at the same sky and the same moon. Maybe they wonder where I am, too." *Are they looking for me? Is anybody looking for me?* he wondered.

Janie's eyes filled with tears again. "It's a great comfort to think so." Her voice dropped to a whisper. "It's too lonely, otherwise."

Danny held her tighter. "You'll always have a place in my heart, Janie McCorkle. And from now on, wherever I am, whenever I look up at the moon, I'll think of you and wonder if you're looking at it, too." *And thinking of me*, he tacitly finished the thought.

Tears began to trickle down her face again. Danny held her, stroking her hair, until she finally fell asleep.

8

The next morning, they ate a few of Dooley's biscuits and set out again for Anuncio. By the time they reached the town, Danny was questioning whether he should leave Janie.

Janie obtained the name of a rooming house from Mrs. Bradford, the wife of a storeowner. The large, plain-looking rooming house was their next stop. Danny carried Janie's belongings inside.

"Janie, I could stay for a few days if—"

"No. I appreciate what you've done for me, Danny. But you have family you need to find. You won't ever feel right until you know." She smiled. "Besides, you aren't one for staying in the same place too long."

Danny took a piece of paper out of his vest pocket. "I told you about Mrs. Bromley and Johanna. You ever need anything—*anything*—you get in touch with me through them. If you need help, go there." He handed her Mrs. Bromley's name and address. He gave her a sheepish grin. "They already know about you. I wrote them from the YT."

Danny kissed her cheek. He pressed his hands over his heart and in an exaggerated brogue declared, "Remember, lass, that you have a place in my heart forever."

Janie shook her head at his theatrics, but she touched his face with her fingertips. She walked outside with him. She said nothing, for fear she might start to cry again.

With an easy grace, Danny swung into Diablo's saddle. "I got a trail driving ex-ranger to find. Wish me luck, Janie."

She smiled and handed him a small purple flower she plucked from a vine growing beside the gate. He twirled the slender stem in his fingers, tucked the flower in his hatband, and tapped Diablo with his boots.

On the way out of town, he stopped at Bradford's Mercantile. He told the gap-toothed, gray-haired Mrs. Bradford that Janie had taken her belongings to the rooming house she recommended. He bought a gold heart-shaped locket. He started to put the small package in his pocket, but instead handed it back to the woman. "I'd be grateful if you'd give this to Miss Janie McCorkle the next time she comes into the store. Give it to her for me. Tell her it's from Danny."

Mrs. Bradford managed a curt nod. "I'll see she gets it." She wrote Janie's name on a piece of paper and placed it and the locket in a small drawer behind the counter.

As soon as Danny left, she turned to another woman who was standing nearby. "Humph! Now I wonder just exactly what kind of unmarried young lady, Aggie, comes into town escorted by a man who buys her a present on his way out."

The customer pursed her lips and raised her eyebrows. "I think we *both* know."

TWENTY-TWO

1

When Helga awoke, she had no idea where she was or whether, in fact, she was alive. She wondered, *Is this was what it's like to be dead? If it is, it's better than living with the Dills.*

She lay on a strange bed, her head elevated, with a fresh white sheet draped over her. She raised her arms and looked at them. They were covered with scratches, cuts, and bruises, and it hurt to move them. She could tell she had been bathed, and when she brought fingertips close to her face, she could detect the pleasing scent of soap. She dropped her arms on the sheet and stroked the smooth cotton with her fingertips.

She scanned the room anxiously from where she lay. She was afraid to get out of bed or make any noise. *Where am I?* She surveyed the room more slowly. The walls were white. There were bowls and utensils on the table beside her. There was a clean, antiseptic smell—not at all objectionable—and other smells she could not identify. Her eyes drifted to a glass-front cabinet filled with rows of neatly labeled bottles. The window had a green shade that had been pulled down. Lace curtains gave the illusion that large, delicate snowflakes floated in front of the shade. She exhaled slowly and began to relax a bit.

At that moment, the door opened softly and a tall man walked in. Helga froze. Her breath caught in her throat as she suppressed a yelp. She pretended to close her eyes but peeked at the man as he raised the window shade a few inches. He wore a full, gray mustache and had ruffled gray hair.

When he approached the bed, Helga reacted instinctively to shield herself. Her arms flew up to form an X in front of her face, and she found her voice. "No! Not again!" Suddenly she could feel hot tears running down her cheeks. She turned her head aside. "Not again. Please, not again," she whimpered.

The man sat down on a tall stool beside the bed but made no move to touch her. "You're safe," he said in a calm voice. He allowed her a moment to compose herself. Then he asked, "Who did this to you?"

Helga's eyes filled with wonder at the sound of his German accent. Her father's voice was the last one she had heard that sounded like that. She lowered her hands to look at him, but she remained silent.

He pursued a different tack. "I'm Dr. Ohlmsted. You've been... through a bad experience." He straightened up and crossed his arms in front of his chest, then leaned farther back from her. "No one will hurt you again. Mrs. Lowell is going to bring you some soup." The cadence of his native language skipped and bobbed in his English. He gave Helga a slight nod, then stood and left the room.

As if responding to some unseen signal, an older woman whose gray braids wreathed her head appeared with a tray. On it was a bowl of steaming broth, a spoon, and a napkin. With a look of a hungry animal, Helga sat up and snatched the bowl, splashing drops of the hot liquid on the sheet and down her front. She tilted the bowl, winced as it touched her split lip, and sucked the liquid down. Mrs. Lowell's eyebrows rose in amazement, but she said nothing. She left and returned with the bowl filled again. Although Helga did not look directly at her, she did not grab the bowl this time. Mrs. Lowell sat quietly beside the bed as Helga finished the second bowl of broth.

"Sleep now," instructed Mrs. Lowell, her voice echoing the same Germanic inflections as her brother's. The warm broth began to ease the pain low in Helga's belly, and she grew drowsy again. She stared at the window as the magical pattern of lace-curtain snowflakes dissolved into a soft, blurry glow. Then Helga drifted off into peaceful sleep for the first time since she was a young child.

2

Nearly twelve hours elapsed after Helga wrapped herself in a cocoon of sleep. When she awoke, Mrs. Lowell came in and raised the shade on the window. Light streamed through the panes and filtered through the lacy curtains, creating a soft pattern of shadows on the floor.

"Where am I?" Helga was startled by the sound of her own voice. It sounded like a rusty door hinge.

"You're in San Antonio. This is Dr. Ohlmsted's home—and also his office. I'm his sister, Elisabeth Lowell. I help the doctor with his patients." Helga's eyes skipped anxiously around the room, resting briefly on each unfamiliar and frightening looking instrument. Mrs. Lowell disappeared and returned with a tray.

"How did I get here?" Helga asked, as if there had never been a break in the conversation.

While Helga ate, Mrs. Lowell busied herself arranging instruments and bottles on a shelf. "You were found lying beside the road just outside of Salt Box. You were hemorrhaging." Seeing that Helga did not understand, she said, "You were bleeding very badly. The man who found you put you in his wagon and brought you into San Antonio. There isn't a doctor in Salt Box. There hasn't been one since Dr. Fraser passed away four years ago." Helga knew vaguely that doctors were supposed to help people who were sick, but she had never seen a doctor or been to a doctor's office.

Dr. Ohlmsted appeared in the doorway. He waited until his sister finished talking and then came in and sat down beside the bed. "What's your name, child?" His voice was kind.

"Helga." She gave him two monotone syllables, no more. She wound a lock of hair around her finger, twisting it nervously.

"Helga what?"

Helga shook her head and looked down at her food, unwilling to say lest she be sent back to the Dills. Dr. Ohlmsted turned to his sister, and in German asked, "What should we do? We can't locate her family if we don't know her name."

Thinking he meant the Dills, Helga screamed, *"Nein!"* and continued in German, "They are *not* my family! I won't go back!" Then she whimpered, "Please, please!"

The shock of hearing the battered girl speak in German registered on both of their faces simultaneously. For several seconds, they simply stared in silence at her and then at each other.

"Did someone in *that* family do this to you?" Dr. Ohlmsted gently touched her bruised face. He curled his lips in disgust. He thought how much she resembled a small, broken bird.

This time Helga glanced at his eyes and answered his question. "Yes." It was barely more than a whisper.

"You do not have to go back to such people," he asserted. "Will they be looking for you?"

She shook her head no. "They hate me. They hurt me."

"You will stay here until we can decide what is to be done."

3

Weeks went by. Helga remained with the Ohlmsteds, growing stronger each day.

"What if we say she's our niece? She's regaining her German very rapidly."

Wil Ohlmsted rested his chin on his clasped hands and considered his sister's suggestion.

Elisabeth pressed, "No one saw her arrive that night. No one knows she's here."

After a moment, he nodded. "She says her parents and a sister are dead, that she has an older sister, but has not seen her in several years and does not know where she is. Her injuries are healing. We don't know which family she was living with. Even if we did, I would never return her to such barbaric people. They do not deserve to have children."

Whenever he looked at Helga, the doctor found his thoughts turning to his own young son. His child and his beloved wife had perished in the 1878 yellow fever epidemic in Victoria. Of the family of three, only he had survived. His widowed sister, Elisabeth, had urged him to join her in San Antonio, to start a new life. Not long after, he had accepted her invitation. He left the coastal town and submerged his grief in his work.

When Helga was well enough, the doctor took her out of town under cover of darkness and returned the next morning as if he had gone to pick her up. He and his sister had no trouble passing Helga off as a relative. She called the couple "Tante Elisabeth" and "Onkel Wil" and, indeed, began to think of them as relatives from the Old Country. Helga listened to Elisabeth tell of her life and Wilhelm's in Germany, and for several weeks, Helga insisted that Elisabeth tell her the same story each night.

"Child, you must be tired of this story!" Elisabeth said to Helga one evening.

"No. But you can tell me more stories. Other stories."

Helga soaked them up like dry earth absorbing rain. "No," she would shake her head, "don't stop!"

So for several months Elisabeth continued to recount stories of her family's early life until Helga, like the rain-saturated ground, had drunk her fill of Elisabeth's memories.

Helga's own memories of Germany were fragile and few, so she adopted Elisabeth's. Helga recounted to Elisabeth and the doctor her sketchy recollections of Germany and her voyage on the ship, then more vivid memories of her life in the New York tenement and at the Home, and finally, the train trip west. Eventually, she began to reveal fragments of her more immediate, painful past. She told them in broken tones and choppy episodes her experiences with the Dills.

Dr. Ohlmsted realized that Helga was aware of neither her pregnancy nor her miscarriage. He learned that she was approximately thirteen, although she herself did not know for sure, and was unable to tell him her birth date. The doctor and Mrs. Lowell slowly pieced into a coherent whole the shards of Helga's life as she spilled out details of her mother's and father's deaths, her separation from her sisters, and her life with the Dills.

Ultimately, her anger and pain gave way to grief over her losses. Many nights, Mrs. Lowell comforted Helga when she was sad and soothed her when she woke up terrified from a nightmare. After a few months, the sadness, bitterness, and pain began to fade.

It was then that Helga began to make up for lost time, filling in innumerable social and educational deficits. She started slowly in school. At the doctor's insistence, she was placed with the younger children. Her progress was unusually swift since the teacher and most of the other students in the small school were German. Within months, Helga was fluent in both German and English. Elisabeth read to Helga at night and listened to her read aloud. The doctor helped her with her arithmetic.

During her first weeks at the doctor's home, Helga ate so much that it concerned the doctor and his sister. Even when she was uncomfortably full, Helga slipped food into her pockets and hid it in her room. When Elisabeth found a cache of shriveled fruit and stale rolls stashed in a drawer, she confronted Helga. "Why are these in your room?"

Even though Elisabeth's tone was kind, Helga's eyes went large with fear. "Come with me, Helga." Even though Elisabeth had never so much as spoken harshly to her, Helga stiffened, awaiting punishment. She followed Elisabeth silently into the kitchen. Elisabeth pointed to a shelf. "Get that basket, please."

Helga did as she was told. She remained apprehensive and silent.

Mrs. Lowell opened the larder. "You can have as much food as you want, whenever you want it." She began filling the basket Helga was holding. When it was full, Helga looked solemnly and suspiciously at Elisabeth, and then quickly retreated to her room. Two days later, Mrs. Lowell noticed that the basket was back on the shelf and that the food had been put back. She also noticed that Helga no longer gorged at meals.

Even so, Helga slowly gained weight. Her sunken cheeks filled in, and her dark hair took on a luster. Her fuller face, along with her frequent smiles and laughter, reflected her burgeoning health and happiness.

Helga liked to watch Elisabeth prepare the hearty meat and potato dishes that left Elisabeth, but not her brother, plump. Although she helped Elisabeth knead potato bread, mix funnel cake batter, and pare apples for apple dumplings, cooking—other than measuring the ingredients—didn't interest Helga. She was happy simply to eat Elisabeth's baked ham and to savor her molasses pie, raisin pie, and corn pudding.

From the beginning, it was apparent to Elisabeth that Helga was more interested in the kitchen equipment than in cooking. In particular, Helga was fascinated by the Great Majestic stove that dominated the cheerful, aromatic kitchen. She quickly acquired the knack of starting the kindling on the first try. Then she added logs until the stove radiated and shimmered with heat. With practice, she mastered what many women were never able to become adept at: to estimate accurately the heat of the six burners. She could see that their temperature depended on the distance from the firebox. She learned how to turn food at regular, precise intervals so that it cooked evenly in the cavernous oven. Each week Elisabeth watched as Helga meticulously applied blacking to the cast-iron behemoth.

Every afternoon, Helga hurried from school back to Dr. Ohlmsted's house. She loved the beautiful exterior. It stood in distinct contrast to the practical, antiseptic interior. After his wife and son died, the doctor had preferred more austere, impersonal surroundings, and his sister had understood.

A small, neatly lettered plaque beside the front door announced, "Dr. Wilhelm Ohlmsted." The outside of the house, however, reflected the same love of color that his sister had shared with his wife. Rust and ochre, and deep red and green imparted a welcoming warmth to the house. There were decorative shingles, ornate porch railings, turrets, lace-cloaked bay windows, an elaborate white picket fence, and a cast-iron hitching post. Elisabeth took particular pleasure in the front door: it held inset squares of colored, translucent glass that threw rich, ever-changing designs on the floor when the sun shone through. Viewed from the outside at night, the panels were illuminated from behind and sparkled like jewels.

Each day a stream of patients trickled into the front parlor that served as the waiting room. The room in which Helga had first awakened had once been the dining room but had long since been transformed into an examining room. It also doubled as the doctor's operatory when surgery was called for.

In the afternoons Helga helped oversee the waiting room, allowing Mrs. Lowell to spend more time assisting the doctor. But it was the other room that inspired both fascination and fear in Helga. The examining room held white, wooden, glass-paneled cabinets, and a table with drawers filled with instruments and bandages. On the table stood a microscope, a clock, and white, rectangular enamelware pans of varying sizes. A metal stand held two circular enamel basins and a pair of towels. A swing-away table on a pedestal base that held a stethoscope and other instruments stood next to the examining table. The wooden table was draped with a white sheet; a small pillow rested at the adjustable end. In the corner of the room was a hall-tree whose branches held the doctor's umbrella, overcoat, and lantern. At its foot rested his black medical bag. The light from the window and the electric ceiling light washed the white-walled room in brightness. Helga loved the clean, spartan simplicity. She marveled that she ever had been surprised by the electric lights or startled and puzzled by the ringing "telephone" box on the wall.

Eventually Helga began helping the doctor when Mrs. Lowell was unavailable, and then she took over the end-of-the-day tasks. She discovered that she much preferred re-shelving vials of medicines, rolling bandages, and washing and replacing utensils to helping in the kitchen. Helga began appearing earlier in the afternoons and on Saturdays, observing Dr. Ohlmsted treat young patients whenever he allowed her to. When he needed assistance and Elisabeth was busy, Helga volunteered.

Helga's fascination with medical procedures developed slowly. Initially she had been terrified. The doctor found himself wondering if her absorption and fear stemmed from witnessing the hog butchering at the Dills, a traumatic introduction to knives and flowing blood.

Once, when he was pondering this, he heard his sister ask, "Should she be allowed to see patients' injuries, Wil? Do you think it's wise? It may be too upsetting." He could hear the concern in Elisabeth's voice.

Dr. Ohlmsted considered the question thoughtfully, as he did any important matter. He leaned back in his desk chair and closed his weary eyes, rubbing them with his thumb and forefinger. Then he said, "I think Helga's interest comes from her desire to see suffering lessened, perhaps because of her own painful experiences. And because she is young herself, she makes children feel less frightened. I discovered that when she came in to calm the Bruners' little daughter so that I could remove a nail from her foot."

The doctor opened his eyes and sat up a little straighter. "But we'll proceed slowly, I promise. Helga says she wants to help, so I'll let her help with children's minor injuries. But if working with patients upsets her or affects her appetite or her sleep, I will *forbid* her to enter the examining room." Elisabeth knew her brother would not deviate from his word.

At the moment, the apothecary room at the back of the house was Helga's favorite room. She loved the milky glass jars that stood at attention in perfect rows. Graceful black script on gold ovals announced the contents of each jar. A set of scales and weights and a mortar and pestle rested on the compounding table. There were chemicals, powders, and medicinal herbs. Neatly stacked papers, cellophanes, small stoppered vials and bottles stood ready to receive slippery salves, soothing syrups, strengthening tonics, tinctures, decoctions, and eyewashes that the doctor formulated. One of his proudest possessions was the McCarty Label Cabinet that he had ordered from Philadelphia. Through slots, marked and gummed labels emerged from rolls inside the small drawers that held them. These he extracted and pasted on the containers. Patients knew to keep their bottles, vials, and corks for refills, and to bring them whenever they came to see him.

It became Helga's task to keep the rows of bottles in the strict alphabetical order that Dr. Ohlmsted required: acacia, acetic acid, aloes, alum, ammonia water, ammonium carbonate, assafoetida. The names themselves soothed her as they rolled off her tongue: hydrochloric acid, tannic acid, and tartaric acid. She slid each container into its proper place. Some of the cloudy jars held pain-relieving morphine, opium, ether, and chloroform. Others held more mundane medical provisions such as castor oil, olive oil, camphor, quinine, and senna. A bottle of yellow-green liquid held soap made from potash and olive oil. There was also silver nitrate, digitalis, canthracides, and brandy—although Helga secretly wondered about the brandy.

Helga talked to herself as she worked, reviewing what she had learned. For the row that contained herbs: "Caraway and chamomile for digestion. Chamomile for arthritis, too. Hawthorn for heart failure. Willow bark—make into tea for headaches. Borage, comfrey, echinacea. Elecampane for bronchial problems and coughs." She read the names on the jars aloud as she placed them in alphabetical order: "…feverfew, foxglove, germander… horehound, hyssop, mullein, salvia… valerian, wormwood, and yarrow." She liked the sounds of the words. More importantly, each one seemed to offer some hope of healing, and Helga barraged the doctor with questions about all of them.

In the evenings, Dr. Ohlmsted showed Helga how to mix and blend the compounds and medications he prescribed most often. "Tonight I'll show you how to make pills," he promised. He demonstrated to her how to compound a stiff paste and extrude it through the row of openings in a hand-held device. "Now, you use this to slice across the end of the rows that stream out"—he picked up a smooth blade—"and you will have produced pellets that harden into pills." He inspected his efforts and was pleased. Under his scrutiny, Helga practiced until she could make pills that were as perfect and uniform as his.

On another occasion, he showed her how to regulate the dosage of powders. "We do it by using evenly sized seashells. They have to be bleached and sterilized first, of course." Helga liked the doctor's intensity and concentration when he worked. At that moment, his whole universe was the row of shells lined up in front of him. "Powdered medication is poured or tamped into a set of small- or medium-sized shells." His actions illustrated his narrative. "And the shells are sealed over with paraffin. The patient scrapes away the wax and adds the powder to a liquid." He held up a finished shell. Helga marveled at the ingenuity of it. "Now, you try making some." He placed the powder, shells, and paraffin in front of her.

The apothecary room adjoined a small chamber that served as the doctor's study. The myriad drawers of his heavy rolltop desk hinted to Helga of all kinds of treasures and surprises. A large, deep, leather chair beckoned to anyone who walked by. Dark, wooden bookcases with glass fronts sheltered the doctor's well-used medical volumes. Helga especially liked the smell of the room: the leather, the polished wood, the books. In the corner stood a complete human skeleton. More than once Helga had run her fingers over a rib or touched the skull and contemplated the set of bones. *Who were you? What kind of life did you live? How did you die? How did you become a doctor's skeleton instead of being buried? Did you have a family?*

Through the doctor, Helga met Dr. Ferdinand von Herff, a German surgeon in San Antonio who had become famous while still in his twenties. "He is a brilliant man, Helga. There is much that all of us can learn from him," Wil told her. She relished Dr. von Herff's visits and plied him with questions to the point that Dr. Ohlmsted sometimes found it necessary to "excuse" her so that he and Dr. von Herff could finish their talk.

Von Herff had, in fact, performed the first hysterectomy in the country and the first cataract surgery in Texas. In his home he had created a center for advanced research in surgery and pathology, and he had investigated treatments for tuberculosis. He had performed restorative surgery on disfigured patients. Although his gray hair was now sparse, he was bedecked with a splendid, full mustache and beard, and he looked upon the world through small, oval, wire-rimmed spectacles. Dr. von Herff had helped develop licensing programs for young Texas doctors, and it was because of this remarkable doctor and her Onkel Wil that the idea of becoming a nurse first entered Helga's head.

4

When Elisabeth suffered a stroke a year later, Helga continued to attend school in the morning, but came home early each afternoon to care for her and assist the doctor. In her room at night, Helga pored over medical books she borrowed from his bookcases. She would visit "Bones," the skeleton, and recite to him the names of each of his segments.

Elisabeth's condition deteriorated imperceptibly at first, but then it accelerated. One evening, as Helga and the doctor sat on either side of Elisabeth's bed recounting the day and the patients they had seen, Elisabeth signaled that she wanted something. Using her "good hand," the one not impaired by the stroke, she reached for Helga's hand and placed it near her heart. Then she took her brother's hand and placed it over Helga's. Finally, she placed her hand over both of theirs and squeezed them. In the recesses of her mind, Helga saw herself at the train station, with Johanna placing her sisters' tiny hands together and clasping her own over theirs. The thought hit her like a jolt: *It was the last time I ever saw Johanna.*

Zusammen! Helga cried suddenly. "We must stay together, Tante Elisabeth."

But Elisabeth could no longer hear her. Her eyelids had drifted shut, and she had a serene look on her face.

Helga rested her head on the bed beside Elisabeth and sobbed. Dr. Ohlmsted walked around to her and placed a hand on her heaving shoulder. "Elisabeth's at peace now. And we'll be all right. We still have each other."

TWENTY-THREE

1

Danny surveyed the room while the aging ex-ranger poured himself a cup of coffee. His eyes came to rest on two faded photographs, in plain frames, tacked to the wall. One showed the ranger standing behind a woman who was seated in a chair. His hand rested on her shawl-draped shoulder. The other photograph showed two men astride horses, the ranger and a younger man with the similar features. Danny wondered if it was his brother, but he refrained from walking over to look more closely. The ranger seated himself at the table and gestured for Danny to do the same.

The ranger cradled his cup in gnarled but powerful hands, rubbing his thumb slowly back and forth over the curve of the handle. Then he began to talk. "Your uncle died from being snake-bit by a diamondback. A rattler." In his mind, the ranger could still hear Shamus's startled cry, could see the two puncture wounds on his hand that seeped blood and urine-colored venom. Saw his hand and arm quickly swell and become discolored with mottled blotches. Saw the blood blisters form and rupture. Remembered Shamus's tongue bulging and later, his gums beginning to bleed. He could still picture all too clearly the vomiting, sweating, and chills, and Shamus's eyes rolling back in his head, but the old man kept these recollections to himself. Instead, he took a deep breath and sighed. "Aidan was off gathering wood. I saw Shamus collapse. I held him until he died." The ranger paused at the memory: Shamus had gone into convulsions just before dying. "I had a boy who died young, of a fever. If he'd lived, he'd have been the same age as your uncle then—nineteen."

The blood drained from Danny's face. He closed his eyes and sank back against the hard chair. *When Shamus died, he was only a little older than I am now.* He had always thought of Shamus as a man, not a boy. He'd always thought he'd be glad, or at least relieved, to know his uncles' fates. Now he wasn't sure. *What was it Dilue had said? Sometimes it's better not to know.* Danny tried at first not to imagine the scene when his uncle died but found it impossible. He closed his eyes to hold back a tear. *At least Shamus didn't die alone,* he comforted himself. After several seconds Danny opened his eyes. He cleared his throat, but his voice was hoarse and dry. "Tell me what happened."

The older man began to spell out details. "You wouldn't have figured it would happen this way. They'd only just joined the drive. We were still following the Pecos River. It was dusk, and we'd called it a day. Shamus sat down on a fallen tree near the

river and took off his boots. Said he was going to wade in the water." The old man
thoughtfully sucked down a mouthful of steaming coffee. "There was a rattlesnake
under the log." To give Danny time to absorb the implication, he began mumbling
about snakes instead of continuing with the story: "Snakes don't like the sun. If the
weather's too warm, they spend their days under logs, in holes, and in rock piles. They
only come out after sunset. They look for rabbits, rodents, lizards, and such..."

Danny had heard nothing the old man said after the word rattlesnake. "A rattler
hit my uncle's foot?"

The ranger shook his head and repeated his words. "You wouldn't have figured
it would happen this way. No, the snake hit his *boot*. Your uncle leaped off the log.
Barton Riley shot the snake on the spot and held it down with his foot behind its head
while another man chopped its head off. The hindmost part of the snake kept twisting
and moving, and its mouth opened and closed a time or two. They do that, you know."
He looked up at Danny, whose eyes were riveted on him. The ranger looked down at
his cup again. "Well, your uncle walked back over and before anyone could even yell,
he reached down to pick up the snake's head. That's when it bit him. Bit him between
his thumb and his forefinger." He held up one hand and with the other pointed to the
spot.

Danny leaned forward. "But you said the snake was dead." His voice rose at the
end of his words.

"It *was* dead, but a rattler can still bite for while after it's dead. Like I said, you
wouldn't have figured it would happen that way."

Danny propped his elbows on the table and then slumped forward, gripping his
head in his hands. The ranger thought he heard him mutter something about "the
O'Brien luck," and then Danny sank back into his chair.

After a minute the old man spoke up again. "Your uncle died brave." Then he
answered a question that Danny had not yet thought to ask. "We buried him beneath a
hackberry tree beside the river." He drank the last of his coffee and, rising, shoved the
cup aside. The ranger rambled on to fill the uncomfortable silence. "They used to say
there's just two things cowboys feared: the Pecos River and rattlesnakes." He stood
leaning against the table, his hands pressed flat on it, and stared at the empty cup.

"What about Uncle Aidan?" Then Danny had second thoughts. He wasn't sure
he wanted to know if it meant finding out that Aidan was dead, too.

"I can't say for sure. He finished the drive with us. He was sorely grieved. Never
said much after that, but he sang sorrowful Irish tunes all the way to the Wyoming
Territory and back. He took off just as soon as we got back to Texas. Didn't say where
he was going."

Danny was thinking of Brody and his doleful ballads when the ranger smiled.
"Matter of fact, it was on account of their singing that the outfit I was with ran across
your uncles in the first place." He eyes twinkled at the remembrance. "Trail boss knew
we needed more hands. When we were trailing along beside the Pecos, we heard
voices wailing an Irish song. We followed the sound and over the next rise, we spotted
two men wandering along. When we got closer, we could see that they were sun-
baked. They were pitiful thin. Their clothes were torn, and their hair was matted. We
were smack in the middle of nowhere, and I couldna've been more surprised if I'd
encountered Moses and the Israelites. Come to find it was your uncles. They told us

about making it to shore after the ship went down." He chuckled. "A bedraggled lookin' pair, they were, but we signed them on. They said that they'd be happy to be as far as possible from the ocean for a while. Said they'd floated around in the gulf for two days before they washed ashore. All I could figure was that they must have followed the Rio Grande and then wandered up the Pecos. It's a tributary, you know. They were eager to see some of the country and make some money, but they made it clear that as soon as the drive ended, they were heading for Galveston." The ranger laced his fingers across his chest and leaned back in his chair. "I'm mighty glad they joined us. Good men, both."

Danny nodded in agreement and appreciation. Then he recounted his experiences with cattle on the YT, of Brody and his nightly serenades, and of Brody's death. The ranger listened with interest, for he'd heard tales of the sprawling YT. Then he asked Danny, "You plan to stay with cowboying?"

Danny shook his head. "No."

"Can you handle a rope and a gun?"

"Yes."

"Well, it's clear you can handle a horse." The ranger had noticed Diablo when Danny first rode up.

Danny gave a single, modest nod. Astride a horse, he always felt taller, stronger, larger.

"You hungry?" It was already midday.

Danny hesitated, suddenly aware that he might have overstayed his welcome. He also realized that he was hungry. *I must look as if I'd welcome any food that was put in front of me,* Danny thought.

"I got some beans and bacon." The ranger placed a pan on the stove where the coffee pot had been and threw another piece of wood into the belly of the stove. He fussed with the beans for several minutes until he was satisfied they were hot enough. The odor made Danny's stomach growl in anticipation.

"Tell me about the rangers," Danny said as the man ladled up two platefuls of beans.

The old ranger captain tore off a crust of bread and sopped it in the hot beans. "It started with Stephen F. Austin needing some men to protect his colony. That was near three-quarters of a century ago. They 'ranged' the area around the colony to keep it safe from Mexican bandits and Indians. I heard once their wages was fifteen dollars a month, but most of 'em did it purely voluntary. Returned to their day-to-day doings after each emergency." The corners of his mouth turned up in a faint smile. "The pay sure ain't improved much over the years, but I'd bet my hat that if need be, every last man would still do it voluntary, even today."

The ranger shoveled more beans into his mouth. "A half century ago, after the war against Mexico, a ranger captain bragged that his men could 'ride like Mexicans, track like Indians, shoot like Tennesseans, and fight like the devil.'" With unmistakable pride the old ranger thumped the table. "And that's *still* a pretty fair description."

He poured more coffee and set the pot back on the stove. "In '40, San Antonio was established as the Ranger headquarters. In '41, they introduced the Colt to the West—or maybe I should say they introduced the West to the Colt. The Colt Paterson 5-shooter, that is."

Danny suddenly felt even prouder that he owned a Colt.

The older man ate several mouthfuls of beans, talking between and through bites. "During the War Between the States, there was a whole cavalry of rangers led by General B. F. Terry. It was the 8th Texas Cavalry, but everyone called them 'Terry's Texas Rangers.' Two-thirds of 'em gave their lives for the Confederacy, but I can guarantee they put up one hell of a fight first."

The old man was about to move his story forward another quarter century but digressed. "Did you know that Robert E. Lee came to Texas with General John Wool's army during the Mexican War? You said you once lived in San Antone. Did you know that Lee later commanded a regiment there? He lodged at the Menger part of the time."

Danny nodded. He had passed the Menger Hotel countless times; it was only a few hundred yards from the Alamo.

"I've spent some time at the Menger myself." The ranger arched one eyebrow as if to suggest he was a man of the world, then he picked up the thread of his tale. "Anyway, that's how I heard Lee had stayed there. He was called from Texas to Washington to take command of the U.S. Army. Instead, he resigned and joined the cause of secession."

The ranger finished his beans, bacon, and bread, then bit off the end of a small, tightly rolled cigar and spat it out. He struck a match on the stove and established an ash on his cigar.

Danny was still eating, but he waved his spoon to urge him on. He swallowed and wiped his hand across his mouth. "What happened to the rangers after the War Between the States?"

Danny's host took a long, thoughtful drag on his cigar and exhaled a lazy cloud of pungent smoke. "They disbanded. But the governor reactivated them in the mid-70s. Mexican bandits and rustlers near the Rio Grande, you know."

The ranger pointed an arthritic finger at the photographs. "My younger brother served in the war. He wasn't much more than a boy when he ran off and enlisted. He was never the same after he came back. He was restless. Tried several things but couldn't hold a steady job. Around that time my wife, Theodora, died. She was a fine woman, and I sorrowed for her constantly. I'd decided to quit rangering. My brother said I was in the doldrums and that a change of scenery would do us both some good. So it was him that talked me into my first trail drive. That drive cost him his life—a stampede—but he'd always said that he'd rather die a has-been than a never-was." He grew silent and watched a smoke ring expand gently outward, drift apart, and disappear.

After a minute, Danny asked him, "How does a—I mean how does someone— become a Texas Ranger?" He was afraid his question sounded presumptuous. He diverted his eyes to his plate.

The former ranger realized that Danny was inquiring for himself. "If I was you, I'd get me some experience in the law—see if I liked it. It takes more than just being able to ride and handle a gun. It takes using your instincts and wits, knowing when to back down and when not to. Nobody can teach you that, but if you don't know it, you get yourself killed. If a man loses his head, his butt usually goes with it."

In his mind, Danny could hear Artis Dunside's refrain, "Use your head, not your fists," and Tom Bartlett saying, "Keep both eyes open, O'Brien."

"Rangers got to use their wits," the man repeated, triggering the recollection of one last story to illustrate his point, one that he knew would be of interest to Danny. "There was once a ranger who saved his prisoner, and possibly himself, by singing Irish songs." He took a long draw on his cigar, taking pleasure both in it and in the story he was telling.

"Yup. McCafferty was bringing a prisoner in, but there was a vigilante party on their tail, hell-bent on dispensing their own justice at the end of a rope. McCafferty was outnumbered five to one. They kept a-following at a steady pace, biding their time. Now McCafferty knows they're waiting for dark. He also knows—having picked up his prisoner near old San Patricio—that they're smack in the heart of the South Texas Irish belt." The ranger noticed a stray bean on his plate and flicked it into the stove. Satisfied with his shot, he went on, "So round about sunset, McCafferty starts singing. He sang and he sang, each song getting a little sadder and slower than the one before. He had a fine voice, and he kept singing for hours."

"What happened?" The suspense stopped Danny's last spoonful of beans midway to his mouth.

"McCafferty flat sang those Irish vigilantes out of steam. He serenaded them with every Hibernian ballad and love song he ever knew, some of them a half-dozen times over. The self-appointed posse took to listening to McCafferty. They got homesicker and more sentimental with every mile and every song. By sunrise, they'd lost their taste for vengeance. Finally, just turned their horses around and walked back the way they come."

Danny's eyes sparkled with amusement and admiration. "McCafferty used his head," he laughed, "and his lungs."

The residue of beans had begun to harden on the tin plates, and the ranger's cigar had been reduced to a pile of cold ashes. "I don't get many visitors out here. I got two daughters. One lives in Missouri. Jefferson City. The other settled with her family in the Oklahoma Territory." He rubbed his throat and smiled. "I believe our chat cleared some rust out of my pipes. I ain't talked this much in the last few years put together." Then he added in a quieter voice, "Sorry I couldn't give you better news about your uncles."

"I'm obliged nonetheless. And I'm sorry about your son and your wife and your brother." Danny rose to leave. The old ranger walked outside with him. They shook hands, and Danny mounted his horse. He touched the brim of his hat, spurred Diablo, and trotted off towards a familiar destination and a new destiny: to San Antonio to become an officer of the law. He thought to himself, *I might even be able to track down Uncle Aidan.* Danny paused when he reached the road and looked back. Then he turned towards San Antonio. He was humming "Mary McCrae."

2

When Danny reached the Pecos, he dismounted slowly and stared at the river. He walked over to a small log and kicked it towards the water, half disappointed there was no snake underneath that he could vent his rage on. He picked up the log and heaved it into the murky water. He picked up one stick and then another, hurling them into the river. "It wasn't fair!" he yelled in a hoarse voice. He flung sticks and rocks in a blind fury. "It wasn't right!" He lost his footing and slipped farther down the bank. Reduced to hurling impotent handfuls of dirt into the patient water, he slumped against the trunk of a sturdy tree, exhausted but still quaking with rage. He stared at the ground around the foot of the tree, wondering if it was the tree his uncle was buried under. His voice constricted to a whisper. "It wasn't right." He picked up one last pebble and flung hard it into the river.

TWENTY-FOUR

1

"Is that it, Papa? Is that the Chicago's World's Fair?" Inga was bursting with excitement, but instead of pointing to the fair, she was pointing at Midway Plaisance, across the street from it. The midway was a mile-long strip of sideshows, rides, restaurants, and theaters. Anna gave a frown of disapproval. She had heard that for fifty cents, one could watch "Little Egypt" do the "hootchy-kootchy." "Look at that! What is it?" Inga shouted. The object of her fascination was George Ferris's giant steel wheel that towered more than two hundred and fifty feet above the ground.

"That area is called Midway Plaisance. And that enormous contrivance is the Ferris wheel. Perhaps we'll ride it later, but we're here to see exhibits. This is also called the World's Columbian Exposition because it commemorates the four-hundredth anniversary of Columbus's landing in America. In fact, there's a full-scale replica of the *Santa Maria*, Columbus's flagship." Albert realized his history lesson was falling on deaf ears and gave up. He steered Inga towards the fair's entrance. "Look! There's a photographer. He can use my Kodak." Albert held up a small black leather box, a fifty-dollar luxury he had treated himself to.

"*Another* picture, Papa?" Inga realized that they were headed for the fair, not the midway as she had hoped, and that there would be a picture taken first. But after getting a glimpse of the fair, she was eager to go inside.

"Yes, a picture here at the entrance." Albert centered Inga between himself and Anna, and paid the photographer to take a picture of them standing beneath the large arch. He marveled that their adolescent daughter, now a beautiful young woman, was taller than Anna. "Someday, Inga, you will be able to tell your children that you went to the Columbian Exposition of 1893."

The photographer unsnapped and opened one side and extended the lens, delighted to have a chance to try a Kodak No. 4 folding camera, the first one for roll film only. "Hold very still!" he said. He snapped the picture, and they were done.

Inga tugged her father's hand. "Let's go in!"

Once inside, Albert surveyed the park and was awed by the grandeur and the scope of it. White, neoclassical buildings looked as if they had been lifted intact from Renaissance Italy and deposited in Chicago. In contrast to the sprawling midway, their symmetry, order, and simplicity suggested other aspects of the Victorian era: self-control, sobriety, industriousness, modesty, and manners. A white wall of false marble surrounded the park and its trove of milky-white buildings. "No wonder they call it the White City!" he said out loud, and then murmured, "an ideal model city." In the center of the graceful buildings was a lake with an imposing, hundred-foot-high statue of a toga-draped woman. He pointed it out to Inga. "That statue is entitled 'The Republic.' I read about it just the other day—"

Inga paid no heed, but instead ran towards the man-made lagoon. She gaped at the gondolas and swans that floated on its mirrored surface. "Oh, Papa," she gushed, "it's beautiful!"

Albert churned his head up and down. "Didn't I tell you it would be wonderful!" He felt as he often did the pleasure of seeing the world through his daughter's eager eyes. He winked at his wife. Anna smiled back at him a mother's contented smile.

Albert stood and stared. The breeze was cool and the sunshine warm. Groups of swans swam in graceful Vs, the delicate ripples behind them the only disturbance of the flawless surface.

"Papa," Inga cajoled, "please, can we ride in the boat? *Please!*" She raised her eyebrows expectantly as she ran back to him, took his arm, and steered him towards the languid green pool.

"A gondola-ride *would* be nice." It seemed impossible to him to deny Inga any request. As they strolled to the lagoon, Albert looked with tenderness at his beautiful fifteen-year-old daughter. "Let's have our picture taken on the gondola!"

Inga gave him a good-natured roll of her eyes. "Papa, we've had our picture taken *everywhere!*"

"Then one more won't matter!" He squeezed her arm. "Besides, Mama is going to fill a separate album with pictures of our trip to Chicago. Our album for 1893 won't hold all of them."

By the end of the week, the Jäegers had been dazzled by the exhibits in the dozens of domed, turreted, and gilt-embellished buildings that dotted thousands of acres. Albert, Anna, and Inga had taken carriage rides through miles of wooded parks. They had been captivated by inventions that offered a heady glimpse of the coming century. They had wandered through exhibit after exhibit: the Moorish Palace, the Persian Theater, the Turkish Village, the reproduction of old Vienna in the Austrian Village, and the model of St. Peter's. They'd wandered through the Donegal Castle, the East India Bazaar, Egyptian temples and tombs, and the Javanese Village. They'd spent time at the Chinese Theater, the Japanese Village, and had enjoyed dinner at the restaurant in the 1776 log cabin. At the Blarney Castle, Inga had kissed the Blarney stone. They had marveled at the miniature Eiffel Tower. The German Village, with its exhibit, museum, and concert garden, temporarily transported Albert and Anna back to their life before coming to the United States.

Inga was delighted at the Hagenback's Menagerie and sweet-talked her father into buying tickets to see the circus show. Anna finally agreed to ride the Ferris wheel, but only after being assured that the fifty-cent ticket bought customers only two revolutions. Anna flatly refused to go on the Balloon Ascension, and she fretted the entire time until her husband and daughter were safely back on the ground. "Too high! Be careful!" she had called out, but Albert insisted that seeing the fairgrounds from 1500 feet in the air was the only way to comprehend and appreciate the magnitude of the exposition.

In deference to Anna's wishes, they visited the Venice-Murano exhibit to see the delicate, colorful glass, and the Libbey Glass Works exhibit. Although Inga had lobbied in favor of seeing a different exhibit, she found herself entranced by the demonstration of glass molding and glassblowing. For the price of admission, each person was given a custom, glass souvenir. Inga had already decided she would put hers in the curio cabinet in her bedroom.

Albert was eager to tell his friends about the elevated electric railway, the first ever built, and to describe the movable sidewalk. "Such machines!" he would tell them, as he showed them pictures he had taken. He had spent most of one day wandering through buildings devoted to electricity, transportation, mining, machinery, and manufacturing. While he was doing this, Inga and her mother had spent their time exploring the horticultural building, the fine arts building, and the woman's building.

The family admired German sculptress Elisabet Ney's monuments to Stephen F. Austin and Sam Houston at the Texas Pavilion. "I read that there is a million dollars of statuary here, and I believe it," Albert said to no one in particular as he moved from one monument to the next.

The crowd—200,000 to 300,000 a day and topping 700,000 on one day—was international and affable. The multitude of languages Inga heard fascinated her, and then she realized why: it reminded her of the days in the tenement. She felt a pain in her heart. *My sisters should be here with me.*

Each day the Jäegers had been tempted by odors of foods that were tantalizingly sweet, spicy, or salty. They tasted many of the new items introduced at the Fair: Shredded Wheat, Cream of Wheat, Aunt Jemima Syrup (Anna's favorite), Juicy Fruit gum, Cracker Jacks (Inga's favorite), hamburgers, and Pabst Beer (Albert's favorite). "The food has been... interesting," Albert reluctantly admitted, "but nothing matches the chili we Texans have introduced at the fair." He was right; it was a spectacular success.

On the last day they were there, he announced, "I have a surprise. This evening we go to a concert." He paused dramatically. *"John Philip Sousa!"* he exclaimed, unable to contain his enthusiasm.

That night as they entered the concert hall, Albert explained, "Although Mr. Sousa is known for his marches, he's equally knowledgeable about classical music. And did you know that he has perfect pitch, Anna?" Albert turned to Inga. "He's an expert horseman. And a skilled trap shooter, just like your Papa!"

Soon the houselights dimmed and the gaslights on stage went up. There was silence in the vast hall. Musicians in impeccable uniforms entered single file from both sides of the stage. At precisely the moment the show was scheduled to begin, Sousa strode on stage. The short, neatly bearded, bespectacled man bowed once to the audience. The gold braid of his uniform and hat glittered in the bright light. Then, at a signal from his immaculate white-gloved hands, the band burst into a glorious march. The rest of the concert was every bit as exhilarating.

"A fine finale to our trip!" was Albert's assessment.

2

Having sampled fully the exposition's wonders, the Jäegers set out for home the following day. They were elated but weary, and Albert was doubly glad he had purchased round-trip tickets on trains that featured luxurious Pullman sleeping cars.

Albert settled back in his seat and turned to Inga. "Did you like the exposition?" he asked, even though he knew the answer.

Inga was studying the stack of postcards and stereopticon prints she held in her lap. "It was even better than Fiesta San Antonio! Better than the parade to Alamo Plaza!"

Albert smiled. This was high praise indeed.

As the daughter in a prominent family, Inga had been among the young women who enjoyed the privilege of riding on the flower-covered floats and waving to the throngs of spectators who lined the streets at the city's annual celebration. "The exposition was better than even the Battle of Flowers!" she exclaimed. She loved the fiesta's culmination in which the crowd split in half and pelted each other with flowers in a mock fight. "But now I'm ready to go home. I want to tell my friends about it and show them my pictures." She held up one of a gondola.

That night, as Inga lay in the berth listening to the sound of the train wheels, she felt again deep sadness and longing for her sisters. *Where are they now?* Along with sadness, she felt guilt. Although she tried to convince herself otherwise, she kept thinking, *Their lives can't be as happy as mine.* When she was finally lulled to sleep by the sound and the motion of the train, she dreamed that she, Helga, and Johanna were children again. They were riding west on a train to Texas.

3

It was late afternoon when the train pulled into San Antonio. Albert arranged for a wagon to deliver their baggage and sought a carriage to take them home.

They rode in silence, lost in their separate thoughts and memories of the trip. Inga leaned back, smiled, and closed her eyes.

A bump in the street jostled her back to wakefulness. She glanced out the window and then let out a startled cry. "Stop!"

Albert and Anna jumped.

"What is it?" Anna never ceased worrying about her daughter's health, and Inga's face had lost all traces of color.

"There! I saw her! I *saw* her!" Inga shrieked. She was shaking, gesturing frantically towards the street they had just passed, and fumbling with the handle on the door.

"Saw *who*?" Albert asked, looking past her, trying to see out the window.

"*Helga!*" she cried, "I saw *Helga!*" Inga yanked at the door of the carriage and shoved on it. Despite her desperate attempt, the door would not yield to her quaking hands. "I have to find her!"

Albert grabbed her flailing arms. "Inga! That wasn't Helga."

Inga abruptly ceased any movement. "Yes it was! I *saw* her!" She began to cry. "*Please, Papa,*" she sobbed, "we *have* to go back. We have to look."

"Inga, it can't be Helga. Helga's…" Albert struggled to say the word. He had known that he might have to tell Inga someday, but now that he needed to, he couldn't get the words past his lips. He looked at his wife. Anna looked at him with sad eyes and nodded. He took a deep breath. "Inga, Helga died. Several years ago."

Inga looked as dashed as if Albert had struck her. She sat in stunned silence, taking in gulps of air and laboring to breathe. Huge tears rolled down her cheeks. The drops fell on her dress and merged in expanding circles.

Tears flowed from Anna's eyes, too. She put her arm around her daughter. "Several years ago, Inga, your father met a man who had seen Helga. He knew she had come West on the train and that she looked just like you. He said that she had been run down, killed by a horse that had bolted."

Inga put her hands over her face. An image flashed through her mind: a child lying in a New York street, limp and bleeding, rendered lifeless by a runaway horse. The joy of the Chicago trip was shattered and forgotten. Then she looked at her parents and sobbed in an angry, breathless burst, "If you knew, why didn't you—" She saw the anguish in their eyes and didn't finish her question.

"Inga, there was never a time, a right time," Albert said softly. "We tried to find Helga. If we could have Helga, we would have taken her to be our daughter, too."

Inga cried the rest of the way home. Anna held her close, and Albert anxiously patted her hand. *She looks so fragile,* he thought. His heart ached for her, but he took consolation in knowing that time would help her heal.

4

For two months Inga barely spoke to her father and didn't speak much more to her mother. Whenever the Jäegers tried to broach the subject of Helga, Inga cut them off. "You should have told me!" she shouted at them repeatedly. "You should have told me about Helga!" She would retreat to her room and close the door. They could hear her crying but knew not to follow her.

Little by little the strain lifted. After a while and as if by tacit agreement, none of them spoke of Helga again. Once her anger began to soften and her sadness became less acute, Inga realized what a terrible secret her parents had been burdened with. She was able to see that their not telling her about Helga was to spare her pain.

Inga also knew that as a Jäeger, she was blessed with a life that most people could only dream of. The family was among the well-to-do San Antonians who arrived at Alamo Plaza by phaeton, carriage, surrey, or buggy to patronize the elegant stores, to dine at the Bismarck, to attend performances at the Grand Opera House, and to enjoy treats at Harnisch and Baer's confectionery.

Sitting in her room one day, Inga recalled that when she was a little girl, she had insisted over and over again Albert tell her the story of how he and Anna had come to the United States. "Your mama and I came on a ship," he told her, "just like you. We had to start a new life in Texas, just like you. And we hurried to get here first so that we would be here when you arrived." She remembered she had smiled and hugged his neck whenever he told her that.

He told her how he had worked hard and prospered from the beginning. San Antonio's livestock industry had become the backbone of the local economy, and along with the factories, stockyards, hotels, and breweries that had thrived, so had his sausage and meatpacking business.

Inga had become aware only gradually that Albert was among the wealthiest German citizens in the city and that the men he counted among his closest friends were also highly prosperous and influential. William Gebhardt's chili factory could hardly turn out enough of the fiery powder to meet the demand. Nearly a dozen breweries, including William Menger's, were producing the much-loved German beer. The Finck Cigar Company was only one of many highly successful cigar factories. There were no less than eighteen German newspapers published in the city, and Albert knew the owners of several of them.

But the Jäegers' dearest friends were Emil and Katje Braun. Albert and Emil, along with other powerful men, belonged to the Casino Club, a prestigious social club on Market Street that was the focal point of German culture in the city. The Club regularly sponsored operas and other artistic performances that the Jäegers and the Brauns attended. Both Albert and Emil were active in local politics and in the life of the city's German community. Both belonged to the Grand Order of the Sons of Hermann, a benevolent fraternal order named in honor of a German folk hero. Both families belonged to St. Joseph's Catholic Church, a hub of German religious life in San Antonio. And it was the Brauns' oldest son, Dieter, whom Albert had picked for Inga to marry one day.

Art, music, literature, the church, and a rich social and family life formed the fabric of Inga's childhood and adolescence. There were theatrical societies, singing societies, athletic associations, and clubs—*Vereine*—of every sort. Albert, Anna, and Inga all participated in singing societies. They attended performances at the Beethoven *Maennerchor,* the Southwest's finest concert hall. Anna and Katje belonged to literary, music, and service societies, the same ones that Inga and the Brauns' daughters would join as soon they were old enough. As the children of prominent German families, as neighbors, and as schoolmates at the prestigious German English School, Inga and Dieter saw each other daily.

The bonds of *Deutschtum*—Germanness—and tradition fostered an enduring sense of family and community. Religious and secular holidays, as well as the rituals and celebrations associated with baptisms, birthdays, weddings, and funerals, punctuated the Jäegers' lives.

Inga's birthday celebrations, *Geburtstags,* were joyous occasions. As was the custom, the Jäeger mansion was made immaculate down to fresh paper linings in the drawers. Linen tablecloths and gleaming silver serving pieces adorned tables laden with cakes, cookies, sandwiches, and urns of coffee. Relatives and close friends began arriving midafternoon. The children hurried over the moment school was let out. As guests arrived, they joined the others who were seated in a circle on the gallery, the porch. They moved around the circle and shook hands with each person before joining the convivial group. Since the Jäegers had not known Inga's birth date, they selected September 4. It was on that day, so many years ago, that the doctor had pronounced Inga fully recovered from the pneumonia that threatened her life.

The Jäegers and the Brauns lived a few houses apart, and the two families regularly shared social activities and special occasions. Inga had always thought of Dieter merely as the son of her Onkel Emil and Tante Katja. She thought of him and his brothers and sisters as cousins of hers. It was just after her seventeenth birthday that Inga realized her father intended for her to marry Dieter.

"Dieter, he's a fine young man, *ja?*" Albert never missed a chance to bring up his name. It was "Inga, did you know Dieter won the prize last week at the shooting club?" or "Emil tells me Dieter plans to go into business with him. That boy has a bright future."

Inga would shrug, but over time she felt the ripples of her resentment swell into waves.

Emil Braun also had in mind for his son to marry Inga. Dieter had no objection. In fact, he found Inga pretty and accomplished.

"Papa, Dieter's nice, but I don't want to *marry* him! I don't love him." Inga and her father had argued about it countless times.

Albert waved his pipe in the air. "You marry him. The love will come later. You'll see. There will be children, and you will be glad you listened to your Papa."

Inga would leave the room in tears. Anna would try to calm Albert, then go to Inga to calm her.

When she returned, she would chide, "Albert, you don't know about young girls. Don't upset her so." Based more on sympathy for Inga than on reality, she always added, "You know her health is delicate."

5

It was a boy in her class, Günther, the son of a fine furniture-maker, about whom Inga dreamed her adolescent dreams. He was shy, but he drew exquisite pictures and gave them to her. He had anthracene eyes, and she often caught him looking at her. It was Günther she yearned for, not Dieter. Not sensible, familiar Dieter.

Two years older than Inga, Dieter finished the German English School in 1895. "Emil tells me that Dieter is going to Germany to complete his education. He won't be back until after you have graduated," Albert informed Inga one night during an argument. He hoped Dieter's impending absence would cause her to reconsider her feelings towards him.

"Good!" Inga shouted as she retreated to her room. "I'm *glad* he's going! I hope he *stays* there!" She slammed the door, threw herself on the bed and cried. *I shouldn't have talked to Papa that way,* she told herself once again, but the thought of being forced into a marriage with Dieter made her feel worse. *Maybe if Dieter's gone, Papa will forget about him. And maybe Dieter will forget about me, too.*

But Albert did not forget about Dieter, nor did Dieter forget about Inga while he was in Germany. He wrote her frequent letters, despite the fact that the only ones he received from her were brief and perfunctory, ones her parents insisted she write. Letters from him lay untouched on the parlor table until Albert made Inga open them. "Either you open it or I will," he would threaten.

When Albert sensed Inga's interest in Günther, he refused to let her see him. Inga choked back her resentment, bitter at first and angry with her parents. Over time, though, she began to wonder perhaps if her parents were right. *What if they do know best? What if I chose Günther and then discovered they were right?* It was a frightening thought.

She began to avoid Günther at school, leaving him puzzled and hurt. She told herself, *I owe Papa and Mama my very life. Is it so much they ask? That I marry Dieter, a fine, well-educated young man? Now a worldly young man who has studied abroad?* As the time for Dieter's return grew closer, his letters took a more personal turn. *Perhaps I could grow to love him,* Inga mused.

She was proud to be among those in the school's final graduating class in 1897, and she was flattered that Dieter made a point of returning from Germany in time to see the ceremony. To Inga, he seemed wiser, more knowledgeable, more grown-up— more like her father and Emil.

A month later, Inga, to the Jäegers' and the Brauns' mutual delight, accepted Dieter's proposal.

Only Inga knew that when she had said yes, she had her fingers crossed behind her back.

TWENTY-FIVE

1

Danny strolled through Alamo Plaza. Music and the aroma of chili wafted in the warm, spring air. Fabiana called out his name and waved him over to her table. "You eat chili tonight." Her inflection rendered the pronouncement simultaneously a statement and a question. She ladled a serving of the steaming concoction into a bowl, and Danny flipped her a coin. He sauntered to a lamppost and leaned against it while he gulped down the spicy-hot mixture of chiles and meat.

Another chili queen a short distance away chided the young law officer. "You don't like *my* chili? Is better than Fabiana's!" She pouted with feigned indignation. "Next time you have Yolanda's chili!" For emphasis, she held up her lantern and tapped a large, chili-coated spoon against the rim of her simmering kettle.

Another voice called out, "No! Leticia's!"

Danny grinned and shrugged to show that he was helpless to choose among them. "Too many good chili queens—what can I do?" He had walked only a little farther on his rounds when he heard a ruckus coming from a bar on the other side of the street. Danny broke into a lope and placed his hand on his Colt as he crossed over to El Fandango.

The second he strode through the open door, a drunken young firebrand careened into him. Danny spun him around, locked his forearm around the man's neck, and pressed his gun into the small of his back. Despite his inebriation, his prisoner understood the hard metal of the Colt barrel. He immediately raised his hands over his head. "Don't shoot! We was just celebratin'."

At the sound of his terrified plea, the brawl abruptly stopped. His five comrades froze, and those scuffling with them loosed their grip. "Line up against the bar! Now!" Danny boomed.

The troublemakers stumbled towards the bar. One quickly dropped the chair leg he was holding. Danny gave his prisoner a rough shove in their direction.

The Fandango's owner pushed his way through the ring of patrons who had positioned themselves on the periphery of the action. He sputtered and gesticulated wildly in the direction of the bar. A huge spider web of cracks radiated from the center of the etched mirror that spanned the wall behind it. "A fortune! That's what it's going to cost to replace!" he shrieked. Along with angry words, small sprays of spit flew from beneath his black mustache. "A fortune!" He whirled around towards the young men. He stabbed the air with his finger as if leading a charge. "Deputy, arrest them!" he screamed. "I demand you arrest them!"

"I'll handle this, Francisco," Danny replied in an even tone. One of the young men started towards Danny to explain. "Don't move!" Danny barked as he scanned the lineup with his Colt. "Don't *any* of you move!" The man sheepishly fell back in with the others. Bluffed into submission, the rest shook their heads to show they would offer no resistance. Danny holstered his gun as patrons began to upright the chairs and tables. The deputy surveyed the mirror, then the broken whiskey bottles and shattered furniture. Danny's head jerked slightly when he spotted a body beneath a table. "Francisco, who is—"

"That mirror came all the way from St. Louis," Francisco wailed, still fixated on what had been the showpiece of his saloon. He shook his fist at the troublemakers. "You should be locked up forever!"

Francisco was too distraught to be helpful, so Danny walked over to the body and nudged it with his foot. He pushed the table aside and knelt on one knee to take a closer look. "Well, I'll be damned." He felt a smile spread across his face. *Looked the same way the last time I saw him.* Even though a decade had intervened since he and Johanna had sneaked away from the Mutts' farm, Danny recognized Cletis instantly. Danny kept his head down so no one could see his broad grin. He uttered in a low voice, "Well, I never expected to see you again, fella, and I sure didn't expect to see you passed out on some barroom floor."

Still brawny and sturdy, Cletis lay serene and unconscious, a pleasant expression on his face. Danny pressed his ear to Cletis's chest. Then he glanced back over his shoulder and looked at the man he had shoved towards the bar. "You—" he called out, "Tell me what happened here tonight."

"Yes, sir." His tone was deferential. "It was like this. The seven of us met at the fairgrounds this afternoon. We heard Teddy Roosevelt's speech about Spain, about how it's mistreating prisoners in Cuba. Well, sir, we felt roused to action. We decided right then and there that it was our patriotic duty to join the volunteer cavalry and straighten them Spaniards out." He wiped his sleeve across a cut on his cheek. His eye was now black and swollen shut.

The man beside him rubbed his broken nose with his raw knuckles and stepped forward to continue the tale. "We made a pact to volunteer first thing Monday morning. So tonight we was celebrating our decision—"

Francisco cut him off. "You been celebrating your decision all afternoon!" He turned to Danny. "They were half drunk when they arrived. I let them have a drink, but they got too loud, and I asked them to leave. They refused, so I asked Carlos, Hernando, and Juan to show them the door."

Danny raised Cletis's eyelids as he listened to the rest of the facts: in the fight that erupted, fists, chairs, and whiskey bottles had flown, and one of the airborne bottles had shattered Francisco's prized mirror.

A rotund man with large jowls peered down at Cletis and shook his head. "I wouldn't put a plug nickel on him in a fight. He could barely stand up. Just teetered this way and that." The man tilted his raised whiskey glass back and forth as he said "teetered," sloshing whiskey over the sides. Some of it splashed on Cletis's face. "He tried to come to the aid of his friends, but all he could do was wobble. Just sank back into his chair, then slid to the floor. Out cold." The man took another gulp of whiskey and hooted in derision. "That boy done missed the entire fight."

Danny raised his palm to silence the man. He took his drink from him and poured the remainder of it on Cletis's face. Cletis's eyelids fluttered. When he opened his eyes, his unfocused stare locked on Danny's face. "You never could hold your whiskey," Danny said ruefully, scratching his ear and trying once more to suppress a grin.

Cletis squinted. With great effort, he struggled to make sense of the blurry image he was seeing and hearing. "Danny?"

"Yup."

Cletis suddenly wrapped his hands over his head. "You ain't gonna give me another haircut, are you?" he blurted.

This time, a laugh did escape Danny's lips. "No," he shook his head. "No haircut."

Cletis exhaled in relief, dropped his hands, and drifted back into insensibility.

Satisfied that Cletis was merely drunk and not injured, Danny signaled for two of Cletis's companions to come get him.

With great fanfare, Danny herded his prisoners to jail, the conscious lugging the unconscious Cletis. Sheriff George Ewing locked the subdued band in a cell, and Danny left to finish his nightly rounds through the bawdy dance halls and boisterous saloons.

2

The next morning, Danny returned to the jail in hopes that Cletis had sobered up enough to carry on a conversation. Judge Kohler, a portly, gray-haired man, was already there. Misled by his easy-going manner, those on the receiving end of his sentences were often surprised by their severity. Wretched hangovers, soreness from the fistfight, the heavy damages and fines, along with the five-day jail sentence Judge Kohler had already pronounced on the prisoners had extinguished any trace of their previous exuberance. They protested loudly—all except Cletis, who sat hunched against the wall of the cell. He crossed his forearms on his knees and rested his head on them. "We were fixing to sign up with Roosevelt come Monday," one wailed in vain.

Judge Kohler was unmoved.

Danny stood back, arms folded, listening to the judge upbraid them again. When he was through, they sat sullenly in their cell. Danny approached the judge. In a low voice, he said, "Judge Kohler, I have reason to believe that one there"—he pointed to Cletis—"was guilty of public drunkenness, but he wasn't one of them who busted up the place." After hearing Danny relate what happened at El Fandango, the judge reluctantly volunteered to let Cletis go.

"Judge, I'm not asking you to do that!" whispered Danny. "Besides, these other yahoos would pound him to a pulp if you just let him walk out the door. They were too drunk to know that he didn't do nothing. And the owner of the Fandango is insisting they're *all* guilty. Can he go to trial? What about that?"

The judge considered the matter, then hollered to the sheriff, "George, bring that tall one over here."

Sick, pale, and shamefaced, Cletis emerged from the cell and shuffled towards the magistrate. Then he saw the deputy sheriff. "Danny!" he brightened. He held out a shaky hand. "I thought I had a dream about you last night."

Because he was still in view of the others, Danny ignored Cletis's extended hand. He whispered to him, "No. It's wasn't a dream. It was me."

The judge interrupted. "You stand trial Monday morning."

The others protested. "We want trials, too."

To them he boomed, "You're guilty. Your sentences stand."

"That's unfair!" one continued to rail.

"The judge didn't say this man is off the hook," Danny retorted. "Only that he's going to trial. The jury can determine whether he was involved."

Before Cletis went back into the cell, Danny muttered to him, "I've got to go now, but I'll get you a lawyer." Then he winked. "See you at the trial."

Danny exchanged a few words with the judge and the sheriff, who both laughed out loud. He strolled out the door, tipping his hat to Cletis and the others on the way.

Cletis unconsciously reached up and touched his hair. As he did, he felt a tremor of apprehension flutter through him.

3

Cletis sat in the small courtroom, his shirt tinged with sweat despite the cool spring air. He felt confused by what was going on, and he was terrified he would have to speak in front of the spectators. He had heard that the prosecutor, Martin Hawkes, rarely lost a case.

Danny arranged for Henry Schemler to serve as Cletis's lawyer. Danny entered the courtroom, sat down, and glanced at the sheriff. While bystanders and witnesses milled about and situated themselves on the benches, Sheriff Ewing sauntered to the table where Henry Schemler was standing and whispered something to him. Schemler's look of disbelief was quickly replaced by a bowl-shaped grin. Cletis hung his head, too frightened to look anywhere except down at the table.

The crowd began to titter. The source of their amusement and attorney Schemler's soon became apparent.

"Order! Order!" Judge Kohler gaveled them into silence. As if there was nothing out of the ordinary, the judge directed the attorneys to proceed.

The prosecutor stood waving his arms and sputtering. "This is an outrage!"

The sheriff had summoned a panel of prospective jurors, but at Danny's instigation and with the judge's blessing, he had rounded up only cross-eyed and wall-eyed men.

"By gobs, get on with it, man!" the judge thundered at Hawkes.

So thrown was Mr. Hawkes by the turn of events that he accepted the first twelve men as jurors. The dozen stumbled their way into the jury box.

The judge looked pleased. "Let's commence, gentlemen," he urged the attorneys in a dry voice, "so we can get this over before we all grow old."

Prosecutor Hawkes was unnerved by the jurors' twenty-four eyes, no two of which seemed to be gazing in the same direction. Unable to determine where to look when he addressed the members of the jury, much less to tell when they understood a point he was making, Hawkes grew more and more frustrated. His concentration and then his composure deserted him. In his summation, he declared, "Cletis Mutt was wall-eyed drunk!" Flustered and embarrassed at his unfortunate choice of words, he compounded his error: "I mean, he was drunk, but while the fight was going on, he was still cross-eyed—I mean still *conscious*." Perspiration had begun to trickle down the sides of his face. "I hope you'll have the good squints—*sense*—to find him guilty…" Mr. Hawkes trailed off in a lame voice and sagged in his chair, the picture of misery. Danny noticed that Judge Kohler, on the other hand, seemed to be enjoying himself.

Then it was Henry Schemler's turn. He adjusted his bow tie and straightened his cuffs to show that he was in no particular hurry. He sketched the scene the evening of the fight: spirited boys galvanized by Roosevelt's words, invigorated by the spring air and by being young, full of exuberance and, yes, a little whiskey. He portrayed Cletis as well-intentioned and patriotic, as a farm boy who had gone along with the others, but who had not initiated the fight or even participated in it.

Schemler walked over to the jurors and turned to Cletis. "Hold up your hands, Mr. Mutt. Turn the backs of them where we can all see them." Cletis complied, unsure of the reason for Schemler's request. Then Schemler clamped his own beefy hands on the rail of the jury box and leaned towards the jurors. "Take a close look, gentlemen." A sea of crossed eyes peered in Cletis's direction. A few cocked their heads to see better with their good eye. "Do you see any bruises? Cuts? Swollen knuckles? Any signs that he was in a fight?" He answered his own questions. "No!" he bellowed, "because he wasn't *in* the fight. The worst this boy is guilty of is not being able to hold his liquor—not and stay conscious anyway." The spectators laughed, and even a few jurors found themselves smiling. And, perhaps with the jury's inadvertent help, attorney Schemler was able to raise doubts in the minds of El Fandango's owner and the patrons as to whether they had actually seen *all* of the young men take part in the brawl. Without Cletis taking the stand, the defense rested.

The jury foreman collected a slip of paper from each man. "Not guilty," came the unanimous verdict.

Disgusted and exasperated, the prosecutor slammed through the swinging gate, stormed down the aisle and out of the courthouse.

Judge Kohler was beaming as he stepped down from the bench. "Windbag! First time Hawkes ever ran out of words!"

Danny pumped Henry Schemler's hand in congratulation and then Cletis's. "Looks like the jury saw *eye to eye* with you fellers," Danny hooted. "But the verdict was a surprise! When they voted, I was sure the '*ayes*' would have it!" He stood there waving his hands helplessly, laughing so hard that he shook.

Walking out of the courthouse with Danny a few minutes later, Cletis said in a sheepish voice, "I reckon I owe you a thank you."

"I reckon I owe you an apology, from several years ago. I'm sorry about that licking in the cornfield, and I'm sorry about the haircut."

"Had it comin'," Cletis conceded. "Well, the lickin' anyway."

Danny chucked him on the arm as a way of changing the subject. "Now tell me about yourself and your family."

4

"Well," Cletis began, slowly gathering his thoughts, "my sisters, they run off with a drummer who come through Sulphur Creek a while back. Had him a whole wagon full of ribbons, lace, and gewgaws. Turned them foolish girls' heads in a flash." Cletis walked a few more steps and stopped. "Like to have broke Ma's heart."

Danny cringed at the thought of what Oleta must have been like after her daughters ran off.

Cletis quickly confirmed his suspicions. "She took to her bed. Stayed there a week with a rag over her face." Cletis shook his head. "She's been in a mood ever since. It got to where Pa and I both stayed clear of her." Cletis shook his head again. "Them two girls never was grateful for nothin'."

Danny gave Cletis a sympathetic look and nodded in commiseration.

"When it got to where I couldn't take no more, I just plain left. I figured if you and Hannah and my sisters managed to leave, that I could too. When Pa sent me into town one day, I took my money with me and just kept going. Got on the train in Sulphur Creek and rode until I thought I'd gone far enough. Got off in San Antone. Been working as a farrier ever since." He was silent a minute. "Ain't never regretted leaving neither." He straightened and thrust his shoulders back. "And now I'm going to be a soldier. With Mr. Roosevelt." Cletis conjured up a mental picture of himself decked out in a blue flannel shirt, bandanna, brown pants, leggings, boots, and a slouch hat, carrying a Winchester rifle or a Krag-Jorgenson carbine. The image thrilled him.

"Make a man out of you!" Danny boomed. "I like being a lawman, and I wager you'll like being a soldier."

Then, as if the question suddenly burst into his head, Cletis asked, "Where'd you and Hannah go?"

"What?"

"You and Hannah. After you left the farm. Where'd you go?"

Danny's grin looked like the crescent moon. "You're going to like this…" he began. He told him how he and Johanna hid back from the road and watched Oleta, Angus, and their daughters return from the revival and baptisms.

"Ruby and Opal were sick as dogs," Cletis interjected. Then, telling Danny what he already knew, "And so was I—only from whiskey."

"I bet they were sick!" Danny exclaimed. "That Malto-Lax is a powerful dose. I don't suppose your ma and pa got sick, too?"

"Uh-huh, but not so bad as them two brats." The implication of what Danny had said began to dawn on him. "You mean…?"

"In the syrup."

Both of them burst into loud guffaws. "Well, I'll be jigged," Cletis kept muttering in amazement. "Like I said, Ruby and Opal were dog-sick by the time they got home. Ma sent them right to bed." He felt his face flush as he realized that Danny also knew about the molasses in their bed.

"Ma was furious over her hat and the mess. She and Pa would have killed you and Hannah if they could have found you."

"Did they try?"

"They couldn't remember Hannah's last name. Pa asked around about a Danny O'Riley, but he couldn't find out nothing."

"O'Brien," Danny said. "Danny *O'Brien.*"

"Well, no wonder he couldn't find nothing." Cletis looked skyward and then shook his head. "It's kinda funny, though, ain't it?"

"What is?"

"You turning out to be a lawman."

Danny scratched his head and grinned as if he'd been caught misbehaving. "Hadn't never thought about it. But I have to say it's a stretch from where I started out," he conceded. Then he told Cletis that Johanna was in San Antonio, but he was no more specific than that. He told him briefly about his train travel throughout Texas and about some of his experiences in Galveston and at the YT. Danny clapped Cletis on the back. "You need to get on over to the fairgrounds to sign on with Mr. Roosevelt's outfit, but meet me here at seven o'clock. We'll finish our talk at dinner. I'm buying. Steaks." He looked over at Cletis. "It's the least I can do for a fightin' man."

Now Cletis's head was bobbing up and down like a toy on a spring.

Danny walked on a few paces, but then turned back. "And, Cletis," he grinned and called out, "I'll buy you a whiskey."

TWENTY-SIX

1

Inga scanned the graceful interior of the gothic church: the vaulted arches of the ceiling; the exquisite, thirty-foot-tall lancet stained-glass window; the German inscriptions in German script. She looked at the magnificent main altar and at the paintings of the Assumption and the Ascension on the walls above the side altars. Her eyes drifted over the smaller paintings depicting the fourteen stations of the cross. She had been in St. Joseph's thousands of times, and until this moment, she'd always felt a deep sense of peace as soon as she entered. But now, with the dazzling panoply of wedding flowers and scores of blazing candles, the church seemed overwhelming, dizzying, suffocating.

The sound of the pipe organ jolted her from her thoughts. The music reverberated from the sanctuary's stone walls, and the bridal procession began to move down the aisle. Inga tightened her grip on her father's arm. Albert patted her hand, smiled at her affectionately, and then walked her down the aisle in view of hundreds of guests.

Now Inga stood stiff and still in her lavish, lace-trimmed wedding gown. For good luck, she had sewn inside the wrist of her left sleeve the button from her father's coat. Dieter, standing beside her at the altar, looked at her approvingly. In return, she gave him a small smile. Behind the bouquet she held, she touched the hidden button with the fingertips of her right hand.

As they knelt for the priest's final blessing, Inga prayed, *Dear God, help me to be a good wife to Dieter*—she peeked sideways at him—*and to learn to love him.*

After the ceremony there was an extravagant party at the Menger Hotel. Guests filled the ballroom to dance to the music of both an orchestra and a band. Albert led Inga to the floor for a dance and then relinquished his daughter to the arms of her husband.

Damask-draped tables were laden with food, coffee, and wine. There were kegs of dark beer. Ribbons, streamers, and flowers bedecked every surface except the floor. A mountain of wedding gifts overflowed tables that occupied one corner of the room. As was the custom, Inga unwrapped them during the musicians' intermissions. One gift took Inga by surprise: it was a beautiful sketch of her. It was signed "Günther" and was set in a polished, hand-carved frame. *Did Günther know what I was thinking at the altar?* she wondered. She scanned the crowd for him but could not find him.

At midnight, Dieter and Inga went to their suite in the hotel. She undressed, brushed out her hair, and went to Dieter. But even as he began to make love to her, she found herself wishing it was Günther, not Dieter, and she felt her eyes fill with tears.

2

The Jäegers' wedding present to Dieter and Inga was a house in the same stately neighborhood in which both sets of parents lived. "Lots of bedrooms," Albert remarked to Anna in front of their daughter and new son-in-law, "for lots of children." Inga had blushed. Dieter's parents filled the house with splendid furniture, much of it, to Inga's dismay, crafted by Günther's father.

3

"Dieter…"

Dieter was fussing with a collar stay. He stood in front of the hall-tree mirror, stooping a bit to keep his image within the confines of the silvery rectangle. Inga sighed. *He looks like a tall comma,* she thought to herself. *A tall comma with a crooked collar.*

"Dieter," she repeated. Inside the pocket of her dress, she drummed her fingers in irritation.

Finally satisfied with his collar, he moved to the next object of scrutiny. With his palm he pressed a stubborn cowlick against the crown of his head—the same cowlick he unsuccessfully battled every morning of his life. The pale blond lock refused to stay flat. It bounced back like a spring that had been pressed sideways and then released. He frowned. He disapproved of unruliness and untidiness. He quickly inspected his dark gray jacket for lint, stray threads, and hairs.

Just like his father, thought Inga. *Emil is always straightening pictures and picking threads off things.* She realized how much the habit irritated her. "Dieter!" she practically shouted.

His entire frame jerked in a startled reflex, and he whirled around towards his wife. "Must you shout?"

"You never even hear me! What are you thinking about that's so important?"

"A new machine."

"What?"

"A new machine. At the plant. Father and I are thinking about buying a new type of machine."

Inga's shoulders slumped. "A piece of machinery is more interesting than I am. You never even hear me or see me anymore." *If you ever did,* she almost added aloud.

"That's not right." Dieter gave her a perfunctory kiss on the forehead. "I'm just busy. Mama says that having the first baby makes women high-strung and prone to tears. That's what's wrong with you."

"Me! What's wrong with *me*!" Her tone sounded almost menacing. "What's wrong with me is *you*!"

To Dieter, her frustrated tears confirmed his assessment. He patted her arm. "Now, don't forget. It's Tuesday. We have to be at Papa and Mama's by seven. Mama's fixing dumplings." He surveyed Inga and straightened the ribbon that was threaded through the lace ruffles at her neck. "Why don't you wear your new green dress tonight?"

"I don't want to go anywhere tonight!"

"What? Why not?"

Inga spewed angry words of exasperation. "I'm sick of having dinner with your parents every Tuesday night. I'm sick of all of us going to church and having dinner on Sundays. I'm sick of going to coffee klatches and clubs—" Dieter looked shocked, but Inga plunged ahead, "—and I'm sick of everyone telling me what to do! I'm sick of *you* telling me what to do! *What* to wear! *What* to prepare for supper!" Inga's words frightened even her, but there was no turning back. "Even my own *papa* didn't do that!"

"I am *not* your papa." Dieter's words, liked everything else about him, were definite and controlled—equally spaced syllables that reflected no emotion whatsoever.

"You're certainly not! You're not like him at all. That's the problem."

Dieter winced visibly, as if a flash of bright light had hit him squarely in the eyes. Then he picked up his hat, placed it on his head, checked in the mirror to be sure it was on straight, and walked out the front door.

Inga sat down in a chair and cried. She knew that she would be ready at seven and that she would be wearing the green dress.

4

On their first anniversary, Dieter had Goggan's Palace of Music deliver a piano for Inga. Their son Karl was born the next day, and Ulla a year later. After the babies were born, Inga understood more of what Albert and Anna had so often told her.

She rarely thought about Günther now. Although Dieter had objected, she had kept his sketch of her. It was tucked away in a drawer. She was a married woman now, a young matron with children. Like her mother and mother-in-law, she belonged to literary, music, and service societies. She understood her place in the world.

With children of her own, Inga marveled at the richness of her life. To her relief, Dieter was no less devoted to the children than he was to his work. He seemed to relax with them in a way that he was incapable of with adults.

Albert and Anna had told Inga many times that once they had brought her home from the train, they had felt as if their life was complete. She understood that now. She felt her own life was nearly complete. All it lacked was her sisters.

And even though her parents had told her of Helga's death many years ago, a small voice inside her told her that it just wasn't so.

TWENTY-SEVEN

1

Once again a free man after the cross-eyed jury's unanimous decision, Cletis enlisted with the Rough Riders. The recruiting officer was required to certify that each volunteer was sober at the time of enlistment. A slight shudder had rippled through Cletis as he recalled his brush with the law.

Competition to join the Rough Riders was fierce: twenty thousand men had vied for a thousand openings. Like many prospective recruits, Cletis could offer brawn. Further, his work as a farrier had equipped him with an extensive knowledge of horses. But it was his unabashed fervor and earnestness that ultimately tipped the scales in his favor.

He was the most ardent of recruits. He was in awe of Colonel Leonard Wood, the commander who had been sent to organize the troops. "I heard tell Colonel Wood fought Geronimo, the Apache chief," Cletis burbled to another equally green recruit, a star quarterback at Harvard. The young man rolled his eyes.

Colonel Wood went about his job with the same efficiency he had demonstrated as an army surgeon. Mustering his courage, Cletis had ambled over to the colonel and blurted, "I'd be pleased to help you any way possible." Then he quickly added, "sir." Cletis felt honored when the colonel called upon him for several tasks, despite the fact that they were menial ones. It was enough for Cletis just to be in the presence of such a commanding figure.

Then on May 15, 1898, Theodore Roosevelt arrived. Looking dashing on a fine dun horse, the flamboyant Roosevelt drilled the men intensively every day for two weeks. The citizens of San Antonio were enthralled by the charismatic Roosevelt, and they quickly dubbed the cavalry regiment "Teddy's Terrors." The troops were so popular with the townspeople that Colonel Wood had to institute measures to prevent the enthusiastic crowds from overrunning the camp. "You two!" The colonel pointed to Cletis and another recruit. They scrambled over to the colonel. "What are your names?"

"Cletis Mutt, sir." Cletis started to offer his hand in a handshake but remembered just in time. He gave a salute.

"Dewey Beckworth, sir."

"Mutt, Beckworth, stand guard at the gates," he ordered. He pointed to the townspeople who crowded around the drilling troops. "Too many gawkers. Keep them out of the way."

The two recruits nodded, flattered to have been singled out.

Cletis's awe for Colonel Wood paled in comparison only to his reverence for Teddy Roosevelt. Later that afternoon, Cletis had momentarily and unintentionally gained his hero's attention when he diverted a large sorrel just seconds before the horse would have stepped on a toppled pair of Roosevelt's pince-nez. In anticipation of his military service, Roosevelt had ordered a dozen pairs of the steel-rimmed spectacles to help his weak but lively blue eyes. A pair of glasses inhabited every pocket, and a pair was even tucked in his hat. "Bully good save!" Roosevelt bellowed to Cletis, as he reached down and clapped Cletis's broad shoulder. Roosevelt returned his pince-nez to their rightful position atop the bridge of his nose. "You join me and some friends for a drink at the Menger tonight."

"Y-yes, sir," Cletis stammered, unsure whether or not he should salute. "I'll be there, sir!" Cletis knew it was a sincere invitation; it was widely known that Roosevelt often bought his men beer at the temporary saloon that had opened near the regiment's camp at the fairgrounds. But this was different.

Roosevelt was inviting him to the Menger.

2

Cletis removed his hat and clutched it against him as he entered the Menger bar. He glanced self-consciously around the hazy, smoke-filled taproom, eyeing the rich cherry wood panels, the beveled French mirrors, and the polished glass-front cabinets on the wall behind the bar. Why, he had heard that the cabinets alone had cost sixty thousand dollars! For a moment, Cletis tried to imagine how that number might look in writing but gave up. *Made a mistake*, he chided himself. *Shouldn't have come.* He turned back towards the door.

"Over here!" The hearty, booming voice stopped Cletis in his tracks. Lieutenant Colonel Roosevelt waved the young recruit to his table where he sat with other officers. In his enthusiasm Cletis tripped against a brass spittoon, nearly upsetting it. He felt relieved to make it to the table without further mishap.

With a sweep of his arm that took in the entire saloon, Roosevelt said, "An exact replica of the one in the House of Lords in London." Though not sure what a house of lords was, Cletis nodded approvingly and sat down, grateful to be handed a glass of beer. Since Cletis seemed tongue-tied, Roosevelt continued, "I first came to the Menger in '92. I was twenty-nine, not much older than you, and I was on a trip hunting javelina." A long, satisfying draft of dark German beer prompted his next comment. "There are tunnels under the hotel that they roll the barrels of beer through. Did you know William Menger founded the first brewery in the state?"

Cletis shook his head, and offered gamely, "No, sir, but I'm truly glad he did." The others at the table laughed.

Cletis would have felt foolish except that Roosevelt immediately concurred. "Me, too, my boy! Mr. Menger had so many customers from the surrounding towns that he finally had to build a place for them to sleep it off overnight before they headed home again. That's how he got into the hotel business." To those at the table,

Roosevelt announced, "We're part of an illustrious tradition, gentlemen. Both Ulysses S. Grant and Robert E. Lee had drinks at the Menger. In fact, General Lee rode Traveller right into the lobby."

"Was that *after* he had been drinking?" Cletis asked in utter seriousness.

Everyone at the table hooted, and Roosevelt guffawed. "That's a good one! Maybe I should ride Texas into the lobby later tonight. What do you think?"

Cletis was too awed by his expansive hero to respond with anything other than a foolish grin. He drained the last of the beer from his glass. Not wanting to overstay his welcome, he rose to his feet. "Thank you for the beer, sir."

"Thank you for rescuing my specs this afternoon. Rest up," Roosevelt instructed, "because we have a full day of drilling tomorrow."

"*Yes, sir!*" Cletis replied. It was clear that he actually relished the prospect. He turned and with a slight swagger, strode out of the bar. He was proud to be one of Teddy's Terrors.

3

A few days later, on May 28, Cletis helped load the cavalry unit's horses on the trains, only to discover that the horses alone filled all seven railroad cars. There was no room for the men. All one thousand recruits slept beside the tracks that night. The next day they boarded another long train for Tampa, Florida, the jumping-off point for Cuba. Cletis felt a rush of excitement and apprehension as he stepped aboard. When Dewey Beckworth pulled a map out of his pocket and pointed to Texas and Florida, Cletis slowly ran his finger from one to the other, connecting the two states with an invisible line. He furrowed his brow and gave a solemn assessment: "It's *far.*"

A nearby recruit, the former captain of Columbia's crew team, shot back, "Hell, yes, it's far, country boy!" Then stabbing at the map, he mocked Cletis's accent and rural speech, "And looky here. There's water around most near all of Florida, and around *all* of little ol' Cuba."

The realization began to sink into Cletis's comprehension that he was going to Cuba, a faraway place he did not know, to fight Spaniards, whoever they were, and that he was going to have to go on a boat across the ocean to get there. *I might drown on the way over. I might even be killed once I get there.* The thought exploded in his brain. Somehow that hadn't seemed like a possibility when they were drilling on the fairgrounds before the admiring eyes of local citizens. The back of his neck prickled with fear like a cornered dog's, and droplets of sweat began to roll down his face.

Cletis ran his finger around the inside of his blue neckerchief, then freed the knot so he could mop his brow. He realized that he had begun nervously humming "There'll Be a Hot Time in the Old Town Tonight," and abruptly became silent.

4

After four sweltering, miserable days, the train delivered the recruits in Tampa— almost. For unknown reasons, the train stopped seven miles short of its destination.

The men mounted up and rode on horseback the last few miles to the sprawling tent city that served as the army's camp.

"Men, I'm afraid ill fortune has struck again." So began Colonel Roosevelt on June 6, as he made a painful announcement to his eager cavalry regiment. "I have been informed that only officers will be allowed to take horses to Cuba." He drew a breath and then delivered even more devastating news: "And I am sad to inform you that I will be allowed to take only slightly more than half of this fine regiment to Cuba."

Those not going cursed their fate, so at first Cletis felt a burst of joy and relief when he learned he was among the five hundred and sixty who would continue as Rough Riders. The next day, he and the others began to question their luck. The train that was to take the regiment to the point of embarkation failed to show up. Nor did a train appear at the other track they were then directed to. When he least expected it, Cletis heard Roosevelt's familiar stentorian voice shouting, "Get aboard, men! Get aboard!" So determined was he to move his men that he had commandeered some coal cars.

As they scrambled aboard, Cletis heard a former Apache fighter and Arizona sheriff mutter, "Coal cars! And worse than that, the engine's facing the wrong direction!" A moment later when the train began to move, he gushed in delight, "Damnation!" Colonel Roosevelt, looking every inch in command in his tan uniform with its bright yellow trim, gave a victorious wave as the train began to back its way to its destination.

The Rough Riders' troubles weren't over yet. "I heard two other regiments were assigned to the same ship as our outfit and that there won't be room for us," complained a frustrated recruit from Yale. Suddenly, though, Cletis and the others scrambled to their feet as Roosevelt boomed orders from his barrel chest. "Get on board! On the double!" The colonel figured that once his regiment was on the ship, it would be difficult to remove them. The men flooded aboard. Later, when the other troops arrived, Roosevelt, without a trace of guile, told them, "Sorry. We're under orders to hold the gangplank."

Six more days passed in agonizing slowness. The looming presence of unidentified warships prevented the Rough Riders from receiving permission to sail. Cletis and the others waited restlessly in quarters that were airless and hot. Provisions began to spoil, water was becoming undrinkable and, to Cletis's dismay, horses were dying daily. He did all he could to help the ailing animals, yet his spirits sank further with each senseless death.

5

When they at last set sail, Cletis felt a surge of pride. The thirty-one transport ships that fanned out over twenty-five miles of ocean gave the appearance of invincibility. But it was not until they had sailed for several miles and the fleet turned due southwest, directly towards Cuba, that the officers and troops knew for certain that they would not be held at some intermediate point. Cheers erupted from the decks of the ships. On Cletis's transport, the men witnessed an exultant Teddy Roosevelt wave his hat and perform an impromptu Indian war dance.

More determined than ever not to miss out on the war, Roosevelt managed to have his transport land first. The Navy made it safe for the troops to land by bombarding the coastline and blockading Spanish ships inside the Santiago harbor.

Cletis was frightened by the waves as he slid over the side of a smaller boat and struggled to the shore. He watched in helpless dismay as the horses were lowered into the ocean to swim to shore. "Rain-in-the-Face!" Cletis screamed as he watched one of Colonel Roosevelt's two horses drown. It was almost more than he could bear. His only solace was that the colonel's remaining horse, Texas, made it safely ashore.

Once on shore, Roosevelt exhorted his men, "To win the war, we must take Santiago." He pointed in the direction of the city. "Heavily defended hills stand between us and our goal."

Roosevelt refused to ride while his men walked. Sodden from a deluge, he began the march across seven difficult miles to a point where they could go inland. "He's a hero even if we don't take Santiago!" declared Dewey, who was trudging alongside Cletis. "He don't ask anything of us that he won't do himself. I'd follow that man to Kingdom Come and never look back!" Cletis nodded mutely in his comrade's direction.

Dewey continued a patchy conversation with Cletis as they worked their way through the jungle. The congenial young man swatted absent-mindedly at the voracious mosquitoes. He seemed untroubled by them, although Cletis was miserable.

6

Like the others, Cletis and Dewey were overwhelmed by Cuba's exotic but dangerous nature. Sometimes they were choked by the dust; moments later, they found themselves in a tropical downpour. Brilliantly colored birds screeched and darted about. Lizards crawled along overhanging branches, and snakes slithered over protruding roots.

Cletis and his comrades discovered that these were as much their enemies as the Spaniards were. The jungle, with its tangles of deceptively beautiful, flower-bedecked branches above and overgrown ground beneath, was ruthless. There were insects everywhere: in the steamy air, hovering around trees, crawling on the verdant ground. Swarming mosquitoes landed on any exposed bit of the soldiers' skin.

Cletis felt a jolt of fear electrify him when Roosevelt announced, "Along with regular army regiments, we've received the order to attack the Spanish troops that hold the forward positions." Cletis tried to cheer with Dewey and the others, but no sound came forth from his dry, constricted throat. He noticed with shame that his hands had begun to tremble. Dewey's confidence made Cletis feel better, so he positioned himself next to his comrade.

Without warning, the buzzing of the insects was infused with a hum that sounded like someone was ripping silk. Within minutes, men began to drop, groaning and bleeding, and Cletis discovered what the sound was: Mauser bullets slicing through the air.

Where to fire? Cletis and the others were at a loss. The Spaniards were using smokeless gunpowder. When Roosevelt's men sighted cone-shaped hats, however, they cut loose. The Spaniards scattered, and Teddy's Terrors quickly captured the red-tiled buildings from which the enemy had fled.

7

Later, in camp, Cletis and other able-bodied soldiers tended the wounded, rinsed bloody uniforms, and searched for food to compensate for supplies that still had not arrived. Men had already begun succumbing to dysentery, malaria, and yellow fever.

Then came July 1. Inspiring, courageous, and supremely calm, Theodore Roosevelt led what was left of his regiment towards San Juan Hill. Astride Texas, the broad-shouldered colonel was a conspicuous target, yet he somehow managed to avoid being hit. The regiment waded through a creek clogged with bodies and red with blood. The men kicked at the scavenger crabs and shook their fists to scatter the circling vultures. Finally, the soldiers crawled through the tall, protective grass on the other side of the creek. "We're almost there, Cletis!" Dewey called out. "We'll by god show those Spaniards what happens when they tangle with Teddy's Terrors!"

Then it happened.

Cletis screamed. "Dewey!" His companion's sweat-caked face had gone slack. A trickle of red sprang from his forehead. The young soldier toppled forward on his rifle, jabbing it into the dirt. He appeared to rest on it momentarily, as if it were a cane. Then he crumpled like a rag doll.

No! No! No! Cletis's mind reeled. *Dewey's my friend. He ain't no older than me!* Cletis threw down his own rifle and knelt beside Dewey. "Dewey, get up, man, get up! C'mon! I'll help you!" His voice was desperate, strident, shrill.

Within minutes, huge land crabs with clattering claws scuttled towards the body, and vultures began to swoop down from the sky for their share of the war's spoils. Cletis cursed at them as he tried to fend them away from Dewey's body.

An older man shouted to Cletis as he passed by. "It's no use. Grab a rifle. We have to press on."

Even Cletis recognized the futility of the situation. The perspiration that ran down his grimy face camouflaged angry tears. He now turned his wrath on the Spaniards. For the first time, they took on a tangible identity in his mind. *They're the ones who killed Dewey.*

Cletis was filled with rage. He grabbed Dewey's rifle and hooked his finger on the trigger, ready to kill every Spaniard on the island. Before he had a chance to raise the rifle to his shoulder, he stumbled and lurched on the uneven terrain. At the same second, he heard the rifle shot, he felt the impact of the bullet. Searing pain radiated through his foot. Blood poured freely onto the ground, attracting insects. Cletis went numb. He stood staring at his mangled, throbbing foot, oblivious to the maelstrom around him.

A cohort shoved Cletis to the ground and quickly bound his foot with his neckerchief. "You've been shot." Cletis's face was blank and uncomprehending. "Don't move! Stay here!" the voice commanded.

His companions pressed on and captured Kettle Hill. The decisive Roosevelt moved them past army regulars whose commanders were reluctant to storm the hill from their equally unfavorable positions below the Spaniards.

With his bushy mustache flying and his pince-nez clinging precariously to his nose, Roosevelt led the final charge: San Juan Hill. The Rough Riders were the first to reach the top. The colonel had remained dogged in his determination, despite a wound to his elbow. He even managed to kill a Spaniard with his sword.

Afterwards, the victorious Roosevelt paced the crest of San Juan Hill, his hands clasped behind him, opening and closing his fists. Over and over again he proclaimed to both his men and a reporter who was traveling with the regiment, "It was a bully fight!"

Cletis still sat halfway down Kettle Hill. He wasn't among those who heard Roosevelt's words. Eighty-nine Rough Riders had laid down their lives, the greatest percentage of any regiment. And although Cletis wasn't among the fallen eighty-nine, he was among those who had taken a bullet. But unlike the others who were wounded, Cletis wished that he had died.

TWENTY-EIGHT

1

"There's no uniform. You supply your own horse, saddle, and weapons. And you make your own badge." A badge with a five-pointed star in the center was the only identifying mark of membership in the Texas Rangers, but even their badges varied. A hammer and a Mexican ten-peso silver coin were the favored starting point for a badge, but each man devised his own. The speaker, a ten-year veteran of the Rangers, named Virgil Bragg, continued Danny's orientation. "There's two Ranger bibles: the Good Book, and this." He handed Danny a list of the men wanted by the Rangers. "We go where we're sent, wherever and whenever there's a problem. Our boundary is the whole state. We get called in whenever the problem's too much for the local law enforcement to handle."

There was informality among the men, both enlisted men and their captain alike. Virgil introduced Danny to the others in Company D who were on hand. Noah Dixson, a slight but intense man, was dwarfed by Sergeant B.J. Coffee, a seventeen-year-veteran whose huge physique could fill a doorway. Clancy Stephens and Billy Clark, two younger men, both privates, were given to ready laughter and lively conversation. Six-year veteran Henri LeBlanc, a corporal, had become "Ornery" LeBlanc, due to both his temperament and his fellow rangers' lack of familiarity with French. Short and stocky, Corporal Kirby Pearson resembled a toadstool when he donned his wide-brimmed hat. His appearance gave him a comical look, but several outlaws had regretted dismissing him on that basis. Kirby was acknowledged by the others as the finest marksman in a company of sharpshooters. He had once blown off a robber's thumb when the man tried to draw on him. "Welcome to *Los Diablos Tejanos*—the Texas Devils." Kirby spoke in a mock Spanish accent, for this was the name the Mexicans had given the fearsome and fierce rangers after the Mexican War. Kirby beamed with pride as he tipped his oversized hat in Danny's direction.

It had been obvious to Danny before the captain introduced himself that this man was indeed the captain. Rangers had no flags, no insignias, and no outward indications of rank, yet one could sense in any company the man the others identified as their captain.

Danny himself instinctively knew that Robert James was the one the others looked to for leadership. Once chosen as their captain, he, like other ranger captains, was the sole decision maker as to who was accepted into the close-knit unit. Initially

Danny had been nervous, but the captain had put him at ease. When Danny was invited to join Company D, he was elated.

"I'll do my best." The newest ranger pumped the captain's hand. *Rooster proud,* Danny thought. *That's how Twigs would describe the way I feel.*

2

For two decades, Robert James had served in the Rangers. He was, quite simply, a presence. When he spoke, others listened, and when someone else spoke, he turned his full attention on the speaker. He had the ability to draw out the best in those around him, in large measure by the example he set. Among the rangers, his courage and integrity were legendary, but no less so than his humility.

His hair had been snowy white since he was in his twenties. It crowned his smooth, unlined face and contrasted with his startlingly blue eyes. He stood an erect six-foot-three, and Danny noticed that each man seemed to stand a bit taller when the captain was nearby. The captain's easy manner in the saddle reminded Danny of Tom Bartlett.

At his first meeting with Captain James, Danny's eyes had drifted downward to the captain's sleek boots. Despite the dust, the patina of burnished leather gleamed through. From his days as a cowhand, Danny knew what a fine pair of boots cost, not that he had ever owned so fine a pair. He guessed that Sam Lucchese, the city's premier bootmaker, had crafted them. And when Danny discreetly assessed the hats that hung on a row of pegs, he was easily able to identify the captain's. One stood out as relatively pristine. A simple, superbly tooled band encircled its deep crown. Danny speculated that a hat such as that, assuming one could be found around here, would have set a cowboy back a month's pay or more. No one ever asked the captain where his boots or hats came from, and no one seemed to begrudge him in the least these fine accouterments. They seemed consistent with who he was, and it seemed right that he should possess them.

During the ensuing months, Danny heard stories about the captain that left him more intrigued than ever. Noah Dixson volunteered, "Once when Ornery and Kirby was bickerin', Ornery turns to the captain and says, 'Cap'n, tell him that the biggest fool on earth is the man who thinks he knows everything.' Captain just smiles and says, 'Ornery, the biggest fool on earth is the man who wastes his breath arguing with the man who thinks he knows everything.'" Noah laughed at the memory.

Then Kirby told Danny a story that involved B.J.'s oldest son, Benjamin Josiah, Jr. Danny mentally settled in because Noah had a way of recounting a story that sounded like one continuous sentence. "Round about two years ago, Ben took a terrible fall into a ravine. He was climbing on a railroad trestle when he slipped. He bounced all the way down and landed in a heap at the bottom. His head was cut, he busted a couple of ribs, and the bottom half of his left leg looked like it had sticks inside instead of bones. When they got him to the doctor, the doctor shook his head and says, 'Looks like that leg might have to come off at the knee.' Only time I ever knowed B.J. to cry. The captain says, 'Why don't you wait a few days, B.J.? There's time to decide.' Three days later a doc from Boston appears at the hospital that knows all about bones. Says he was passing through and young Ben's situation looks interesting. Would B.J. mind if he took a look? B.J. says, 'Doc, I can't pay you.' The doc says, 'I'll do this one for the experience.' So he *says*." Kirby's inflection made it clear B.J. didn't believe the doctor's words. "To make a long story short, he did an op'ration on Ben and pretty much put all the pieces back the way they was before Ben took that tumble. He's got a hitch in his get-along, a bit of a limp, and like as not always will. But he still got both legs, and they both work. Captain says, 'Well, it sure was a stroke of luck that doctor happened through.' But B.J. knows wasn't no luck involved, unless 'luck' is the captain's middle name."

Kirby continued, "There's more. Last year a train robber named Ryan tried to put a bullet in the captain's back. B.J. and the captain had been trackin' Ryan and finally got him holed up in a cave. At least they thought they did. Ryan discovered another way out and circled back around the captain and B.J. When B.J. heard the click behind them, he jumped up and took the bullet in his shoulder." Kirby pointed to a spot on his own shoulder. "Anybody with less heft than B.J. wouldn't have survived." Almost as an aside, Kirby added, "I don't have to tell you that the captain shot Ryan deader 'n hell." Kirby inspected a fingernail he had just pared with his pocketknife and then resumed his story. "So the captain starts working on B.J. He always keeps alumroot or powdered yarrow in his saddlebag to stop bleeding. He digs out the bullet, mashes up a mess of nearby plant leaves—hyssop, I think—mixes it with the powder and stuffs it in the hole in B.J.'s shoulder until he can get him to a doctor."

Danny nodded his understanding. His thoughts flickered first to Janie and her knowledge of herbs, and then to a train trip he'd made with the captain. During the trip, the captain had told him part of the story of the Trojan War and had explained how Achilles used yarrow to stop the bleeding of his wounded men. After hearing Kirby tell about B.J.'s wound, Danny had a new appreciation for the ancient story and the captain's knowledge.

Danny became aware of Kirby's voice again. "…so the captain says, 'I owe you one, B.J. I don't know how you repay a man for saving his life.' And B.J., who's thinking about his boy, Ben, says, 'Captain, you already did.'" Kirby closed his knife with a satisfied snap and shoved it back into his pocket.

Billy Clark had been listening to Kirby's story, too; and although he had heard it many times, he seemed as interested as if he were hearing it for the first time. "Captain says, 'Never forget your friends, and never take your eye off your enemies.' It's a good rule." In a departure from his usual joviality, Billy said solemnly, "The captain lets us make mistakes and learn from them, but he don't ever put us at unreasonable risk. At one time or another, darn near every one of us has had to trust our lives to him." Then Billy switched to a lighter note. "Captain's had book schooling, too. A barrelful. But he don't lord it over anybody. And he remembers *everything.*"

Danny found this wasn't an exaggeration. The captain soaked up information of every sort regardless of whether he heard it or read it. A few months later when the captain handed Danny a book, he told him, "The man who wrote this lived in New York, where you started out. He was orphaned, by the way." The captain glanced at Danny to make sure he had not ventured into too personal an area. "He had every type of job from schoolteacher to cabin boy to whaleman in the Pacific. He died in '91. His books haven't received much attention, but I like this one. You probably will, too, especially since you already know something about life at sea from, was it a Mr. Dunside?"

Danny nodded and ran his finger over the title of the book.

"After you've read it, tell me what you think."

"Sure. And thanks." Danny looked down again at the embossed words, *Moby Dick*. The title told him nothing.

It was the first of many books the captain would share with him.

3

No matter when Danny went to Ranger headquarters, he was there. "Where'd he come from?" Danny asked B.J. one day, as he flicked his thumb in the direction of a small dog sleeping beside the captain's desk.

"Who? Scrap?"

At the sound of his name, the little dog instantly raised his head. One ear lopped down; the other seemed perennially cocked as if scanning for stray noises.

B.J. set down the newspaper he was reading. "Scrap latched on to the captain about five years ago. He came trotting down the other side of the street one morning, just as purposeful as sin. He stopped and crossed the street to where the captain was standing. He sat down square in front of the captain and barked at him. Captain ignored him, but it didn't do no good. When the captain moved on, so did the dog. It was like that critter found his rightful place in the world and just fell in step. He finds the rest of us tolerable, but the captain is the only star in his sky."

Scrap lowered his head again, resting his chin on top of his paws, and closed his eyes.

"Every time the captain takes a step, that dog moves with him. He still scrambles whenever the captain stands up." B.J. smiled. "Captain would never admit to it, but he's just as stuck on that mutt."

Danny studied the small, wiry dog. His back had a peculiar arch in it, and his tail curved up like a sentry's salute. His tail ended abruptly and bluntly, mute testimony to an earlier, unsuccessful encounter of some sort. His fur was mottled and curly. Danny gave B.J. his considered opinion: "Looks like he got whopped with the Ugly Stick."

B.J. concurred. "He ain't much to look at, but he sticks like glue. Him and Captain are a regular Pete and Re-Pete." He chuckled at his own humor. "When the captain goes to the livery, that dog marches right alongside him, then comes back here. Same thing if the captain goes to the depot. Once, the captain got a call and had to leave on short notice. We didn't know where he'd gone. Virgil got the bright idea to 'ask the dog.' Virgil's walking around talking to the dog, saying, 'Where's Cap'n? Find Cap'n!' Kirby almost busted a gut laughin', but sure enough, Scrap goes out the door and heads straight for the livery. We got three rangers following this here dog down the street and looking like fools. But at the livery, Harold Beckley says, 'Sure, the captain left first thing this morning. A disturbance of some kind over in Holt.' Pointing to Scrap, he says, 'That dog came over with him around dawn.' Well, I can tell you that put an end to Kirby's laughin'."

BJ stared at the Scrap, studying the animal. "Cap'n says the reason dogs has got so many friends is that they wag their tails instead of their tongues."

Danny looked down at the scruffy lump of fur. "Why's he called Scrap? Like a leftover, that kind of scrap? Or because he's such a snip of a dog?"

"Not neither," said B.J. "Captain said he named him Scrap because he likes to fight."

Danny stared in disbelief at the diminutive, unprepossessing clump of fur that was now sprawled spread-eagled, snoozing on the floor.

B.J. rubbed his chin thoughtfully. "I don't know for sure, but I think the captain was funnin' us."

Scrap opened one wary eye, then slowly closed it again. To Danny, it looked suspiciously like a wink.

4

As a lawman, Danny learned about parts of San Antonio that he had known nothing about as a boy. The "sporting district" at the southwest end of downtown was one of the country's most notorious red-light districts. At the YT Danny had heard some cowboys discussing San Antonio's "high-class brothels." They had hooted when he asked what a brothel was. They told him, then quickly explained that it was the wealthy ranchers and businessmen who patronized these establishments, not ranch hands and working men. The city's brothels were housed in fine mansions and featured gambling and whiskey of every sort, paintings of naked women, velvet-covered furniture and drapes, even player pianos to provide music for dancing. Danny recalled that although Dooley hadn't used the word brothel, he'd told him that a well-to-do gent might pay to spend an entire week with one of "them ladies."

As a deputy, Danny had acquired some knowledge of the red-light district. As a new ranger, he was given a tour of the area by Clancy and Billy. Billy instructed Danny on the fine points. "There's also 'houses' upstairs in saloons and in second-rate hotels." He rattled off the names of several.

"And then lastly you got your sporting women who work out of rundown shacks and attract customers off the street. A turn with them will set a man back a quarter," Clancy explained. "Those are your two-bit whores. Your saloon and hotel houses run a half a dollar, whereas your brothels run a full dollar."

Billy took over again. "There ain't much trouble in the district. Saloon and brothel owners keep the peace because it helps business."

"But a few years ago," Clancy interjected, "there was an evangelist that come through town. She declared that this was the wickedest city in the universe 'cept for Washington City, which she said was the wickedest of hell."

Billy grinned, revealing an uneven row of teeth. "I guess that makes us famous now, don't it?"

5

Danny leaned back in his chair and sipped a sunrise cup of coffee. His thoughts drifted to Janie, as they often did at odd moments. His hat rested beside him; without thinking he ran his fingers over the hatband. "B.J., you got a missus…" The way Danny said it made it sound like the preface to a question.

B.J. continued cleaning his pistol. "Yup. And three young uns—a pair of jacks and a queen: eight, six, and four." He beamed and clicked the cylinder into place. Then seeing Danny's surprise, he deadpanned, "And to answer the question you're thinking, no, I ain't been mistook for their grandpa."

Danny blurted out another question instead. "Don't your wife worry about your safety?" What he really wanted to ask was, "Why would a woman marry someone who might be killed at any time?" He had been thinking a lot about Janie lately.

"Sure, Althusa worries. But risky situations is a fact of life in this work. To please her, I left the Rangers—for a while, anyway. I farmed, carpentered, tried lots of things, but I was plain miserable. And we weren't no better off. So I signed on again. Never been happier. I'd never go back to anything else." Then B.J. asked a question in return. "You thinking about getting hitched?" He raised his eyebrows expectantly.

Janie crossed Danny's mind again, but he quickly shook his head no and gulped more coffee. He looked over at the captain. "What about you, Captain James? You got a missus?"

The captain shook his head without looking up from the report he was writing.

B.J. was now polishing the handsome, engraved barrel of his Colt. "Cap'n never had a missus," he teased, "but at least he has Rose."

Captain James paused and raised his eyes without raising his head. He looked briefly at B.J. and then resumed writing. In a level tone, he said, "B.J., I think you need a better command of the English language."

Ranger B.J. Coffee developed an intense interest in the trigger of his pistol and began examining it closely. Danny finished his coffee in silence.

"What did he mean?" Danny asked B.J. later.

B.J. grinned. "He meant I need to learn to keep my mouth shut."

6

Three days later Danny and the captain set out on horseback through the open space and silence of the Edwards Plateau. Danny surveyed the country, enjoying the easy roll of his horse's gait and the beauty around him. Large stands of sycamore, cypress, and pecan trees dotted a landscape splashed with great patches of bright gold coreopsis and wildflowers. Yellow-cheek warblers fluttered in trees. At dawn and at dusk, whitetail deer came out to graze. Ambling along on horseback, Danny was struck with a realization: *I love this land.* For the first time, it occurred to him, *It feels like home.*

Danny and the captain were traveling west to take into custody two men alleged to have robbed several small-town banks. The captain filled Danny in on the details. The men had shot a teller point-blank and then killed a shopkeeper who unwittingly entered the bank during the robbery. In another town, they left the teller severely wounded. They had escaped once after being captured and had nearly beaten the deputy to death in the process. They were headed for Mexico when they were captured and brought back to Dawson. Since they had already eluded captivity once, the sheriff requested a ranger to escort the pair to trial in Flat Rock, the site of the first robbery. The captain thought it would be good experience for Danny to come along. "We'll travel to Dawson, pick up the prisoners, and take them back to Flat Rock. We'll stop at Placita on the way to Flat Rock," he told Danny.

Danny nodded. Anywhere the captain wanted to go was fine with him.

7

Danny and the captain rode for long stretches, alternating conversation with silences. Danny thought about Dilue and Bartlett, people of few words. He thought about Artis, who had fascinating things to tell once you got him started. He thought about Twigs and Dooley and Brody who were never without something to say. "Captain, why is it some folks never run out of talk and others never get started? Tom Bartlett and Dilue—I told you about them—they never said much, but it was worth listening when they did."

"Well, maybe the quiet ones prefer to be observers. Or maybe they're thinking instead. If you're talking, then you only know what *you* know, but if you're listening, then you also learn what the other person knows." The captain smoothed the ends of his reins. "Of course, there's another possibility. Maybe they just hate to use up all the silence by filling it with talk."

Danny looked at the captain. There was a trace of a smile on the captain's face.

After a while the captain volunteered, "It's also been said that it's better to be silent and be thought a fool than to open your mouth and remove all doubt." This time the captain smiled broadly, and so did Danny.

They camped along the way beside streams that were fed clear, cold water from springs deep underground. Danny showed the captain some of the more complicated knots Artis and Ples had taught him. He learned them easily. While Danny and the captain sat beside the campfire tying knots, they talked.

"Have you ever gone into Mexico?" Danny asked.

The captain nodded. "Many times." He finished tying an intricate knot and handed it to Danny to inspect. An owl they could not see hooted in the distance. Although Danny was not surprised that the knot was right, he remembered that as a boy it had taken him nearly a week to master it. He handed the rope back to the captain, giving his approval of the serpentine coils.

Captain James noticed that Danny seemed preoccupied. Sensing that he was uneasy about the coming day, he broached the matter. "This kind of business can make you a little jittery at first. When I feel that way, I remind myself that during the days of the Republic, the rangers and their first captain, Jack Hays, were the only protection people had against the Indians to the west and Mexican troops to the south. It always makes my task seem a little less formidable by comparison." Although Hays had been dead for decades, the captain spoke of him as if he had just left the room. Danny noticed that rangers seemed to do that when speaking of their legendary predecessors.

Danny smiled. "Thanks." He appreciated the captain's willingness to acknowledge that he still felt apprehension, too. Setting aside his fears about the prisoners they were going to escort to Flat Rock, Danny changed the topic. "South Texas. I have a friend, Janie McCorkle, who lives there, in Anuncio." Danny recounted tales of meeting Janie at the YT and gave a vivid account of her father's bizarre death. The captain listened and asked questions.

Danny felt the topic was exhausted, and it made him feel forlorn to speak of Janie. He unconsciously touched his hatband, running his finger back and forth over it. He switched to a more impersonal line of conversation. "At the YT, Dooley told me ranchers got cattle through droughts by feeding them prickly pear—with the thorns off, of course. He also said the core of it, the tuna, is sweet and good and that Indians ate it. Dooley said to find a good one, you watch the birds, see which ones they choose."

"You ever try any?" the captain asked.

"Once. It tasted slippery. It tasted—" Danny searched for a word to describe it. "It tasted *green.* Dooley said you can sun dry it, too. He told me he once made a pie out of it. Called it South Texas apple pie. He made a bet no one could figure out what the fruit was, and he won." Danny felt warmed by the memory of Dooley and his endless yarns.

Then the captain spoke. "There's another name for prickly pear: nopal cactus. If you get in a pinch, it's good to know about the thin, red juice in it. Prickly pear has several medicinal purposes, too." The captain stopped when he noticed Danny was shaking his head. "What?"

"I don't know why I thought there was anything you don't already know *something* about," Danny said with a grin.

"I like the land. Knowing about the land and what's on it can save your life. Especially in this job. Look how it's changed the farther west we've come."

He was right. As they had traveled west, the terrain had grown more austere. It was big, but it was empty, with little water and infrequent rain. The captain pointed out mockingbirds and thrashers that darted among tough, brown-green creosote bushes adorned with tiny yellow flowers. Then a brief shower yielded a surprise as unexpected as the rain itself: a pleasant, spicy odor.

Danny sniffed the air and inhaled the sharp fragrance. The captain pointed to the delicate creosote blooms to indicate its source. "There's a plant called the night-blooming cereus that can be smelled downwind for a quarter of a mile. I've only seen one cereus in my life."

Danny looked skeptical. "A quarter of a mile? And it blooms only at night?"

"It opens one single night at sunset in the early summer. White petals that you can actually see unfold. They look lustrous, probably because they reflect the moonlight. Then the petals die and fall away. It's all over by daybreak." The captain pointed to a thorny, sword-leafed agave. "Now *that* one is called the century plant. It grows for years and never blooms. Then one spring, it suddenly blooms, a flower on top of a tall stem. Then the agave dies."

A whole lifetime that leads to one brief moment. Then it's over. A moment, maybe even a lifetime, that might go unnoticed by anyone. Danny was still thinking this baleful thought when the captain halted beside one of the yuccas that studded the desert-like terrain. He snapped the end off a leaf. "The thorns at the tips are so hard that they can be used to puncture rattlesnake bites. Good to know around here." The captain reminded Danny again to keep an eye out for rattlers since they favored dry, loose, rocky ground. At the mention of rattlesnakes, Danny thought of Shamus and blanched.

The young ranger scrutinized the landscape. "I can see the value of knowing how to use whatever you got at hand, especially out here in the open."

The captain nodded. "As a matter of fact," he continued, "yucca thorns can also be used to stitch something together." He stopped, leaned down and snapped off another thorn. Carefully, he peeled it back. He held it up to show the long fibrous strand trailing from it. "Needle *and* thread," he proclaimed.

Danny smiled. "And I thought West Texas was just coyotes, rabbits, hawks, and kangaroo rats."

8

The following day, Danny and the captain moved into even more desolate country. Its sand dunes were crisscrossed with the stitchery of bird tracks. In the distance, Danny could see areas that were rocky, even mountainous.

The captain lifted his hat and wiped his forehead with his sleeve. He took a sip of water from a canteen and handed it to Danny.

Danny took a grateful gulp. "It's sure hot enough."

"Dawson is only a few miles ahead."

Danny could make out its hazy contours emerging over a hummock. He poured a little water on his bandanna. "Whoever said 'Everything in Texas sticks, stings, or bites' should have added 'or scorches.'" Had it not been for his hat, his face would have been blistered. There had been few clouds to offer any relief, and now the late afternoon sun glared in his eyes. He handed the captain back his canteen. His throat felt dusty despite the water.

The captain secured the canteen to his saddle. "General Philip Sheridan once said if he owned both Texas and hell, he'd rent out Texas and live in hell."

Danny and the captain reached the town at twilight. "We're due a hot meal and a night's sleep in decent beds, Danny. We'll go over to the jail first thing in the morning."

The Dorset Hotel was a gray, two-story building with a white-railed balcony. Although the accommodations it offered were basic, they were a welcome change from sleeping on saddle blankets among prickly pears, scorpions, spiders, and snakes.

Danny and the captain registered at the hotel and headed for the dining room. A meal of steak and fried potatoes, accompanied by whiskey, contributed to a sense of camaraderie. Aglow with a full stomach and flush with whiskey, Danny blurted out, "Who's Rose?"

"Rose," the captain repeated. "Rose is my little sister."

Danny sat in silence, puzzled. Then he asked meekly, "Is she still alive?"

The Captain nodded. Another silence ensued.

"Do you ever see her?"

"Every few years, when I can. Lives in New York."

Danny sensed the conversation was at an end. Lost in separate thoughts, they finished their whiskey and retired for the night.

9

After breakfast, the captain and Danny walked over to the jail where Charley Clayburn and Louis Gibb would be remanded to their custody. Sitting sullenly in their cell, they appeared uninterested in the rangers' presence. Clayburn was the leader of the two, a grim, brooding fellow with a fresh scar that started on his forehead, leaped over his eye, and continued its erratic path down his left cheek. Gibb was tall and gangly, but what captured an onlooker's attention was the lumpy, oatmeal-like texture and color of his skin.

The sheriff reviewed the pair's alleged crimes with Captain James. Danny knew that when they returned to San Antonio, the captain would recall the information verbatim, from the amount of money stolen in each robbery to the names of the hapless tellers, the battered deputy, and the slain shopkeeper.

An energetic Mexican man who ran the local livery brought horses to the jail for the prisoners. The captain went outside and spoke to him for several minutes in Spanish, then he handed the man some money.

The sheriff handcuffed the prisoners and brought them out of the single cell that made up the town's jail. Danny pushed the prisoners towards the office door. When Clayburn was even with the captain, he glowered and spat at him. He missed the tall captain's face and hit instead the bandanna around his neck. Never taking his chilly blue eyes off Clayburn's face, the captain untied his neckerchief and knotted it around the offending dampness. Without saying a word, he shoved the knot into Clayburn's mouth and tied the ends behind his head. He put his face close to Clayburn's. "You provoke me again, Clayburn, and I'll trade that bandanna for a bit made of rope."

Once under way, with their prisoners stringing along on horses a rope's length behind them, Danny asked, "How'd you learn to speak Spanish so good?"

"I learned early. My father negotiated agreements between the U.S. and Mexico. When I was a boy, I spent my summers with him in Texas. Sometimes I traveled to Mexico with him, too."

Danny recalled Kirby telling him once that the captain lived in a fine house in San Antonio, out a distance, and surrounded by high walls. "It belonged to his father," Kirby reported. "None of us has ever seen it, except B.J. When the captain had to go to Austin for a week to testify in a trial, he asked B.J. to check each day on Jacinta, his housekeeper. She was ill. B.J. said she worked for the captain's father and has took care of the captain ever since he was a little boy. The captain was already a young man when his father died. He stayed on after that, and Jacinta stayed with him."

Danny's thoughts drifted for a moment as he tried to contemplate the captain as a child. All he could conjure up was a smaller version of him, a picture so silly that he smiled and dismissed it. Kirby had told him, "Toward the end of the week, Jacinta got to feeling better. She made B.J. a whole heap of hot bizcochitos. We only got to hear about them, of course. B.J. polished them off before he got back to headquarters. I always regretted that." Then he had added other remembered details: "Oh. B.J. said there was flowers everywhere. Outside the house and inside. Don't that beat all? And there was a whole room filled with nothin' but books. Shelves full! Can you imagine? Wonder what the captain does with all of 'em?" At the time, Danny had simply shrugged rather than admit his own fondness for books.

Danny realized he'd let the conversation with the captain lapse, and worse, he felt it must be obvious that he had been speculating about the man's private life. Danny glanced back to check on Clayburn and Gibb. Both stared ahead impassively. He cleared his throat and resumed, "And your mother? Did she come to Texas?"

"Only once. After that she stayed in the East. She said Texas was too uncivilized." He laughed. "That was the very thing I liked about it. By the time I had finished school, New York City had begun to feel claustrophobic. I liked the openness, the challenge, of living in Texas. I wanted to be part of something newer, something that was still being formed. To my mother's eternal dismay, I came to Texas one day and stayed."

"And Rose?"

Captain James smiled. "My sister felt the same way as my mother. Our parents are gone, so now there's just Rose and me. She still lives in New York City." He shook his head in distaste. "'Hurry-up City,' I call it. Rose runs a highly regarded finishing school for young ladies and has a fondness for literature. We write to each other on occasion, and I visit her every now and then."

Mary Ceara crossed Danny's mind. The captain understood what it meant to have a younger sister, and much better than he did.

"Rose is the one who sends you the books?" Danny had seen some of the packages when they arrived at the Ranger headquarters.

The captain nodded. "She and I both like them. They're a lot easier to get there than they are here, so she sends me ones she likes." Captain James shifted in his saddle and looked back to check on the prisoners. "Anyway, several years ago, after Rose's husband died, she made a trip west to visit me. She said it was just too different here, and she returned home a month later. Except for me, everyone and everything she loves is in the East. Except for my sister, everything I love is here." He made the fact that he had no family within nearly two thousand miles sound unimportant, but he and Danny rode in silence for the next half hour.

Danny noticed a small sheaf of papers protruding from one of the captain's saddlebags. "What's that?"

"Those are some stories written by by a man named William Sydney Porter. Apparently, the only formal schooling he had was at a school run by his aunt. Later, he trained with his uncle as a pharmacist. When he was about your age, he came to Texas because of his poor health. He worked on a sheep ranch, and after that, worked as a bank teller over in Austin." The captain looked back at their prisoners. "Fortunately, he never encountered any like those two. Unfortunately, though, he's in prison now for embezzling money from the bank. When he was first indicted, he fled to Honduras on a banana boat, but he returned when he learned his wife was dying of consumption." Danny was assimilating this when the captain added, "I've sent Rose a couple of his stories. Lots of them are set in Texas, although I'm not sure I'll ever convince Rose that there's *anything* worthwhile here. The stories have unusual twists at the end. You'd like them."

Danny made a mental note to borrow the stories from the captain once they returned to San Antonio. He had been enthralled with *Moby Dick* because of his own experience of crossing the ocean and Mr. Dunside's tales of life at sea. And he and the captain had enjoyed spirited discussions about *Moby Dick* and damnation and fate.

10

They traveled several hours in comfortable silence. Towards dusk, Danny said, "The sun'll be down soon. What do you want to do with Ahab here?" Danny gestured towards Clayburn and his scarred face. "And Fedallah?" He pointed to Gibb.

With a slight nod, the captain acknowledged his appreciation of Danny's allusion to the diabolical sea captain and his prophetic servant. "We'll take turns watching them throughout the night."

Danny and the captain had barely finished their sparse supper when Clayburn began his taunts. "You know, Captain, we killed one of you peso-badges outside of Liberty Point last month." He gave Gibb a look of satisfaction as he let his revelation sink in on the rangers. "Did it just for the hell of it. He wasn't even tracking us. We followed him out of town. I shot him in the leg, then Gibb shot him in the gut once he fell to the ground." Clayburn paused again. "We let him twist on the ground like a snake, and when we got tired of watching the show, I plugged him in the back of the head. Like shooting vermin." Even with his hands handcuffed in front of him, Clayburn was able to mimic with his index finger and thumb the firing of a gun. He gave a contemptuous smirk.

Both Danny and the captain knew Clayburn was telling the truth. There had been no clues in the case; it appeared to have been an unprovoked, random murder. They had both read the report. Danny wondered if Clayburn knew the implication of his boastful confession. No ranger would let the killing of another ranger go unavenged.

Danny watched the captain out of the corner of his eye. The captain's expression never changed, but even in the glow of the campfire, Danny could see twinges of suppressed anger in the captain's clenched jaw.

Clayburn belched. "Did you know the law has no way of connecting us with our proudest achievement, Gibb? Now that's a genuine pity. In fact, they're going to have a difficult time proving for sure we done those robberies."

He was right. The stolen money had not been found. They'd kept their faces covered during the robberies. It was only witnesses' sketchy descriptions that led to their being suspects. There was also a question as to whether or not a third person had helped them escape. The deputy had been choked unconscious near the cell and then severely beaten. The captain made no reply, but when they arrived in Placita the next day, he exchanged the prisoners' horses for a wagon. He gave Danny no explanation for his actions, and Danny did't ask.

The captain gestured for the prisoners to climb inside the wagon. They sat down, and Danny handcuffed them to the wooden ribs on opposite sides of the wagon. Then he tethered his horse to the rear of wagon. As he sat in the sun and drove the team, he envied the prisoners the shade inside. The captain rode stone-faced alongside.

When they stopped for the night, the captain instructed Danny to seat the prisoners on the ground, their backs to the wheels, on opposite sides of the wagon and tie them around their chests to the wheels. He tossed Danny two more pairs of handcuffs. "Cuff each hand to the rim of the wheel so they can't untie the rope."

Clayburn continued to mouth off to the captain. "Afraid we might slip through your fingers? Well, no matter what, you'll be rid of us tomorrow, Scarecrow."

"Maybe sooner," came the terse reply. Had the captain bothered to look, he would have seen the first and only trace of concern flicker across Clayburn's face.

Hours later Danny was startled awake. He scrambled to his feet in confusion, his heart racing at the sound of screams and galloping horses. In the moonlight, he could see the wagon careening wildly across the landscape. The captain stood near the spot where the wagon had been. "Saddle up," he said. He did not hurry.

They followed the tracks for the better part of a mile before they spotted the overturned and shattered wagon on the other side of a rise. The two horses stood placidly nearby, still linked together and trailing their broken reins. Gibb's limp body was splayed on an upturned wheel, still bound by the ropes. Clayburn, no longer recognizable, lay face down on the hard ground. He was still lashed to the wagon wheel that had crushed him, his arms and legs twisted at grotesque angles.

Danny's eyes darted over the spattered tangles of ropes, wood, and flesh. He felt his stomach contort. When he was able to speak, he choked out, "What happened?"

The captain did not answer immediately, but when he did, he uttered a single word: "Justice." He surveyed the corpses dispassionately and removed the handcuffs. Then he scooped up a handful of dirt and trickled over the bodies. He remounted his horse and gathered the reins of the two horses that had been hitched to the wagon.

As the two rangers traveled to Flat Rock, the silence expanded into a chasm that was so uncomfortable that the young ranger finally spoke. In a muted voice, he said, "Neither a hearse, nor a coffin. Death by hemp."

The captain's eyes never deviated; he stared resolutely ahead. Danny was correct: Fedallah's prophecy had again come true. The monstrous Ahab and Fedallah had been carried to their deaths lashed to a thrashing whale by twisted harpoon lines. Clayburn and Gibb had been taken to their deaths bound to a wheel, flung in jarring and terrifying revolutions before crashing into the unforgiving West Texas earth.

At last the captain spoke. "They had choices. They made bad ones. Gibb made a bad one last night. I went over to unhook the team so I could stake them to picket pins, and when I walked past him, he began kicking at me. The sudden commotion spooked the horses and set off the final chain of events." He offered no further explanation and no apology.

Danny rode in silence, pondering. Had the captain set Gibb up? Even if he had, it was still Gibb who startled the horses. It was Gibb who had made the decision to strike out at the captain. And what if Gibb and Clayburn had been taken to trial and, despite their confession to the captain and him, had gone free for lack of evidence or witnesses? Danny's head ached.

In Flat Rock, the captain reported to the sheriff that Clayburn and Gibb had been killed in a wagon accident the night before. "We were transporting the prisoners by wagon. They were bound. The horses got spooked, and the wagon was destroyed. The bodies were so badly mangled that we left the remains there." He didn't mention that the prisoners had been bound to the front wheels of the wagon.

"You bury 'em?" The sheriff cocked one eyebrow.

"We put a little dirt on them," came the captain's careful reply.

The sheriff made a sucking sound with his tongue, then flicked a piece of tobacco from his teeth with the blade of his penknife. "Well, the world's a better place without them, that's for sure," he said in a monotone. He ran his fingers down the sides of the small knife blade to clean it. "What caused the horses to start?"

It was Danny who spoke up and answered the sheriff's question. "A snake." To himself, he thought, *A snake named Louis Gibb.*

"A snake?" said the sheriff. Now he was studying Danny.

"Yes," Danny repeated, returning the lawman's gaze, "a snake."

He eyed Danny a moment longer. "Well, you got to be mighty careful nowadays. There's lots of 'em out there."

"Lots of what?" Danny asked.

Still without dropping his gaze, the sheriff flipped his knife shut and slipped it into his vest pocket. "Snakes," he replied. "Lots of snakes."

TWENTY-NINE

1

"The year, the decade, and the century are drawing to a close. This may be the last time I witness the conclusion of any of them." The person speaking was Artis Dunside, and the occasion was New Year's Eve, 1899. Gathered around the dinner table with him were Danny, Johanna, Mrs. Bromley, and Dilue.

"Now, now, Mr. Dunside," Mrs. Bromley chided, "you're just a bit under the weather. The changing of the year, the decade, the century! Gracious, they mark a beginning, not an end."

Mr. Dunside shrugged off her words. "No, the future belongs to these young ones." He glanced with affection at Danny and Johanna.

"We couldn't make it without you, Mr. Dunside!" Danny said, trying to cajole him into a more sanguine mood. It troubled him to hear Mr. Dunside talk as if the end were near. He directed his attention to Dilue. "We're at a special moment in history, Dilue. Tell us what you think the future holds."

Dilue demurred, but Danny was insistent.

"I will tell only your future since you are the one who asked."

Danny felt his pulse quicken.

"It is this: You will find what you are searching for, but you may not recognize it when you find it." Dilue would say no more.

There were several seconds of silence. Finally, Mrs. Bromley spoke up. "Well, my dears, it's growing late. We older folks will have to leave it to the two of you to see in the New Year."

"Leave the dishes. Danny can help me with them," Johanna told her.

The three older ones arose from the table and bid Danny and Johanna goodnight.

Danny and Johanna sat and talked for a long while. Then they carried the plates to the kitchen. "Do you think Dilue meant your uncle?" Johanna asked.

"I don't know," Danny replied in a pensive voice.

"Danny, do you think you'll ever see any of your family again?" Johanna sounded sad.

He set the dishes down. "I don't know, Johanna. I just don't know."

"Do you think I'll ever see either of my sisters again?"

The clock chimed midnight, resonating in rich, heavy tones. Danny smiled at her. "I hope so. After all, it's the beginning of a new year, a new decade, and a new century."

2

"Your first assignment of the new year." Captain James handed Danny the telegram he'd just finished reading:

NEED HELP. STOP. THREE TRAPPED IN BEECHES NEWSPAPER OFFICE BY MOB. STOP.

It was signed by the deputy sheriff of Beeches, a town halfway between San Antonio and Austin.

After Danny had read it, the captain said, "We're spread thin here. Think you can handle this alone?"

"I'll do my best." Danny could feel his scalp tingle with excitement and fear. Never before had the captain sent him out of town by himself.

"The train comes through in fifteen minutes. You'll be in Beeches within an hour. I'll wire them that we're sending a man. Size up the situation. If you can't solve the problem, just keep a lid on it. If I don't hear from you, I'll assume you need help, and I'll come tonight."

"I'm sure that won't be necessary, Cap'n." Danny hoped his words projected more confidence than he felt. He was determined to do whatever it might take to handle the situation by himself.

An hour later, Danny stepped off the train in Beeches, a town named for an incorrectly identified grove of nearby trees. The young ranger was greeted by a deputy who looked even younger than he did. The deputy's dismay was as great as Danny's. His eyes darted to the train. "They sent *you?*" He looked past Danny, hoping more rangers would appear. "They didn't send you by yourself, did they? I mean, there *are* more, aren't there?"

"Nope." Danny stared at the deputy. His hair was chopped off above his ears; he had a square jaw and a pointed chin. Danny sighed and shook his head imperceptibly. *He's not only a kid. He's a kid whose head looks like an acorn.*

"...a bad problem."

At the sound of the word "problem," Danny tuned in to the deputy's voice again. The young man was clearly frightened. He was almost breathless from swallowing large gulps of air. *Take charge,* Danny told himself. *That's what the captain would do.* "Nope, just me," Danny repeated himself. "So let's start walking and you tell me about this problem."

The deputy spewed a terse account of the facts. The newspaper editor, the townspeople, and the surrounding farmers were angry because Senator Lovell Burgess, who once had lived in Beeches, had foolishly traded away some of their water rights. An aquifer, their primary water source, ran beneath acreage the senator had bargained away. Horace Sinclair, editor of *The Beeches Banner*, had published a series of pieces condemning the legislator and demanding that he rectify the situation. The deputy poured out more of the story: "The senator was on his way back to Austin. He stopped in Beeches to try to explain himself and mend fences." The two lawmen hurried towards the newspaper office.

The deputy quickly explained the rest. "It got ugly. What began as a speech in the town square turned into shouting and rock throwing. The senator couldn't calm the crowd. Neither could the sheriff, even when he emptied his Colt overhead into the air. The crowd flat ignored him. That's when the sheriff, Mr. Sinclair, and the senator made a run for the newspaper office." The deputy pointed to the nearby *Beeches Banner* office. "And that's where they've been ever since."

All three were barricaded inside, but Danny could see that some windows had been broken. Even the unseasoned deputy had enough sense to know that whatever was going to happen would occur at nightfall, under cover of darkness.

The deputy was trembling when he approached the newspaper office. He called out to the crowd, "This here is a Texas Ranger." His voice came out sounding like a defiant eight-year-old's.

A belligerent, red-faced man held up a rope. "Save yourself a lot of trouble and just send out the senator. We'll give him a 'suspended' sentence!" The crowd laughed and cheered.

Another man spat tobacco juice on the ground and then pointed to Danny. "Let him go in. He can't do nothing." Then he thought better of it and added, "But leave your gun with the deputy, sonny."

Danny gave him a look of seeming indifference and said nothing. While he was removing his gun, he scanned the crowd, noting again the man he had identified as the leader. Then Danny entered the newspaper office through a door opened barely wide enough for him to slip in sideways.

"Ranger Danny O'Brien," he said in a perfunctory tone, as he surveyed the office and sized up the trio who had taken refuge in it.

Horace Sinclair was a sturdy, round-shouldered beetle of a man who very much looked like a newspaper editor. He peered myopically at Danny through small round lenses that magnified his eyes and glinted beneath bushy, black, caterpillar eyebrows. Agitation caused his thick brows to twitch up and down like they were parts of a puppet's face. "Personally," he sputtered, "I think what Senator Burgess did is reprehensible, but I won't be a party to that mob's lawlessness." He bobbed his head as he cast anxious glances towards the barricaded window.

The senator's puffy face glistened with sweat. He reminded Danny of a plump, plucked goose that had been greased for baking.

The sheriff was a quiet, tired-looking man in his sixties. His solemn visage and the wisps of gray hair that curved up in small points above either ear gave him the appearance of a horned owl. Danny surmised that he probably did an adequate job as long as he was making his rounds or escorting the town drunk to jail. This situation, however, was a different matter.

"You have a gun in here?" Danny asked.

"A shotgun." The newspaper editor gave an embarrassed frown. "But no shells. I have empty shell casings and everything to make shells." Sinclair's voice dropped a notch. "Everything except buckshot, that is."

The sheriff looked away and shook his horned-owl head. "I'll swear, Horace, you fancy, educated types don't have enough sense to…." He snorted in disgust.

Sinclair turned to the sheriff. "It isn't my fault. Several months back, I gave Calvin Dobbs my shells and extra buckshot. He was going hunting." He raised his palms in lame apology. "I meant to get more."

The sheriff looked at Danny. "Calvin was outside earlier, so I reckon he's told 'em we don't have protection. I reckon he—"

"Gentlemen!" Burgess interrupted them in a voice shrill with fear. "I don't have to remind you, do I, that I'm a state senator! What are you—what are we—going to do?"

Without looking up from what he was doing, Danny answered the question. "We're going to *think,* Senator. We got some time. Nothing's going to happen before nightfall." Danny continued to move around, exploring the contents of the office.

The senator glanced nervously at the Regulator clock that occupied a prominent position on one wall. "How do you know it'll be nightfall?" His voice was hoarse.

"Because bullies are also cowards." The young ranger spoke as matter-of-factly as if he were reciting the days of the week. He peered into a cabinet, rummaged through it, and slammed it shut again. "They don't have the nerve to do anything in broad daylight except stand around and make threats."

Silenced, the senator slumped into a chair and dabbed his florid face and damp neck with a crumpled handkerchief.

Danny yanked open a large, flat drawer of a dusty cabinet that stood in the back of the office. "What's this?" He pointed to trays filled with neat rows of tiny metal letters.

"They belonged to my grandfather. They used to have to set the type by hand." Sinclair's tone was irritable. "Look, this is no time for the history of printing. We have a problem, young man." His confidence in the boyish law officer was no greater than the deputy's.

But Danny had already pulled the drawer out and dumped the trays of type on a table.

"You can't do that!" Sinclair shouted. "You can't just come in here and—"

Danny ignored his protests and cut the man's tirade short. "Where are the casings you mentioned? The packing? The gunpowder?"

Still protesting, Sinclair retrieved a box from another cabinet. Danny pulled out a casing. He put in the primer and gunpowder, and then packed in a wad. He held the shell up, and from his cupped hand poured in the typeset. He added another wad, then crimped the end. He inspected it, and held it up in front of the other men. "We have work to do."

They understood and clustered around the table. The tiny tin letters danced on the tabletop as they trickled through the senator's jittery fingers. But the other men deftly corralled the rectangular bits into the shell casings. As the afternoon drew to a close, the finished shells began to accrue. They stood at attention, rows of small, red-jacketed soldiers.

An occasional rock thumped against the building or crashed through a windowpane, and angry taunts periodically pierced the air. The crowd had thinned a bit, but it had not dispersed.

The minutes ticked by, the clock registering the passing of each half hour with a dull clang. By dusk the tension inside and outside the newspaper office had risen to the boiling point.

Anticipating a break in the stalemate, the crowd had now swelled again to its original size. As the sun set, the rabble-rousers grew bolder and more vocal. Rocks began to fly. The torches the men carried cast sinister shadows across their faces. "Send the senator out!" a strident voice shouted.

"Turn that traitor over to us!" screamed an angry, scowling face. Peeking around a cabinet and out the window, Danny could see one man still holding a rope.

Danny felt it was time. To maintain the semblance of authority and control, he decided to go outside rather than allow the mob a chance to break in. He opened the door and walked out unarmed. The crowd, surprised by his boldness, nevertheless jeered and repeated its demands. When Danny said nothing, they grew quiet, curious about what the young lawman had to say.

Danny surveyed the crowd. He spoke slowly, trying to think what the captain would say. "Gentlemen, you're going to have to disband. If you have a bone to pick with the senator—and I ain't saying you don't—then you're going to have to settle it through lawful means. If you want to vote him out of office, that's your choice. That's your right. And frankly, I wouldn't blame you a bit." Danny's voice began a strong, clear crescendo. "But regardless of what he's done, I'm responsible for seeing that the senator gets out of here in one piece, and I intend to do just that."

Discontent rippled through the crowd. A couple of rocks landed near Danny. Then one hit him squarely in the chest. He made an involuntary grunt as the stone thudded against him, but he did not flinch. Instead, he cast a cold, unwavering stare at the rope-brandishing man who had thrown the rock. In a loud voice Danny called out, "Sinclair, hand me your shotgun." An outstretched arm handed Danny the gun through a crack in the door.

A voice from the back of the crowd scoffed, "Ain't gonna do you much good, sonny. Everyone knows Calvin Dobbs borrowed the shells. You can bluff all you like, but that gun don't got nothin' in it."

Danny kept his eyes on their leader. "I'm asking all of you one last time: Move on. Let's end this peaceably."

The man was still fingering a rope when his anger got the best of him. He had been reluctant to fire at a ranger, especially one who looked so young, but he was even less willing to be humiliated by so youthful an adversary. He reached for his gun.

Danny fired at his feet, spraying him with dirt and ricocheting buckshot letters. The startled man dropped his rope. Before he had a chance to react further, Danny fired again, causing the man and those nearby to hop and then leap backwards.

The crowd began to surge forward. Danny met them with another blast at their feet. It took the crowd a few seconds to assimilate what had just happened. Danny pulled out more shells and shoved them into the chamber. The leader spun to avoid having his shins peppered again. With that, the crowd began to turn and run. Danny fired at their backsides, and they scattered even faster.

"This ain't over!" the red-faced man screamed over his shoulder.

The deputy appeared from the shadows and handed Danny back his Colt. Danny called to the sheriff, shoved the shotgun into his hands, and began issuing orders. "I'm taking the senator to the tracks just beyond the depot. If anyone has a mind to follow us, you keep him at a distance." To the deputy: "Tell the stationmaster to signal the mail train to slow down to a crawl when it comes through at 11:00 p.m." To the editor: "Wire Captain James in San Antonio." Danny stood a little taller. "Tell him he won't be needed here tonight."

Just then, the senator spoke up. "But I want to go to Austin. That train's going the wrong way."

Danny couldn't contain his irritation. "The point is, that train's *going.* You wait around for a train to Austin and you might not make it out of here. Ever."

The senator, still damp and bedraggled, held up both hands in acquiescence. But he was unable to squelch his satisfaction at his tormentors' retreat. "They'll be picking the alphabet out of their backsides for weeks!" Then he gave a smug grin and sneered, "It's probably as close to formal learning as most of them will ever get."

Danny folded his arms across his chest. "Well, Senator, I guess they've become just like you."

"Like me! How?"

"This morning they were just sons of Beeches. Now they're educated asses."

3

The captain strode into headquarters and extended his hand to Danny. "Good job in Beeches, Corporal O'Brien."

It took Danny a minute to register what he had heard. *He said* Corporal *O'Brien, didn't he?* He set down the gun he was cleaning, scrambled to his feet, and began pumping the captain's hand. "Yes, sir! Thank you, sir!"

Scrap wandered over to the captain and sat down in front of him. The captain reached down and scratched the dog's head.

"To be honest, Cap'n, I didn't know how it was going to end." The compliment and new rank thrilled Danny, but he had to admit to himself that he was glad to be back at headquarters, glad to be polishing his gun, and more than relieved that he hadn't had to use it the day before. "I keep thinking how bad it could have turned out, Cap'n. I keep thinking, *what if*—"

"A man can ask 'what if' about everything." The captain sat down, but continued to stroke Scrap's head, despite the dog's closed eyes.

Danny sat down again. "I know. All my life I been asking myself things like, *What if* my family had stayed in Ireland? *What if* my mother hadn't died? Or *if* I hadn't been put on that train to Texas? Or *if* I hadn't ended up with Mr. Dunside—"

"Stop." Captain James held his hand up in front of Danny's face and looked directly at him. "It's like this: Some things you don't have a choice in. Some you do. When you do, you try to make the best choice you can. And then you take the consequences. When you don't have a choice, when you don't have a say, you make the best of it." He resumed stroking the sleeping dog's small, bony skull. "And sometimes you have to live with the consequences of someone else's actions."

Danny fiddled with the rag he was cleaning his gun with. "I know, but what if—"

Again, the captain cut him short. "Look, Danny, you could spend your whole life asking 'what if' instead of living your life. There are a million 'what if' lives each of us will never experience."

Danny made no reply. He inhaled and cast his eyes towards the ceiling, searching his memory. *What was it Dooley had said about not making yourself miserable over things you couldn't change? About moving on? "When the horse is dead, get off."*

The captain's voice was quieter now, but just as firm. "Danny, we have to live the questions, most of us all our lives. And if we're lucky or we live long enough, we might just live our way into a few of the answers."

Danny stared at the oily rag as he repeatedly folded and unfolded it, but the captain knew he was listening.

The captain—then Scrap—walked over closer to the table where Danny was sitting. "There's a story the Indians tell about the 'Mountain of Sorrows.' Everyone in the tribe is complaining about their tribulations. The Great Spirit tells them that they will each be allowed to take their worst hurt, affliction, or sorrow and lay it at the foot of the mountain—free of it forever."

Danny stopped toying with the rag and looked up at the captain.

"There is one condition, however. The Great Spirit tells them that everyone has to select something that was left by someone else. They quickly agree. Each person walks around slowly, looking at what the others have put there." He paused. "Do you know what happens?"

Danny was silent for a minute. Then he gave the captain a wistful smile. "They each take back what they brought to the mountain?"

The captain gave a single nod.

Danny looked back down at his Colt, unfolded the rag, and began thoughtfully rubbing the barrel again.

He felt the momentary warmth of the captain's reassuring hand on his shoulder and then heard the door close softly behind him. But a peculiar feeling settled over Danny that, despite the August heat, left him chilled. It was the feeling that he would soon see the mountain and glimpse for himself the sorrows others had laid at its foot.

THIRTY

It was Friday, September 7, 1900. Cletis had been in Galveston only a few days when it happened. He had barely been there long enough to get the lay of the land: the island itself was a long, narrow strip of sand three miles wide and thirty miles long. Like grappling hooks, three railroad trestles and a wagon bridge spanned the bay and linked the island to the mainland. The south side of the island was gloriously open to the Gulf of Mexico.

Strolling down Broadway Boulevard, Cletis stopped to stare at the elegant homes—Victorian and gothic mansions adorned with balconies, chimneys, towers, turrets, pilasters, and cupolas—that flanked the prestigious street. The boulevard's wide esplanade was studded with fragrant oleanders; palms from the West Indies dotted it at regular intervals. The oleanders and palms reminded Cletis of the garden at the Menger Hotel in San Antonio. He had walked over to see it after he heard Colonel Roosevelt describe the luscious ice cream made from the mangoes that grew in it.

A clanging sound intruded on Cletis's reminiscing. Mule-drawn streetcars plied their way back and forth to the beach, but trolleys traversed the length of Broadway, and at night they sparkled with colorful electric lights.

Cletis sauntered along the grassy esplanade, luxuriating in the sunshine and inhaling air redolent with the oleanders' heavy sweetness. Mingled with this scent were exotic odors of South American fruit being unloaded at the dock and the pungent smell of fish and ocean brine. When Cletis walked at a leisurely pace, as he had been doing, his limp was barely discernible. But even though no one else might notice it, he was aware of it—a perpetual reminder to him of his failure and shame.

He headed down Postoffice Street and paused to gape at the four-story building that held the Hotel Grand's shops, cafes, and the Grand Opera House. Cletis peered into the Opera House. He was awed by its magnificent staircase, marble foyer, and parquet floors. Wandering from 20th Street, a few more blocks down Postoffice, he found himself in the heart of the island's red-light district. He felt ill at ease and conspicuous. He'd heard that the area between 25th and 29th was a center for gambling as well. He kept going, ambling towards the beach. "Learned my lesson about bars in San Antone," he said half-aloud.

He was agog at the Midway, ten blocks of shabby wood-frame shops that proffered seashells, gaudy postcards, and other cheap trinkets and souvenirs. The smells of sticky saltwater taffy, greasy frankfurters, and spicy mustard competed with the aroma of boiled clams and beer. The mammoth, double-domed Pagoda Bathhouse spanned two blocks. It was held aloft by pilings, like a stork perched on spindly legs.

The Gulf. Cuba. Cletis's mind wandered from topic to topic as he walked along the beach, gazing at the sea. He watched the gulls and terns make lazy circles over the water. He scanned the horizon and inhaled the sea air. Then he closed his eyes and exhaled, the image of the white clouds and brilliant blue sky still visible in his mind's eye. He was now profoundly thankful just to have survived his military experience. *How could it have been so different from what I expected?* In Cuba, the feeling of terror had never completely left him, although it had been obscured briefly in the fury of battle. He was too ashamed to admit to anyone that he had felt relieved when his injury took him out of action.

He felt even more ashamed that the injury was his own fault. Cletis watched the entire awful scene replay itself on the inside of his closed eyelids. Dewey moaning, lurching forward, and slumping in a grotesque, twisted heap. Realizing Dewey was dead. *Not Dewey!* The rage that had suddenly consumed him. Yanking Dewey's rifle tip out of the dirt. Firing blindly through his tears. Then the pain. The searing pain in his foot. The shock of seeing his shoe fill with blood. Wondering how it happened. An older man, a former Texas Ranger, binding his foot, then coming back for him later when the fighting was over. Finally, the terrible, shameful realization that he'd shot himself with Dewey's jammed rifle. In the noise and confusion of battle, it never occurred to his comrades that his injury was caused by his own anger and ineptness, and not by the enemy.

Cletis could feel heat burning his cheeks. He hoped it was only the sunshine, but he suspected it was the shame. His dreadful secret was a bitter gall to him. It had gnawed persistently at him during the remainder of his short stint as a soldier, and it never left his thoughts completely.

He'd felt the shame most deeply almost exactly two years ago. He often replayed that scene in his mind as well. It was in August 1898. The triumphant Rough Riders arrived at Montauk Point on Long Island. An enormous, cheering crowd greeted them. When the troops mustered out a few weeks later, Teddy Roosevelt shook each man's hand and called him by name. Cletis had kept his eyes lowered, glancing up only long enough not to appear rude, but unable to manage even a weak smile.

I can't go home again, he had decided, *at least not back to the farm or to my blacksmith's job in San Antonio. Everyone will ask me about the war.* So he had stayed and worked on the docks in New York. Eventually, he had begun to rethink the matter: the winters were just too cold. He'd heard a ship was sailing for Galveston, and he recalled Danny's appealing description of the city. Immediately he decided to go there, but not without feeling sorry for himself. *Don't really matter where I go. It's not like I got anyone anywhere waiting for me.* Now in Galveston, he was again awash in feelings of self-pity.

The joyous shouts of children abruptly jarred Cletis from his musings. The glare of the dazzling sunlight on the sand and sea hurt his eyes when he opened them again. Once his eyes adjusted, they came to rest on a sign that informed him he was standing on a stretch of beach "Reserved on Sundays for Baptisms." According to the sign, one section was reserved for "Whites" and one was reserved for "Coloreds." Cletis wandered over to the "White" water. He dabbled his hand in the surf and then licked his salty fingers. Trying to be inconspicuous, he moved to the "Colored" section and did the same thing. A look of surprise registered on his face. *Why, they're the same! Look the same! Feel the same! Taste the same! Them signs made it sound like there was something special about one or the other!* He harrumphed in disgust, and walked away not only feeling duped, but disappointed.

Cletis had wondered about baptisms ever since Ruby and Opal had gone to the revival and he had been left at home. He chuckled, again remembering Danny's yarn about it in San Antonio. Then his expression changed; it seemed very long ago. *Shoot, I was a kid then,* he told himself. Now he felt burdened, older. Much older.

"Sunday," he declared aloud. "I'm coming back on Sunday to watch the baptisms." He strolled a few more yards, his limp more pronounced. He picked up shells and pieces of driftwood and idly chunked them back into the surf. He wrinkled his forehead as an idea struggled to form. "Hell, I might even *get* baptized." He instantly felt sheepish for swearing in the same breath that he mentioned getting baptized.

It occurred to him that a baptism—being reborn—might lift the heavy stone of cowardice and shame from his troubled heart. *Perhaps I could start over, with the sin and guilt washed away.* He smiled and quickened his pace. *Yes. Washed away.*

But Cletis's baptism came one day early, and like war, the experience was not what he had expected.

THIRTY-ONE

1

The rain started after midnight, and by nine o'clock Saturday morning, Galvestonians found themselves wading in calf-deep water. Walls of water began crashing against the island, despite the peculiar fact that the north wind was blowing against the tide.

By early afternoon, the wagon bridge and the trio of railroad bridges that arched over the bay and joined the island to the mainland had disappeared beneath the rising water. By sundown, torrents of icy rain were pelting the city. Families began moving to higher ground, such as there was of it on the island, or at the very least, to the second stories of their houses. The tide was rising at an astonishing two and a half feet per hour. Within another three hours, the winds reached one hundred and twenty miles per hour, the tide climbed to fifteen feet, and twenty-five-foot breakers were smashing the Gulf side of the island.

In the early morning, Cletis had removed his shoes and socks and rolled up his pants legs. Like the others on the island, he had splashed and rollicked in the ankle-deep, then calf-deep water. But as the sky, wind, temperature, and sea turned sinister, and the ominous rain continued hour upon hour, he began to feel the same alarm the others did—and then the same bone-deep terror he had felt in Cuba.

The fear was well founded, for the black of night brought terrors unimaginable. Battered by the roiling water and lashed by furious winds, entire buildings and houses cracked up and washed away. Whole rooftops flew through the air, tumbling and swooping like gargantuan prehistoric birds. Furniture, wagons, bricks, telegraph and telephone poles, crates, and heavy barrels were flung about like toys hurled by a petulant child. There was a deafening din of cracking timber and earsplitting thunder. Great flashes of lightning intermittently illuminated the ghastly scene.

Earlier in the afternoon, a mother and father, struggling to hold onto their brood of six children, signaled to Cletis. "Where you headed?" the man screamed, trying to make himself heard. Cletis shrugged and raised upturned palms to show that he had no destination. The father gestured for Cletis to join them. When Cletis was near enough, the man motioned for two of the children to take Cletis's hands. "St. Mary's," the father screamed hoarsely. Cletis did not understand, but he was relieved to be part of a group that seemed to be moving purposefully. They soon joined many others who had taken refuge in the church.

That evening, priests circulated among the frightened, bedraggled citizens. Some people knelt in prayer or recited the rosary. Some sang hymns of their own faith. Others sat in mortified silence or tried to comfort the injured or soothe the grief and fear of those who did not know the whereabouts of their families.

Like a snake uncoiling to release the full fury of its strike, the malevolent storm continued to unleash itself. Sensing the end, the priests began administering the last rites.

Suddenly the stained-glass windows exploded into vicious shards. Massive cornices crashed to the floor. The church's slate roof tiles flew through the air like saw blades, severing victims in half or decapitating them.

Cletis gasped, then gagged, as roof beams collapsed and crushed those huddled below. *Maybe God is trying to punish me for entering a church,* he thought. Choking with nausea at the death and destruction around him, Cletis forced his way out into the dark, down the steps and into the deep water as another roof beam cracked like rifle shot, buckled, and crashed down. It was no better outside. With one arm, he tried to shield his head and face from the flying debris. With the other, he clung to a lamppost.

Cletis's mind reeled. The shrieks. The screams. The cracking timbers. *Like rifle shots.* He hugged the lamppost and clapped his hands over his ears. He felt as if his head and lungs and chest would burst. *Dewey.* Something in Cletis snapped. He was angry, angrier than he had ever been in his life. Angrier than he had been in Cuba at the Spaniards. Angry at the storm. Angry at the senseless death and destruction.

He slogged through the raging water and fended off loose boards and bricks to fight his way back up the steps past those who were now trying to flee the sanctuary. Once inside, Cletis struggled to pull pews and beams off of those buried beneath them. He shoved and hurled aside pieces of the fallen roof and pulled people and bodies from the rubble. He worked as if endowed with superhuman strength. He worked like a man possessed, until there was nothing more he could do.

A priest cried out to him. "Surely the Lord sent you to deliver us! You are God's angel of mercy!"

"No," Cletis demurred, embarrassed. "I'm just Cletis. Cletis Mutt." He then felt more embarrassed. *Of course he didn't mean I'm an actual angel.*

Out of respect, and no less out of embarrassment, Cletis lowered his eyes. The priest placed his hand on Cletis's head. Straining to hear and to make himself heard, the priest shouted, "Well, Cletis Mutt, God bless you. You may not be an angel, but you *are* a hero. We will remember you in our prayers, my son."

Cletis felt free. The priest's words, "hero"—*he had said "hero," hadn't he?*—and "my son," filled Cletis with gratitude and warmth. The creaking and groaning of the church's bell tower and foundation abruptly replaced those feelings with one of claustrophobia. "I have to leave."

"Where will you go?" the priest asked.

"Out there."

"But it isn't safe!"

"It isn't safe anywhere. I can't stay inside any longer. I'll—I'll suffocate."

Sensing that further protest was futile and that he himself would not survive the night, the priest removed his crucifix. "Then take this." He slipped the chain over Cletis's head. "Perhaps it will protect you." He blessed Cletis and watched him disappear into the storm.

Cletis again waded into the swirling, chest-deep, brown water. During phosphorescent lightning flashes he could see that whole buildings and houses had disappeared. Driftwood, flotsam, and battered bodies of people and animals floated by him. *Like the war.*

Exhausted, Cletis could no longer maintain his footing or balance. He clung to a large piece of a wall that came floating by. He realized that he was being carried into deeper water, but by then it was too late to turn loose. Airborne pieces of wood and metal battered and bruised him and ripped his clothing and skin. When an upside-down rooftop floated by, Cletis scrambled aboard. He snared a loose piece of tin, pulling it from the greasy foam. He drew it over his head, and struggling against the wind, shielded his head and shoulders from the icy, stiletto rain and the fusillade of flying debris. During explosions of lightning, he could see people hanging onto pieces of lumber or furniture, or riding a roof they had perhaps retreated to before it was dislodged from the house beneath it.

During a lightning flash, Cletis glimpsed a woman nearby. She was clinging perilously to the sideboard of a decimated delivery wagon. She had one hand wrapped around the heavy board; with the other she clutched her small son against her. Like corks, they bobbed in the inky water, choking and sputtering whenever they emerged.

"Please, *please*," she beseeched Cletis, "I can't…" In a frantic gesture, she thrust the child towards Cletis, but the child slipped from her exhausted arms. Cletis lunged for the child but missed. He clambered over the edge of the roof, and still clinging to it, plucked the thrashing child from the water. He kept the child pressed against his chest, and with his free hand, struggled to pull himself and the baby back aboard his roof-boat.

"Hold on!" he screamed to the wild-eyed woman. Stretching himself out flat and bracing the toddler between himself and their rooftop raft, Cletis extended his hand to the woman. She sputtered, rising and sinking beneath the frothy water. She looked at Cletis and then at her baby. She released her grip on the board and flailed her arms towards Cletis. A look of surprise crossed her face, as if she had suddenly realized she was late for an appointment. Then she simply disappeared. Cletis moaned in anguish. He rested his weary head flat on the roof, cradling the baby against him, and pulled the protective piece of tin over both of them. Then he began talking to the child. "It's all right, little feller. Cletis will keep you safe. We'll make it." Cletis repeated his words over and over again as he wrapped the chain of the crucifix around the baby's chest to help secure his hold on the limp child.

2

After hours of being pelted by debris and cold rain and tossed about by surging currents, Cletis and his small passenger were carried by the waves towards higher ground. Tattered survivors huddled there, shouting encouragement to Cletis and extending a pole to him. They hauled Cletis in like a large fish. A heavyset woman, whose uncoiled gray hair was strewn in wet clumps about her shoulders, took the shivering baby from Cletis. "Is he yours?"

Cletis shook his head and compressed his lips. "His mother drowned right after she handed him to me."

"What's his name?"

Cletis shook his head again. At that moment, he sank to his knees and slumped over in exhaustion, grateful that the sensation of motion had stopped. His entire body hurt. He was bleeding in several places, as if he had been the target in a shooting gallery. A ragged gash gaped above his right eye.

"What's your name?" the woman asked.

"Cletis Mutt," he mumbled in a weary voice.

The woman hugged the child to her breast and peered into the darkness. She cradled the baby closer against her ample bosom, stroking his small head and soothing him. "I have two nearly grown children I can't find. I'll care for this lamb until we find out who he is." Then she added softly, "*If* we find out."

3

After midnight the water began to recede rapidly. The storm had passed. The beleaguered group stayed where it was until sunrise, thankful for solid ground and the salvation it had provided.

No one was prepared for the scene that the dawning sun revealed. One by one, the survivors rose to their feet. "Oh my God…" There was awe in the woman's voice. "It's a mountain. A mountain of bodies and debris." It protruded from the island like the spine of some hideous leviathan, a ghastly twenty-foot high wall of twisted wreckage, corpses, animal carcasses, household furnishings, and splintered lumber.

In the distance, the band of survivors could see a mud-caked man struggling to make his way towards them. With every step, there was a sucking sound as he pulled his shoes from the muck and slime. He was panting by the time he reached Cletis and the others. "The wreckage is six, maybe eight blocks wide," he reported in gasps. "And on the other side there's…" He fought back tears. "There's nothing. The ground's scraped as clean as if God took a scythe to it." He wiped his eyes and nose on his grimy sleeve.

The gray-haired woman, with the exhausted toddler now asleep on her shoulder, covered her mouth with one hand and began to cry softly. She regained her composure enough to utter, "My two boys are out there somewhere. Late yesterday afternoon they said they wanted to go to the beach to see what the waves looked like. They're big, strapping boys. Even so, I begged them not to go. They just laughed and said I worry too much. They thought it was exciting. They promised to meet me half an hour later at my brother's house—it's on higher ground—but…" She choked out the last words. "They never showed up."

A woman stepped forward and put her arm around the gray-haired woman. "There, there," she soothed. "They're probably fine. They'll turn up and tell you what an adventure they had. That's the way boys are." She led the woman away and seated her on a plank propped up to serve as a bench.

"I hope her boys are all right," the man offered. He hesitated until she was out of earshot. "I was at the beach before I came here. I saw the Pagoda Bath House. It ripped loose from its pilings. It's not much more than kindling. That wall of debris flattened everything in its path. And I heard that the east end of the island was destroyed, too. The Gulf and the bay actually merged over it." He shook his head. "Can you imagine? And in places where the wreckage piled up, it created lakes right on the spot. Why, I heard some of them were twenty feet deep—"

"What about the south side of the island?" an old man interrupted. "I have property there. Do you know what happened to it?"

The mud-caked man could offer no encouraging news. "A policeman told me practically every structure on the south side was demolished. He said it was scraped clean as a fresh-shaved face."

The old man's shoulders sagged at the news.

"Some folks are starting to gather in the center of the island. The Tremont Hotel was spared. We can go there for shelter. Any of you want to try?"

Several of them, including Cletis, nodded. The old man volunteered to stay with the rest of the women and children until help could be sent. Cletis fell in with those headed for the central business district, to the Tremont.

"Watch where you step." The man hardly needed to warn the band of trekkers. A greasy, foul-smelling, inch-thick layer of slime coated everything. Downed electrical wires performed macabre, jerky dances and made popping and crackling sounds to accompany their spastic movements. In the distance, Cletis could see railroad track twisted at grotesque angles. Ruptured water lines were contaminated by the brown bilge water that had inundated the city. There was already an unbearable stench.

The band of survivors helped steady each another as they slogged their way through the debris and muck. Mostly they stared at the ground, picking carefully the next place to step. Occasionally one of them would look up and gasp. The island lay in shambles. Bodies hung on the branches of trees like gruesome decorations on a Christmas tree. Other corpses were wedged in the train trestles. Some were fixed in the very spots where they had drowned; others had drowned and been deposited there by the storm.

A young woman shrieked. Then she moaned and pointed to a live oak tree. Along with moss and seaweed, a crystal chandelier had become lodged in its branches. From the chandelier, a scalp dangled forlornly, a hank of tangled brown hair the only trace of its former owner.

The leader of the group tried to make sense of the ghastly sight. "Her house must have filled with water. She was probably floating near the ceiling. Her hair got tangled in the chandelier and when the roof ripped away, it tore off her scalp."

The young woman gagged, then turned her head aside and vomited.

Cletis took her by the elbow to support her. "Try not to look," he said. But it was useless. There were corpses everywhere, the horror made worse because other than their sizes, they were nearly indistinguishable. Broken glass, splintered wood and metal, and boards with nails had left them naked, shredded, and bludgeoned into anonymity. Most were unidentifiable other than by a remnant of clothing, a ring, or some other piece of jewelry that by chance remained on them.

A woman's face contorted in pain. "It's Addie's boy, Andy, and Buster!" she cried. "There. Beside that pile of debris. He's my neighbor's child. You've got to help him!" A young boy's battered body rested limply in the wreckage that had snared him. In one arm he held a lifeless black and white terrier.

Cletis made his way over to the child and knelt beside him. There was nothing to be done, but he felt the need to help in some way. He raised the child's dangling left arm and draped it gently across his thin chest. Cletis felt sickened and angry and helpless. "This ain't right," he muttered. "This just ain't right." He wished that he knew a prayer he could say. Instead, he brushed the child's wet hair from his pale face.

The woman peered anxiously and called out, "Is he all right, mister?"

Despite the stench, Cletis took a deep breath. Then he stood up and shook his head.

The woman began to weep. "Poor Addie. She loved that boy so." She pressed her knuckles to her mouth, choking back sobs. "Poor little thing must have been terrified. At least he had Buster with him. They went everywhere together, you know." She fell silent, and they began walking again, each lost in separate thoughts.

In little more than an hour, they reached Broadway Boulevard. "By damn! Will you look at that!" The words exploded from the leader's lips. He was staring at the stone and brick mansions, the jewels of Broadway Boulevard. What was shocking was that most of them were intact. "Ain't it *always* that way! The rich get spared and the rest of us get wiped out. It's peculiar, ain't it?"

In another thirty minutes, they reached the five-story Tremont Hotel. Although damaged, the aristocratic hotel had been spared from destruction. The city fathers were beginning to assemble there to develop a plan for coping with the disaster. A crowd of citizens had already gathered, and more were arriving every moment. They traded tales of terror and swapped scraps of information. Cletis hung back and listened. He was a newcomer trying to piece things together to make sense of what he was hearing: Old Red—*one of the medical school buildings?*—had fared better than most. Ball High School, which he gathered was in the middle of town, was reasonably undamaged. The Deep Water Saloon—wasn't it ironic?—emerged largely unscathed. The roof at St. Mary's Orphanage had collapsed, crushing the nuns and ninety of the ninety-three children. "The sides of buildings had been sliced away like they were crusts on a loaf of bread," the voice added.

He continued to listen to the talk among the small knot of men. Ships had been marooned, left aground far inland. Why, some people had been carried thirty miles across the bay. A voice was saying, "...and then they clung throughout the night to one piece of debris after another. Must have felt like polar bears scrambling from one ice floe to another in a frozen river that had broken up."

After a while, the conversation blurred into a buzzing sound in Cletis's head. He walked back outside. He slumped against the wall of the hotel, squatting on his heels and staring in disbelief at a world unrecognizable from twenty-four hours earlier. He pressed his fists against his red, watery eyes for several seconds. The thought that kept running through his mind when he opened his eyes again was, *How can this be?* There was chaos, devastation, and death in every direction. And yet the day shone as radiant and tranquil as if no drop of rain had fallen, no breeze had blown, and no grain of sand had been disturbed the night before.

THIRTY-TWO

1

"Galveston?" Surprise registered in Danny's voice.

"You leave tomorrow." The captain looked up from the papers on his desk. "You already know the city. A hurricane has nearly destroyed it. The death toll is high. Some looting has already been reported."

Danny looked at the calendar: September 9, 1900. It seemed as if a lifetime had passed since he had first gone to Galveston in search of his uncles.

"The island's telegraph and telephone lines have been destroyed. They're having to send dispatches from the mainland. I don't have much more than this." The captain picked up one of the pieces of paper and handed it to Danny. "This is the name of the law officer you need to contact when you arrive."

The next morning, Danny rolled a change of clothes, his Colt, and a blanket into a pack and headed for the depot. He closed his eyes as he waited for the train to pull out. He tried to envision Galveston as he remembered it.

He did not expect to encounter anyone in Galveston he knew, although he hoped to find Seb Pendleton, Mr. Dunside's old shipmate. Sitting there on the train, he did not know that he would learn nothing of Seb, that he would be left to wonder whether Seb had died before the hurricane or perished in a watery death long after he had given up life at sea. And sitting on the train, Danny did not know that in Galveston he would discover four former acquaintances, as well as a man who was wanted by the Rangers.

2

Danny traveled by boat across the bay. Even descriptions and newspaper accounts he had read could not have prepared him for what awaited in Galveston. The state's premier city, which had boasted a population of forty thousand, was devastated. Seawater sixteen feet above normal had surged five feet deep over the city.

Each day Danny saw new and horrifying sights that astounded him. He was stunned by the gruesome wall of debris strewn along one edge of the city and by its sheer magnitude: it was thirty blocks long.

Later, when the death toll was assessed, it would stand at six thousand, although the exact number would never be known. *How many had perished?* he wondered. *How many had simply fled, thankful to be alive, and vowing never to return?*

Initially, the city had been at a loss in dealing with the bodies. One of the men in charge explained to Danny, "When we dug trenches for mass burials, they filled with water. When we tried 'burying' several dozen bodies at once by putting them overboard at sea, they washed back ashore. It was drawing sharks, too." He shook his head. "The threat of disease just kept increasing. We finally had to resort to this"—he gestured to a smoldering heap of bloated, rotting corpses—"burning corpses wherever and whenever we find them." He sighed. "Damn distasteful. They deserved better." He raised his eyes. "The task is so loathsome that we have to ply men with whiskey or force them at gunpoint to do it." That came as no surprise to Danny. The stench, even the smell of the smoke, was almost unbearable.

Well into November, funeral pyres of debris would still be burning as many as seventy bodies a day.

3

Looting in Galveston turned out to be slight, Danny discovered, and the city had immediately begun the slow process of recovery. A few days after he arrived, he was preparing to return to San Antonio when he received a message from a marshal to come to Ball High School, one of the makeshift hospitals that dotted the Island.

"I think you'll be interested in this." The lawman handed Danny a fearsome-looking knife. Danny immediately recognized the name engraved on the handle. It was that of a man wanted for murders in San Antonio and Houston: Mashburn Dill. "There was no identification on him other than the knife. I guess it's his." The lawman started walking down the hall and motioned for Danny to follow. "This way. He's down here."

When they came to the improvised ward, Danny stared at the man on a cot. "Can't much tell what he looks like with his head swathed in all those bandages, Marshal."

"No. His head must have looked like a ripe cantaloupe that was cleaved." A broad band of bright blood faded into a rusty line of dried blood, suggesting that the vital fluid was still seeping at a glacial but steady rate. "If you think he might be your man, you can talk to the woman who owns the Delta Queen. That's the saloon where he got hurt. It's down around 27th and 28th Street, not that there are any street signs left. Actually, it's more than a saloon—they got girls there, too."

Danny slogged, slipped, and picked his way through mud, slime, and debris to the Delta Queen, wondering all the while whether the half-dead man was worth the effort. But the thought of finding a man on the Rangers' Wanted List spurred him on.

The saloon was dim. Light that filtered through the grimy front windows provided the only illumination. The floor was still covered with mud, although a path of sorts had been scraped— *or worn?*—between the door and the bar. After Danny's eyes adjusted to the shadowy interior, they opened wide when he saw the owner. It was like discovering a peacock, a plump peacock, in a barnyard. She was resplendent in a purple dress. Her hair, which hung in ringlets far too youthful for a woman her age, had a preternatural burgundy cast. Jewels—*were they real?*—flashed from various extremities.

Danny stared at the faintly familiar-looking woman who owned the saloon and the brothel it housed. "'Scuse me, ma'am. Are you Miss Queen?"

She smiled and waved him in with a ripple of jeweled fingers. "Sure am. We're in shambles, honey, but we're selling whiskey!"

Then Danny showed her his badge and identified himself as a Texas Ranger.

Her smile abruptly changed to a frown.

"I'm here simply to get some information. Did you know the man they brought to the hospital at Ball High School last night?"

She shrugged. "Nope. He's just some feller who got hurt." Then she asked, "Who is he? And why are you interested?"

Aware of her side business, Danny pressed ahead, hoping to enlist her aid. "I have reason to believe his name is Mashburn Dill. Dill is wanted for brutal assaults on several—" He started to say "painted ladies," but after glancing at her heavily rouged face decided instead on "ladies of the evening." He continued, watching her reactions. "Two of them died at his hands, one in San Antonio and one in Houston. He left some others cut up along the way."

Her face contorted in disgust and anger, and she hissed, "I hope the son of a bitch dies. I had a bad feeling about him." She ducked her head. She had said more than she intended.

"Tell me what happened here last night."

She glanced around the room, hesitating too long before responding. She pointed to a beam that lay in the corner with other debris. "That ceiling timber hit him on the head. The storm must have loosened it, and it fell." She snapped her fingers. "Bam. Split his skull just like that."

Danny locked his gaze on her eyes. "Couldn't have happened that way," he said bluntly. She started to protest, but Danny said, "That beam would have crushed his skull, not split it open." He let the uncomfortable silence run. The woman's fingers darted to her hair, her nose, her eyes. He pressed her further: "You're lying. Tell me what happened last night." His tone had become impatient.

She seemed to reassess the situation and consider her options. Then she said in a weary tone, "Look, I don't need any more trouble." She gestured to the damage around her. "I got enough already."

Danny continued to watch her eyes.

Then she dropped all pretenses. "Aw, hell. A bed fell on him." When Danny's eyebrows shot up in disbelief, she persisted. "I swear. That's exactly what happened." She tipped her head in the direction of the baldheaded bartender who was pushing mud and splintered furniture towards a door. "Curly heard one of the girls scream." She didn't elaborate as to who "the girls" were, and Danny refrained from asking the obvious. "She ran screaming from a room upstairs. She was bleeding here." She touched a spot on her collarbone near her throat. "Curly grabbed his club and charged up there. The man was waving his knife. He started swearing at Curly like a madman." She stopped to see if Danny was following—and believing—her story. Satisfied that he was, she went on. "Curly knocked the man's knife to the floor with his club. When it slid under the bed, the man dived after it. He was scrambling back out. That's when

Curly jumped over him and landed on the bed."

"And that's when the bed collapsed on him."

"Yes." She took Danny to the room and opened the door. A heavy oak bed frame lay tilted to one side. "We could tell he was hurt bad. The knife must have been under his forehead when the bed came down on him. We wrapped a towel around his head. Curly closed the knife up and put it back in the man's pocket. Then we carried him downstairs."

"Curly will verify all of this?"

She nodded.

"And the girl?"

"She was lucky. More scared than hurt. She came around the next day and I gave her some money. I don't look for her to come back."

"I see." Danny leaned down to examine a bloodstain on the floor beneath the bed. "From what you've told me, I'd say the man in the hospital is definitely Mashburn Dill. I appreciate your help. I won't trouble you further." He reached up to put on his hat. "And your full name, Miss Queen?"

"Ruby. Ruby Queen."

Danny lowered his hat and looked hard at her. "Ruby Queen? That your real name?"

She ignored his question. A trace of irritation flashed in her eyes. "I am not the kind of woman who likes to be questioned. I think I've been subjected to more than my share of unpleasantness." She pursed her lips and drummed her fingertips against her thumbs. "I took that name when I came to Galveston. Hell, everyone here has known me as Ruby Queen for years." She made another sweeping motion, this time to show who "everyone" was, despite the fact that there were no patrons in the saloon.

Danny squinted and peered closely at the brightly rouged, ringlet-framed face and at the plump form that was squeezed into a tight dress. Given the circumstances and the mud and destruction around her, the dress itself was incongruous and absurd. Its low-cut bodice had not escaped Danny's notice. A smile passed his lips. In his head, he could hear Dooley's description of the neckline of such a garment: *Any lower and she could step through it.*

It was obvious to the saloon owner that Danny was inspecting her, not admiring her. Her vanity asserted itself, and she bristled at his scrutiny. With one hand she self-consciously covered her partially exposed bosom. She raised her chin and sputtered, "See here. I'm a respectable woman, and I run a respectable business. No use your coming in here trying to make me feel like a common criminal or some sinner."

Of course! Danny began to laugh.

Ruby flared at him. "Just exactly what's so funny?"

"Sin."

"What?" She was yelling now.

"I said sin. You must have been baptized in a *river* of sin."

Now she was genuinely angry. Her eyes narrowed to small bullets. "What the hell are you talking about? Just who do you think you're talking…"

Her dark, painted eyebrows became twin arches. "You! The skinny boy. On the farm. Back home!"

"Danny O'Brien, at your service, Miss *Queen*. Miss *Ruby Genesis Mutt* Queen."

Danny was smiling broadly. He had made a point of pronouncing "Ge-NE-sis" the way Oleta had.

Ruby smirked in embarrassment and defiance. "Well, I couldn't very well run a saloon callin' myself Ruby *Mutt*." Her thoughts turned to the last time she had seen Danny. Memories rushed out like birds released from a cage, and she suddenly sounded like the Ruby of old: "You know, Pa just about killed Cletis when we got back from the revival. And Ma would have skinned Hannah if she could have gotten ahold of her. You two ruined her hat, you know. On top of that, Opal and me was took down with the miseries. Why, there was folks in the cemetery that felt better 'n we did. And then we come home to find our bed filled with molasses. A damn mess." In spite of herself, she started laughing. "And Hannah? Whatever happened to—" Just then, two men entered the saloon. "Honey, I got me some *paying* customers." She scribbled something on a piece of paper and handed it to Danny. "Come to this address tonight. It's where I'm staying. My room here ain't fit to stay in."

Confused, Danny thought perhaps he was being propositioned or being invited to become one of Ruby's customers.

"Don't look so bent out of shape," she scolded. "There's an old friend of yours who'd like to see you again." Ruby closed up like a morning glory in the afternoon sun. She sashayed off, fluttering over to the men who had just come through the door.

Both Danny and Ruby knew that he would show up that night: he could think of no one else he knew in Galveston.

4

Danny received his next surprise when he returned to the Ball High School hospital. He found himself staring at a woman who was a few years younger than he was. She was absorbed in her work. She moved from patient to patient, assisting a haggard-looking doctor.

Her appearance and her slight accent triggered a vague sense of a past encounter with her. Danny tried to dismiss the feeling as having been triggered by his reunion with Ruby, but the feeling persisted. The young woman was diminutive and was dressed in a simple uniform with a red cross pinned on it. Danny had heard that Galveston had sent out an urgent call for medical volunteers and supplies. Clearly, she was among those who had responded.

Danny stood in the background, not wanting to interfere with their work, but the doctor recognized him and waved him over. "I'm nearly through." The doctor pointed to Mashburn Dill. "Did you come back to see about him?"

Danny nodded. "There's no hurry, though." He watched the nurse comfort a little girl who had stripes of abrasions on her torso, a blackened eye, and a nasty knot above her ear.

The doctor inspected the child's injuries. "You're a mighty lucky young lady," he told her. As he bandaged her head, he explained to Danny, "When her father realized the strength of the storm, he had the presence of mind to tie each child high up on the trunk of a palm tree. Then his wife. Then himself. He wound long ropes around them so they couldn't be washed away. Every last one of them survived—a little worse for the wear, but alive." The doctor finished wrapping the child's head as if he were demonstrating her father's actions with the rope. He patted the child's hand. "There you go!" She scampered away, back to her mother, who was waiting nearby. "Poor little thing was unconscious when they brought her here. She must have been clipped by something. A flying board, maybe."

Danny nodded and followed the man over to Mashburn Dill's bedside. The doctor removed the bandages to examine the gaping wound. Danny flinched and looked away. The jagged, exposed bone gave the impression of a ghastly, toothy grin carved across Mashburn's forehead. The doctor palpated the patient's puffy, bruised face. When he lifted an eyelid, a pupil the size of a dime stared blankly into space. The physician sighed and shook his head almost imperceptibly. "You can bandage him up again, nurse."

She understood his meaning: *Nothing can be done. This patient isn't going to survive.* She deftly rewound the bandages. A small crimson stain began immediately to seep through the gauze.

The doctor gave instructions for sheets to be draped from the ceiling on either side of the cot. All at once, he seemed too exhausted to complete a sentence. "This poor fellow… He's going to… The others on the ward don't need…"

Danny and the nurse understood his point: There was no reason for the other patients to watch the life ooze from this inert body. The doctor signaled his departure and left. When the nurse looked up, she was flustered to find Danny staring at her.

He was embarrassed to have been caught staring. "I was here earlier." He rummaged in his vest pocket and pulled out his badge and a piece of paper. "I'm a Texas Ranger. I've determined this man's identity. He's now a prisoner as well as a patient."

"Well, I hardly think he'll cause you any difficulty." The young woman's tone suggested impatience with the ranger's very presence.

Danny ignored it and handed her the piece of paper. "This is the man's name. You'll need it for the hospital records. I want to talk to him if he comes to. I'll check back later." Still distracted by her familiar delicate features and dark hair, he blurted, "I see the red cross on the apron bib of your uniform. I was wondering if you came to Galveston from somewhere else."

She was taken aback by his boldness. After a hesitation, she answered. "San Antonio."

"Me, too! Danny O'Brien, Ranger Company D, San Antonio."

She relaxed a bit. "Perhaps we met there?" She was hoping there was a simple explanation for his forward behavior.

"I don't think so," he said slowly, still turning the puzzle over in his mind. Her accent tickled at his subconscious once more. "What's your name?"

She was leery again. "Nurse Buehler. Nurse Helga Buehler."

Buehler! "Do you have a sister?" Danny practically shouted the question.

Helga looked shocked. "I *did.* Two, in fact. One died many years ago. I don't know where Johanna is."

Before she could ask Danny if he knew Johanna, he volunteered, "You had a twin sister."

Helga's face blanched an even paler white. She sank into the bedside chair. "You *knew* Inga?"

"No, but I know Johanna!" Danny crowed. "And I remember you and Inga. From Five Points in New York, then later at the Home. And we were on the same train to Texas." Danny slapped his thigh and almost let out a whoop before he remembered that he was in a makeshift hospital.

Helga's astonishment temporarily stripped her of her power of speech. From the look of expectation on her face, though, Danny knew she wanted to hear more. "Johanna lives in San Antonio."

He helped her up, and they moved into a hallway, where she besieged him with a flood of questions. He answered as many as he could, but it was already turning dark outside.

"Miss Buehler—Helga—I know you still have work to do, and I have to go now. I promise that tomorrow I'll come back and I'll tell you everything I know."

5

Danny looked at the address on Broadway Ruby had given him. He looked at the mansion, and then back at the paper. *This has to be it.* Despite some damage, it had withstood the storm. Danny climbed the wide, stone steps. For a second, he felt as if he were ten years old again, climbing the steps of the Aid Society Home in New York. The mansion's massive, carved doors had the same effect. The twenty-five-year-old lawman felt like a small boy as he rang the bell.

A portly man opened one of the doors. "Come in, Mr. O'Brien!" He gave Danny such a hearty clap on the back that Danny felt as if a bear had cuffed him. A thick cloud of cigar smoke wreathed the man's head.

Danny was buffaloed. *Who is he?*

Over his shoulder, his host bellowed, "Ruby, darlin', our guest is here."

Since he did not recognize the man, Danny glanced around surreptitiously to see if there was anyone else there besides the three of them. He surveyed the high ceilings. He discreetly eyed the lavish furnishings. They were grand despite some breakage and water damage. Someone had already scraped the slime and mud from the marble floor of the foyer. "This is quite a house," Danny remarked.

His host beamed. "Just bought it a couple of days ago! Whole kit 'n caboodle. The previous owners vowed they'd never set foot on the island again. Took a few of their clothes and left." He held up his glass. "Fortunately, they left their whiskey." He took a large gulp. "I bought the house for ten cents on the dollar. I really haven't had a chance yet to look around to see what all I bought. I always swore that one way or another, I'd live in a fine house on this street." His attention shifted to the doorway, and he raised his glass. "Ah, here she is!"

Awash in yards of frothy yellow material and gaudy jewels, Ruby flowed into the room like a foamy wave. She rustled as she moved, her ample bosom rising and falling like the tide with each step.

The man grinned as he ogled her breasts and tipped his glass in her direction. "Eighth and ninth wonders of the world!" He drew a profile of Ruby's torso in the air.

"Yessir. They provide warmth in the winter and shade in the summer."

Ruby shot him a tolerant glance. Clearly, this was not the first time she had heard his jokes. "I know," she anticipated his next remark. "If this dress were any tighter, *you* wouldn't be able to breathe."

Danny concluded that her companion, judging from his girth, didn't miss any meals either. And he, too, displayed a fondness for fussy clothes. Beneath his jacket, he wore a two-tone, gray, striped silk vest. A shiny gold watch and chain winked from the pocket. A maroon silk tie adorned his fleshy neck. Glossy leather shoes peeked out beneath his white spats. Clearly, he hadn't been in town when the hurricane hit.

The man ushered Danny to a heavy, plush couch. He opened a walnut humidor and tilted it towards Danny. "Cigar?"

Danny declined.

Without inquiring, the man poured whiskey into two crystal glasses. He handed one to Ruby and the other to Danny, and then he refilled his own.

Danny took a long sip. The whiskey tasted as good as it smelled. He closed his eyes momentarily as he felt its warmth travel down his throat and into his empty stomach. As he sampled some crackers and potted meat Ruby had found in the pantry and placed on a silver tray, he waited for an introduction to his host. But Ruby and her companion were enjoying the suspense and were in no hurry to end it. Danny felt that he should know this man, yet he was still blank.

Ruby strewed hints before him. "Danny, this fine man is a politician." She patted her companion's arm. Now it was her turn to have fun at his expense and Danny's, and she was relishing it. "You know what a politician is: one of those fellows who thinks *twice* before he says *nothing*. Somebody who *stands* for what he hopes most people will *fall* for. So slick his *socks* won't stay up."

The man gave the pretense of a frown but did not bother to dispute her characterizations.

Ruby exhaled another volley. "Give a politician a free hand, and it will wind up in your pocket."

Danny sensed that these were meant to be clues, but he was no closer to recognition. The only politician he knew firsthand was Senator Lovell Burgess, who, now that he thought about it, seemed to have a lot in common with his host.

Ruby poured more whiskey in the man's glass as an excuse to replenish her own. "After all these years, he still knows his whiskey, and he can still estimate the amount in the collection plate just by eyeballin' the crowd."

Whiskey. Collection plate. Working the crowd. "Arthur! I mean, Gabriel!" Danny roared.

"You know it!" The man's face glowed like a jack-o-lantern. "I figured there was even more money in politics than in religion. I decided to go by 'Gabe.'" He winked. "Who knows, after all these years, they may still be looking for me in a couple of counties."

Danny barely heard his host's words. He stared at the man's prematurely thinning hair and expansive paunch, but once he looked past them, he could see a glimmer of the skinny acquaintance he remembered from childhood. "What happened? You used to have a hiney like a hummingbird."

Gabriel drew himself up in mock indignation and downed a sip of whiskey.

"Watch it, my boy. I'll have you know you're talking to Gabriel Arthur Blower, state senator from Galveston."

"Well, at least he has the right initials for his profession," Ruby interjected, "although I'm not sure there's that much difference between politicians and preachers. They both stand up and rock the boat, and then they try to convince you they're the only one who can save you from the storm. And speaking of storms, Galveston is lucky to still have a state senator!" Ruby was feeling the whiskey now and enjoying it. "We were in Houston when the hurricane hit. Otherwise, we might both have perished." She dipped a jeweled finger into her drink and sucked the whiskey off. "That's also the reason I still have clothes—dry clothes—on my back. Gabe was able to get us and our luggage back to the Island. He had to arrange for a boat and bribe somebody to take us across the bay. Because he's the senator, he was able to get through the protective lines they set up around the island to fend off looters, scavengers, and curiosity seekers." She flashed a huge smile at Gabriel. "And then they let *politicians* back in. What in the world were they thinking?"

"And how exactly did you meet this fine man?" Danny inquired.

Ruby explained that she and Gabriel had crossed paths again in Galveston many years after her baptism in the river. Before Gabriel became senator, he had been a regular at the Delta Queen, playing cards, imbibing whiskey, and availing himself of the services provided by Ruby's girls.

"They were fine, but none of 'em could hold a candle to *this* stunning creature." Gabriel extended a bent right elbow and began to recite in a singsong voice,

> "He offered his arm.
> She honored his offer.
> And all night long,
> It was 'honor' and 'offer.'"

Gabriel threw his head back in a hearty laugh, once again enormously pleased with his wit. Danny suddenly recalled their childish verses about Miss Darden and Mr. Rice, and found himself grinning. *Some things just don't change.*

Ruby rolled her eyes at Danny. "No better than a schoolboy. Just ignore him, honey. Him *and* his bawdy jokes. It's the whiskey. It's better than what he usually drinks, and he probably isn't used to it." She folded her hands demurely on her ample lap. "Now, where was I before I was so rudely interrupted? Oh, yes. I remember. Gabe won a considerable sum of money playing poker, and his prestige rose steadily with his winnings." She threw Gabe a pointed glance. "He was more successful at cards than at horses, but only because he couldn't shuffle the horses." Then she gave him an affectionate smile. "But he was generous with his winnings, and he made lots of friends. Even lent me money once when I was in danger of losing the saloon. And when he accumulated enough money to become respectable, he decided to run for office." She flashed Danny a boozy smile.

"Did you know that I was sweet on Ruby from the first moment I saw her?" Gabe asked Danny.

Danny tried to envision both of them at the revival more than a decade ago. He smiled at the thought.

"'Course she was an uppity young thing. Had her nose stuck so high in the air that she'd have drowned in a thunderstorm."

"You're a pair, all right!" Then Danny noticed that there was no wedding ring on Ruby's jeweled fingers, so he ventured, "You two contemplating getting hitched one of these days?" It was obvious to Danny from their comfortable familiarity that they had been keeping company for years.

Both of them looked shocked. The senator made a clicking sound with his teeth. "Now you know as well as I do that the only perfect marriage would be between a deaf man and a blind woman." In spite of his facetious protest, he and Ruby had the ease of a couple who knew each other's strengths and weaknesses, which they appreciated or tolerated accordingly. Gabriel gazed affectionately at Ruby. "Father Time hasn't been able to take away what Mother Nature gave her."

Ruby brushed his compliment aside. "He should go by 'Gab' instead of 'Gabe.' He's such a smooth talker, you could pour it on a biscuit. And that," Ruby concluded, "is also how Gabriel Blower came to be *Senator* Gabriel Blower." Ruby tossed her curls. "Besides, I wouldn't marry the old cuss anyway. It'd be bad for business."

"Yours or mine?" Gabe jibed.

Now Danny rolled his eyes.

Ruby folded her arms across her chest. "It's obvious that you and Gabe chose the opposite sides of the law, but tell us how you've occupied yourself since you and Hannah hitched a ride with Gabe and the reverend that day."

Danny felt warm and happy as he told them some of his experiences, including the one with Senator Burgess. He told them about Johanna, and now Helga. Then he asked Ruby about her sister and brother.

She looked dispirited. "I don't rightly know. After you and Hannah took off, I decided to do the same. You two were my inspiration, I guess. I hated doing farm work, and I didn't like school. Opal and me run off with a drummer. A couple of days later, Opal got scared and said she was going back home. I guess she made it."

"And Cletis?"

"Well, I can't say for certain about him either. He was still at home when Opal and me took off."

"Then you don't know that he ended up in San Antonio?"

Ruby lowered her glass from her lips. "*Cletis*? Why, I didn't think he had enough gumption to leave the farm."

Danny recounted the one-eyed jury story to a chorus of appreciative howls. "The last time I saw Cletis, he was set on joining Teddy Roosevelt's army unit. I hope he made it. I went out of town for a couple of weeks after the trial. I never saw him again after I got back."

Ruby continued to look somber. Danny felt bad for having brought up her family. He changed the subject. "Say, Ruby, why do you call your establishment the Delta Queen?"

Ruby jumped at the change of topics. "Honey, I'm not even sure what a delta is. But I know it's got something to do with water. I heard of a high-class bar in New Orleans called the Delta Queen." She smoothed the fabric of her dress. "I thought it sounded downright refined."

"She thought 'Ruby *Queen*' sounded refined, too." Gabe gave her a broad wink.

Danny was enjoying himself, but he was too exhausted to stifle a yawn. "I'm going to have to call it a day, but I thank you for your hospitality." After politely turning down their offer to stay the night, he rose to his feet a bit unsteadily. His hosts did the same. Gabriel pumped Danny's hand and gave him a bear hug. Ruby grinned and smothered him in a perfumy embrace. "Who ever thought I'd be hugging the likes of you!"

Gabriel handed Danny a lantern at the door. "Take this. You'll need it to keep from disappearing in a mud puddle."

Danny walked out into the night and towards the hospital. *Helga. Ruby. Gabriel.* He concluded that perhaps the old bit of folk wisdom was true: Things do come in threes.

6

It was after midnight. The walk to the hospital cleared Danny's head. Trying to pick his way by lantern light demanded all of his concentration.

He noticed how much quieter the hospital was at night. A weary nurse recognized him and allowed him to pass unchallenged into the ward. Noiselessly, he approached the curtained cubicle where the comatose Mashburn lay.

Danny peered around the edge of the curtain and froze where he stood. Helga, as if in a trance herself, clenched a pillow in her hands. She was pressing it hard against Mash's face. Motionless, they resembled a sinister tableau in a wax museum.

In order not to startle Helga or create a commotion, Danny moved silently but swiftly beside her, resisting the impulse to wrest the pillow from her. Instead, he placed his hands over hers. He lifted the pillow and eased it from her grip. Mashburn Dill lay slack-jawed and ashen.

Helga's eyes were vacant. They seemed to follow the movement of her head, as if an invisible force delayed them. All of her actions seemed to occur in slow motion. He reached down and rested his fingertips on Mash's neck. Helga offered no resistance as Danny took her quaking hands in his.

After a moment she spoke. "I've killed him." Her voice was low and flat. It was as if she were talking to no one in particular and reporting a fact that had nothing to do with her. "Now I'm a murderer, too. Just like him."

"He's still alive," Danny lied. "He's been near death for two days now, but he's still breathing." *She's in a state. There'll be time to deal with this later.* He took Helga's arm and guided her away from the bed and out of the cubicle. "You've been working twenty hours a day, Helga. You need to get away from here." *Had the pressure become too much?* he wondered. *It's understandable; there's death and devastation everywhere. But why would she do that? Why? To end his suffering?*

He walked her to a nearby church that was providing shelter and food for victims of the storm. Helga drained two cups of coffee, then sat in silence staring into the empty cup and twisting a lock of hair around her finger. When Danny thought she was able to answer, he asked her one question. "Why?"

Helga began to chew on her thumbnail. Her voice sounded small and remote, as if it belonged to someone else. "It was the Dills who chose me off the train. Mashburn Dill… did… unspeakable things to me. Things with knives… snakes… rats. Terrible things. He never missed a chance to hurt me or scare me. I was afraid every day I was there." Her voice faded out. Danny started to speak. She held up her fingers to silence him, determined to tell him all of it. "Stup Dill, Mashburn's father, taught Mash to be like him." Helga spewed out a bitter stream of words: "Stup was a *Schweinhund,* a swine-dog, a mean, repulsive man who—" Her shoulders sagged. She could go no further.

"Mashburn Dill's father?" Danny was unable to make sense of what she was saying.

"Mash and his father both treated women bad." Her eyes flickered upward, making contact with Danny's only long enough to see if he comprehended. She could see that he still did not understand. She took a deep breath. "Stup Dill treated his wife and his daughters bad. He treated *me* bad. He beat me. He hurt me. He hurt me in even worse ways than Mash did. I hadn't thought about either of them for a long time. Then you handed me a piece of paper with Mashburn Dill's name on it. All of a sudden, I realized I was taking care of the same monster who…"

"Helga, what exactly did Mashburn Dill do to you?" Danny spoke gently and was prepared to drop the subject if it upset her too badly.

Helga fidgeted with the cup and saucer. Her eyes filled with tears.

"I'm a law officer, but you don't have to tell me about it if you don't want to."

She looked up. "No. It's all right. It was a long time ago. I just never thought I'd see any of the Dills again. At least I hoped not." In a halting voice, she told Danny about Mash. Then she pressed her hands over her face and began to talk about Stup. She had to stop periodically to regain her composure but told him the all that had happened to her. When she was through she bit her lip to prevent further words from escaping, but they exploded anyway. "I *hate* Stup. And I hate his son." She shuddered. Her vehemence surprised Danny.

As he had listened, he felt his own anger towards Mashburn Dill and his father escalate. He thought about Johanna and how much this knowledge would hurt her. *What if she had been placed out to someone like Stup or Mashburn?* For the first time in a long time, Mary Ceara crossed his mind. *What if my sister was placed with people like the Dills?* Danny unconsciously clenched and unclenched the badge he carried in his pocket. *Bastards. Both of them.*

Helga told Danny how she ended up in San Antonio. As she talked about her life with Dr. Ohlmsted and his sister, her voice grew stronger. Finally, she managed a weak smile.

After nearly an hour of talking, she slumped in exhaustion. She cradled her cup in her hands. "Mashburn is going to die anyway," she said in a flat voice. "I hope his father is dead. And I hope Mashburn soon will be, too." She looked up at Danny with weary eyes. "That's a terrible thing to say, isn't it?"

"I'd feel the same way if I were you," he said in a quiet voice. "You need to rest, Helga. Have you taken a day off since you came to Galveston?"

She shook her head.

"You take a day away from the hospital tomorrow. I'll tell them. And I'll tell you all about Johanna when you come back."

Helga was too tired to argue. Danny took her by the arm and helped her stand up.

After she left, Danny sat back down and placed his badge in front of him on the table. For a long time, he sat there, running his thumb back and forth over it, thinking about what Helga had told him. He thought about the law. He thought about justice.

7

Helga stayed away from the hospital the next day. When she returned, the bed that had held Mash was empty. Another woman with a red cross pinned on the bib of her apron explained, "Oh. The head injury. He died a couple of nights ago. It was expected, you know."

Dead. A tear of relief rolled down one of Helga's cheeks. She quickly brushed it away and turned her head aside.

The woman's expression suddenly changed. "Oh, I'm sorry, dear. Was he someone you knew?"

Helga shook her head no.

"Well, I understand it's hard, but as a nurse, you can't let yourself get involved. There's so much sadness." She scanned the others in nearby beds, patted Helga's arm, and moved on to a patient who needed help.

Helga was ashamed of the satisfaction she felt at hearing that Mash was dead— and relieved that she had not been the cause of his death after all. Then she remembered the nurse's words: *He died a couple of nights ago.* Helga shook off the possibility. *No! Danny had said that Mash was still alive when they left the hospital. He must have died during the night.* She fumbled with the red cross, straightening and re-pinning it. She told herself, "I'm *glad* Mash is dead. I'm *glad* he finally saw fit to die. It's the only good thing he ever did."

Helga realized that she no longer felt tired. In fact, she felt lighter than she had in years. As she went about her work, she forced away any further thoughts of Mashburn Dill. Instead, she focused on a happy one: *Johanna is alive. What was taken away has been given back to me.*

8

Danny opened the battered door of the telegram office and strode over to the counter. Years had passed since Stup Dill had beaten Helga and driven her from his farm. *Was Stup still alive?* He considered the matter and then addressed his telegram, "To the Family of Mashburn Dill."

Danny had made a vow to himself that if Stup Dill were alive, he would bring him to justice for what he had done to Helga. Her words echoed in Danny's head: "Stup's evil. He'll die of his own meanness."

Now Danny mentally added, *Not if I find him first.*

9

Farley Edgecock delivered the telegram to Stup. "Want me to read it to you?" He suspected that Stup was illiterate.

Stup was in the pigpen feeding the hogs. He shrugged and nodded. "I got slop on my hands. You go ahead."

Farley cleared his throat and adjusted his spectacles. "It says,

> MASHBURN DILL NEAR DEATH AFTER GALVESTON HURRICANE. STOP. BALL HIGH SCHOOL, TEMPORARY HOSPITAL. STOP. MONEY FOR TRAIN TICKET WIRED AT YOUR SON'S REQUEST. STOP.

Farley looked up. "It's signed 'DANNY O'BRIEN.' Don't say who he is, though."

Stup stood still, holding a bucket in one hand. Farley volunteered, "The money arrived, too. More 'n enough for the cost of a ticket." Farley handed Stup an envelope.

Stup set the bucket down and walked past Farley. Without stopping or looking at Farley, he muttered, "Can I ride back to town with you?"

The door banged shut behind Stup as he entered the house. A few minutes later he emerged holding a stained and worn bag. Althene hung back in the shadow of the doorway. Stup called over his shoulder, "Mashburn's been hurt." He offered no further explanation as he climbed onto the wagon with Farley.

Stup got off at the depot, and without thanking Farley, disappeared into the small building.

10

Danny was at the hospital when Stup arrived. "I'm sorry, Mr. Dill. Your son died a few hours after I sent the wire."

A jolt of pain flickered across Dill's red, weather-beaten face, and his eyes watered as if he'd swallowed turpentine.

"He asked me to give you this." Danny produced Mash's knife.

Stup fingered the handle and continued to stare at the knife. "Gave this to him when he was a boy." Then, "How'd he die?" His voice was husky.

Danny was vague. "The storm. He took a blow to the head."

Stup glanced up and narrowed his eyes, but he remained silent.

Danny continued, "Mr. Dill, you're lucky to know your son's fate and to have his knife. Most people on this island still don't know what happened to their loved ones, and they never will."

Stup still did not reply.

"The city is burning bodies around the clock to prevent contagion. The ground is too wet for burials, and there are thousands of bodies. They've given up trying to identify them. They're burning them wherever they find them, just as they are, with rings still on their fingers and earrings on their ears."

Stup's eyes flickered at the last bit of information. Then he grunted, "My son's body?"

"Burned," replied Danny, taking a modicum of pleasure in telling Stup.

Stup's face puckered again. In a more subdued voice, he said, "Well, then. I guess I can go home."

Danny nodded. "Next train out isn't 'til tomorrow afternoon. It'll be a while before all of the trestles are repaired and regular service is restored."

It was nearing dusk as Stup walked out of the building. Danny picked up his coat. His Colt was wrapped inside it. He slipped his coat on and tucked his .44 in his waistband. The last thing he did before he followed Stup out of the hospital was to put on his badge.

11

Controlled fires were burning all over the island, as they had been since the Tuesday afternoon after the storm. Even so, the stench was not something that the nostrils ever became accustomed to. Carbolic acid, lime, and putrefaction mingled with the odor of burning flesh. The stench was made all the worse by the fuel oil used to ignite the bodies and the debris.

It took days for a corpse to be reduced to ashes. As bodies were found, they were piled atop a section of debris to be burned. Men with cloths over their mouths and noses tended the smoldering heaps, poking air holes in them with long poles. Clouds of flies hovered above the carrion-laced mounds.

Danny followed Stup at a distance, staying out of sight. Stup pulled a small bottle out of his pocket and downed half of it. He shuddered, as if hit by a small convulsion. As he walked along, he muttered to himself and drank the rest of it in angry gulps.

Danny didn't have to wait long before he saw what he expected.

Stup moved beyond one of the burning heaps. He flung the empty bottle into the fire, taking satisfaction in the sound as it shattered. He looked around furtively, then he knelt unsteadily beside a female corpse at the edge of the pile. The rotting earlobes offered no resistance as Stup stripped away the earrings and pocketed them. Then he used Mash's knife to severe a finger from the left hand. He removed the diamond wedding ring and crammed it in his pocket.

The instant he sliced the finger, he was transported back to his childhood. In his mind's eye, he could see himself, a young boy trembling as he set the log on the stump and held it for his father to split with his ax. *Pa, I don't want to hold it!* He heard his father taunt him for his cowardice. *Please, Pa! Not again!* He saw his severed fingertips fly from his hand. He saw them land in the snow, saw the blood seep into the snow and stain it. Saw his drunken father's belligerent scowl as he flung the ax down in disgust. Then Stup heard his own nine-year-old voice scream at the pain and at the blood that spouted from his open fingertips. He heard his father yell at him to shut up. Now, standing on the beach, Stup unconsciously pressed his fingers into his mouth to stifle a nine-year-old's scream and to staunch blood that wasn't there. Even so, he could again taste the peculiar metallic taste of blood. *No,* he had vowed, *I'll never treat a son of mine that way.* And he hadn't.

The heat from the fire made Stup aware again of where he was. *Mashburn loved me. And now Mash is dead.* Bitterness crept over him like a chill. *The only person that matters to me is dead.* Stup drew his sleeve across his eyes and his nose.

Then he stood up and moved a few feet farther down the beach. He hovered over another body and repeated his vile act. He took the woman's gold ring and yanked off her cameo necklace.

"Mr. Dill!" Danny's voice rang out.

Startled, Stup whirled around on wobbly legs. He cursed at Danny and waved the knife at him. The ranger walked towards him but stopped a few feet away. "Get out of here!" Stup snarled.

"Mr. Dill, martial law has been declared on the island. I'm a lawman. Looting is a crime." Although Danny kept his Colt in his waistband, he added, "We've been told to shoot looters on sight. Throw your knife down, now. You're under arrest." Danny took a step closer but was careful to remain out of Stup's reach.

"You go to hell!"

"Your son was lucky, Mr. Dill. He had a good nurse who took care of him before he died. You know her, in fact. When she was a girl, you took her off the train to live with you and your family."

Stup was now silent, but his agitation showed in his eyes.

"Her name was Helga, although you called her Hilda. She told me that you hurt her, Mr. Dill. She told me that you hurt her real bad and that you hurt her in terrible ways. You *and* your sorry son."

Stup made a bellowing sound and lunged at Danny, slashing the air with his knife. Danny pulled his pistol and fired point-blank into Stup's left shoulder.

Stup looked shocked. He dropped the knife and stared down at his chest in disbelief, then he looked back at Danny. Stup extended his arms and fell towards Danny, but the young ranger stepped aside. Stup fell face down into the greasy sand. With the toe of his boot, Danny flipped him over.

"You won't ever hurt another child or another woman again, Mr. Dill. And neither will your sorry son." Stup glared at Danny with unadulterated hatred. "Did you know that he killed women, Mr. Dill? Also cut up a few. And I bet he learned how to use a knife from you."

Enraged but impotent to respond, Stup lay there, blood gurgling from his lips.

A deputized citizen who was patrolling for looters materialized from the other side of the smoldering pile of debris and corpses. "I heard a shot. Is everything okay?"

Danny gestured to Stup. "It is now. I caught a ghoul stealing from the dead." Danny pointed to the two bodies Stup had defiled. He fished the rings and earrings out of Stup's pocket. It was getting too dark to see, but the jewelry sparkled in the eerie glow of the fading conflagration.

The man grimaced and spat in disgust. "He's no better than a damn vulture." He could think of nothing to say other than, "Well, we'd better get them bodies on the fire."

Danny pointed to the corpses that Stup had defiled. "Those are the only ones that need to be handled with respect."

The man tightened his bandanna over his mouth and nose, pulled his gloves up, and tugged gently on a corpse's legs, dragging it towards the pyre. Danny took a pair of gloves from his back pocket and dragged the other corpse.

Danny pointed to Stup. "I can get the last one."

The man raised a weary hand to signal his gratitude. Danny picked up Stup's legs and dragged him towards the fire. Stup was near death and too weak to offer any resistance, but he gurgled, and his eyes opened wide with fear as they neared the fire. His mouth twisted into a contorted epithet, but no sound came out.

Danny stared at Stup and then at the fire, fighting with himself. He thought about Helga and Johanna. Mary Ceara flickered through his mind. Then he lifted the dying man and shoved him face down onto the white hot, smoking pile of debris. "Burn in hell, Stup Dill. You *and* your worthless son."

Danny turned and walked off into the darkness. He did not look back.

12

Early the next morning Danny headed to Ball High School. As he turned the corner, he saw her approaching from the opposite direction. "Helga!"

Before he could say another word, she told him her news. "Danny, I met her! *Clara Barton.* I heard her give a talk last night. Imagine! Heroine of the War Between the States. President of the American National Red Cross Society. And she came all the way from Washington, D.C., Danny. A dozen aides came with her. She's no bigger than I am, barely five feet tall. She may be slight and in her seventies, but she's a barrel of energy. She's staying at the Tremont Hotel—"

"Helga, I need to tell you something." The excitement faded from Helga's face; his tone sounded ominous. "I notified Stup Dill that his son was dead. He came to Galveston yesterday."

Helga sucked in a sharp breath and an involuntary jerk coursed through her thin frame. The color drained from her face. She clutched Danny's vest with both hands. "Don't let him find me, Danny. Please don't let him find me! It was terrible enough knowing that Mash was here in the same hosp—"

"He's dead, Helga. Mr. Dill's dead. He came to Galveston to claim Mash's body, but it had already been burned. And after Mr. Dill left the hospital last night, he was shot for looting corpses."

Helga covered her mouth with her hand. The image of him defiling bodies made her gag. She swallowed hard. Then she lowered her hand slowly. "Then he can't ever hurt anyone again." It was a question.

"No. Not anyone. Ever."

She sagged against Danny, trying to collect herself. He could feel her shaking. "Well, I guess justice has finally been done." Her voice was a whisper.

"Are you all right?"

She gave a slight nod.

"I'm going to notify Mr. Dill's wife. She doesn't know."

Helga again nodded mutely. She asked for no details of Stup's death, but at the mention of "Mr. Dill's wife," the image of Althene and the Rabbits flashed through her mind, and she found her voice. "Althene. His wife's name is Althene. She and her daughters will be as relieved as I am that he's dead. Maybe more."

Danny went to the telegraph office and wired Althene Dill that her husband, like her son, had died in Galveston. When Danny reached into his pocket for change for the telegram, he felt the earrings, rings, and necklace. He handed them to the operator. "See to it that these are sent to the same person. Say in the telegram that her husband wanted her to have them to sell or keep as she sees fit." Danny paused. "And tell her that he said he's sorry for every bad thing he ever done to her and their daughters."

Then Danny sent a telegram to Captain James. It read:

> MASHBURN DILL DEAD. STOP. JUSTICE DONE. STOP. WOULD LIKE TO REMAIN IN GALVESTON UNTIL NEEDED ELSEWHERE. STOP. DANNY.

THIRTY-THREE

1

"DISASTER PRODUCES MANY HEROES," declared the *Galveston News* headline. Danny sipped a cup of scalding coffee and scanned numerous vignettes that described acts of heroism and sacrifice during the storm. There was a boy who drowned, but first saved his younger sister by holding her above the water long enough for her to make it to safety. He read of two sisters who had clung to an armoire and thereby survived a nightlong, aquatic roller-coaster ride across the bay before being dumped on the mainland. There was the mother who let go of a piece of driftwood and perished when she realized that it could not support both her weight and that of her three young children. "Hang on!" she had admonished them. "Don't turn loose!" The stories were endless: a man who had handed his daughters to his wife through a second story window of their house but was unable to crawl out himself before the opposing wall fell on him; a lad who was hit by flying debris and killed as he tried to swim to his cousin to free him from the storm wreckage and seaweed that entangled him.

Then Danny read a priest's account of an "angel of mercy." A strapping young man—"Cledis Munt," as he recalled—had single-handedly freed many of those trapped by fallen beams and cornices at St. Mary's Church. "Not even an Islander," the priest had marveled, "and very possibly, not even Catholic. I gave him my crucifix when he went back out into the storm. I pray that it protected him." Danny reread the piece, wondering if it was Cletis. He had last seen him in San Antonio two and a half years ago. *Had he signed up to serve with Theodore Roosevelt? If it was Cletis, why was he here? Was he still on the island? Was he still alive?*

Sipping his coffee and leafing through the remaining pages, Danny happened upon another item that piqued his curiosity: "Winfield Seeks Man Who Saved Grandson." In the article, Laughton Langley Winfield II, patriarch of one of Galveston's most prosperous and illustrious families, expressed his gratitude for his only grandchild's survival. Danny read the article again:

> Laughton Langley Winfield IV, barely
> eighteen months old, was rescued from his
> drowning mother's arms the night of the
> hurricane. The child is now thought to be the

only surviving Winfield heir. When word of the disaster reached them, Laughton Winfield and his wife, Lillian, returned straightaway from New York City, where they were visiting Mrs. Winfield's relatives.

The Winfield's son, Laughton Langley Winfield III, is the baby's father. He is missing and presumed dead. The baby, Lawt, was located after his distraught grandparents initiated a massive search for their son, daughter-in-law, and grandson. Their daughter-in-law, Catherine, has not yet been found and is presumed to have drowned.

It is reported that at the height of the storm, Mrs. Emmalou Watkins was handed the terrified baby by a man who had clung to a rooftop with the boy throughout the night. He said the child's mother handed the baby to him just before she disappeared beneath the water. According to Mrs. Watkins, the toddler had a large crucifix fastened around him. She recognized a picture of the Winfield child in the newspaper. His identity was later confirmed by his grateful grandparents who will assume guardianship.

The article described the Winfields' tearful reunion with their grandchild and then concluded,

The Winfields are seeking the "tall, robust, sandy-haired man in his late twenties" who rescued their grandson and whose first name may be "Cleavis." Mrs. Watkins could not remember the name with certainty, nor could she recall his last name. She described him as "limping, bruised, and battered, with a severe cut over his right eye." Anyone with knowledge of this person is asked to notify Mr. Laughton Winfield.

Danny flipped back to the front page. Thoughts raced through his head. *The descriptions are certainly similar. The names the priest and the woman gave are both similar to "Cletis." And there's also the crucifix.*

He gulped down the rest of his coffee. Tracking was one of the things rangers did best. Danny folded the newspaper and put it inside his vest. *If Cletis Mutt is on this island, I'll find him.*

2

It took Danny a week to find his man, and it was, indeed, Cletis. Danny asked every law officer he met, whether he was a deputized citizen or an actual militiaman, to be on the lookout for Cletis. At the temporary hospitals and medical tents, Danny gave Cletis's description in case he had sought treatment for his injuries.

On a demolished stretch of beach, a militia member told Danny about a young man who had appeared several times, although erratically, to help pile and burn debris. A few days later, Danny spotted his man.

Cletis had a rag tied around his lacerated forehead, and he still sported numerous large purple and yellow welts. Otherwise, he looked much the same as he had when Danny had last seen him in San Antonio. So intent was Cletis on his task that he did not notice Danny.

"Buy you a drink."

"What?" Cletis looked up, sure he had misheard.

"Now don't argue with me. I'm a ranger."

Cletis squinted in the morning sun, shielding his eyes with his hand. He studied Danny's face for a minute, and then threw his shovel down on the greasy sand. Simultaneously, he began muttering his familiar, "Well, I'll be! Well, I'll be!" Like a giant bear that had spotted a honeycomb, Cletis clamped his big arms around Danny and began pounding him on the back.

"Buy you a steak and a whiskey tonight," Danny said, continuing to replay the conversation of their last meeting. "I know a good saloon. Well, one that's still standing, anyway."

"But where'd you come from? How long have you been here? In Galveston, I mean."

Danny gave Cletis a congenial wallop on his brawny arm and just smiled. "We've got a lot to catch up on." Without answering Cletis's questions, he turned and began to stroll off. Over his shoulder, he called out, "Find a place to clean up later. Then meet me at eight o'clock on the other side of the island at a saloon called the Delta Queen."

3

Danny was already in the saloon when Cletis arrived. Cletis had bathed and shaved, and he had slicked down his hair. His shirt, though badly wrinkled and musty, looked reasonably clean. A fresh bandage replaced the rag around his forehead.

When Danny spotted Cletis, he strode towards the saloon door and shook hands with him. "Well, you look a damn sight better than you did this morning." Danny carried a worn but neatly folded newspaper under his arm. He gestured to a table in the corner; his hat rested squarely in the middle of it. "Over there."

The tavern was slowly returning to normal. The piano had a strange ringing sound, but the music, the reassuring clink of glasses, and the partially restored lights gave the saloon a congenial atmosphere. However, the shattered mirror behind the bar had been removed, and its absence gave the wall a blank, forlorn look. Broken tables and chairs had been stacked to one side. "Kind of reminds me of El Fandango after you and your friends finished with it," Danny teased.

Cletis looked sheepish, but he smiled.

As they reached the table, Danny called out, "Curly!" He held up two fingers, and the bartender sent over two whiskeys. Cletis downed his in a single gulp. Danny signaled for another, but he couldn't resist: "Better slow down, Cletis. Do you know how hard it'd be to find a dozen cross-eyed men in this town?"

Ruby stood at the bar talking with a tall man, occasionally pressing herself against him and laughing too loudly at his jokes. She patted him on the chest, and then, like a good proprietress, circulated among the other patrons, welcoming them, whispering in their ears, and seeing that their glasses were kept full. Her voice carried across the room. "Ain't no such thing as too strong whiskey, honey." She chucked a gray-whiskered patron on the chin and delivered the rest of her assessment in a consoling tone: "There's only weak men." Those at the bar voiced good-natured agreement. Before the man could respond, Ruby flashed a huge smile at him and bobbed like a buoy to another table. There, she draped her arms around the shoulders of two German lads who were chattering in animated, guttural voices. "Say, boys, is that German"— she paused for effect—"or do you have throat ailments?" More laughter. They shrugged and grinned. "The remedy is to drink more beer. It'll smooth the gravel out of your vocal chords." She gave them a maternal pat.

Danny marveled as he watched her in action. "She's something!" he declared as he pointed her out to Cletis.

At the next table, Ruby chided a man who made a face as he tasted his glass of whiskey. "Why, Harlan, you think coffee's got to be saucered and blowed before it's tame enough to drink!" There was the predictable pause, followed by, "Maybe you'd better leave the stronger stuff to the grown-ups!"

"Oh, I think I can handle the 'stronger stuff,' Miss Queen." The man patted the seat of an empty chair beside him, but Ruby just winked. "I'm working, sugar, but I know just what you need." She glanced at one of the attractive, nubile women who hovered near the bar. Without saying a word, she made herself understood, and the young woman approached the table. "Raney, this is Mr. Harlan Hanks. Perhaps you'd like to invite Mr. Hanks to share a drink with you upstairs?" A minute later, Raney steered Harlan to the stairs at the back, her arm linked in his. Ruby called out in mock indignation, "Now, Harlan, you know I'm just pure *jealous* of Raney for getting all your attention! Yes, indeed, it's a real shame. Why is it the seat of the pants does the work, but it's the vest that gets the gravy?"

Without skipping a beat, she moved to the next table. "Hello, Griff!" She eyed his bruised face and broken arm. "I'm happy to see you survived." He gave her an appreciative smile, displaying a set of beautifully even teeth. "I declare, honey," she went on, "you got teeth like piano keys." Those nearby had to wait only a half a moment. "Fortunately, the *white* keys." The man grinned and tapped his front tooth with his fingernail.

It was clear that a similar ritual was played out every evening at the Delta Queen and that regular patrons took it as a compliment to be singled out by Ruby, even for a ribbing.

Swishing in layers of frothy peach-colored taffeta, Ruby finally floated over to Danny and Cletis. She recognized Danny and chirped, "Hello again. I trust this is social and not business?" She arched her eyebrows. "Who's your friend?"

Cletis stared dreamily at her, the whiskey having quickly spread its welcome, relaxing warmth through his tired body.

Ruby crossed her arms over her ample chest and pressed her fingers into her pale, fleshy biceps. She glanced at Cletis again, then back to Danny for an answer to her question.

"This is an old friend of mine from San Antonio, a military man." He abruptly turned to Cletis. "You *did* join the Rough Riders, didn't you?"

Cletis lowered his eyes, studying in detail the glass in which his whiskey had been served. He nodded miserably.

"Well, as I was saying…" Danny was relishing every minute of the conversation; he remembered Ruby and Gabriel stringing him along the previous week. But Ruby's rising impatience forced him to move ahead. "Yessir, this man is a genuine hero!"

Cletis groaned softly to himself. *If only he'd asked me first. I might have told him that my bein' a soldier wasn't… like I thought it was going to be.* Cletis had to stave off the impulse to flee.

But Danny's next words caught Cletis by surprise. Danny unfolded the newspaper, smoothed it flat, and thumped a small square of it with his finger. Then he pointed to Cletis and said, "This is the hero who saved those folks at St. Mary's that terrible night."

Cletis shot Danny a look of gratitude so strong a tightrope walker could have traversed it.

I knew it had to be you who saved them! Danny congratulated himself on having pieced the events together correctly.

Ruby looked at Danny's companion with new and heightened interest.

"There's more," Danny announced, turning two pages of the newspaper. Running his finger beneath the caption, he read, "Winfield Seeks Man Who Saved Grandson." He cleared his throat and read parts of the article aloud.

Ruby had now forgotten about everyone else in the bar as she leaned forward to hear about the rescue of little Laughton Winfield IV and about the handsome reward his grandparents wished to bestow upon the heroic man who had saved him.

Cletis was sitting up straight, assimilating in increments Danny's revelations.

"Me? They're looking for me?" Cletis asked in disbelief.

"Yup. And a hero deserves a drink!" Now it was Danny's turn to pause dramatically. "Ruby, pour your brother Cletis another whiskey."

At the sound of their respective names, Ruby and Cletis both jerked their heads in the direction of the other.

"Cletis?" It was the quietest voice in which Danny had ever heard Ruby speak.

"Um-hmm," Danny interjected. He laced his fingers behind his head and leaned back in his chair. "This is the man the Winfields have been looking for!"

"Ruby?" Cletis was still studying the image before him: the rouged cheeks, the piled-up ringlets of hair, the rosy lips, the fancy jewels, and the bread loaf bosom that overflowed the neckline of her dress like yeasty dough.

"Well, I'd *think* a long-lost brother and sister would have a lot to talk about." Danny put some money down on the table. "Bring Cletis a steak, Ruby, or whatever you got that's good." Then he turned to Cletis. "You and I can visit tomorrow. Meet me here at ten, Cletis. We're going to see the Winfields. I'm sure they'd like to talk to the last person who saw their daughter-in-law alive and the man who saved their grandson."

As Cletis was struggling to absorb what Danny had just said about the Winfields, Ruby settled into the chair beside him. Danny glanced back over he shoulder as he walked out the door of the saloon. Ruby's jeweled fingers were flying at a rate that matched her animated speech. Danny smiled. She and Cletis looked deep in conversation, although Ruby was doing all the talking. *Some things,* Danny thought, *never change.*

4

It was overcast the next day. The smell of burning fuel oil from the fires saturated the clammy morning air. Danny and Cletis picked their way among uprooted trees and other debris, trying to stay on the improvised paths of boards that had been laid over the slimy ground.

"It's going to be fine," Danny reassured Cletis, but he had to take Cletis by the arm and steady him as they climbed the steps of an imposing Broadway mansion. Danny rang the bell.

"You do the talking," Cletis begged.

A dour looking man answered the door. After Danny identified himself as a Texas Ranger, the man silently ushered them into the foyer. Danny removed his hat and cleared his throat. "Mr. Winfield, the reason we're here is because—"

"Sir, I am *not* Mr. Winfield," the man practically sniffed.

"Well, we're here to see Mr. Winfield. We have information about his daughter-in-law."

The man's demeanor instantly changed and his tone became conciliatory. "Wait here, please."

Within minutes, the Winfields appeared and introduced themselves. They gestured Danny and Cletis towards a brocade settee in the spacious parlor and made an effort to put them at ease. Danny could see how anxious they were for knowledge about the tragic night. In halting words, Cletis told them what had happened. Over and over again, Mrs. Winfield dabbed her eyes with a lace-embroidered handkerchief. Mr. Winfield struggled to keep the emotion out of his voice. "I can't tell you how profoundly grateful we are to you, Mr. Mutt, and to you, Mr. O'Brien, for locating Mr. Mutt and bringing him here."

Mrs. Winfield reached for a small bell and jingled it. The same man who answered the door appeared with a tray of tea and cookies. As he served them, Mrs. Winfield issued some other instructions. A few minutes later a woman appeared at the doorway to the drawing room. She wore a white uniform; her braided white hair was looped in a figure eight and secured on top of her head. She held a bright-eyed toddler by the hand.

Cletis recognized Lawt immediately. "Hey, little feller!"

The child smiled at Cletis but then ran over to his grandmother and climbed in her lap.

After asking Cletis every detail about the night of the hurricane, Mrs. Winfield suddenly realized the one thing she had not asked. "Mr. Mutt, I apologize for not asking sooner. Please tell us about yourself."

Cletis recounted his history as briefly as possible. He glossed over his stint as a soldier by saying that he'd "been in the Volunteer Cavalry for a short while."

Danny interrupted, announcing with pride, "Cletis served in the Rough Riders and fought at San Juan Hill with Teddy Roosevelt."

Mrs. Winfield pressed her handkerchief over her heart. "My glory! Being a hero just comes naturally to you, doesn't it, Mr. Mutt?" Cletis looked pained and embarrassed, which only endeared him further to the woman.

Danny spoke up again. "It was Cletis that saved those people at St. Mary's."

"Of *course!*" erupted Mr. Winfield, smacking his fist on his open palm. "The priest told us about it when he came to offer condolences about the children." Mr. Winfield blinked. "And the crucifix is *his!*" He looked directly at Cletis. "What can we do to thank you, Mr. Mutt? There's the reward, of course, but what else?"

Cletis fidgeted with the white lace napkin and delicate rose-colored teacup he was attempting to balance on his knee. "Nothing. Really. I didn't do none of it for a reward." He looked at Lawt. In a smaller voice, he added, "I'm so sorry I couldn't save his mama."

Mr. Winfield nodded his understanding, and Mrs. Winfield again dabbed her eyes. Then he pressed Cletis, "Do you have work, Mr. Mutt?"

"Nope. When I got here, I was planning to work on the docks. Ain't much left of them. So for now, I'm just helping with the cleanup." His voice trailed off. What he couldn't say was that he, Cletis Mutt, war coward, couldn't go home again. He added feebly, "I have everything I need. At night I sleep in one of the warehouses the Red Cross is using as a shelter. Everyone is real nice. They feed us, too."

Mr. Winfield strode over to an intricately carved desk and extracted a pen and paper from the drawer. He talked while he wrote. "I'm going to arrange for my banker to put one thousand dollars in an account for you, Mr. Mutt. If you leave Galveston, the money will be transferred to a bank of your choice, of course. And as long as the city is in shambles, you'll stay with us as our guest. There are many empty rooms in this house, and it's the least we can do. We won't hear otherwise."

Cletis sat open-mouthed, but mute. After several seconds, he managed to stammer, "Thank you... but you don't need to... I mean, that's a fortune..." His voice trailed off: he had the feeling the Winfields were not the kind of people a person refused. Then in a tentative voice he asked, "But I can still help with the cleanup, can't I?"

"Certainly you may!" soothed Mrs. Winfield. "It's just that by staying here, you'll have a comfortable bed and as much good food as you can eat." She turned to her husband. "Laughton, we're donating a stained-glass window to St. Mary's in memory of Lang and Catherine. Don't you think it would be fitting if we also donated one in honor of the courageous Mr. Mutt?"

He nodded in wholehearted agreement with his wife's suggestion. "A capital idea, Lillian." He folded the note he had written and tucked it in his coat pocket.

Cletis's head was still spinning. He raised one last feeble protest, but the Winfields would hear none of it.

"It's settled," Mr. Winfield declared. "And I'll arrange to have your things brought over today." The moment he had spoken, Mr. Winfield recognized his error, but it was too late.

Cletis was matter-of-fact though. "I don't have no things, Mr. Winfield. At least nothing that I can't carry in a sack. But I'd be pleased to sleep in a bed instead of on a cot."

Mr. Winfield extended his hand. "Well, this has been quite a morning, gentlemen."

As the three men shook hands, Mr. Winfield told Cletis, "There *is* one other thing I can do. I'm a member of the Public Safety Committee that was created after the storm. We have appointed Major L. R. D. Fayling to act as Commander in Chief of the Military and Special Deputies of the Police. Fayling is a former deputy U.S. marshal who served proudly in the Spanish-American War, just like you."

Cletis began to feel alarmed. *Why is he telling me this?*

Mr. Winfield continued, "The major is in charge of the three hundred men we pulled together to maintain order after the storm: local militia, the Galveston Sharpshooters, deputized citizens, artillery men, and police officers. You know, they patrolled thirty-six hours straight following the storm. Did a damn fine job, and they still are." He spoke with fierce pride. "Since then, two hundred well-armed and uniformed militiamen have arrived by train from San Antonio and St. Louis. And, of course, tens of thousands of rations have arrived, along with a thousand Army tents."

"Dear, now what exactly is the other thing you plan to do for Mr. Mutt?" It was Mrs. Winfield's way of letting him know her husband had gotten sidetracked.

Mr. Winfield quickly came to the point. "Mr. Mutt, I'd like to personally recommend you to Major Fayling. He'd appreciate a fine, brave soldier such as you."

Cletis looked mortified. "No, Mr. Winfield. I'm mighty grateful, but—"

Mr. Winfield cut him off with a wave of his hand. "Nonsense! I've already penned him a note." He tapped his breast pocket. "You'll work directly for the major. I won't hear otherwise."

And with that, Laughton Winfield shook hands with Cletis and Danny and walked them to the door.

5

Standing before Major Fayling, Cletis felt like he had when he was a schoolboy and Miss Cooper summoned him to her desk. He shifted his weight and stared at the tops of his dilapidated shoes. Then he mumbled, "Sir, I have something to tell you, sir." Cletis burned with shame.

Major Fayling sat behind a battered table at the temporary headquarters. He nodded and pointed to a chair. Cletis sat down. The major said nothing further, but steepled his fingers and waited for Cletis to begin.

"I'm a coward, sir," Cletis announced in a flat voice. He looked like a deflated balloon. His head sank even closer to his brawny shoulders.

The major seemed unfazed by Cletis's admission. "The facts of the last few weeks refute that."

"No. I mean…" Cletis swallowed hard, determined to spit out the bitter truth. In an even lower voice he said, "In Cuba." The major remained silent, so Cletis took a deep breath and continued. "At San Juan Hill. My regiment's job was to fight its way up the hill. There was lots of Spaniards shootin' at us."

The major suppressed a small smile and nodded his understanding of these obvious facts. Still he did not speak.

It was coming more easily now for Cletis. Each detail of his disjointed confession seemed to lighten his burdened soul. "Dewey Beckworth was shot standin' right next to me. Fell like an uprooted tree. Dewey wasn't no older than me. I grabbed Dewey's rifle. I was gonna shoot every Spaniard in sight. I took off in a lather, firing at them as I went. I didn't get more than a few feet before I stumbled." Cletis looked down at the desktop and whispered the last few words. "That's when I ended up shootin' myself in the foot." *There. The truth's out. You finally said it, you coward,* Cletis assailed himself.

Major Fayling rippled his fingertips together. "Private Mutt, did you deliberately shoot yourself in the foot?"

Cletis looked shocked. "Gosh, no!" Not only was he taken aback, he was also offended by the very question.

"Were you able to fight after that?"

"I tried, but my shoe filled up with blood, and I couldn't step down on my foot on account of it hurting so much."

"Up until the time of the *accident*, you fought with your unit?"

"Yessir." Cletis decided to make a clean breast of it: "But I was scared *all* the time 'cept when I was firin' at 'em at the end."

The major ignored Cletis's last comment. "And you were wounded while attempting to fight the enemy?"

"Yessir, but I shot *myself* instead." Cletis felt frustrated. *How can I make him understand?*

"And you were wounded while *attempting* to fight the *enemy?*" The major repeated his question in a slightly louder voice.

In a meek voice, Cletis responded, "Yessir."

"Then you did nothing wrong, Private Mutt. You acted honorably."

"But I didn't tell the others I'd tripped and bumbled the rifle and shot my own self. They thought it was the Spaniards." He hung his head. "And I let 'em think it." He slumped against the back of his chair.

The major extracted a small notebook from his front pocket and turned the pages until he found the one he wanted. "Private, let me read you something Lieutenant Colonel Roosevelt said." He cleared his throat. "This may not be verbatim, but I believe I captured the essence of his remarks." Major Fayling began to read. "Far better it is to dare mighty things, to win glorious triumphs, *though checkered by failure,* than to take rank with those poor, timid spirits who know neither victory nor defeat." He closed the notebook with an authoritative snap. "Private, there were many who couldn't fight because they contracted malaria, yellow fever, or dysentery. Do you think they were cowards? Should they feel ashamed?" Before Cletis could respond, the major answered his own question: "Certainly not! And what about those who died from malaria before ever firing a bullet? More men died in Cuba from malaria than in battle. Should they be considered cowards? Should their families feel shame? Of course not! The point is, no soldier, not even a general, can control everything in war, or even in a battle."

Cletis sat up a little. He was listening to every word.

"Henceforth, Private, you are to regard yourself as a veteran who served the cause of freedom honorably in the Spanish-American War. The precise circumstances of your injury are no one else's business. You may have been less than skilled with a rifle under conditions of extreme duress, Private Mutt, but you are *not* a coward."

Cletis didn't understand all of it, but he understood the last few words. He sat up straight to accommodate the gratitude and relief welling in his chest.

The major rose to indicate that their meeting was over. Cletis scrambled to his feet as well. "Private, report to me again tomorrow morning. There's much work yet to be done."

"Yessir!" Cletis exclaimed, and saluted.

The major saluted. With military bearing, Cletis turned and walked outside, feeling warm and standing proud in the brisk autumn air and the sunshine of a clear conscience.

6

Two months later Senator Gabriel Blower and Ruby hosted a farewell dinner for Cletis at the senator's home. Danny escorted Helga, explaining on the way more about his and Johanna's experiences at the Mutts' farm.

When Ruby greeted them at the door, she embraced Danny and gushed about "what a beautiful little thing" Helga was.

Helga was taken aback at first by Ruby's effusive manner and coquettish appearance. *"Schmeichelkätzchen,"* Helga scoffed under her breath as she and Danny followed Ruby into the cavernous parlor.

Danny shot her a quizzical look. "What?"

"A kitten. One that purrs sweetly. *Too* sweetly." Helga searched for words in English that conveyed the idea. "A flatterer. A flirt."

"Ruby's okay. She's all wool and a yard wide," Danny tried to reassure her.

"She's what?" The figure of speech was lost on Helga.

"It means that underneath all that face paint and fluff is a genuine, warm-hearted woman."

Later, Ruby, Cletis, Danny, Helga, and Gabriel sat around the immense, mahogany dining table. Holding his sides, Danny groaned, "That was much too good! I won't need to eat for a week."

Mellowed by the food and the wine, Ruby and Cletis recounted stories about Johanna and Danny on their father's farm, and how Johanna and Danny's departure had ultimately emboldened them to leave as well. Danny and Gabriel regaled Helga with the baptism story. Then Danny had everyone shaking with laughter over the cross-eyed jury and Senator Burgess's near-lynching in Beeches. For the first time, Cletis talked freely and proudly about his experience in Cuba.

Helga described her life with Dr. Ohlmsted and his sister, but said little about her life before that, other than it had been "unhappy." Neither she nor Danny mentioned Mashburn or Stup Dill. "I'm eager to return to San Antonio and Uncle Wil," Helga declared, "but I've vowed to stay in Galveston as long as Clara Barton does." It would be December before either woman left the island.

Gabriel had an endless supply of raucous tales. The convivial group talked until the early hours of the morning.

Those gathered at the table had told stories and laughed until tears flowed. By the end, Helga leaned over and whispered in Danny's ear, "I was wrong about Ruby. I like her, even if she is a bit... flamboyant."

Gabriel emptied the last of the wine into their glasses and lifted his own. "As Helga would say, *Prosit!*"

A chorus of "*Prosits!*" seconded his toast.

"I swear, Gabe's the only man I know who's determined to ruin his health drinking to everyone else's!" Ruby teased.

Gabriel gave a radiant smile and raised his glass one last time. "To friends, old and new!" he proclaimed.

"To friends!" they echoed.

7

The following afternoon Ruby met Cletis at the train station to bid him farewell. She gave him a clumsy hug. "I'm proud of you, brother."

Cletis looked embarrassed and did not reply, but Ruby could tell he was pleased. He looked handsome, although clearly uncomfortable, in his new blue suit, a gift from the Winfields.

"You have the photograph for Mama?" Ruby inquired. They had had their picture taken together, and a copy made for their mother. Ruby had also hung one behind the bar at the Delta Queen and took every opportunity to tell patrons about her "famous brother." "You're good for business," she joked to Cletis.

Cletis tapped his handsome valise, another gift from the Winfields, to indicate that the photograph was safely enclosed. It also held a copy of the newspaper that described his heroic deeds the night of the hurricane. "Ruby, what do you want me to tell Mama? About you, I mean."

Ruby was silent for a minute, then raised her head high. "You tell her I'm a fine lady, Cletis. That I wear fine dresses. That—" Ruby gave a wry smile. "Tell her that people call me 'madam.'"

Even Cletis had to smile at that.

Then Ruby pressed a large, ribbon-trussed package into his hands. "And give her this for me, Cletis. Tell her she can wear it to church on Christmas day."

"What is it?"

Ruby smiled. "My fanciest hat."

8

Even inside the train station, the damp December chill permeated the air. Helga shivered. She had ambivalent feelings about leaving Galveston, but the city was well on its way to recovery, and she was eager to go home to San Antonio.

Lost in her thoughts, Helga was horrified when Danny suddenly snapped a pair of handcuffs on her. "What in the world!"

Danny ignored her and walked over to the ticket window. "I'm Ranger Danny O'Brien," he announced, showing his badge, "and that woman is my prisoner. I'm escorting her to San Antonio, and we need passage on this train."

Several people turned and looked at Helga. Her cheeks flushed deeply, but she feared that speaking up would only draw more unwanted attention. As the ticket agent issued the tickets, he stared at Helga with bald curiosity. "What did she do?" he asked Danny in a confidential tone. "She sure don't look dangerous."

"Well, looks can be deceiving," Danny tantalized the agent, but said no more.

Helga had turned her back to those in the station and kept her now scarlet face turned towards the wall. She closed her eyes, as if doing so would make it all go away.

Danny walked back to her, touched her arm and held up the two tickets.

"How could you?" she hissed. "How *could* you?"

"Oh, pish," Danny imitated the voice of a young girl who had received her first compliment from a boy. "It was just pure inspiration, I guess." A look of satisfaction suffused his face. "You don't have any more money than I do, and you may need what little you got."

"*Du Esel!* You donkey! You're enjoying this!" Her angry words flew like chips of wood. She raised her linked fists and shook them. "If my hands were free, I'd pinch your ears off!" The loudness of her voice even startled her.

For Helga's benefit, Danny cast a "see-what-I-mean" look in the direction of the man selling tickets. He turned back to her. "That being the case, I reckon you'd best keep wearing those bracelets." Danny crossed his arms over his chest. "I told you I could get us back to San Antonio on the first train, and I'm doing exactly that." He touched the brim of his hat with his forefinger. "A ranger always keeps his word, little lady."

9

As soon as they boarded the train, Danny removed the handcuffs. He sat and stared out the train window watching Galveston recede behind him. Although Helga closed her eyes, she was not asleep. Now that she was leaving the island, she wanted time to reflect on the events of the past months, to begin to absorb all that had happened.

Danny found the motion and sound of the train oddly soothing. Riding along and listening to the metallic click of the wheels, he found himself thinking about where other train trips in his life had taken him. He thought about his first trip, the one that had brought him and Helga and Johanna and Gabriel to Texas so long ago. His thoughts drifted to his early life in San Antonio, his first train trip by himself to Sulphur

Creek to see Johanna, and then later to Galveston. The trip to South Texas and the YT. His numerous train trips as a ranger. It occurred to him that his trip back to San Antonio was different from any previous trip. Instead of thinking, *I'm going to San Antonio,* he found himself thinking, *I'm going home.*

His thoughts turned to his father and his uncles. *They helped build railroads. Maybe my father is laying track right now.* It was impossible for Danny to envision his father any older than he was the last time Danny had seen him. *Maybe I come from a family of railroading men.* The idea pleased Danny, some sort of tradition that linked the men in his family who had come to America. *Railroaders.* The notion was broad enough for him to include Mr. Dunside among the railroad men in his "family."

Danny's bleary eyes drifted to the window, to the men laboring below to repair the last storm-ravaged trestle. Viewed in the distance, they reminded him of ants as they toiled. Nameless, faceless, and clad in drab coats on this chilly, overcast December day, they worked steadily, hauling and laying new timber and steel.

The train pulled onto the mainland to continue its journey. Danny looked behind him one last time. *Good-bye, Galveston.*

What he did not know, could not know, was that one of the faceless men he had been peering down at was his Uncle Aidan.

THIRTY-FOUR

1

Dr. Ohlmsted grasped Helga's hands affectionately and surveyed her with paternal pride. "It's good to have you home again!" He pointed to a pleasant-looking woman who was visible in the kitchen. "Mrs. Roemer is the housekeeper I employed after…" He still couldn't bring himself to say "after Elisabeth died and you went to Galveston."

Helga called out a hello to the chubby, square-jawed housekeeper who was stirring a bowl of batter. The woman stopped to wave a welcome, then wiped her hands, and came out to meet Helga.

Dr. Ohlmsted glanced at Helga's spare frame. Normally slender, Helga looked gaunt after the months in Galveston. "Mrs. Roemer, could we have veal chops tonight?"

Helga was aware he was sizing her up. "Too many meals of rations, Uncle Wil."

"I know just the remedy for that." He turned to the housekeeper. "And may we have potato cakes, brown bread, and cabbage, Mrs. Roemer?" He looked at Helga's thin frame again. "Also strudel and wine, please."

Helga rolled her eyes in delight. She laced her fingers across her stomach to show what a treat the meal would be. The doctor continued, "Wait until this evening to tell me all about your experiences. You look exhausted, my dear."

Helga nodded. She realized she *was* tired. She and Danny had traveled throughout the night. The train had been uncomfortable and cold.

"You also look older." The doctor lifted her small chin and raised an eyebrow in an appraisal of her face. "Older and wiser."

"There's so much to tell, Uncle Wil: the hurricane, Clara Barton, Danny, Ruby and Gabriel, Cletis, the Dills. But most of all, Danny knows Johanna!"

"Slow down," the doctor laughed. "Clara Barton, *ja?*" The mention of this famous woman overshadowed the other names Helga had poured out. "You go rest now. I have patients to see. We'll talk at dinner." He squeezed her hands again and kissed her cheek.

Helga disappeared up the stairs. At the sight of her featherbed, a cumulative, bone-deep fatigue overwhelmed her. She stopped only long enough to remove her hat and shoes and to loosen her bodice before sinking into her bed. By the time she pulled the comforter over herself, she was asleep.

2

"Mmmmm! Good to be home!" Danny declared through a mouthful of hot, buttered biscuit. "Nobody in Galveston can make biscuits like these, Mother Bromley." He reached for another one and juggled it in the air. "Hot!"

"You've only been back a day, Danny. You don't have to make up in one meal every biscuit you missed during the last three months." Johanna pretended to move the basket of biscuits out of his reach.

"No, but I'm sure going to try." He broke the biscuit apart, lavished butter on it, and topped it with jam. "Perfect!" Unexpectedly he asked, "Mother Bromley, can I invite a friend to join us tomorrow for Sunday dinner?"

Johanna's ears perked up. "What kind of friend?" She gave him an inquisitive look. "A *lady* friend?"

Danny sank his teeth into the flaky pastry and pretended to swoon. Opening his eyes again, he wiped some jam from his lips and licked his finger. "Yes, as a matter of fact."

Johanna tried to decide whether the swoon was occasioned by the thought of his "lady friend" or by the jam-laden biscuit he was devouring. She swallowed the bite of potato she was chewing. "Well, just who would that be?" She was annoyed at the feeling of jealousy that had suddenly asserted itself.

Danny played coy. "Someone I met in Galveston, but she's from San Antonio. She's younger than you. And she's a pretty little thing." He popped the last of his biscuit into his mouth and licked the melted butter off his fingertips. "I hope you'll be nice to her," he said with feigned sternness. He extended his plate towards Mrs. Bromley. "Another pork chop, please. Oh, and more fried potatoes and onions. They're delicious."

Mrs. Bromley filled his plate and handed it back to him. It still gave her pleasure to see him eat. "Of course she can come, dear, and of course we'll *all* be nice to her. Any friend of yours is welcome."

Mr. Dunside was trying his best to follow the conversation. "Eh?" he half-shouted. Danny looked with fondness at the old man. He seemed much frailer than when Danny left in September.

"Tell you later," Danny called out in a loud voice, patting him on the shoulder. Then to Mrs. Bromley he said, "Will you make a spice cake for tomorrow? In Galveston, I had dreams in which I could just about *taste* your spice cake."

"Certainly, dear," clucked Mrs. Bromley, trying not to let her pleasure show. "Certainly." To herself, she thought, *And I certainly want to meet your friend.*

3

During church, Johanna peeked at her watch, anxious for the service to be over. The fact that the sermon was about Job and the virtue of patience only increased her guilty feelings. The final hymn. *At last!* she thought.

Along with the others, she pressed her way towards the door of the church, giving a cursory "good morning" to other churchgoers, but not stopping to visit. Then a thought struck her. *Could Danny's "friend" be one of the young ladies in church with them right this minute?* She looked around uneasily. *No,* she decided. *He said he met her in Galveston.* She tried to focus on other matters, but her thoughts kept returning to Danny's mysterious dinner guest.

On the way home, she was no longer able to stifle either her curiosity or her anxiety. "Danny, are you… serious… about your 'friend'?" She tried to sound as indifferent as if she were asking about the weather. She pulled her coat collar closer to block out the chilly December air.

"Why?" Danny asked playfully. "You jealous?"

Johanna's face flushed in embarrassment and annoyance. She and Danny walked in silence the rest of the way.

When they entered the house, they were met by tantalizing odors of roast, potatoes, carrots, and onions. Mr. Dunside and Mrs. Bromley had ridden home with neighbors in their carriage. He had gone to his room to rest, but Danny could hear Mrs. Bromley bustling about in the kitchen. She was happily humming the final hymn from church that morning. Johanna removed her bonnet and coat and went to help her. Danny went into the parlor.

Johanna was putting plates on the table ten minutes later when there was a light knock at the door. It was soon followed by the ringing of the bell.

Danny made no effort to answer the door. He continued to sit right where he was, pretending to be engrossed in last week's newspaper.

"*Danny!*" Johanna called out in an urgent voice from the dining room. "I'm busy! For heaven's sake, answer the door! It's cold outside!" Johanna hurriedly set down the last few plates. She did so with a loud clatter. "Besides, she's *your* friend."

He still did not look up. "I'm reading. You answer it."

The bell rang again.

A growl of irritation emerged from Johanna's clenched teeth as she shoved her way past Danny, deliberately bumping his arm and jarring the newspaper. She quickly collected herself, smoothed her hair and dress, and opened the door.

A diminutive young woman with dark hair stood before her. The visitor stared at Johanna in wide-eyed astonishment. Then she said in German as softly as a prayer, "Sister, it's Helga."

For a few seconds, Johanna stood as if moored in quicksand, her hand still clutching the doorknob. When the realization had sunk in, she embraced the diminutive figure and then pulled her into the house. "Helga! Helga!" she sobbed over and over again.

"Yes! And look at you!" Tears streamed from Helga's eyes, and she clasped her hand over her mouth to choke back happy sobs. "Oh, Johanna! Even after Danny told me, I couldn't believe it. I still can't. But it's really you!"

Johanna locked her arm in her sister's and tugged Helga to the settee in the parlor. "Mother Bromley! Come quick! Come see who's here!" There was a torrent of happy words, tears, and laughter. Each sister continued to touch the other's hair and face, as if to reassure herself that she was seeing a living person and not a ghost.

"Look!" Helga reached into her pocket and produced a small, black object.

Seeing the button, Johanna burst into tears again. "I still have mine, too. I wonder if…"

There was an immediate silence. It was Helga who finished the thought: "If Inga still has hers? Johanna, do you know if she's all right? Danny said he didn't know."

Johanna was silent. She shook her head and shrugged as she let out a defeated sigh. "Danny never saw her once he left the train in San Antonio. The agent—what was her name?"

"Miss Darden," Danny chimed in, shaking his head at the memory of her.

"Yes. Miss Darden told him that she didn't think Inga would live. That a man was going to take her to a doctor." She paused, then went on, no more comfortably. "But Danny never saw anyone carry her off the train."

They both looked to Danny for confirmation. He clasped his hands together and took a deep breath. "I'm sorry," he said gently.

There was another sad silence. Then Johanna and Helga held each other and cried.

Danny felt a tightening in his throat. Overcome first with their joy, and then unable to bear their grief, he slipped out of the room, unnoticed.

Mrs. Bromley appeared in the doorway, wiping her hands on her apron as she entered the room. "Johanna, what's going on here? Is this Danny's friend?"

"This is Danny's friend, but this is also my *sister*, Mother Bromley! My sister, Helga!" Still holding Helga's hands and pulling her towards her again, she exclaimed, "My sister, Helga."

"Heavens to glory!" the tiny woman declared. She scurried to embrace Helga. Then she dabbed her eyes with the hem of her apron and turned to Johanna. "Oh, Johanna, the Lord works in mysterious and wondrous ways! Truly he does!"

"Oh, yes!" Johanna nodded. Only then did she notice that Danny had disappeared. She gave a small, lopsided smile. "And so does Danny."

4

Later that afternoon, Johanna gave Danny a satisfied assessment. "It's going to be a happy Christmas! You're back, and Helga's here! Thank you, Danny. I still can't believe it." Johanna dreamily rinsed cups in the sink. Then, as if waking up, she turned to him and lowered her voice. "I'm so thankful you're home. Mother Bromley has been worried to pieces about Mr. Dunside, although she won't admit it. But now that you're here, I can tell she feels better, and I can see how happy *he* is to have you here again. He really missed you." She wanted to say, "And I really missed you, too." Instead, she handed him a cup to dry.

"I'll talk with Mother Bromley about him. I'm glad to be back, too." Danny put the cup on the shelf. "Johanna, I'm happy for you and Helga. I had a chance to get to know her while I was in Galveston. She's a remarkable person."

"It's hard to believe that she's a nurse! As soon as I finish at Kirchner's tomorrow, I'm going to go visit her."

Johanna rinsed and stacked the plates from their noonday. As Danny dried them, she took one and put helpings of food on it. "I'm taking supper to Mrs. Hartgate," she explained. "She's down in her back again." Danny picked up the plates and put them on the shelf. Then, as if it were the next logical comment, Johanna said, "Oh, Janie lives in San Antonio now." She mentioned it as casually as if she were announcing a shipment of new tools had been received at Muehlenberg's. "In fact, she lives close by."

Danny felt his equilibrium shift, and along with it, the stack of plates he was holding. They slid sideways and he struggled to keep them from crashing to the floor. He set them back down unsteadily and turned towards her. "What did you say?"

Johanna continued preparing the plate of food without looking up. Danny was instantly at her side. He clamped his hand on her forearm, forcing her to stop what she was doing. "Johanna, what did you say?" His voice sounded strained.

"Janie."

"Janie McCorkle?"

She nodded.

"How do you know? Where is she?" He suddenly felt a desperate need to see her.

"But it's Janie Prescott now," she corrected him. "And she has two children."

The fact that she was married cut through Danny like a knife through a ripe peach. He released his grip on Johanna's arm. He felt as bereft now as he had felt thrilled at the mention of her name a few seconds earlier.

Johanna saw the joy disappear from his face. *Why does he have to feel that way,* she silently lamented. She struggled momentarily with feelings of jealousy, then anger, and then shame. *It was Danny who brought Helga back to me,* she chided herself. She realized Danny was waiting for the rest of the explanation. "Janie came to San Antonio just after you left for Galveston. She had the paper you gave her with Mother Bromley's name on it. She said not to tell you she was here, that you had work to do, that she'd see you when you got back. She and her children have come for Sunday dinner several times. Her children are wonderful." In a tone that sounded less than convincing, she added, "Of course, I like *her* very much, too."

Danny blurted out his next question, aware that it revealed too great an interest, but too curious and desperate to hold back. "What about her husband? What's he like?"

Johanna wrapped a cloth over the plate of food she had prepared and turned to face Danny. "She's a widow." Johanna walked over to a covered dish on a shelf and lifted the lid. She extracted a small card. In neat script it read, "Mrs. Foley Prescott." Beneath it were written Janie's address and telephone number. Johanna picked up the plate of food and handed the card to Danny on her way out of the kitchen.

Danny had never grown completely comfortable using a telephone. The disembodied voice on the other end made it seem unnatural and untrustworthy. But as soon as Janie said hello, his distrust evaporated. *There's only one voice like that.* Just hearing it produced joy and relief in him. *Nothing has changed.*

But his own voice stuck in his throat. He hadn't thought about what he was going to say. "This is Danny," he finally blurted.

The excitement in her voice banished all awkwardness. "Danny! When did you get back?" Before he could reply, she insisted, "You're to come for a visit this very afternoon." She didn't have to ask twice.

5

Danny walked up to the gate of a new, colorfully trimmed house. Because it stood by itself near the undeveloped end of a street, it appeared even more imposing. A Christmas tree laden with cookies, silver stars, and red bows sparkled through the parlor window.

As he made his way towards the door, he realized that he hadn't felt so jittery since the first time he swung onto Diablo's back. He also noticed that he was perspiring despite the December cold. He hesitated, then knocked. Through one of the glass panels that flanked the door, he caught his first glimpse of Janie in years. He inhaled sharply. He felt his knees go weak, and he reached for the doorframe to steady himself.

She opened the door looking herself like Christmas: her rich red hair caught up in a soft twist, a cream-colored silk blouse that tapered to the waist, a billowy, deep green skirt. Danny caught his breath. *She looks the same: beautiful, but more. What was that word the captain had once used to describe rich, lustrous copper? Burnished? Yes, burnished.*

She stood there, smiling. Danny once again found himself at a loss for words. "You look—grown up!" He instantly cursed himself for such an idiotic statement.

"Well, so do you, Danny O'Brien!" Her laughter dissipated the tension like a gust of wind scattering a puffball. "Come in!" She reached for his arm.

Danny was no sooner absorbed into the house than two children appeared, curious about the visitor. "Sul, Augusta, this is Mr. O'Brien," Janie said, but by the time she could finish her sentence, the small boy had clasped him by the hand. "Come see the Christmas tree," he urged, and he tugged Danny in the direction of the parlor.

6

Danny and Janie sat in the drawing room, the children occasionally running in and then disappearing again to play. "Sul, don't leave those marbles on the floor. You'll slip on them and fall," Janie called out. She looked back at Danny. "My husband's name was Foley Sullivan Prescott," she began. "Sul's named for him."

"He's a fine-looking boy."

Janie looked pleased in spite of herself. "Sul's as rambunctious as his father was quiet."

"How did you and Foley meet?" Danny hoped his question wasn't too personal, but he wanted to know about this man Janie had chosen and how their union came about.

Janie smiled. "Foley owned the only hotel in Anuncio." She spoke as if she were resuming an ongoing conversation. "When the railroad was extended to the town, it prospered—and so did Foley's hotel. Shortly after I arrived in Anuncio, Foley gave me a job at the hotel posting entries in the ledger, ordering supplies, and improving the meals in the hotel's dining room." Wisps of curls that framed her face shook as she laughed. "Looking back, I think he just made up the job because I needed work. I was too inexperienced and too desperate and grateful to realize it at the time."

Danny learned that Foley had been forty-two when they met. Janie explained, "Foley never married, although lots of ladies had tried to interest him. He said I caught his eye because I showed no interest in him whatsoever!" She smiled at the irony of it. "At the YT, I grew up around men. I guess I'm comfortable with their ways." As she spoke, it occurred to Danny that her sense of ease was part of what had drawn him to her as well. "From the beginning, I always accepted Foley just the way he was. I never tried, like so many other ladies did, to change the way he dressed or combed his hair, or the way he ran his hotel."

Danny was reluctant to ask more questions but nodded in hopes of encouraging her to go on.

"You'd have liked Foley. He was a good, honest man. He was kind, but he wouldn't let anybody push him beyond a point. He was stubborn that way."

Danny grinned. "*He* was stubborn?" He pretended amazement that she would describe anyone else as "stubborn."

She couldn't repress a smile, but she ignored his question and went on with her story. "After Foley and I married, I moved into the hotel. That's where he lived. Several of the ladies in town never got over it that Foley didn't choose one of them or their daughters. The judge and his wife, in fact, had Foley picked out for Lolly, their eldest, and still unwed, daughter. It got worse after Foley became successful. The ladies in the town criticized us for living at the hotel. Foley wanted to buy me a house, but I couldn't see the sense of it." She sighed. "They made remarks about Foley being so much older than me. There was endless speculation about where I'd come from since I had no family, and because you and I rode into town together. Foley was never bothered by any of their idle talk. His people, what few of them there were, were mostly in Missouri and were distant relatives he hadn't seen in twenty years. He always told me not to pay any attention to the women in Anuncio. He'd say, 'Janie, those biddies are so small-minded that their ears probably touch in the back.'" Janie unconsciously fingered a fold in her skirt. "Anyway, the important thing was that we were happy, even though I was never really accepted in town. Not even after the children were born."

"It's hard when you feel you don't fit in." Danny understood the feeling only too well.

"Well, it taught me one thing: Not ever to let other people's opinions or gossip shape my life. You can never please folks like them anyway. They'd just find something, or someone, else to whisper about." Danny liked it when Janie's fiery spirit flashed in her eyes.

She had endless questions for Danny about his life since leaving the YT, about being a Texas Ranger, about Galveston. "Mrs. Bromley and Mr. Dunside and Johanna told me about some of your experiences, Danny, but what about your uncle? They told me one of them died a long time ago. Did you find your other uncle?"

Danny shrugged. "I never did learn what happened to Aidan."

"I'm sorry."

"Well, at least I know what happened to Shamus. He was only nineteen when he died." Danny explained the circumstances of his uncle's untimely death. Then he brightened as he told her about Helga and Johanna's reunion earlier that day.

The clock on the mantle chimed, and Janie looked up at it. The afternoon was slipping away. "You'll stay for supper, I hope."

"No. I've imposed enough." He spoke with sufficiently little conviction to make it clear that he would indeed like to stay. He wanted to reach out and touch Janie's face, to draw her close, but he was happy just to be near her once again after so many years.

"Of course you'll join us. I won't hear otherwise, but I should warn you that Sunday supper isn't much because of the big noonday meal. What's more, we'll have to continue our visit in the kitchen."

"Janie, I reckon you and I have spent more time talking in kitchens than anywhere else." He felt a longing as he thought about their conversations in the Big House at the YT. *What I wouldn't give now to feel her pressing a poultice to my shoulder!*

Danny added wood to the stove. The kitchen was cozy, and before long, the fragrant aroma of simmering stew and cornbread began to waft through the house.

Drawn by the aroma, Augusta appeared in the doorway where she stood silently holding a doll. She was four, a tall slip of a girl whose yellow-green eyes dominated her face like luminous lanterns. Her skin was delicate and pale, and her flat cheekbones, clearly Foley's contribution, and large oval eyes gave her face an inscrutable cast. In this child, Janie's flaming copper-colored hair had been moderated to strawberry blonde, and it hung like limp silk in dainty hanks around her solemn face.

"It's ready, Augusta. Go get Sul," Janie told her. The child did not reply but turned and scampered off. "Augusta's a watcher," Janie told Danny. "She's an observer who hangs back, but those eyes see everything!" Janie ladled the stew into a large tureen. "Now Sullivan, on the other hand, never met a stranger. He'll talk your ears off."

Danny had already concluded that for himself. Sul was a year younger than his sister and seemed her antithesis. Even sitting at the table, he exuded energy from every part of his small frame. It made Danny think of Brody and his perpetual motion. "Your father would have loved them. Sul even reminds me of Brody."

"Me, too." She wrapped the cornbread in a napkin and carried the basket to the table. "I wish my father had lived long enough to know them. Maybe you can tell them about him sometime, about working with him at the YT. Other than me, they don't have any family."

"Dilue says family is a feeling. She says home is a feeling, too."

Janie turned to face him. "She's right."

7

After supper, while Janie cleared the dishes, Sul climbed into Danny's lap without any trace of self-consciousness and presented him with a picture book. It was obvious that he expected Danny to turn the pages and explain the story to him. This Danny did, enjoying the feel of the child's warmth against him and the sweet, mingled odor of milk and Castile soap that emanated from him.

A few minutes later, like a watch that had run down, Sullivan's movements ceased, and halfway through the book his eyes floated closed. Danny untied the boy's small, scuffed shoes and removed them. Janie motioned for Danny to follow her. "If you'll carry him up the stairs, I'll put him to bed." Janie tucked Sul and Augusta in, turned out the lights, and came back downstairs.

On a tray, she brought cups and saucers and a pot of coffee into the parlor. "Thanks for helping me with Sul. Even though I don't yet have any neighbors close by, the ones down the street have been kind to me and the children. They look in on us from time to time to be sure we're all right." She sipped her coffee and smiled. "I know they were curious about me at first. Understandable since I showed up with two small children and no husband, and as a widow was able to buy a nice house. But I've made more friends here than I ever had in Anuncio."

"I'm glad for that. It must be hard being by yourself. Without Foley, I mean." Then, "Janie, what happened to Foley?" Once again, he hoped that his question wasn't too forward.

Janie twisted the gold wedding band on her finger. "A year ago September, Foley died. He woke up that morning fine. Midday, after dinner, he had a pain in his arm and his chest. He kept saying that he was just a little over tired and that it would pass. Then he started having a hard time catching his breath, and he began to perspire. I insisted he go lie down. I knew he must have felt awful, because he finally agreed to. Foley wasn't a complainer. He never put in less than a full day's work in his life. By the time I got him settled and came back with a cold compress, he was unconscious. By the time the doctor arrived a short while later, he was dead."

Janie told this in a level voice, but Danny could see that her eyes had filled with tears. She sipped her coffee, cleared her throat, and continued. "After Foley died, I learned that he had bought railroad stocks. He had seen what the railroad had done for the town. The stock turned out to be worth…"—Janie searched for a genteel way to phrase it—"…a considerable amount. That only increased the resentment against me."

She quickly concluded her story. "I stayed in Anuncio for almost a year. When things didn't get better, I decided it was time for the children and me to make a new life for ourselves. I vowed I wasn't going to spend another day in a place my children and I weren't wanted. I had kept the scrap of paper you gave me with Mrs. Bromley's name on it. So many years had gone by that I wasn't sure if she still lived here, but I took a chance and wrote to her last September. She wrote back immediately. I sold the hotel and a month later, we were here. She's been wonderful about making us feel welcome. The children adore her. She bakes cookies for them the size of saucers, and Augusta chatters like a magpie around her and Dilue."

Janie stood up and offered in a half-apologetic tone, "Now *I've* talked your ears off. I guess Sul comes by it honestly!"

Danny thought perhaps it was a signal that the evening had ended and that it was time for him to leave. But instead, Janie walked over to the clock on the mantle. She pulled open the tiny drawer at its base and removed a tattered piece of brown paper. "Do you remember this?"

He recognized the scrap of paper he had given her years earlier when he left her in Anuncio. A feeling of tenderness filled him. She turned back to the small cavity in the clock and exchanged the paper for something else. "Do you remember this?" In her palm she held a small gold locket. "Mrs. Bradford gave it to me when I went into the mercantile." She smiled at the memory of receiving it when she was a young woman starting out on a life of her own, and she clutched the locket to her breast.

Danny thought about *his* memento of the last time he saw Janie. He'd left the purple flower in his hatband until it had deteriorated and disappeared. Eventually, all that was left was a small purple stain, which he had treasured. He'd taken his hat off hundreds of times, at sad or lonely or just quiet moments, and touched the spot with his fingertips.

Danny walked across the room to Janie. He took her hand in both of his and gently opened her fingers. Lifting the heart-shaped locket, he undid the clasp, and moving closer, encircled her neck with the delicate gold chain. He fastened the clasp behind her neck and ran his fingers down either side of the chain, smoothing it, until his index fingers came to rest on the locket, directly below her chin. Janie kept her eyes on Danny's. She searched his face with the same curiosity as she had so long ago on the plains under that sad, starry sky.

Danny knew that he was going to kiss her, and so did she. This time, however, there was nothing tentative. He kissed her once and then again, engulfed in her warmth and his desire. Danny pressed his face into her soft hair and held her closer. *Home.* He had the thought that he was in the one place in the world he was meant to be, like a traveler returned at last from a long journey.

Janie said nothing, but laced her fingers with his. Then she led him to her room.

One by one, she slid the hairpins from her hair. Each pin made a tiny *plink* as it hit the polished wood floor. Her hair tumbled down in waves around her shoulders.

Button by button, Danny undid her blouse. Blouse, bodice, skirt, petticoat—the layers fell away until there was only the locket. She shivered in the cold air. Danny quickly removed his vest and belt, pulled his shirt off over his head, and drew Janie close to him. After a minute, she gently withdrew from his embrace, lifted the bed covers and slid beneath them. Then she held them aside to make room for Danny. He took off his boots, stepped out of the rest of his clothes, and slipped into bed beside her.

Danny pulled her to him and lost himself in her softness and warmth.

It was as if two rivers had finally and inevitably merged. And in an instant, Danny found himself swirling in the lovely, faint fragrance of lilac.

8

"Christmas, 1900, will be one I remember forever." Danny was speaking to those gathered in Mrs. Bromley's parlor that day, but he was looking at Janie. Johanna and Helga immediately chimed their agreement, and the others echoed theirs as well.

Augusta sat on the floor pulling a tiny blue dress over her doll's head and arms. "Look! We match!" She paraded around the room holding aloft a doll whose outfit was a miniature version of her own. "Grandma Bromley made us dresses that match!"

Sul was sprawled on the floor building a fort of brightly painted wood blocks. He showed no interest in the sailor-collar shirt Mrs. Bromley had created for him until

Mr. Dunside began to entice the child with the promise of a story about a ship. "Come sit here, Sul," he half-shouted, patting one of two small chairs beside him. For Christmas, he had fashioned chairs for the children and for Augusta's doll, and Dilue had caned tiny chair seats. "I'm retiring from the railroad at the first of the year," the old stationmaster announced unexpectedly. The fact was, he could no longer keep up with the demands of the job. He quickly directed his attention back to Sullivan. "You can wear the hat to my uniform whenever you come to visit, Sul. And I'll show you how to tie some sailor's knots."

An awkward silence followed Mr. Dunside's revelation that he was retiring from the railroad. It heightened further Mrs. Bromley's concern that his health was failing.

Not wanting the festive mood to turn somber, Janie pointed to a large rolled bundle that was propped in the corner. "That's for you, Mother Bromley. Merry Christmas!"

Mrs. Bromley protested as Danny unfurled a rich, jewel-toned rug. "Much too lavish a gift!" she protested. "Why, this is from a specialty store in the East. It's lovely, dear, but you've spent far too much." As soon as Danny placed the rug in front of the settee, though, Mrs. Bromley's protests subsided. She studied the effect and clasped her hands in front of her chin. "Why, it's perfect!"

9

During the weeks after Christmas, Danny visited Janie and the children whenever he could, and Janie often brought the children to Mrs. Bromley's house.

So much had happened that Danny found it hard to concentrate on his job. He was already at Ranger headquarters one morning when the captain arrived, but he was sitting at the table tracing squares on it with his finger. Lost in thought, he hadn't heard the captain enter. *There have been other women, but it wasn't the same. No, not the way it is with Janie.*

"Danny?" The captain's voice startled him. "Are you all right?"

"Huh?"

The captain repeated his question, then added, "I have an assignment for you, but you've been acting strange ever since Christmas."

Danny looked as if he had been caught fishing when he should have been milking cows. "Janie. Remember I told you about her a long time ago?" The two men had not spoken of their respective romantic interests since the captain had made it clear his personal life was a topic he rarely discussed.

"The girl from the ranch?"

Danny nodded. "She's lived in San Antonio for a few months now. Her and her two children. I found out when I got back from Galveston. When I saw her again, Cap'n, it was like all the years in between, they never happened. And she's still pretty as ever. Prettier, in fact."

"So are you going to let her get away? Again?"

Danny retraced a square with the knuckle of his index finger. "I know that a man who doesn't learn from his mistakes is a blamed fool." Hesitation laced his words like threads through a cloth.

"But?"

"It's just that I been on my own for so long. Since I was a kid." He chose his words carefully. "I don't know how I'd feel about…" He struggled to put his feelings into words. "Well, it's just that I been moving around all my life. Even now, as a ranger, I like coming and going. Going wherever there's something to be done."

The captain walked over to Danny and clapped him on the shoulder. "In that case, you're in luck!" Scrap scrambled to his feet to follow the captain across the room. "Could be that what you need is some time to sort things out. And I have a job for you that will give you a chance to get your perspective. From a distance, of course." He reached down and scratched the ragged-looking dog behind the ears. "I'm sending you to Gladys City."

Danny narrowed his eyes. "Where?"

"That big oil well that we've all been reading about."

"Spindletop? In Beaumont?"

"Yes. But it's actually in Gladys City, near Beaumont."

Danny rocked his chair back on two legs. Along with everyone else in the state, the country, and even various parts of the world, he had combed the papers daily since January 10 for details of the one hundred thousand barrel-a-day gusher. "Why am I going? What do they need a ranger for?" Danny was puzzled, but excited at the prospect of seeing this phenomenon firsthand.

"In Galveston you had extensive experience with a chaotic situation. Gladys City has gone crazy. The sheriff, Ras Landry, is bright, capable, highly respected, fearless. And smart enough to know that all he can do is try to keep the lid on. I'm making you available to him until things settle down a bit." He reached down and ran a hand over Scrap's lumpy fur.

"What's it like there?"

"The ground is mucked with mud and oil. Ras says the mud is three feet deep on the hill. The air is thick with oil droplets and reeks of sulphur gas."

Danny wrinkled his nose. "Sure *sounds* like Galveston. And that ain't a compliment."

The captain nodded. "But unlike Galveston, the population has mushroomed. A lot of those who showed up are folks wanting to make a fast buck: wheeler-dealers, hustlers, and whores. Fights break out constantly. Saloons, gambling halls, disorderly houses operate twenty-four hours a day, seven days a week. There's disease, of course. No sanitation. Oh—and water costs six dollars a barrel."

"Six dollars! How much is oil?"

"Nickel a barrel." When the captain's expression didn't change, Danny realized he was serious. "I want you to take the train to Houston. Because of Spindletop, six trains now run daily from Houston to Beaumont. Once you get there, hire a hack to take you to Gladys City. Then find Ras Landry. He'll help you arrange a place to stay. People are sleeping on rooftops, in barber chairs, store windows, wherever they can find a place they won't be stepped on."

Danny thought of Janie and the comfort of her deep, warm bed, of how he hated to be away from her. "Cap'n, you're sending me off again, and January ain't even over yet!"

The captain fished around in his vest pocket for a piece of jerky and tossed it to Scrap. He smiled at Danny. "The year's started with a bang, hasn't it?"

<h1 style="text-align:center">10</h1>

Johanna struggled with her feelings towards Janie, a fact that was not lost on Janie. On a warm spring day, the two sat in silence sipping lemonade on Mrs. Bromley's back porch, watching the children dart among the emerging flowers, and listening to the steady hammering of Anton Wernicke as he repaired the front porch and the railing around it. Mrs. Bromley had shooed the children and the two women out of the house, insisting that the fresh air would be good for all of them.

Since Danny was still in Beaumont, Janie decided it was time to broach the delicate topic, and it was she who finally broke the silence. "Johanna, you don't like me very much, do you?" The question was a difficult one for Janie to ask; it brought back hurtful memories of Anuncio.

Johanna felt her face flush, and rather than look at Janie, she looked out towards the back garden where the children were splashing the water in the birdbath.

Janie persisted. "It's Danny, isn't it?"

Johanna's injured pride prevented her from responding. Janie could see Johanna's grip tighten on the cloth napkin in her lap. Slowly, painfully, Johanna sought words. "I'm glad Danny has someone he…." She could not bring herself to say "loves."

"Danny loves you, too, Johanna. It's just *different.*" She hesitated, afraid she had already pressed the matter too far, but then she resolved to go forward. "Danny doesn't know you feel that way about him."

Small explosions went off inside Johanna's head. "How could he *not* know?" Her voice was constricted with pain. She would have liked it if she could have hated Janie, but she couldn't. Worse, she actually admired her strength and independence. Johanna looked away. She despised herself for her own weakness.

"Johanna, Danny doesn't know you feel that way about him any more than you realize how Anton Wernicke feels about *you.*"

Johanna jerked her head in Janie's direction. "What?" Completely flustered, she dropped her napkin, and when she reached for it, she tipped her glass over. The lemonade splashed on her skirt and on the floorboards below.

Johanna began to blot it up, but Janie caught her by the wrist. "Johanna, listen to me. For some reason, none of us ever seems to be able to recognize or appreciate what's right under our noses. Do you think Anton has come here straight from the lumberyard for the last four Saturday afternoons because he likes repairing porches?" Johanna had not yet pulled her hand away, so Janie hurried on. "What Danny feels for me will never change what he feels for you. There's room in his heart for both of us, and I would consider it a great honor to be your friend, too."

Now Janie was struggling. Johanna was resisting her words. She turned loose of Johanna's wrist. In frustration, she said, "Look, Johanna, even if I weren't here…." She stopped short. She did not want to be unkind.

Johanna's eyes filled with tears. Janie had only told her what she already knew, and in fact had known for a long time. *Even if Janie weren't here, Danny still wouldn't think of me in a romantic way.* Johanna bit her lip and nodded in agreement. "I suppose in a way, Janie, it's a relief."

Janie reached over and held Johanna's hand. They sat in silence for a few minutes. Janie gave Johanna's hand a squeeze. "I'll clean this up. You go change your dress. It's time for the children and me to leave anyway."

Janie rinsed away the sticky lemonade with a pitcher of water and tidied up the table. She called the children, and they said her good-byes to the others. She called out a good-bye to Janie. From the top of the stairs, Johanna replied, "Janie—." There was a long pause, and then, "Thank you."

"You're welcome."

As she and her children walked down the street and rounded the corner, Janie glanced back. A look of pleasure came over her face: Johanna had put on her favorite yellow dress, and she was handing a smiling Anton Wernicke a large glass of lemonade.

THIRTY-FIVE

"Please open an account in the amount of $1,000 in the name of Mr. Cletis Mutt," read Mr. Winfield's instructions. Terence Bains, mayor and owner of the Sulphur Creek Bank, picked up the check, studied it, and exhaled a long, slow breath. He removed his spectacles and leaned back in his chair. A sizable account such as this would certainly help the bank. But who was the person in whose name the account was being opened? *Mutt. Cletis Mutt.* The name Mutt flickered in his memory as perhaps belonging to a farmer to whom the bank had once made a small loan for crop seed.

Mr. Bains put his glasses back on and shook the rest of the contents out of the heavy, cream-colored envelope. It was a collection of newspaper clippings. He sifted through them briefly and then picked up the letter and resumed reading. The letter, also written on paper that had the weight and feel of wealth, explained that Cletis Mutt had acted heroically during the Galveston hurricane. The banker was intrigued. Most of the country, and all of Texas, had read with morbid fascination everything they could learn about the terrible storm. "The newspaper clippings provide the details of Mr. Mutt's heroic deeds. You should also know that Mr. Mutt was a member of Lt. Col. Theodore Roosevelt's Rough Riders, and as such, fought with valor in Cuba during the Spanish-American War. I am sure that Sulphur Creek's newspaper will want to share this information with its citizens and that they will want to welcome this hero home again." The letter concluded, "Mr. Mutt will be arriving by train on Thursday afternoon." It was signed Laughton Langley Winfield II.

Mr. Bains lost no time notifying the editor of the *Sulphur Creek Chronicle*, who was only too glad to have an exciting story. As Mayor Bains pointed to various articles, he declared, "I think we should greet this hometown hero at the station tomorrow. You know, patriotic music and flags."

"I agree," came the vague response. The editor was already engrossed in the clippings about Cletis and had begun composing his own article in his head when he heard the mayor repeat a question about flags. "There are some flags stored at the town hall," he said in a distracted voice.

Thursday arrived, and so did Cletis. Wearing his rumpled blue suit and clutching a fine valise and a circular box, he alighted from the train. In disbelief, he found himself greeted with applause, cheers, waving flags, and the sounds of a small, ragged but enthusiastic band.

The mayor motioned for Cletis to join him at the makeshift podium that was festooned with red-white-and-blue streamers. A little girl called out, "That's him! He's here!" Other children waved their flags and shouted "Welcome home!" A small boy poked his friend and pointed animatedly to the red scar above Cletis's right eyebrow. "Look there! At his head! Probably a war injury!" His friend responded with an admiring nod.

Mayor Bains raised his hand to silence the music and the crowd. Then he began the proceedings. "As mayor, it gives me great pleasure and pride to offer a warm welcome home to a hero of both the Spanish-American War and the Galveston hurricane, Sulphur Creek's own Cletis Mutt." The townspeople applauded, whistled, and cheered. Cletis stood there, embarrassed by the attention, but grinning and waving back at them.

The mayor signaled an older couple to come forward and join him and Cletis. Angus and Oleta Mutt emerged from the crowd looking a little tentative, but then they began to beam. Oleta's eyes overflowed with tears. "My boy! My boy!" she chanted as she locked Cletis in an awkward embrace. Cletis stood stiff as a stork in a blizzard. Angus remained in the background looking pleased. Then Oleta turned to the crowd. "We always knowed our Cletis would do us proud!" she blubbered and wiped her strawberry nose with a hanky.

Angus nodded in agreement. "He was always a good boy."

Oleta snuffled and resumed her role of family spokesperson. She didn't mention that Cletis had run away from the farm as a boy and that they'd never heard from again. Instead, she bleated, "We're proud as punch, but mostly we're just real happy to have our boy home again!" She waved her hanky, a signal for a tight cluster of people to come forward. "Come up here, Opal, and say howdy to your brother!" A young woman holding a baby, flanked by a gangly man and a gaggle of small children, nudged her brood towards the podium.

Opal stopped directly in front of Cletis. She held aloft the arm of a scrawny child whose ears and hair stuck out. "This here's Otis." Pointing to her daughters, she went down the line. "These here are Pearl and Sapphire." Large, floppy bows clung precariously to their thin hair. She tilted the infant sleeping in her arms towards Cletis. "And this here's Daisy." She saw Cletis frown at the baby's name. "We run plum out of jewels, so we started on flowers." The crowd laughed, so Opal hurried on. She turned to her children and announced loud enough for the crowd to hear, "This is your Uncle Cletis. He's a hero that fought in the Santiago-American War and helped capture Cattle Hill." The crowd laughed again. Opal was not sure what provoked their laughter, but they immediately burst into a good-natured round of applause, and she smiled. "And this here is my husband, Miller Nance."

Miller extended a callused hand to Cletis. "Me, Opal, and the chilrun live outside of town, a short piece down the road from your folks. At the old Peavy place." Cletis could imagine how all this had come about. *Opal lost her nerve and came home after she and Ruby ran off with the drummer. Ruby called her a scaredy cat, and declared that she was never going back to the farm. Once Opal got home, Ma reminded her daily of the endless suffering she and Ruby had caused her. When Miller Nance showed an interest in Opal, she jumped at the chance to leave home. Probably secretly married him and then told Ma after it was too late. Ma had her nose out of joint until the first granddaughter was born. Then with the birth of each grandchild, Ma's bitterness most likely faded further. And now she's stuck on Opal and Miller's children. Probably has grand plans of "making ladies" out of them little girls…*

Cletis's speculation ended when a man stepped in front of the crowd and set up a camera tripod. Oleta fussed with her granddaughters' bows and her grandson's unruly sprigs of hair. The photographer snapped a picture of the entire family, setting off a flash that startled the children. To the photographer, Cletis called out, "I'll be wanting a picture to send to our sister, Ruby."

Oleta's ears perked up and she scowled. "Ruby? That one like to broke my heart," she wailed. "I'd as soon a-swallowed a keg of nails as to have gone through the suffering that girl caused me."

Cletis ignored her remark. "She sent some things for you." Right on the spot, he unfastened the valise and took out a paper-wrapped package. Oleta's martyred expression evaporated. She squealed as the paper fell away and she saw the photograph of Cletis and Ruby. Oleta zeroed in on Ruby and her flowing garb. Cletis hurried to explain. "Ruby's a fine lady now, Ma. She wears fancy dresses and everyone calls her 'madam,' just like you always hoped. She lives in Galveston. And she's keeping company with a state senator."

Oleta stared, speechless. Then she held the picture high and made a slow panoramic sweep with it. "My daughter, Ruby," she announced proudly. Opal leaned closer and peered at the picture. Her surprise equaled her mother's.

"And there's this, too." Cletis handed his mother the large box that rested beside his grip. Oleta relinquished the photograph to Opal and tore at the ribbon on the box. When she lifted the lid, a chorus of admiring "ooohs" arose from the women in the crowd. Oleta triumphantly extracted a pink silk hat that boasted two large plumes, a multitude of shimmering beads, and rows of green satin ribbon ruffles.

The crowd applauded. Thinking that the celebration was over, Cletis walked around to the front of the podium. A throng of townspeople surged forward to shake his hand and congratulate him and the Mutts. Mayor Bains waited respectfully for the excitement to abate and the crowd to begin to clear. Then he motioned to a young woman, and she made her way to the podium. The mayor cleared his throat and took her by the elbow. With obvious pride, he announced, "Mr. Mutt, may I present my daughter, Miss Francine Bains." A stout, pretty, giggling young woman in a fine pink dress and matching hat made fluttery gestures and then clasped Cletis's hand in her pudgy ones. Franny had already concluded that he couldn't possibly be the loutish boy who had sporadically attended grade school with her so many years ago.

She chattered effusively to Cletis about his bravery, but Cletis barely heard her words. He was overcome with the heavy, sweet fragrance of her rosewater perfume, and he felt woozy from the nearness of her.

He did, however, hear her when she warbled, "I do hope you'll favor us by coming to supper one night and telling us the details of your courageous deeds in Cuba and Galveston, Mr. Mutt."

Franny's father seconded the invitation. "We insist. And, son, if you're interested, I think I may have a place for you at the bank."

THIRTY-SIX

1

"He's been waiting for you to get back." Even before Mrs. Bromley raised her red-rimmed eyes to meet Danny's, he knew she had been crying. She was hoarse, and she twisted a damp handkerchief in her blue-veined hands.

Danny had spent most of the winter and spring in Beaumont, punctuated by occasional trips back to San Antonio and to other towns where the captain had sent him. "I'm glad I got here in time, Mother Bromley." Danny couldn't think of anything to say that would assuage her grief, so he simply put his arm around her shoulder.

"I'll be all right, dear," she said after a minute. "You'd best go on up."

Danny felt his throat tighten and his own eyes fill with tears. He ascended the stairs two at a time in long, silent strides. Without knocking, he turned the knob slowly and entered Mr. Dunside's small, tidy room. It still left the impression of a properly stowed ship's cabin despite the fact that the nearest ocean was more than a hundred miles away. Mr. Dunside lay in bed, a smooth cover pulled up to his chin, his frail hands folded neatly across his chest.

Danny pulled up a chair and sat down beside the bed. Then he slipped his hand over Mr. Dunside's bony ones. The old man opened his rheumy eyes and smiled when he saw Danny.

"Hello, son," he said, not much louder than a whisper. "They told me you were coming. I been waiting for you."

"I'm here now."

"Yes." Mr. Dunside closed his eyes. Although it seemed to require an effort for the old man to breathe, there was a look of contentment on his face. When he opened his eyes again a few minutes later, he said, "I want you to have that." He lifted his index finger to indicate a carved wooden box and the gold pocket watch that rested on the small bedside table. Then his eyes lighted on a book next to the box. "I liked the book you sent me." He frowned slightly. "That Ahab was a bad one."

"Indeed he was," chimed Danny, trying to project an enthusiasm he did not feel. To cover his anxiety, he rattled on, "We'll have to talk about that book. And I still have so much to tell you about the Lucas gusher. Derricks everywhere, spouting thousands of barrels of oil round the clock. Hundreds of people still arriving every day, and every last one of 'em struck with get-rich fever. And a lot of those folks are, well, they ain't your most upstanding citizens. Some are calling it 'Swindletop.'"

"Yes," Mr. Dunside replied, but his voice sounded far away.

Danny ceased his nervous chatter, and there was silence. He tried to find the words to tell Mr. Dunside all that he was feeling, but his chin was quivering and he found himself unable to speak. Instead, he patted Mr. Dunside's hand.

Then Mr. Dunside spoke up, as if he had been marshaling his energy for this moment. "Everything I have is yours, Danny, other than some money for Mrs. Bromley and Dilue. The three of you is the closest thing to family I ever had."

Danny leaned close so that Mr. Dunside could hear him. "Of course I'll take care of them, but—"

Mr. Dunside continued, speaking over Danny. "Some folks are lucky enough to be born into a family that lasts a lifetime. Most aren't so lucky. They got to put together one of their own, and if they do, then they're lucky, too." He smiled at Danny with deep affection. "I'm lucky, son."

Tears rolled down Danny's cheeks. "Mr. Dunside, you're going to be fine. You just need to rest, eat some of Mother Bromley's soup." He struggled to control his voice, but it cracked anyway.

This time the old stationmaster interrupted Danny by gently squeezing his hand. "We both know better. But it's okay." Then Mr. Dunside offered up one final aphorism: "'Young men may die, but old men must die.' I'm an old man, Danny." In a fading voice Danny heard him say, "You were mighty small when you got off that train." He turned his face towards Danny's. "I'm mighty glad you rode it all the way to San Antone."

"Not half as glad as I am. Not half as glad."

Mr. Dunside's breathing became shallow. Danny leaned closer and heard him whisper, "I got a train to catch, son."

The small stationmaster squeezed Danny's hand one last time. Then he closed his eyes forever.

2

Danny slumped forward, propping his elbows on his knees and his face in his hands. He pressed his palms flat against his eyes. "Mr. Dunside," he repeated softly to himself, "we didn't have long enough."

After several minutes, he went downstairs to tell Mother Bromley, Dilue, Johanna, and Janie. Mrs. Bromley and Johanna held each other and began to cry. Dilue gave a slight nod as if he were confirming what she already knew, but her normally square shoulders sagged. When Danny was sure the women were all right, he said, "I have to make arrangements. The undertaker. The preacher."

Mrs. Bromley nodded.

"Will you notify people, Mother Bromley?"

"I can do that," Janie volunteered. "Mother Bromley, why don't you go lie down. It'll be busy once folks start coming to pay their respects."

Danny moved through the rest of the day numbly. Neighbors began to arrive within the hour to offer their condolences and deliver food. Janie helped Johanna greet them.

The funeral was held the following afternoon, on Friday. Afterward, Danny stood beside the grave and turned his face heavenward to feel the heat of the sun. He squinted at the brightness that made everything below glitter and shimmer. The thought occurred to him: *A perfect blue, green, and gold day.* He felt a cooling breeze. He gazed at the grassy field behind the church cemetery. It rippled in soft waves like the roll of the ocean. In the distance he heard a train whistle. *Yes,* he thought, *this is the right place to lay Mr. Dunside to rest.*

Danny took Janie, Mrs. Bromley, Dilue, and Johanna home. A heavy black veil covered Dilue's face. It was the first time she had ever left the house.

Once home, neighbors helped Johanna set out the food. Glad for any task that kept her busy, Janie brewed coffee and set out more cups and saucers on the sideboard. Fragments of comments floated in the air: "Yessir, as fine a man as ever drew breath." "Never heard him say a bad word about anyone nor anyone speak ill of him." "As responsible an employee as the railroad ever had." "He's at peace now, Eleanor." "Artis lived a long and honorable life." "I remember a story he told me once about a time he was at sea." Friends and neighbors comforted the odd mix of those whom the old stationmaster referred to as his "family."

After the last guest had left, Mrs. Bromley took a small stack of letters out of a drawer. "Danny, dear, Mr. Dunside wanted you to have these." The cord around them was tied with a knot that resembled a woven figure eight.

"What are they?"

"He didn't say. Just that they would be important to you." She pressed the envelopes into Danny's hands and dabbed her eyes with a crumpled hanky.

Danny took them to Mr. Dunside's room, turning through the stack of already opened envelopes as he slowly mounted the stairs. The return addresses were for railroad companies. Danny sat down at the small table and unfolded and read the letters one by one. They were replies to queries regarding Danny's father, Rory O'Brien.

The letters bore dates from the past two years. One letter dated only a few weeks earlier stated, "According to our records, a Rory O'Brien, age unknown, employed to lay track, was killed in an accident along with three other men in a work crew." This had happened in New York only a few months after Danny had been placed out in Texas.

Danny dropped the sheet of paper and leaned back in his chair. The same feelings he had about his uncle's death his crashed through his mind again. *It's not fair! It's not right!* He ran his hand through his hair, then gripped his scalp and forced himself to reread the letter. He ran his finger slowly over the hateful words, "killed in an accident." He took a deep breath. After another few minutes, he refolded the page and put it back in the envelope. He placed it in his front pocket and pressed his hand against it. Danny closed his eyes and sank back in the chair again. *Thank you, Mr. Dunside. You knew how bad I wanted to know about my family.* He understood that although the old stationmaster couldn't bring himself to tell him about his father's death, his final act of kindness had been an attempt to rejoin one of the many broken threads in Danny's life.

Danny fluctuated between sadness and relief. *This isn't the way it's supposed to be. But at least I know.*

He continued to sit at the table in the tiny room. Several years ago he had given up any realistic hope of seeing his father again, but he had never allowed himself to think that his father might be dead, much less that at the time of his death, his father would have been not much older than he was now. Danny walked over to Mr. Dunside's bureau and peered in the dull, crackled oval of mirror above it. He studied his face, wondering if he bore a resemblance to his father.

He sat down on the bed, stroking again and again the pocket that contained the letter. His thoughts turned to Mary Ceara. *I can barely remember what you looked like, other than your hair was red and your eyes were blue. Are you still alive?* Where had his infant sister been taken? *A home of some sort... but a different one from the Aid Society Home where I went.* He closed his eyes tight, as if doing so might force to consciousness the ancient memory. *The Foundling Home. Yes, that was it.* His eyes flew open again. *I'll write them for information about her.* Then he realized with a jolt that Mary Ceara would be almost sixteen by now, nearly grown. His shoulders sagged: *She could be living anywhere, with any name.*

Danny felt as forlorn and empty as he had when his mother died. *In two days, I've lost Mr. Dunside and my father.* For a split second, he could see his father's face, feel the coarse wool of his shirt against his cheek when he hugged him, smell his odor of tobacco, whiskey, and sweat. The intensity of his feelings for these two men overwhelmed him. He sat alone in Mr. Dunside's room running his thumb over the pocket watch, clicking it open and gently snapping it shut.

He tucked the watch in his vest pocket and unfastened the lid of the carved box. When he lifted it, particles of dust danced around it in a beam of afternoon sunlight that pierced the single pane of glass in the tiny window. The box had a musty but not unpleasant smell, the smell of time. One by one, Danny extracted the items and studied them. He was fascinated. There was a faded and worn picture of a woman. *Who? Mr. Dunside never mentioned her.* He held up a lock of brown hair secured by a delicate, yellowed ribbon. There was a penny postcard that bore the cryptic, provocative message "Soon." It was signed with the single initial, "H." The flourish of curlicues that trailed from the initial suggested it had been penned by a woman's fine hand. Danny glanced back at the indistinct figure in the picture. *Had she written it? Why weren't she and Mr. Dunside together?* Another wave of sadness and tenderness for the old man swept over Danny. *Every life has it own sorrows. Maybe some are too private or painful to share.*

There were trinkets and souvenirs from Mr. Dunside's travels. A loop of braided trim from a uniform. A tarnished cufflink. A badge with the railroad emblem embossed on it. One by one, Danny replaced the mementos of the old man's life back in the box. He closed the lid and secured the pin back into the loop of the clasp. He took the packet of letters to his room, and then he walked down the stairs, his heart as heavy as his steps.

Johanna was carrying leftover food to the kitchen. Danny entered the room looking hollow-eyed. Johanna knew that neither he nor Mother Bromley had slept the previous night, but that unlike Mother Bromley, he had shed hardly a tear.

Without acknowledging her, Danny reached for the doorknob.

"Are you going out?" She seemed surprised, but her tone was one of concern.

"I've got to see Janie," he said hoarsely. His grief weighed upon him like a yoke. He felt as if he was suffocating in a house teeming with memories.

She started to touch his arm and speak, but nodded instead. *I wish I could comfort you.* A slight pain pricked her heart. *Be glad there's someone he can turn to. Sorrow is too heavy a burden to bear alone.*

Danny stopped halfway out the door. "Mother Bromley?"

"She's fine. She didn't get any rest last night, so the doctor gave her laudanum. I just looked in on her. She's sleeping soundly."

Danny closed the door quietly behind him.

3

Janie knew before she opened the back door that it was Danny. Johanna had called her. "He looks terrible. And he hurts more than he shows."

Janie drew him inside and closed the door behind him. "I—" Danny choked, but he could say no more. She held him as he sobbed. "Mr. Dunside... he never had to take me in... he treated me like I was his own son. I'm going to miss him."

Tears rolled down her face as well. "I know, I know." She stroked his hair and cradled his damp cheeks in her hands. "You look exhausted, Danny. Come lie down."

She saw him hesitate. "It's all right. The children are staying with the McArthurs tonight. Augusta still remembers Foley's funeral. She was so sad after the funeral this afternoon that I thought it would be good for her and Sul to be with other children. Viola insisted the children go home with them."

Janie took Danny to her room. When she lay down with him and held him, his anguish began to pour out. His whole body was wracked with grief. His lungs burned as if someone had shoved glowing coals into them. The pain poured from a wellspring so deep in his soul that he sounded like a wounded animal. He was crying for his father, his mother, his sister, his uncles, and the small stationmaster who had somehow come to represent all of them. He was pouring out a lifetime of sorrow.

Janie let him cry. It came in small jags for the next hour until Danny had exhausted himself. Janie got up and brought him a cup of tea. Danny sat up in bed and she propped a large pillow behind his back. "It's a terrible loss, Danny, but I'm so glad you and Mr. Dunside had each other."

He swallowed, and his eyes brimmed again. "Janie, I don't think I can go through losing Mother Bromley and Dilue."

"Don't take that on now, Danny."

After a moment of silence, he blurted, "Janie, marry me."

She set the teapot down, then took Danny's cup and set it down. Bending near to him, she said in a low voice, "Danny, I've lost nearly everyone I ever loved. Even marrying someone can't make it permanent. *I know.* And I live with the fear that something could happen to Augusta or Sullivan." She pressed his hand. "Do you remember what you told me that night so many years ago? You told me to try to accept things, not to try to make sense of it all. I'd have worn myself out long ago trying to understand why things turn out the way they do." She clasped his hands in hers. "I love you, Danny, and I'll keep loving you. And that will be enough." She leaned over and kissed his forehead.

Danny felt exhaustion so deep that his bones ached. His eyes and his throat still burned, and his chest hurt. He closed his eyelids over his reddened eyes. "I love you, Janie McCorkle."

"And I love you, Danny O'Brien," she whispered, but he was already asleep.

4

When Danny opened his eyes hours later, he saw Janie asleep in a large, deep chair she had pulled up beside the bed. She seemed like a small child in the cavernous chair. She was turned sideways, her knees tucked, her cheek resting on her arm.

As Danny gazed at this diminutive person beside him, a feeling of tenderness swept over him so powerful that his eyes filled. This feeling was different, though. The pain in his chest was gone. Rather than a burdened heart, there was a sense of peace, a lightness he had not ever felt before. But at the same time, there was a sense of solidity, as if the jagged shards of glass-sharp grief had fused into a smooth, cool core, as if the unifying capstone of an arch had slid into place. He had the clear sense that Mr. Dunside was at peace, too, and that he could carry on for both of them. Danny reached out and ran his finger over the rim of the gold pocket watch on the table beside him.

Leaning forward, he brushed his fingertips against Janie's cheek until her eyelids fluttered open. He sank back on the pillow. Janie didn't move, but she smiled at him and took hold of his hand. Then he gently pulled her to him and made love to her.

5

"No, use the other end of the rope. That's it. Now twist it around and loop it under." Danny was instructing Sul on a simple knot.

Sul's chubby fingers fumbled a minute. Finally, he held up a lopsided piece of rope, a look of pure joy on his face. "Like this?" His voice was a sweet, birdlike chirp.

Danny nodded. "Hey, Sul, did you know there was a Texas governor that had the same name as you? His name was Sul Ross, and he was governor not too long after *I* came to Texas as a boy." The rope rested limply in Sul's lap as he listened to what Danny had to say. "Before that, he fought in the War Between the States. Went in as a private, fought in more than 130 battles, and came out a general." Sul knew from playing with his tin soldiers that a general was important.

Danny could feel a question coming, the same way he had been able to anticipate Mr. Dunside's aphorisms.

"Was I named after General Sul?"

"General Ross," Danny corrected him. "No. You were named after your pa."

"I don't have a pa. My pa's dead." Sul eyed Danny squarely and handed him the rope to untangle. "Can you be my pa?"

"I can't be your real pa because you already had a fine pa, Sul. No one can ever replace him." He pulled the child onto his lap. "But I would have been proud to be your pa, and I know your father would be proud of you if he could see you now."

Sul looked at Danny and confessed, "I can't remember Pa too much."

Danny thought about his own father. He tried to picture him the way he was the last time he saw him.

Sul squinted up at Danny again. "If you can't be my pa, then can you be my uncle? Tommy Marsh has got four uncles. I don't have any."

Danny smiled.

The child's logic was irresistible.

"Sure. 'Uncle Danny.' I'd like that." He touched the child's head. *Uncle Danny.* A new thought occurred to him. *I've spent most of my life searching for my uncles. Uncle,* he mentally corrected himself. *Maybe it's time now to put that to rest and* be *someone's uncle.*

6

Danny was still mulling the tumult of the past week's events as he entered the Ranger office Monday morning. "Hot in here," he muttered to no one. When the captain walked in to the office, Danny was searching for something. "I'm hunting for that piece of wood. Where's the one we use to prop the window open?"

The captain opened a creaky desk drawer and pulled out a thick, Y-shaped stick. "Here." He tossed it to Danny.

"Thanks." Danny placed the notched end at the bottom of the raised window and propped the other end on the sill. "That's better." When he finished, he turned to the captain. "Thanks for coming to the funeral."

The captain nodded. "Mr. Dunside was a fine, decent man. I suspect he lived longer than he might have, because of you. I know how he felt about you, how proud he was." He kept his eyes on Danny's face.

Danny turned towards the window and pretended to adjust the stick.

"Are you okay?"

"Yeah." It took another minute before Danny could turn around again.

7

Several weeks later, Danny told the captain about Mr. Dunside's letters and the one confirming his father's death many years earlier. "My sister was a baby when I was put on the train to Texas. I don't remember much about Mary Ceara other than she was puny and had red hair and blue eyes, and that my father cried when he took her to the Foundling Home. That was a day or two after my mother died."

The captain anticipated him. "And now you're wondering what became of your sister?"

"I always wondered, but Mr. Dunside's letters started me thinking maybe I could find out what happened to her, just like Mr. Dunside found out about my father. So I wrote the Foundling Home." Danny produced a letter from his pocket and laid it on the desk. He slid it towards the captain.

As the captain read it, Danny summed it up. "They flat refuse to give information about children they've placed. I'd go to New York if I thought it'd do any good. But I don't reckon I'd get any further even if I was to show up in person." Danny waited while the captain put the letter back in the envelope. "You think there's anything else I can do, Captain James?"

The captain didn't reply immediately. "I might have an idea or two." He was thinking of his sister, Rose. He handed the letter back to Danny. "By the way, Ras Landry sent me a wire last night." The captain fished the telegram out of his pocket and continued talking as he unfolded it. "I hear from other lawmen that Sheriff Landry has done an admirable job of maintaining some semblance of law and order under impossible circumstances. And Ras himself gives you high praise. He said the only thing the Irishmen there like better than drinking is fighting, and that you were good at both." The captain's eyes sparkled. "I'm sure he meant good at *dealing* with both." He rubbed his chin. "Must be that trace of brogue you still have."

Danny grinned. "Now, Captain, we both know it's my charm. And thinking fast on my feet, of course." Because of his small stature, Danny had learned to rely on his wits, something Mr. Dunside helped him learn long ago that had served him well.

Before the captain revealed the specific contents of the sheriff's telegram, he asked Danny detailed questions about the newly discovered oil fields. Danny had suspected for months that the captain himself had a secret desire to see what all the fuss in Beaumont was about. At that moment, he realized he was right. *Why, he's as curious as the thousands of folks who make excursions every Sunday to view Spindletop.*

Danny focused on the captain's voice again: "Tell me about the Heywood No. 2. Ras says that it's the greatest—what's the word they're using?"

"Gusher."

"—gusher in the world. Over two-hundred-feet tall."

"It hit about a month ago, the first of June. It was something, all right! You can't imagine! It was raining thick, black crude! Thousands of men were screaming and cheering! Everyone went wild!" Just describing the history-making occasion electrified him almost as much as witnessing the actual event. "They just *thought* every wildcatter and promoter had descended on the city." Danny shook his head and let out a long, low whistle. "But that well brought a whole new batch of speculators, card sharks, and prostitutes. They say the city's population has quadrupled since Spindletop hit six months ago. There are upwards of fifty thousand people. And what they call the 'Deep Crockett' section of Beaumont is as rough as they come."

The telegram still rested in the captain's hand. He seemed to have forgotten about it. "Ras indicated that most of the men in Beaumont have sent their wives and daughters away. And those who haven't, don't let them go out unescorted."

Danny nodded and pointed to the piece of paper in Captain James's hand. "The telegram? What did Sheriff Landry say?"

The captain looked down at the paper. "Well, I know you've been back and forth to Beaumont during the last six months, but Ras said that yesterday they had what he called"—the captain scanned the telegram until he found what he was looking for—

"'the first major gas blowout.' He said it destroyed everything in its path. Shot four hundred feet of pipe two thousand feet into the air! Ripped the"—the captain again scanned the telegram for Ras's exact words and ran his finger along the line as he read—"ripped the entire rigging off its moorings and splintered the derrick." He looked up. "He says it gassed a lot of the men working near the well. That it was a terrible situation and he's afraid it will happen again."

Danny blanched. "Damn."

Accidents, mostly small but sometimes terrifyingly awful, were a regular occurrence. Danny remembered the hideous oil field fire in March and how each crisis had proved doubly difficult: Because the enterprise of coaxing oil and gas from the earth was something most men had little or no experience with, they had to figure out how to cope with each new disaster as it was occurring. Further, he knew firsthand the force of a large well. He had no reason to doubt what Ras Landry was describing.

Danny focused on the captain's voice again, just in time to catch the end of his sentence. "…and you know that people do unpredictable things when they're scared. It's one reason Ras wants extra lawmen there."

"Yessir. Fear and greed. Even normally reasonable folks do unreasonable things when there are overnight fortunes to be made." Danny began to catalog and tick off the other sources of violence. "You got people fighting over scarce food, water, and lodging. They're exhausted and irritable from working seven days a week. Whiskey is flowing in the streets every night." He realized he had gone off on a tangent and that the captain had more that he still needed to tell him.

Captain James shoved the telegram towards Danny as if he were pushing away a plate of bad-smelling cabbage. "In light of your appealing description of the situation, I almost hate to say it, but you'll be doing another stint there."

Danny could already feel the sulphur gas assaulting his lungs and feel the fine oil spray settling on him like black dew. So he was surprised by his next thought: *By god, it's exciting, though! Half the world wants to see what's happening in Beaumont, Texas.* Danny looked at the captain and grinned. "Sure."

"Then it's settled." The captain walked over to the Arbuckle's Coffee calendar nailed on the wall near the door. Before he had time to flip the page, Scrap had scrambled to his feet and trotted over to him. "But Ras will just have to do without you for a few more days. I need help here until B.J. and a couple of the others get back. I'll wire Ras to look for you around the end of the first week of July."

"That'd suit me fine." Danny was pleased that he'd have a little longer before he went back to Galveston.

The captain sat down and wrote out a telegram to Ras Landry. "Here, you take this over and send it. And, Danny, I'll give the matter of your sister some thought."

That night, the captain wrote a letter to his sister. Although a widow, Rose remained close to her husband's brothers. One was a prominent New York businessman and civic leader who contributed generously to the city's hospitals and charities. The captain had a hunch that with no more than a telephone call, this man might be able to find out something about Mary Ceara O'Brien.

THIRTY-SEVEN

1

Dr. Ohlmsted finished the last bite of his bacon and eggs. "Helga, will you look in on my patients this morning at the hospital? I'll come this afternoon, but if there are any problems, let me know, and I'll come right away."

"Certainly." Her voice exuded the confidence she felt. After her return to San Antonio the previous December, the doctor had begun asking her to visit some of his patients in the hospital and even to make house calls if he knew the problem was not serious. She welcomed the opportunity to talk with patients, make observations, take notes, and report her findings to him. In the intervening half year, she had become skilled at it, and he had come to rely increasingly on her.

"The months you spent in Galveston proved to be excellent training. In fact, I think you now know more than I do, Helga!"

She dismissed his words with a roll of her eyes, but she was thrilled at the compliment: it came not just from her Uncle Wil, but from a man who was also one of the most respected doctors in the city. She continued to sip her coffee, but then raised an eyebrow of concern. "Uncle Wil," she blurted, "are you feeling all right?" Ever since Artis Dunside's death a few weeks ago, she had worried irrationally about the doctor's health.

"I'm fine. More than fine. Just a little tired. I delivered Mrs. Moehr's baby last night." He wiped his mouth and placed his napkin beside the empty plate. "Another beautiful girl." He counted on his fingers. "That makes five in seven years."

Helga's mouth formed a small "o" of surprise. "I'll go by the Moehrs before I go to the hospital, Uncle Wil, unless you need me here."

"No. On Saturday it's usually quieter in the afternoon. By the way, Dr. von Herff is sending over a young doctor today."

"Why?"

"He'll be working with me while I train him. He starts next week." Her Uncle Wil cocked his head. "His name is Peter Bode. Handsome fellow, I hear."

Helga blushed, drank the last of her coffee, and blotted her mouth with her napkin. "Well, let's hope the pupil will be even half as good as the teacher."

2

Helga had just finished visiting Dr. Ohlmsted's hospital patients when she heard a woman's voice, singing. She followed the sound to a room at the end of the hall, but when she reached the partially opened door, she stopped. She leaned against the wall with her eyes closed, letting the sweet melody wash over her. For a split second, her mother's face flashed through her mind.

> *Schlof, Bobbeli, Schlof;*
> *Der Daadi hiet die Schof.*
> *Die Mammi hiet die Lemmer;*
> *Schlof en Schtundli lenger.*

> Sleep, baby, sleep;
> Daddy's tending the sheep.
> Mama's tending the lambs;
> Sleep an hour longer.

The lullaby was the same one her mother had sung to her and her sisters. She had not heard it since Johanna had comforted her and Inga with it on the train. For years, Helga had searched the deepest recesses of her memory, trying in vain to recall the next-to-the-last line of the other verse. She strained to hear the sweet, clear voice.

> *Schlaf, Kindchen, schlaf;*
> *Der Vater hüt't die Schaf;*
> *Die Mutter shüttelt's Bâumelein,*
> *Da fällt herab ein Träumelein;*
> *Schlaf, Kindchen, schlaf.*

> Sleep, little child, sleep;
> The father watches the sheep.
> The mother shakes the little tree,
> Down there falls a little dream.
> Sleep, little child, sleep.

"Down there falls a little dream." Yes, that was it! A bittersweet feeling coursed through her. Then, to her dismay, the song ended. She hesitated, but then tapped lightly on the door and pushed it open a bit farther.

She was as startled as if the opened door had revealed her image in a mirror: she was looking at herself.

A young woman was leaning over a small boy. He was now sleeping peacefully, and she was pressing a damp cloth to his face and arms to soothe him from the late June heat. When the woman saw Helga, she stopped with her hand in midair and gasped. She blinked several times, as if trying to clear her vision.

Helga moved to her as if drawn by a magnet. When she was close enough to reach out and touch her, she whispered incredulously, "Inga? He said you were dead."

Inga dropped the cloth and touched the face she was staring into. She fought to regain her breath. Even so, her voice was barely audible. "Papa had begun searching for you, but he stopped. The man told him you had been killed."

The back-and-forth movement of Helga's head was ever so slight, but it said *No, I'm alive*. Then she put her arms around her sister and wept.

3

"How did you get here?" Helga asked. "I mean, do you live in San Antonio?" Her eyes darted to the sleeping child. "Is this your son?"

Inga smiled and nodded. "His name is Karl. He's three years old."

"Is he all right?" Helga's voice dropped to a whisper.

"Yes, but he began running a high fever a week ago. Our doctor is away in Mineral Wells. Fortunately, Dr. Blumberg at this hospital was able to help. To think he apologized for having to make us come here instead of the hospital closer to where we live." Inga shook her head at the irony.

Helga placed her hand on Karl's forehead to check for fever, an unconscious habit from dealing with patients. She quickly assessed his breathing and his color, and seemed satisfied. "I've heard of Dr. Blumberg. My uncle is a doctor. He says—" Helga broke off abruptly when she saw the bewildered expression on her sister's face. "The man I live with—" That sounded even worse. She broke off and started over again. "Uncle Wil is like a foster father. He's a doctor." Helga laughed at her own jumble of words. She hugged Inga again. "It's going to take a while. There's so much to tell and so much to ask. Your son is getting well?"

"He should be able to go home in a few days." Inga smoothed the sheet and brushed the sleeping child's hair back from his delicate face. She wiped away the fine trace of perspiration that already dampened his brow again.

"My nephew is a beautiful child." Helga touched his delicate, splotchy cheek as if to convince herself he was real. "I have a nephew."

"Dieter—my husband's name is Dieter Braun—Dieter and I also have a daughter, Ulla. She's two." But before Helga could take in that fact, Inga took hold of her hands. "And Johanna? Do you know what happened to her?" Inga riveted her eyes on Helga's, fearing the answer.

But a buoyant smile lit up Helga's face. "She's here, Inga! In San Antonio! I see her often."

Inga stared open-mouthed. Her mind raced. "Where? How long has she been here?" *What sort of cruel joke is this? The three of us living in the same city and not knowing it?* "When did you find out? How did you learn she was here?" *Have you and Johanna been reunited for several years now?* she wondered. *Am I the only one who had been separated?* Inga continued to flood her with questions: "But Johanna was placed out before we were. How did she end up in San Antonio? When can we see her? Is she married? Does she have children?" Then, "Are you married? Do you have children?"

Helga was giggling like a schoolgirl, and she finally held up her hands to stanch Inga's torrent of questions. "Johanna's been here for several years now. She's not married, but she's keeping company with a fine young man named Anton Wernicke. I'm afraid you're the only one who has made any of us aunts. And Danny brought her here."

"Where does she live? When can I see her? To think we'll all be together again!" Inga's excitement was escalating by the moment. She stopped abruptly. "Who's Danny?"

"Tell you in a minute. You know him." Before Inga had a chance to pursue it further, Helga declared, "If you can wait, let's surprise Johanna! Next Thursday is the Fourth of July. You and your family—Karl should be well enough by then—must come for a picnic supper. I want you to meet Uncle Wil, of course." As Helga mentally raced ahead, she tallied on her fingers. "I'm going to invite Johanna. And Anton, Mrs. Bromley, Danny, and Janie and her children—your children will enjoy them." Then something else occurred to her. "The couple you were placed out to, do they have other children?" Helga realized she found the idea disconcerting, but declared, "Bring all of them. I want to meet them, and Johanna will, too."

"I have no other brothers or sisters. My parents are Albert and Anna Jäeger." The word "parents" suddenly sounded strange, even to her own ears. She stumbled awkwardly on. "They weren't able to have children of their own. They were older when they adopted me. They're wonderful people who—" She quit mid-sentence. *What had Helga's placing out family been like?* Inga remembered a frightening man who had taken her back into the church and shoved her at Miss Darden. She changed the topic. "Helga, tell me who Danny is. And who is Janie?" Karl stirred in bed, and Inga wrung out the cloth again in cool water.

Helga explained who each person was. She explained that Danny was the one who reunited her with Johanna. "He and I decided to surprise her at dinner one Sunday last December. We'd just returned from Galveston." She laughed. "I can't wait to see her face when she sees you, me—*both of us*—together!"

"I'm not sure I can wait until the Fourth of July! But yes, yes, of course we'll be there!" Then the rest of what Helga said registered. "Galveston! Why were you there? Why were you there with this Danny person? There was that terrible hurricane."

"I'll explain about it, but first, tell me about the Jäegers." She was curious about these people, the parents her sister seemed to love so much.

Inga spoke affectionately of them, spinning a loose chronology, looping back here and there to weave in missing pieces.

Helga sat spellbound; Inga was describing a life she could scarcely imagine. Each astounding detail set off a small shock in Helga: *Growing up in a splendid home on the south bank of the river… the German-English School. I would love to have gone there. Parties… birthdays… elegant clothes… going about in a carriage… trips….* She struggled a minute with a wave of resentment. She felt it start to suck her in, but she resisted the feeling until she gained control of it. Still, she felt her jaw clench, and she averted her face in hopes that Inga would not notice. She didn't want her joy at finding her sister tainted by the poison of envy.

Karl stretched his arm and made an unintelligible sound. Inga welcomed a reason to get up out of the hard, wooden chair. She fanned the air to make him more comfortable.

A tiny sigh escaped his lips. The back of his hand draped across his forehead like a limp salute and his mouth fell open as he drifted back into the restful slumber reserved for well-fed dogs and innocent children.

Helga watched the silent dance between mother and child, admiring Inga's instinctive actions. Satisfied that Karl was settled, Inga turned to Helga. "Now you tell me about yourself."

Helga started with her recent, extraordinary experience in Galveston, although with no mention of Stup or Mashburn Dill. Then she recounted events in her life backwards to the time she arrived in San Antonio. She concluded with, "In 1893 I first came here, and Uncle Wil—Dr. Ohlmsted—and his sister were so kind…" Her voice wound down as if that were the end of her story.

"But where were you before that? Before San Antonio?"

Helga brushed the question aside and glanced at her watch. "Goodness gracious, we've talked for two hours. I'll come again tomorrow afternoon." She pulled out her small notebook so they could exchange telephone numbers and addresses.

Karl inhaled sharply, a small shudder rippling through him as he exhaled. As he began to surface towards wakefulness, he murmured and yawned. Helga knew his eyelids would soon flutter open.

"Inga, I'll be back tomorrow afternoon. I'm going to leave before Karl wakes up and thinks he's seeing double. Other than the way we wear our hair, we still look nearly identical."

They embraced as if trying to fill the abyss of lost years. Helga wiped her eyes. "I can hardly bring myself to leave. For so many years I thought that you were—" She hugged her sister again. "The important thing is that you and your entire family come for a Fourth of July celebration. I want us to surprise Johanna."

"I'll try to wait until Thursday to surprise Johanna, but I can't wait until next week for my family to meet you. I'd never be able to keep you a secret until then. I'm going to ask Mama and Papa and Dieter to come to the hospital tomorrow afternoon, Helga, and to bring Ulla with them." Her words spilled out as she unfolded her plan. "You come at two o'clock. They can come at three and bring Ulla. Karl's nearly well, and I'm sure the doctor would let us take him outside for a short while. There's a shady spot where we can sit and visit, and he'll be so happy to get out of this hospital room. Is that all right? Tomorrow, I mean? With my family?"

Helga laughed at her sister's outpouring. "Of course." She was thrilled but anxious at the thought of meeting them. Suddenly, though, she felt a profound need to *see* her sister's life, a life so different from her own. "Inga, does your family have pictures? I mean, of the things you told me about? Christmases? Trips? Your wedding?"

"Too many! You know what large families most Germans have. Can you imagine how many albums my parents have filled with pictures of their one child?" When she said the words, "my parents" and "their one child," Inga saw the flicker of pain on sister's face. She bit her lip, instantly regretting her thoughtlessness. *Had circumstances been different, it might have been the two of us.* In a subdued voice she promised, "Yes, I'll bring pictures."

"All of them." Helga's tone was definite.

"Yes, all of them."

Helga was already at the door when Inga called out, "You bring your picture albums, too." Helga stopped, her hand on the knob. "There aren't any." An odd realization hit her. *I've never had my picture made.* She turned to her sister. "I don't have any pictures. I've never seen a picture of myself."

Upon hearing this, Inga's hand flew to her mouth and she closed her eyes.

"I'll look at your pictures instead. It'll almost be the same." Helga's voice had gone flat.

Inga opened her eyes and nodded mutely, her hand still over her mouth. She watched Helga disappear down the corridor. Then she closed the door softly, leaned against it, and cried.

4

Helga stopped at Mrs. Bromley's house, barely able to contain herself. She gave Mrs. Bromley a hug and then joined Dilue on the back porch. "Dilue, I have to tell *someone*, someone who can keep a secret!" With no more preface than that, she poured out the afternoon's strange experience.

Despite her blind eyes and disfigurement, Dilue's face was radiant. "Sisters should be together." Her voice was, though, was softer than usual, and it seemed to carry a note of wistfulness. She reached out for Helga to take her hand. "You've waited for such a long time. And I will keep your secret safe."

Helga telephoned Johanna that evening. "Johanna, I want everyone to come for the Fourth of July. It's to be a reunion of family and friends. You, Mother Bromley, Dilue. Bring Anton. And tell Danny to bring Janie and her children."

Johanna interrupted her. "It sounds wonderful, Helga, but you know Dilue doesn't leave the house. And we wouldn't leave her by herself, especially on a holiday. Why don't you and the doctor come here instead?"

As if on cue, Dilue appeared in the doorway. Helga could hear her in the background. "No." Dilue's tone was firm. "You and Mother Bromley need to get out of the house. Have Danny take you. I'll be fine. I'll sit on the back porch and enjoy the fragrance of the flowers. You can tell me about it when you get back."

Johanna hesitated, but something in the way Dilue spoke made it clear that they were to go. "All right. We'll be there!" She moved closer to the telephone box and lowered her voice. "Mother Bromley has been so sad ever since Mr. Dunside died. Dilue is right. A happy occasion like this will be good for her." In a louder voice, she said, "We'll bring peach cobbler and cinnamon cake. Mother Bromley loves to cook for a celebration of any sort."

"Good." And in a tone that made it sound like an afterthought, "Oh, and there's someone special I want you to meet that night." Then she hung up.

At first Johanna didn't know what to make of Helga's parting comment. *She certainly didn't give me a chance to reply.* Johanna's smile dissolved into an amused smirk. *Why, of course. Helga has a suitor!*

5

Helga was too nervous to eat much of her dinner after church. She was counting the minutes until it was time to see Inga again, and trying to decide whether to tell her

Uncle Wil or wait until Thursday to surprise him.

"It will be nice to see another young face around here, won't it?" Dr. Ohlmsted announced, breaking off a piece of bread.

"What?" Helga's fork clattered to her plate. *How did he know?*

"Dr. Bode. Peter Bode. He starts working with me next week. He'll be here through the end of the year." He speared a small potato with his fork and popped it into his mouth. Helga admired the doctor's adroit hands. Even in the simple act of eating, his movements were precise and sure.

"Bode?" Helga's voice was vague and distracted.

"I told you about him yesterday." The doctor frowned. This wasn't like Helga. Yesterday when she got home, she hadn't even asked about the new doctor. And she had left her notes from her hospital visit in the kitchen instead of on his desk.

"Oh, yes," she said slowly, trying to reconstruct what her uncle had said about him. "Well, I'm looking forward to meeting him."

"He's very nice. And he's not married." The doctor raised his eyebrows and dropped his chin, giving the impression that he was looking over the top of an invisible pair of glasses.

Helga gave him the look that often passes between headstrong daughters and their indulgent fathers, and she ignored his implication. "Uncle Wil, I want to have Johanna and Danny and Mrs. Bromley—well, I'd like to have everyone over on Thursday for a Fourth of July supper. We can eat outside. A picnic. Would that be all right?"

"So that's what's on your mind." He deftly sliced a bite of roast beef and coated it with horseradish as neatly if he were applying ointment to a skinned knee. "That's fine with me. It sounds very pleasant, in fact. Be sure to let Mrs. Roemer know."

"Good, because I'm afraid I got a bit ahead of myself. I've already invited the Bromley household. Then she thought, *I'm going to tell him.* She felt as if the news about Inga was going to bubble out of her if she didn't. "Uncle Wil, I found my other sister. I found Inga."

The doctor lowered his knife and fork. "You found Inga? Your twin?" This man who was never at a loss for words, whom Helga considered unflappable, looked stunned.

"She's alive, Uncle Wil! She's been in San Antonio since 1886, with a family, a couple named Jäeger. I met her by accident at the hospital yesterday. She's married and has children, and I'm going to go see her again this afternoon—in just a short while—and I want her and her family to come on the Fourth of July. We're going to surprise Johanna."

The doctor could barely assimilate her excited deluge. "Of course, of course! That's wonderful!" He had never seen her so animated. He looked at his watch. "When are you supposed to meet her?"

"At two o'clock."

"Then you need to go." He walked around the table and leaned over to hug her. "You'll tell me all about it at supper tonight?"

She nodded, still breathless.

"I'm happy for you. No one deserves this good luck more than you."

Helga got up.

He shooed her away with one hand. "Leave the dishes. Go see Inga."

She gave him a grateful glance.

"And Helga—"

"*Ja?*"

"You tell her I said *Wilkommen!* Welcome to the family."

6

Helga quietly opened the door to the hospital room and peeked in.

Inga pressed her finger to her lips and pointed to Karl. "You came at just the right time," she whispered. "Karl's stomach is full, and he just fell asleep." She gestured apologetically to the uncomfortable chairs, and they sat down. "I did most of the talking yesterday. Tell me what happened when you left the train. I remember a horrible man. Oh, Helga," Inga clasped her hands as if in fervent prayer, "I hope you didn't have to stay with him."

Helga began slowly. "His name was Stup Dill, and he wasn't a nice man…" She chose her words carefully and glossed over the worst parts of her existence with the Dills, but Inga still listened in shock and horror.

Inga wanted to cover her ears, and yet there was a terrible fascination with the evil that Helga was describing. Her mind reeled. *How could this happen? How could our lives have been so different? Was it only a case of pneumonia that kept me from the same fate?* She shivered in spite of the heat. *If I'd been there with her, could I have made things any better?* She had the deflating feeling that the answer was no. *I could never be as strong as Helga is.*

Inga began to feel dizzy and unable to take in sufficient air. Her stomach hurt. The terrible contrast between her life and Helga's was too much to bear.

Helga talked about her life with the Dills in a low monotone, her head down. She looked up when she noticed the change in Inga's breathing. Inga's fingers were pressed against her mouth, and tears streamed down her face.

"Oh, Inga, I'm sorry! I shouldn't have said so much." She took the damp cloth from Inga, wrung it out in the water, and dabbed her sister's cheeks and forehead. "Are you all right?"

Inga nodded weakly. All she could manage was, "Thank you," as she buried her face in the cloth. She found solace in her next thought. *Helga seems strong and happy. There's a resiliency about her, a confidence.* Helga poured water into a glass and handed it to her. Inga felt ashamed again. *We're together again for the first time since childhood, and Helga's taking care of me.*

Hearing about Helga's early life had left Inga drained and sad. She was relieved when her family arrived at the hospital, and she brightened as she waved to them from the window. Dieter was spreading a blanket beneath the tree while Albert paced and Anna anxiously smoothed Ulla's braids.

Inga tickled Karl's cheek to wake him up. "Want to go outside for a few minutes? Opa and Oma are here, and so is Ulla." Karl gave a drowsy nod and she scooped him up.

"Mama!" he squealed and pointed when he saw Helga.

Helga wondered if he was pointing her out to his mother or whether he was exclaiming about their unmistakable likeness.

"Yes, she looks like Mama, doesn't she? That's *my* sister, Karl. Like Ulla is your sister. My sister's name is Helga."

Helga smiled and rubbed his small hand. "Hello, Karl." Then she reached down and pulled a red and blue top and a toy carousel out of a bag. "These are for you."

"Say *Danke, Tante Helga*. Thank you, Aunt Helga," Inga prompted him.

Karl was too fascinated at the sight of Helga to notice the toys. Instead, he reached out to her, just as his mother had, to see if she was real. *"Two* Mamas!" His voice reflected his amazement and delight as he squirmed to touch Helga.

"Yes! Two of us! Hold still, Karl, so I can carry you." Inga turned to Helga. "Are you ready?"

Helga nodded as she smoothed the already straight pleats on her blouse, and then she followed Inga and Karl outside to meet the others. Her nervousness evaporated as she was instantly welcomed by the waiting group.

"I'm Dieter." The tall, spare young man stepped forward to introduce himself. "We're so happy!" He gave Helga an awkward but sincere hug.

Ulla clutched a china-headed doll in one hand and held out a flower to Helga with the other. "This is for you, Aunt Helga," she said in a shy voice.

Helga took the flower and bent down to the child's eye level. "Thank you, Ulla. It's lovely."

Helga reached into her pocket and pulled out a cord with gaily colored wooden beads strung on it and placed it around Ulla's neck. "And this is for you."

Ulla turned to her grandmother. "Look at my necklace, Oma!"

Inga touched her sister's shoulder. "Helga, these are my par—"

"Tochter!" Anna cried, stepping forward to encircle Helga in her thick, soft arms. Tears streamed down her face.

"No, no," Helga laughed. "I'm only a nurse, not a doctor!"

"Helga," Inga said softly, "Mama said *Tochter*. Daughter."

Anna was already embracing Helga again, and now tears filled her eyes as well. "How we would have loved to have had both of you as daughters. And all three of you would have been even better." She shook her head sadly. "Albert tried to find you. He asked anyone he thought might know anything."

"I know how much Inga loves you." Helga felt self-conscious, but she continued anyway. "And I would have loved for us to grow up together with you." *It feels so good to have this woman hold me in her arms and call me daughter.* Helga struggled to swallow. She thought of her Aunt Elisabeth and how much she had missed her. "I was fortunate to have good people take me in, too."

Helga spotted a large basket filled with picture albums. In a voice not much more than a whisper, she said, "Now, tell me about the life I never lived."

7

Surrounded by Inga's family, the sisters sat on the hospital grounds, chattering, asking questions, and finishing each other's sentences. Helga paged through album after album, entranced by what she saw. Ulla played with her doll, but periodically scrambled over to look at a picture. Dieter helped Karl set up some soldiers in opposing formations and showed him how to wind the string around his new top.

At the beginning of the first album, Anna pointed to the page that had no pictures on either side. "We knew nothing of Inga's first eight years, but she had a life and a family before she became part of ours, so I left this page blank. Perhaps you and she can write about it someday and put those pages here."

Helga nodded and began to turn the other pages. There were pictures chronicling each of Inga's birthdays. She stopped at one in which a young Inga was holding a fine, china-headed doll. It looked similar to the one Ulla was holding now. "Was that a birthday present?"

Inga nodded. "I've always loved dolls. Mama sewed fancy clothes for them." She flushed as she remembered the broken carrot Johanna had fashioned into a doll and given to them in New York, and how happy it had made them. She knew Helga was thinking of it, too.

There are pictures of Inga at every age, Helga marveled. The setting of all of the birthday pictures was the Jäegers' imposing home. It was as grand as Inga had described. There were hundreds of other pictures of Inga: Inga with smiling children from the neighborhood. Inga waving from atop a pony. Inga standing in front of a church dressed in her Easter finery. Inga on a float at Fiesta San Antonio. Inga and her classmates at the German-English School.

"Mama!" Ulla proclaimed with glee as she stabbed at one of the pictures with a stubby finger. She hugged her mother's neck and plopped into her lap.

Helga opened another album, one bound in rich fabric that resembled tapestry. The first page showed fifteen-year-old Inga, beaming as she stood beside the entrance to the Colombian Exposition. Anna had printed "Chicago, 1893" beneath it.

Inga looked again at the date. Suddenly she asked, "Helga, were you living in San Antonio in 1893?"

"Yes. I've been here since I was thirteen or fourteen."

Inga whirled and glared at her father. "It *was* Helga! The day we came home from Chicago. I told you! I told you! She was *here*!" She turned to her sister. "I saw you! I was sure it was you. I told them we needed to go back and find you, but—" Inga's chin was trembling, her lips pressed tight to squelch bitter words she might not be able to retract.

Albert slumped and rested his forehead in his hand. He groaned as he lowered his head farther. "I thought Helga was—"

Inga turned away from her father. He reached out to her, but she shrugged off his hand. No, she shook her head over and over again, and wiped tears from her cheeks.

Anna touched Albert's arm in sympathy. "Inga, he didn't know. We thought Helga was dead."

After a minute, Inga nodded. "I'm sorry, Papa." She turned to Helga, who had watched in puzzled silence. "Mama, Papa, and I took the train back from Chicago. On the way home from the station, I thought I saw you walking down a street we passed. I yelled for them to stop the carriage, to go back and look." She pulled an embroidered handkerchief out of her pocket and wiped her nose. "That's when Papa told me you were dead, that a man had told him years before."

Helga inhaled a breath and held it for minute. "What man?"

Albert shook his head. "I never knew. A man who had come to San Antonio to sell his pigs. They were terrible-looking animals, and he was a terrible-looking man. Inga was with me. When he saw her, he came over to me. He asked me if she had come on the train. I was shocked, and I was afraid he might try to take Inga. Instead, he told me he'd seen her sister, and that she—you—had been run over and killed. Then he just disappeared. After that, I stopped searching for you."

Helga pressed her palms against the sides of her head. "This man, did he have fingers missing, cut short?" She held up her right hand and made a chopping motion with her left hand.

"I don't know. I was so afraid that he was somehow going to try to take Inga away that I didn't notice much about him, except that he was frightening and dirty."

"The man I was placed out to was named Stup Dill, and he sold his pigs in San Antonio. Once, when he returned to the farm, he told me *Inga* had died on the train, from her sickness. He said he had learned it while he was in town. I was too afraid of him to ask any questions."

"*Bastarde*," Albert mumbled under his breath in German. Anna, who normally would have protested such language, said nothing. He rubbed his fingers back and forth across his brow as if trying to massage away a severe pain. "And to think that dreadful man was the one who chose you off the train." All the color seemed to have drained from his face. "I'm so sorry, Helga, so very sorry."

"He nearly took both of us, Papa." Inga blotted her eyes and turned to Helga. "Not finding you the day we came home from Chicago cost us so much time together. That awful man caused us so much pain." She suddenly felt foolish. Who was she to tell Helga about the man's cruelty? To dare to complain about the pain he had caused Helga and *her*?

"The important thing is that we're together now." There was a ring of resolute optimism in Helga's voice. Privately she wondered, *What if they had found me that day? Would I have had to choose between living with the Jäegers and continuing to live with Uncle Wil and Aunt Elisabeth?* Then she had a surprising realization: *I wouldn't have given up my life with Wil and Elisabeth. I would have visited Inga every day, but I wouldn't have been willing to leave them.*

"Yes, you and Inga are together now," Albert echoed her words. "And Inga says you've found your other sister as well. That's good. Families should be together."

Ulla climbed into Anna's lap and nestled against her. The heat was making her sleepy. Albert patted her head. "We hope there will be more grandchildren. The best family is a large one."

Anna added softly, "Germans say that when an older person in a family dies, a baby is born to take the person's place."

In her mind, Helga could see the endless links that transcended time and that together forged a family. For a moment she herself felt the continuity that Anna had described.

Ulla now rested her head placidly against her grandmother's bosom, growing drowsier and drowsier as Anna rocked her and stroked her head. "Until the grandchildren were born, we didn't know our life could feel any more complete." Dieter smiled and so did Inga. It warmed her to watch her parents with Karl and Ulla.

Inga looked at her children. They would never be touched by the adversity that scarred her early years. Another wave of sadness and guilt washed over her as she recalled bits of information Helga had told her the day before. *While I was happy with Papa and Mama in San Antonio, Helga was suffering on a filthy pig farm. I had the World's Fair; Helga had harshness and hard work. I ended up with loving parents; she struggled with a cruel foster family. I had more good food than I could eat; Helga coped with constant hunger. I climbed into my soft bed at night; Helga lay in darkness in a barn.* In an action that puzzled Helga, Inga reached over and squeezed her hand. Her eyes were brimming.

Anna, who had been quietly enjoying the afternoon, spoke up again. "Inga said you heard her singing Karl a lullaby." She hummed a bit of the melody.

"Yes, that very one! I hadn't heard it since I was a child."

Anna smiled and turned to her daughter. "You were too ill to know it at the time, Inga, but I sang you a lullaby the day we took you home from the train." To Helga, she said, "And I still have the little dress and the shoes she was wearing." Helga remembered Althene taking hers away.

"And we still have the button," Albert interjected. "It's in a carved box."

Helga's mouth fell open. "You still have the button!"

Anna tapped the cover of the wedding album. "She sewed it inside her sleeve of her wedding dress, at the wrist, so it would be with her at her wedding."

"I have mine, too. Once I thought I'd lost it at the Dills' and I cried every night for a week. Then I found it in a crack when I was scrubbing the floor." Helga's face flushed with embarrassment. Inga lowered her eyes, pretending as if there was nothing out of the ordinary about scrubbing floors. "Anyway, once I found it, I took Mrs. Dill's needle and thread and stitched it inside the hem of my dress. After I came to San Antonio, Aunt Elisabeth washed the dress and put it in the rag bin. I pulled it out and took the button off. I stitched it on a ribbon so I'd never lose it again."

"Do you suppose Johanna still has her button?"

Helga smiled. "I know she does. She showed it to me. She loved Papa's coat." She unconsciously fingered the button at her collar. "Inga, bring your button Thursday!"

Helga set the album down beside her on the blanket and looked at her sister. "Inga, exactly how old are we? I asked Johanna once, but she wasn't certain about the date."

Both the Jäegers and Inga blanched at the question and its painful implication: There had been no birthday celebrations for Helga. "We think twenty-four." Inga's voice was gentle. "We don't know the actual date either, so we might be twenty-three."

"Or twenty-five."

Helga moved her head up and down in acknowledgment. "Tell me about your wedding." Helga opened a lace-covered album and began examining each photograph in detail. It was obvious it had been a splendid occasion.

Inga felt guilt at describing yet another event in her privileged life. She reached out to close the album. "Helga, this isn't right." She was near tears again.

"No, it's all right. Really." She put her hand on her sister's knee. "I'm happy, Inga, and I'm even happier now that I've found you." Helga ran her finger over a picture of Inga and Dieter standing before the flower-covered altar in a candle-lit sanctuary.

"St. Joseph's Catholic Church?"

"Uh-huh."

"It must have been lovely." Helga studied the picture a moment longer before she looked up. "We're Lutheran. St. John's." Once again, she ran her finger over the portrait of Inga and Dieter, tracing their outline, and lost in thought. *This is like looking at myself in a life I never lived. It feels so odd.*

At that moment, it was as if Inga read her sister's thoughts. "Helga, I can't even pretend to understand what you've suffered. I can't imagine ever having your courage and determination. Enduring the Dills. Going to Galveston by yourself." *Compared with your life,* she thought, *mine has been so safe, so predictable. So narrow.* Inga looked over at her parents, who were busy entertaining the children. *Even now, Dieter and I live in "the Little Rhine," only a few blocks from our parents. We see them or speak to them daily. We consult them whenever there's an important decision to be made. Although Papa and Mama became Opa and Oma after Ulla and Karl were born, we still regard them as the foundation and the final authority in the family.*

Helga finished turning the pages of the album. The afternoon and the visit were drawing to an end.

"Where are *your* photographs, Helga?" Anna chided and playfully wagged her finger. "You must show them to us next time."

The color drained from Inga's face. "*Mama.*"

"I don't have any," Helga said simply. "But today"—she held a finger up in the air like a school marm—"I've had a chance to see how I *would* have looked in pictures. Not many people are that lucky!" Her warm smile dissipated Anna's embarrassment, but not her sadness at discovering that Helga had no pictures of herself. Helga looked at Anna and then at Albert. "Please say you'll spend the afternoon and evening of July Fourth with me and my—" she paused, then said with pride, "with me and my family. Inga and I want to surprise Johanna."

Albert sucked on his pipe and then exhaled a cloud of fragrant, white smoke. "We've waited a lifetime for this day, so we can wait a few more days to meet Johanna."

Then Anna spoke up. "It will be the Fourth of July and Christmas all in one."

8

Johanna, Anton, Mrs. Bromley, Danny, and Janie walked towards Dr. Ohlmsted's door. Odors from the picnic hampers the men carried gave tempting clues to their contents. Sul and Augusta hopped and skipped, brimming with anticipation.

"It's been a glorious day!" Johanna declared. She and Anton had spent the morning with Janie and her children at the city's Independence Day parade. They'd waved flags, sung patriotic songs, and listened to patriotic music. They had listened to a rousing speech by the mayor. They had jumped, shrieked, and covered their ears at the sound of the cannon fusillades.

The children raced ahead to see who would be first to ring the doorbell.

At the sound of it, Helga and Inga opened the door together. Had one not been wearing a blue dress and the other a yellow one, they would have been indistinguishable. Even Danny gasped. Mrs. Bromley could muster nothing more than an astonished "My goodness!"

Johanna looked first at one, then at the other. "Who…" She started over again. "How…" Her eyes filled with tears.

Helga smiled. She took Johanna's hand and placed it in her sister's. Then Johanna and Helga said in unison: "Inga."

Johanna shrieked and flung her arms around Inga's neck. After a long embrace, Inga took her sister's hands and squeezed them. Johanna's eyes lit up and she burst into a big smile: she felt Inga press something smooth and round and flat into her palm.

9

With full stomachs, Danny and Albert sat contentedly in the late afternoon sunshine. An occasional languid breeze fanned them. After a while Danny broke the silence. "I've been wondering, Mr. Jäeger, if you remember me?"

Albert removed his pipe from his mouth, stroked his moustache, and scratched his head. "Well, you do seem familiar, but I can't think why. It's been bothering me ever since we got here, but I'd decided that I was mistaken. That it was just because of Inga being reunited with her sisters."

Danny grinned. "Do you remember a boy who worked at Muehlenberg's? You used to give him sausages."

Albert adjusted his spectacles, leaned forward, and peered into Danny's face. "Great God in heaven." A second realization followed instantly. "Why, you knew Johanna even then, didn't you!"

Danny nodded. "From New York. And from the train."

Albert sank back in his chair and sighed. "We could have found at least *one* of Inga's sisters, Johanna, years ago. If only I'd known."

Sipping cold mugs of dark beer, Dieter and Anton strolled in the garden, deep in conversation. Mrs. Bromley and Dr. Ohlmsted chatted amiably with the Jäegers about their respective "children." Janie watched the children, taking pleasure in their unabashed enthusiasm and boundless energy. Ulla and Augusta, sunburned but still exuberant, marched around the yard waving flags and singing "Yankee Doodle," a parade of two. Karl and Sul played on the ground with a set of wooden animals Albert had carved for them.

Johanna, Helga, and Inga stood in a tight knot in the center of the fragrant garden. The sound of their laughter and chatter pleased Danny. He watched them continually clasp and release each other's hands. They would gesture or shake their heads, and sometimes wipe away a tear. He heard the word *Zusammen* float into the warm July air.

Johanna caught sight of him out of the corner of her eye. Then, to her sisters, she asked, "Would you be willing to give up Papa's buttons?"

"What?" Helga couldn't believe what she had just heard. "You want them back again?" She felt confused, but stammered, "Well, yes, if you'd like them."

"I think it's time to put them back on a coat. No, a vest. One we make for Danny. He came looking for me in Sulphur Creek. He brought me to San Antonio. Then he found you in Galveston last year, Helga, and brought the two of us together. Then you found Inga. And he knew Albert within a few weeks of the time he arrived in San Antonio, although he didn't know you lived with the Jäegers."

"A vest," Helga concurred, "would be very nice."

Inga gave a strong, affirmative nod. "A three-button vest."

10

Earlier, everyone had made a fuss over Albert's delectable smoked meats, as well as Anna's potato salad, brown bread, and spicy mustard. They had devoured Johanna's biscuits and jam, and fresh greens, along with Janie's pickles, cabbage slaw, and juicy ears of corn. As promised, Mrs. Bromley had baked a peach cobbler and a fragrant cinnamon cake. The children had enjoyed all this, but still favored the cold watermelon and the foamy root beer. Everyone groaned in mock agony when Helga brought out a frosty pail of ice cream.

The sun finally sank below the horizon. The children began chasing fireflies, squealing with delight whenever they captured one. They took them to Karl, who rested on a large quilt.

Danny stood by himself at one end of the porch, leaning against a column and studying the moon. *Dilue would call that a full Comanche moon*, he thought. The opalescent moon had risen like a luminous disk in the sky. It cast a brilliant light on the landscape below.

Janie walked over to join him. He put his arm around her shoulder and drew her close. "I wish Dilue and Mr. Dunside could be here tonight."

She nodded softly. Then she looked skyward, her eyes following his gaze. "Still the same moon," she murmured.

He understood and drew her closer. They watched Mother Bromley retie the disheveled red bow in Augusta's pale hair. Sul looked up from where he sat with Karl and waved to his mother and Danny.

Danny looked down at Janie and smiled. He looked at the other faces around him. "Dilue once told me that I would find what I was searching for, but that I might not recognize it when I found it." Emotion reduced his voice to a whisper, but Janie could still hear him: "First time I ever knew her to be wrong."

Dilue sat silent and serene in a rocking chair on her back porch, sensing the radiance of the moon she could not see. At that moment, she smiled.

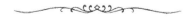

END NOTES

If you are now starting to read the End Notes before reading the novel itself, I encourage you to wait and read them afterwards.

Since the 1800s, American cities have struggled with the problem of their homeless and poor. Between 1854 and 1929, several Eastern cities, and New York in particular, used a controversial solution, one that would ultimately affect millions of lives. For seventy-five years, homeless and destitute children were put on trains headed west and "placed out"—distributed—to families living in rural areas. At the time, the agencies termed this practice "family placement" or "out placement," to distinguish it from placing children "in" institutions, such as orphanages and asylums. The New York Foundling Home referred to its trains as "mercy trains" or "baby trains." It was not until the late 1970s that these trains came to be known more popularly as "orphan trains."

In some ways, "orphan train" is a misnomer. Although there were children on the trains who were, in fact, orphans, most were relinquished to "aid society homes" and "foundling hospitals" by immigrant parents who were simply unable to provide for them. The tens of thousands of immigrant families who poured into New York during the last half of the nineteenth century struggled constantly against poverty, unemployment, alcoholism, hunger and malnutrition, tuberculosis, and cholera. Second, among the train riders there were also teenage boys and girls who went to placing out agencies in order to escape the city and ultimately find work of some sort. Third, many placed out children never rode the trains: they were placed with families in the city. In their records, the New York Children's Aid Society did not distinguish between local and distant placements, and children fostered by local families were counted among those who had been placed out. What is clear, however, is that although the exact number will never be known, more than 200,000 children were placed out. Some researchers estimate the number as high as 400,000, but 250,000 seems more likely.

How did this vast social experiment come about? At mid-century, Charles Loring Brace, a Yale graduate, went to New York City to complete his seminary training. The young minister was appalled at the sheer number of orphaned, abandoned, and neglected children there. An estimated 30,000 homeless children struggled to survive on the streets during the 1850s. Some begged; others sold newspapers or flowers, scavenged rags or coal, or became prostitutes or bootblacks. Many belonged to criminal gangs. At night, these vagrant youngsters slept in alleys, under stairways, and in deserted buildings. Those who lived in tenements did not fare much better as they also endured dangerous, desperate, and squalid living conditions. The photographs of social reformer Jacob Riis, author of the 1890 publication *How the Other Half Lives,* chronicle the plight of these children and their families.

New York attempted to address these children's plight in part with "children's asylums" and "houses of refuge" in which children could live and learn skills. Brace rejected these institutions as a solution. Instead, he conceptualized a "placing out movement" as a way to give these children better lives in rural communities than they would have in institutions in cities. As a missionary, he helped found the New York Children's Aid Society in 1853. Ultimately, children in it and similar institutions were put on trains and placed out to families in rural areas, primarily in the Midwest.

Brace's goal was altruistic: to remove hapless, suffering children from an urban life of poverty and degradation and give them, in his words, "a sweet childhood of air and sky." It also fit with the popular belief that fresh air fostered physical and emotional health in children. This wholesome, rural life would necessarily include hard work, which Brace saw as one key to inculcating children with solid, Christian values. He believed that family traits and character were inherited and that they were transmitted through the blood, a notion prevalent prior to the gene theory that was advanced by Charles Darwin. Unlike many of his day, however, Brace believed that this "bad blood" could be overcome if the children grew up in a better environment. His friendship with Darwin may also explain the minister's belief that better circumstances could help a family's heritability improve and evolve. The young minister was also aware that couples who accepted a child also benefited: They would gain a family member who could help with farm work, do housework, or learn a trade. Childless couples and those who had lost a child could become more complete families, although legal adoption was not required.

Brace's "Emigration Plan" was the forerunner of foster care in this country, and placing out societies attempted to screen potential foster parents. In the towns trains would be passing through, the society representative or the agent accompanying the children sought out a local contact or requested committee of respected town leaders, such as ministers, bankers, and doctors. These distinguished citizens were charged with screening applicants, as well as overseeing local arrangements, which might include providing the children a place to sleep overnight or arranging a location for the agent's public remarks and the subsequent "distribution" of the children. Distribution occurred at the train station, or perhaps at the courthouse, town hall, or a church. Clearly, there was potential ill will if a committee member deemed a neighbor, congregation member, client, or other fellow townsman unfit. For that reason, committees were often reluctant to turn down any applicant. In some instances, especially at the beginning of the placing out movement, agents had to identify a local contact after arriving in a town. As a result, many agents simply bypassed the screening step and allowed children to go with anyone who requested a child.

Applicants had to agree to treat children as members of the family, to send them to school and church, and to feed and clothe them adequately until the age of seventeen. For the most part, the adoptive families fulfilled their obligations and the placements were a positive experience both for the family and the child. This was not always the case, though. Some applicants viewed the children as free labor and treated them badly. Some children suffered harsh treatment or even physical, emotional, or sexual abuse at the hands of their foster parents. Because of their foreign accents, the children were often viewed with suspicion by townspeople and taunted or rejected by classmates. Many rural citizens assumed that the children were the illegitimate offspring or cast-offs of drunks and prostitutes. They perceived the children as coming from inferior stock and incapable of ever overcoming their "bad blood."

It was always the intention of placing out institutions to keep track of the children they placed and the conditions in their adoptive or foster homes. Because follow-up visits weren't practical, this was to be done via correspondence. It is no surprise that for a variety of reasons, including the staggering number of children (nearly 85,000 during the first forty years of the placing out movement), this system proved inadequate and unreliable. Children in unsuitable homes often had to remain there. Some ran away; some were given away to other foster families; others drifted through a series of families. A few of the children who didn't work out were returned to their birth parent(s) or to institutions.

The prevailing wisdom was that the children would receive a fresh, better start if they were separated from their siblings, with each placed with a different family. Once a sibling was placed, he or she had no knowledge of where his or her brothers and sisters were subsequently placed or with whom. With all good intentions, adoptive and foster families typically changed children's names, making it all the more difficult for siblings ever to locate each other. This was compounded by the fact that many of the youngest orphan train riders were too young to know their last name, much less their parents' first names, or their own birth date or birthplace. Further, it was the policy of placing out institutions not to disclose any of the children's records.

Along with the countless more fortunate children, placing out benefited Eastern cities. By relocating their "street urchins," they were relieved in large measure of having to provide facilities and care for homeless children. Moreover, they could feel good about their efforts to provide impoverished children with the opportunity for a better life and pleased they were helping the country as a whole by forging the youngsters into solid, productive citizens.

During its slightly more than three-quarters of a century of existence, the placing out movement relocated children to 47 of the then 48 states. On May 31, 1929, a train rolled into Sulfur Springs, Texas. The placing out of three boys there brought to a quiet close an experiment that altered the lives of scores of thousands of immigrant children and millions of their descendants. In early 2009, it was estimated that only fifteen orphan train riders were still living.

How will history ultimately judge the placing out movement? It may be positive, or it may be summed up by C.S. Lewis's observation: "Of all tyrannies, a tyranny exercised for the good of its victims may be the most oppressive.... [T]hose who torment us for our own good will torment us without end for they do so with the approval of their own conscience." History's final verdict on the placing out movement has yet to be rendered and may never be.

Placed Out is a work of historical fiction. It is based on written accounts given by orphan train riders and their descendants, as well as other research about the orphan trains and the placing out movement. It is also grounded in historical facts about late Victorian-era New York, Texas railroads and their routes during the late 1800s, the World's Columbian Exposition of 1893, Galveston and the Great Storm (the hurricane of 1900), life on early Texas cattle ranches, the Texas Rangers, the Spanish-American War, the Spindletop gusher, late 19th-century medicine, and life in San Antonio during the period in which that part of the story unfolds. Descriptions of flora and fauna are accurate, as are details about daily life, dress, food, speech, household furnishings, and transportation of the time period. Descriptions of houses, hotels, and other buildings, such as those in turn-of-the-century New York, San Antonio, and Galveston, are also based on research.

It's been said that an author will read a hundred books in order to write one. Although "a hundred" turned out to be a gross underestimate, I read with great pleasure. Books, old newspapers, articles, journals—I read these and countless other sources. When I wrote *Placed Out,* at the end of the 1980s, the Internet as we know it today did not exist. Although this made my research more challenging and time-consuming, it carried its own gift: it led me to sources and places I might not otherwise have sought out. I must also have had a "book angel" watching over me: I often had the experience of coming across exactly the information I needed, at exactly the time I needed it, and it often came from unexpected or unlikely sources.

My research included visits to several locations that figure prominently in the story, as well as to relevant museums. I visited Dallas's Old City Park several times. This historic preservation site, which is set up as a village, contains more than thirty reconstructed Victorian-era homes and structures that include a doctor's office, newspaper office, bank, general store, train depot, hotel, and schoolhouse. It allowed me to see and take notes on the equipment, furniture, and furnishings these structures contained. It afforded an opportunity to see firsthand examples of late 19th-century architecture and life, to examine carriages of the time period, and to watch a blacksmith at work.

Texas offered an irresistible canvas on which to paint my story. The state is so vast, and its history so colorful, that it provided the perfect setting for the time period spanned in the novel. Further, "the West," both as a physical reality and a concept, has always captured my imagination. I equate it with challenge, hope, and unlimited possibilities.

My research led me to the fascinating Texas Ranger Hall of Fame and Museum in Waco, Texas. From its collections of homemade badges to Colt pistols, the museum helped fill out my research on ranger lore and life.

Visiting Galveston allowed me to develop a sense of the island's geography, gather information about the Great Storm, and see historical structures that survived the storm. When writing about Galveston in this novel, I could see the palm trees, smell the sea air, feel the breeze, and hear the gulls. The South Asian tsunami (December 2004), Hurricane Katrina (August 2005), and Hurricane Sandy (October 2012) once again brought home how terrifying and horrifying an experience the Great Storm must have been to Galvestonians. A hurricane cannot compare in magnitude with a tsunami, of course. However, both can create torrents of fast-moving water that are filled with furniture, vehicles, and debris and leave people and animals struggling helplessly. It was impossible to see footage of the tsunami without thinking of the multimedia documentary about the Great Storm I'd seen in Galveston years earlier at the Pier 21 Theater.

In colorful San Antonio, I visited the Menger Hotel and absorbed some of its history. Built in 1859 and situated three hundred feet from the site of the Alamo, the hotel is filled with artifacts, paintings, historical photos, and antiques. It has retained its magnificent Victorian lobby. The Menger bar, or taproom, as it was called when it was added in 1887, was built as a replica of the House of Lords Pub in England. Its cherry wood paneled ceiling, booths, beveled mirrors from France, and decorated glass cabinets are the same today as when Teddy Roosevelt and his Rough Riders were there.

In San Antonio, I also visited the Institute of Texas Cultures (ITC), a treasure trove of information about the ethnic and cultural history of the state. The museum's photo collection boasts approximately three million images. Although its fifty thousand square feet of exhibit space chronicle the daily life and culture of twenty-six ethnic groups, I focused on the Irish and German immigrants, and their customs and traditions. My visit to the ITC also allowed me to study firsthand historical exhibits that ranged from buildings in the time period of interest to me, to everyday household items, to a chuck wagon.

San Antonio's charming King William Historic District, which is listed on the National Register of Historic Places, was another destination. The twenty-five-square-block area, with its tree-lined streets, retains the appeal that made it a magnet for fashionable German immigrants during the last half of the 19th century. The restored homes reflect a variety of architectural styles that include Greek Revival, Italianate, and Victorian. The latter was the style of greatest interest to me because of the time period in which my story takes place. Although most King William Historic District homes today are in private hands, two of them are open to the public.

To develop a feel for train travel in the late 1800s, I rode the Cumbres & Toltec Scenic Railroad. It is the best-preserved steam era railroad in the country, and it brought the experience to life. Although the C&TS is narrow gauge and operates in a remote, unpopulated section of New Mexico and Colorado, it was built in 1880. On its sixty-four-mile route, the coal-fired steam locomotive pulls cars over the Toltec Gorge, through tunnels, and across trestles at twelve miles per hour, tops. Standing outside in the open-air observation car, summertime passengers come away sweaty, sooty, and with flecks of coal embedded in their hairlines. Hot cinders float back from the locomotive's black plume. Even for those riding inside a passenger car with the windows open, a necessity in summer, the experience is much the same. Three section houses, which early railroads provided as no-frills homes for crews responsible for maintaining barren sections of track, still exist along the C&TS route.

In Las Vegas, New Mexico, I visited the Rough Rider Memorial Collection, which is housed in a 1940s Works Project Administration (WPA) building. The small museum contains Rough Rider memorabilia, as well as household items, costumes, weapons, ranching gear, tools, and furniture dating from the late 1800s. In addition, there are newspapers, maps, and historic photographs of this era, the time when railroads began displacing agriculture as the primary industry. The museum's photographic collection of more than 1,500 items includes not only black-and-white prints, but also tintypes, stereoviews, and panoramas.

In January 1901, Spindletop, as the Lucas gusher was called, erupted on the little hill in Beaumont known as Gladys City. The oil spray could be seen for ten miles. During the nine days before the mighty gusher could be capped, Spindletop spewed 800,000 barrels. By 1902 Gladys City was a sea of oil derricks crammed so close together that they almost touched. The discovery of Spindletop triggered an unprecedented oil boom in the United States and made the country a player in the oil industry worldwide. Oil companies that emerged from the Spindletop fields became the companies later known as Texaco, Chevron, Mobil, and Exxon. Although fascinating in its own right, Spindletop was a special interest to me for two reasons. First, my father was a petroleum geologist, and second, my paternal grandparents lived almost their adult lives in Beaumont.

In addition to the locations noted above, I visited museums and historical preservation sites in other cities and towns. I studied maps and photographs. Over and over again I would start to write a scene, only to find that I needed more detailed information first. How did the placing out movement come about? What was life like in the New York children's asylums? What was the Five Points area of Victorian era New York like? What were speech, dress, and customs during a particular time, in a certain region of the country or within a specific ethnic group? When did telephones appear in homes? What was late 19th-century medicine like? I researched everything from breaking horses to branding cattle to stampedes—and had fun doing all of it.

The novel includes many actual events and references to historical figures, such as Sarah Bernhardt, Geronimo, Teddy Roosevelt, and John Philip Sousa, who were at the places at the times described in the story. All other characters, events, the names of the placing out societies used in the book, and the names of most Texas towns are fictional.

Five Points, the area that housed the tenement in which Danny's family and Johanna's family lived, refers to that actual area of New York City. This four-square-mile section in the city's Lower East Side, named for the five streets that converged there, has undergone numerous name changes during intervening decades. It held the sad distinction of becoming the nation's first slum, a result of the influx of immigrants that tripled the city's population between 1825 and 1850. Decade after decade, the newly arrived, the poorest of the poor, settled there. It was a cesspool of misery, and those who inhabited it moved away as soon as their circumstances permitted.

Some of the events in this novel that most seem like fiction are based on accounts of actual people and true events. The character of Dilue was inspired by an old newspaper account of a girl who was taken by Indians in the 1800s, tortured and disfigured, and relinquished by them a few years later. She lived out the rest of her life with a caring couple who took her in. The fates of her family members that are described in the novel are the same as in the actual account. Jefferson Dooley's tale of the Indian's death chant and death is also based on an actual account. Bob Lemmons was a legendary black cowboy who could, indeed, make himself the leader of a herd of wild mustangs and walk them into captivity. The episode with the cross-eyed jury was based on a trial that took place in the northwest in the 1800s. The use of typesetters' letters as buckshot is based on a true incident, as is the incident of McCafferty, the Texas Ranger who sang his pursuers into submission. The story of the desperate father who tied his wife, his children, and then himself high up on the trunks of tall palm trees in order to survive the Galveston storm is also true. His actions saved the lives of all four family members, one of whom was a boy who had arrived on an orphan train. In the novel, the character of Oleta Mutt takes the "Bible name" of "Verily." In case you had trouble figuring out where in the Bible it comes from, it is based on the biblical phrase, "*Verily, verily,* I say unto you." Ruby and Opal also have middle names that are "Bible names," but the sources of theirs are self-evident. A college classmate from West Virginia once told me about sharecroppers on their land who named their daughters Genesis, Exodus, and Verily, and unwittingly pronounced them Ge-NEE-sis, Ex-O-dus, and Ver-ILL-ee. I borrowed it for my story. Although I have an imagination, the pronunciation of those names would have been beyond it.

In the story, Danny learns that his uncle, Shamus, died from a rattlesnake bite. The rattlesnake is one of four venomous snakes in the United States whose bite can be fatal to humans. Rattlesnakes normally try to withdraw, but they will strike if startled or cornered. Their venom, like that of other North American pit vipers, is primarily hemotoxic: it destroys blood and muscle tissue, disrupts clotting, and deteriorates organs. Pit vipers are so named because of the pits behind their nostrils; these depressions are covered with a temperature-sensitive membrane that enables the snake to sense warm-blooded animals. These snakes can strike and inject venom from any position, and it is not necessary for them to coil before striking. When the snake opens its mouth to strike, the fangs rotate forward from their folded position against the roof of the snake's mouth. Throughout the snake's life, in roughly sixty-day cycles, new fangs grow, move into place in the roof of the snake's mouth, and stabilize in the sockets; the old fangs are shed. From birth, rattlesnakes can regulate the amount of venom they inject. The same snake can strike again in less than a second, and the movement is too fast for the human eye. Just as humans' reactions to bee stings vary, so do their reactions to rattlesnake bites. The severity depends on several factors, such as the person's health and allergic sensitivities, the strength of the venom, and the location of the bite. In the story, Shamus is bitten between the thumb and the forefinger by the snake's decapitated head, with the venom going directly—and fatally—into a blood vessel. Dead rattlesnakes can, in fact, be dangerous for about half an hour after their death because their jaws continue to open and bite as a reflexive response to heat, movement, and touch. In the story, Shamus's outstretched hand provides the snake's decapitated head with all three. The American International Rattlesnake Museum in Albuquerque, New Mexico, is home to the world's largest collection of rattlesnake species. It graciously provided information I could not find elsewhere. For anyone who is interested, their website is rattlesnakes.com.

Writers also draw on their own experiences because that's what they know best. This was often the case with me. For example, the scene in which Cletis discovers that the ocean water is the same in the "Whites Only" section and the "Coloreds Only" section of the beach was based on a childhood experience I had. In the 1950s, segregation was a fact of life, and our neighborhood grocery store had separate water fountains marked "White" and "Colored." As a five- or six-year-old child, I concluded that the water from them must *taste* different since the water from the "Colored" fountain wasn't colored and the water from the "White" fountain wasn't white. The fountains flanked the stockroom doors at the back of the store, and when no one was around, I surreptitiously sampled water from the "Colored" fountain. I was surprised and greatly disappointed: it tasted exactly the same as the water from the "White" fountain. I walked away disgusted with adults and baffled that they were, for some reason, unable to see that there was no difference.

The flyer at the front of the book is based on one sent to towns at which the orphan trains would be stopping. I've changed certain elements to match the story, but otherwise the wording is the same as in the original circular.

Nobel Prize-winning American author Toni Morrison once said, "If there's a book you really want to read but it hasn't been written yet, then you must write it." I wanted to read—and understand—more about how the lives of early orphan train riders placed out in Texas might have unfolded. It became clear that if I wanted to read such a story, I was going to have to write it.

The idea of building a novel around orphan train riders stemmed from several sources. The first was an article I read several decades ago about the placing out movement. I was stunned at the sheer number of children involved. The second was a newspaper article that told of two brothers in Texas who had been among the last groups of orphan train riders. (It was also the inspiration for the scene in the novel in which two brothers, Kieran and Dillon, are separated.) They had been placed out in different towns, and each had had his last name changed by the foster parents. At the time of the article, the late 1980s, they were in their sixties or seventies, and they had just been reunited. They had spent their lives wondering what happened to each other and, as adults, searching for each other. Once open records laws were passed and orphan train riders associations were established, they were finally able to locate each other. The sad irony was that the two brothers had lived one town apart all their lives and had never known it. As their situation exemplified, the obstacles to locating a sibling prior to the availability of open records and the Internet were two-fold. The first was that after a child was placed out, he or she never knew where or how far on down the line brothers or sisters ended up: it could have been the next town or the next state. Second, foster parents often changed the children's first name, last name, or both. The poignant article stayed with me. I also wondered what life must have been like for the very youngest children who were placed out, those who were too little to have known who they were, where they came from, their birth date, and who their birth parents were. Undoubtedly, the youngest ones must have always wondered whether they had siblings, and, if so, what happened to them. In the story, the incident of the baby who is placed out represents the smallest orphan train riders who experienced this fate.

Another influence on this novel arose from my early years as a teacher. When I began my teaching career in the 1970s, I taught for three years at a huge, new high school whose students came from all over the city. They included those living nearby at a large, institutional children's home. Founded in the late 1880s as an orphans' home, it eventually changed its name in the 1900s to a "children's dome" to reflect the reality that, in addition to providing a home for orphans, it had begun providing short-term and long-term foster care for non-orphans. In fact, most of those who lived at the home had at least one living parent, but for various reasons, the parent or parents weren't able to care for them. Some of my students had lived there for a short while; others had lived there most of their lives. I knew every Monday there would be students whose parents were supposed to have visited during the weekend, but never showed up. For some of my students, this happened regularly. My heart hurt for them. Many were understandably sad and angry, but despite the repeated letdowns, most managed to remain hopeful. "Next weekend," they'd say. And, of course, there were those who had no one, or at least no relatives, who lived close enough to visit. At the end of my first year of teaching, I bought from the yearbook staff the pictures of as many of my students as I could find. (As a fundraiser, the yearbook staff sold the simple, black-and-white headshots for a dime each.) Most of my students couldn't afford to buy a yearbook, and I thought they would enjoy having at least their yearbook pictures. When I gave one of my students from the home her picture, she stared at it for a long time. When she finally looked up, she thanked me profusely, explaining that she'd never had a picture of herself before. She was matter-of-fact, but I felt devastated at the realization that there'd never been a parent or family member to snap pictures. Nor, for that matter, had there been the usual childhood occasions at which family pictures would normally be taken, such as birthdays, holidays, or the first day of school each year.

Although I had many students from the children's home, the majority of my students were African-Americans who lived in poverty in the Dallas housing projects. The projects were dreadful, a blight that should have been a source of shame to every city leader and citizen. The first semester of my first year I opted to accompany a homebound teacher to the projects on a faculty development day in lieu of the other activities. I wanted to understand more about where my students lived and what their lives were like outside of school. I'd grown up in Dallas. Throughout my life and from a distance, I'd seen the rundown housing projects that flanked some of the freeways, but I'd never been inside one. It was a stunner: peeling paint, broken windows, broken doors, broken steps, cracked floors, filth, rusted pipes, broken plumbing. The common areas, the only areas in which children could play, consisted of hard-packed dirt and a few weeds. They were strewn with broken glass and litter. I had a new appreciation for my students' simply making it to school each day.

Another motivation for writing this book was that every large city has its share of homeless people, including families. I was fascinated at how major Eastern cities, via the placing out movement, had tried to address the problem more than a century ago. The intervening decades have not yielded a solution, and cities continue to struggle with the issue today.

My experience with many of the college students I taught also influenced the writing of this book. For three decades I taught college freshmen and sophomores, and during that time, I had innumerable students whose families had immigrated to the United States. These students came from everywhere. They were thrust into a bewildering, new culture, and many spoke little or no English prior to coming here. Nearly all of them worked one or more jobs. They always had my deepest admiration. I could only imagine how I would have fared had the circumstances been reversed, and I'd found myself abruptly relocated to Vietnam, Cambodia, Bangladesh, or Guatemala. I'm sure I could not have dealt with the challenges even half as gracefully or as well as they did.

On a more practical level, I wrote this book because I wanted to understand how to put a novel together and try to figure out aspects such as how to keep several separate story lines moving forward at the same time, how to maintain a consistent point of view, and how to handle dialog. I'm still not sure I know how to write a novel, but I had a wonderful time. Even so, on more than one occasion, Dorothy Parker's trenchantly witty assessment of another book rolled through my mind: "This is not a novel to be tossed aside lightly. It should be thrown with great force." Presumably, if you've made it to the End Notes, you managed not to throw this book aside, and I thank you.

A final motivation for writing the novel was that I have long been interested in the general question of free will versus determinism, which is probably a clear indication that I need a hobby. The concept of placing out seemed to lend itself to that exploration, as did the inclusion of identical twins as characters. Perhaps former Indian Prime Minister Jawaharlal Nehru had it right: "Life is like a game of cards. The hand you are dealt is determinism; the way you play it is free will."

Those who write can attest that writing provides a vehicle for examining their own values and beliefs, as this book did for me. These lines from T.S. Eliot's *Four Quartets* beautifully and eloquently describe the process for me:

> We shall not cease from exploration
> And the end of all our exploring
> Will be to arrive where we started
> And know the place for the first time.

Herman Melville describes life as "a voyage that's homeward bound." In this novel, "home" is clearly a recurring theme. Is it the end of all our exploring, the place where we started? A feeling? A physical or geographical entity? In "Death of the Hired Man," Frost writes, "'Home is the place where, when you have to go there, / They have to take you in. / 'I should have called it / Something you somehow haven't to deserve.'" William Jerome expresses a different point of view in his 1901 song lyrics: "Any old place I can hang my hat is home sweet home to me." And, of course, it's impossible to think of "home" without pondering the message of Thomas Wolfe's book title, *You Can't Go Home Again.* Undoubtedly, "home" means something different to each of us, and I leave it to readers to define it for themselves, just as the characters in the novel must ultimately do.

Writers' values and beliefs permeate their work, whether they consciously intend it or not. I believe that all of us "ride the train" at various points and to varying extents in our lives: we experience circumstances beyond our control, sometimes ones that are life-changing, and we have to figure out how to proceed from there. Further, I am convinced that one of life's great gifts is being able to create, in addition to or in lieu of our families of origin, "families" of friends of our own choosing. I've been fortunate in this way, and I am profoundly grateful.

For additional information on the placing out movement, the orphan trains, or the immigrant experience in 19th-century New York, these are good starting points:

- National Orphan Train Complex, Concordia, Kansas: orphantraindepot.org
- Children's Aid Society of New York: childrensaidnyc.org (Type "orphan trains" in the search box.)
- Tenement Museum, New York City, Lower East Side: tenement.org
- Riis, Jacob. *How the Other Half Lives: Studies among the Tenements of New York.* Originally published in 1890, this remains a seminal work in the history of social reform. Along with the narrative, Riis used drawings and halftone images to document life in the city's squalid slums during the 1880s, as well to expose sweatshops and the plight of working children. In later reprints, photographs replaced many of the drawings.

ABOUT THE AUTHOR

Janet R. Elder, PhD, is a former college professor and top-selling textbook writer. Although her roots are in Texas, she and her husband live in the foothills of Santa Fe, New Mexico. She loves the city's 400-year-old history, blend of cultures, cuisine and rich, varied cultural life. An avid reader, Janet also enjoys the many opportunities for outdoor activities and being with friends. She relishes the beautiful vistas that surround the city and tries never to miss a breathtaking sunset.

You can contact her at janet.elder.fiction@gmail.com.

Made in the USA
Monee, IL
27 January 2021

58758202R10208